Redolfo looks down at her and smiles with a cruelty she hopes is meant for someone else, somewhere else.

"And when you slight someone greater than you," he adds, "vengeance may be slow, but it will be complete. That is what the story means. We will succeed." He squeezes her shoulders. "I will still succeed."

The girl looks up at the spirals of smoke and thinks of Melosino, inert beside a cold campfire in the mountains. None of this feels like success, but then, perhaps the story hasn't ended. And if it is foolish to doubt a god, then what is it to doubt Redolfo Kirazzi?

Praise for
ERIN M. EVANS AND
EMPIRE OF EXILES

"What makes this book special is the world Evans weaves around these characters. Detailed and mysterious, a place to explore and relish. Highly recommended!"

—R. A. Salvatore, author of the Legend of Drizzt and DemonWars Saga novels

"*Empire of Exiles* has it all: characters I love, intertwined compelling mysteries in the past and present, plot twists that keep coming, and a unique and fascinating world and magic system!"

—Melissa Caruso, author of *The Obsidian Tower*

"The beginning of a truly epic tale. Deft worldbuilding and wonderful verbal fencing that is a delight to read. In these pages, you are in the hands of a master."

—Ed Greenwood, creator of the Forgotten Realms

"Readers will be drawn in by the memorable cast, vibrantly drawn fantasy cultures, and vivid prose. Epic fantasy fans will be eager to see where the series goes." —*Publishers Weekly*

"Beautifully wrought and equally ensnaring, this book lived up to and then surpassed all my expectations."

—Cat Rambo, author of *You Sexy Thing*

By Erin M. Evans

BOOKS OF THE USURPER

Empire of Exiles
Relics of Ruin

RELICS

of

RUIN

Books of the Usurper: Two

ERIN M. EVANS

orbit

orbitbooks.net

Copyright © 2024 by Erin M. Evans
Excerpt from *Books of the Usurper: Three* copyright © 2024 by Erin M. Evans

Cover design by Alexia E. Pereira
Map illustrations by Francesca Baerald
Cover images by Shutterstock
Cover copyright © 2024 by Hachette Book Group, Inc.
Author photograph by Kevin Goodier

Orbit
Hachette Book Group
1290 Avenue of the Americas
New York, NY 10104
orbitbooks.net

First Edition: April 2024

Orbit is an imprint of Hachette Book Group.
The Orbit name and logo are registered trademarks of Little, Brown Book Group Limited.

The publisher is not responsible for websites (or their content) that are not owned by the publisher.

The Hachette Speakers Bureau provides a wide range of authors for speaking events. To find out more, go to hachettespeakersbureau.com or email HachetteSpeakers@hbgusa.com.

Orbit books may be purchased in bulk for business, educational, or promotional use. For information, please contact your local bookseller or the Hachette Book Group Special Markets Department at special.markets@hbgusa.com.

Library of Congress Cataloging-in-Publication Data
Names: Evans, Erin M., author.
Title: Relics of ruin / Erin M. Evans.
Description: First edition. | New York, NY : Orbit, 2024. | Series: Books of the usurper ; 2
Identifiers: LCCN 2023037969 | ISBN 9780316441049 (paperback) | ISBN 9780316441148 (ebook)
Subjects: LCGFT: Fantasy fiction. | Novels.
Classification: LCC PS3605.V36494 R45 2024 | DDC 813/.6—dc23/20230828
LC record available at https://lccn.loc.gov/2023037969

ISBNs: 9780316441049 (trade paperback), 9780316441148 (ebook)

Printed in the United States of America

LSC-C

Printing 1, 2024

For Laura, who was exactly herself
1981–2023

IMPERIAL·CARTA
OF·PEOPLE·AND·ALL·THAT·WAS
CHARTED·AND·KNOWN

YEAR·OF·THE·REIGN·OF
EMPEROR·ESCHELLADO

Strait of Anwialad

NARJIT RIU

ANWIALAD

KHIRAZJ

HUTENNA

Pidemaki
River

SHEQAMF

DJAUBELMON

SEMILLA

Salt Wall

BENTURAN

NYMAND   OROZHAND

CHAVRESH   DADOHKO

AL-KUAL
RED DESERT

EDAWE

DOLATEMSE

ICHI

Maanfu Se

Endless Ocean

E

Pidemaki

LOST LANDS
OF THE RONQU

BINGORUT

BORSYA

POLMUNDA

Black Mother
Forest

RIZIWA   GOMGORA

Nkuanshi Mountains

IPICHAN   YATENSI

ALOJA

CHATUNJUN

NOLUCHOCH

BEMINA   KAACHYE

GHONEOCH

Sansamung
Steppe   GANKA-KEI

ZHOCHA SAN   MIN-SE   DORIYE

MEIDEUN

ASHTABARI
LANDS   BELLERANUE

Arm of Couvoton

PASHUNTANA
KINGDOM

SURATH

TAUNGHWA

DATONG

MUNUTJANG

LAIYAHKA

Sea of Siminamwi

for the Imperial Cartography Archives

RAGALE

SHADORMA

ARLABECCA

TERZANELLE

GINTANAS

Salt Wall

SESTINA

AUTHORITY·SEATS·FOR
EACH·PROTECTORATE

*Arlabecca
Imperial Authority*

Khirazj	Sestina
Min-Se	Hyanjja
Orozhand	Magaina
Bemina	Isefa
Rongu	Ragale
Ashtabari	Tornada
Datong	Caesura
Borsya	Bylina
Aloja	Hyanjja
al-Kual	Arlabecca

SAINT ASLA OF THE SALT

MARTYR OF THE WALL

DRAMATIS PERSONAE

Ahkerfi of the Copper: a sorcerer of Kuali ancestry

Alletet: the lion-headed Khirazji wisdom goddess; rules over the day

Alomalia of the Paint: an Orozhandi saint whose bones are kept in the Chapel of the Skeleton Saints

Alzari yula Manco: partner of the yula Manco nest; nest-mother of Tunuk; of Alojan ancestry

Amadea Gintanas: archivist superior of the imperial collections (South Wing), of uncertain ancestry, mostly Semillan; previously Redolfo Kirazzi's "Grave-Spurned Princess"

Anarai of the Silver: a sorcerer of mixed ancestry

Appolino Ulanitti: "the Fratricide," a former emperor of Semilla; Clement's second-eldest brother

Asla of the Salt: a martyred sorcerer whose affinity magic helped form the Salt Wall, an Orozhandi saint

Aungwi of the Corundum: a pre-Sealing sorcerer of Datong

Aye-Nam-Wati: the snake-tailed Datongu wisdom goddess

Bayan yula Manco: partner of the yula Manco nest; father of Tunuk; of Alojan ancestry

Beneditta Ulanitti: the Masked Empress of Semilla and Grand Duchess by Custom of Her Protectorates; wife of Ibramo Kirazzi, daughter of Clement

Bijan del Tolube: corundum specialist; married to Stavio Jeudi, of mixed ancestry, Kuali and Beminat

Biorni: a horned rabbit skull

Bishamar Twelve-Spider ul-Hanizan: reza of the ul-Hanizan clan and partial holder of the Orozhandi ducal authority; Nanqii's grandfather; of Orozhandi ancestry

Bucella del Vodopma: a wood specialist of the Imperial Archives, sub-affinity for cedar; of primarily Beminat ancestry

Chizid del Hwana: a previous bone specialist of the Imperial Archives, of Kuali ancestry; married to Qalba ul-Shandiian

Clement Ulanitti: previous emperor of Semilla; Beneditta's father and target of Redolfo Kirazzi's attempted coup

Clotilda Ulanitti: former empress of Semilla; mother of Clement, Appolino, and Iespero

Conzi yula Manco: Tunuk's younger sister

Corolia: a coffee shop owner of Kuali ancestry

Djaulia Ulanitti: daughter of Empress Beneditta and Consort-Prince Ibramo

Djudura of the Salt: a pre-Sealing sorcerer of Khirazj

Doba of the Pottery: an Orozhandi saint whose bones were not safely translated; one of the wooden skeletons of the Chapel of the Skeleton Saints

Dolitha Sixteen-Tamarisk ul-Benturan: reza of the ul-Benturan clan and partial holder of the Orozhandi ducal authority; Yinii's great-aunt; of Orozhandi ancestry

Dushar Six-Agamid ul-Shandiian: reza of the ul-Shandiian clan and partial holder of the Orozhandi ducal authority; Oshanna's grandfather; of Orozhandi ancestry

Duwan yula Manco: Tunuk's younger sibling

Egillio: a dog, deceased

Eizem del Dolatemse: a seller of sorcerer-wrought charms; of Kuali ancestry

Eschellado Ulanitti: Semillan emperor who reigned during the Salt Wall's sealing

Fastreda of the Glass (Fastreda Korotzma): a sorcerer of Borsyan ancestry; coconspirator of Redolfo Kirazzi

Golden Innocent: a Datongu household god who averts misfortune

Gunarro del Hwana: a fabricator of the Brotherhood of the Black Mother Forest; half brother to Chizid del Hwana; of Kuali and Borsyan ancestry

Hazaunu of the Wool: an Orozhandi saint whose bones were not safely translated; one of the wooden skeletons of the Chapel of the Skeleton Saints

Hezetha of the Sandstone: an Orozhandi saint whose bones are in the Chapel of the Skeleton Saints

Hulvia Manche: the Kinship of the Vigilant Mother Ayemi's imperial liaison; of Ashtabari ancestry

Ibramo Kirazzi: the consort-prince; son of the Usurper, Redolfo Kirazzi; former lover of Amadea Gintanas

Ichenda of the Pottery: a sorcerer of Beminat ancestry

Iespero Ulanitti: former emperor of Semilla; Clotilda's eldest son; killed with Sestrida and their four children by Appolino; of Semillan ancestry

Iosthe of the Wool (Iosthe del Sepharin): a sorcerer of Ronqu ancestry

Isecco of the Acacia: a pre–Sealing sorcerer of Semilla

Jautha Fourteen-Horse ul-Chavresh: reza of the ul-Chavresh clan and partial holder of the Orozhandi ducal authority

Jeqel of the Salt: an Orozhandi saint whose bones are in the Chapel of the Skeleton Saints

Jinjir yula Manco: partner of the yula Manco nest; nest-father of Tunuk; of Alojan ancestry

Joodashir of the Salt: a sorcerer of Minseon ancestry

Karimo del Nanova: a scrivener of Parem; murdered by the machinations of the Shrike

Katucia Ulanitti: Iespero and Sestrida's daughter; killed by Appolino; of Semillan ancestry

Khoma Seupu-lai: advisor to the Duke Minseo; mother of Quill; of Minseon and natal Semillan ancestry

Kulum yula Manco: partner of the yula Manco nest; father of Tunuk; of Alojan ancestry

Lamberto Lajonta: former Ragaleate Primate of the Order of the Scriveners of Parem; Quill and Karimo's superior; murdered by the Shrike

Lireana Ulanitti: daughter of Emperor Iespero and his heir presumptive; presumed murdered by Appolino but claimed to be discovered alive by Redolfo Kirazzi; "the Grave-Spurned Princess"

Lord on the Mountain: the supreme god worshipped in Min-Se, often depicted in a pillar of flames surrounded by his thirteen sage-riders

Maligar of the Wool: an Orozhandi saint whose bones were not safely translated; one of the wooden skeletons of the Chapel of the Skeleton Saints

Manith ul-Chavresh: representative of the ul-Chavresh clan; of Orozhandi ancestry

Melosino Ulanitti: Iespero and Sestrida's infant son; killed by Appolino

Micheleo Ulanitti: son and heir of Empress Beneditta and Consort-Prince Ibramo

Mireia del Atsina: head archivist of the Imperial Archives; of mixed ancestry, predominantly Ronqu

Nanqii Four-Oryx ul-Hanizan: a procurer of questionable goods; grandson of the ul-Hanizan reza; of Orozhandi ancestry

Nimar Eight-Myrrh ul-Shandiian: cousin of Qalba One-Fox; of Orozhandi ancestry

Ninaoku: a Beminat honored-spirit; the pet of the storm god, who fetched fire for humanity

Noniva: the Ashtabari mother goddess

Obigen yula Manco: Alojan noble consul; partner of the yula Manco nest; nest-father of Tunuk; murdered by Karimo del Nanova

Oluali of the Marble (Oluali del Dizifia): a sorcerer of primarily Beminat ancestry

Ophicida: a former Empress of Semilla

Oshanna Eleven-Sand Iris ul-Shandiian: granddaughter and assistant of the reza ul-Shandiian; first cousin, once removed of Qalba One-Fox; of Orozhandi ancestry

Pademaki the Source: the Khirazji river god, as well as the name of the river that ran through that ancient kingdom

Palimpsest (Imp): a cat

Per del Huigas: a former generalist of the Imperial Archives, assigned to the bone workrooms; of mixed ancestry

Qalba One-Fox ul-Shandiian: a previous bone specialist of the Imperial Archives; of Orozhandi ancestry; married to Chizid del Hwana

Qarabas of the Limestone: an Orozhandi saint whose bones are in the Chapel of the Skeleton Saints

Qilbat of the Cedar: an Orozhandi saint whose bones are in the Chapel of the Skeleton Saints; the maker of the wooden skeletons

Quill (Sesquillio Haigu-lan Seupu-lai): third son of House Seupu-lai and Scrivener of Parem; of mixed ancestry, predominantly Minseon

Radir del Sendiri: a generalist of the Imperial Archives; of mixed ancestry

Redolfo Kirazzi: the Usurper; former holder of the Khirazji ducal authority

Richa Langyun: member of the Kinship of Vigilant Mother Ayemi, of mixed ancestry, predominantly Datongu

Rosangerda Maschano (Rosa del Milar): the identity of Redolfo Kirazzi's assassin, the Shrike; killed by Yinii Six-Owl ul-Benturan

Salva Nine-Scorpion Gaitha-hyu: a member of the Kinship of Vigilant Mother Ayemi road cohort; of Orozhandi and Minseon ancestry

Senca yula Manco: partner of the yula Manco nest; nest-mother of Tunuk; of Alojan ancestry

Sestrida Pramodia: consort-princess to Iespero; killed by Appolino

Shaliath of the Gold: an Orozhandi saint whose bones were not safely translated; one of the wooden skeletons of the Chapel of the Skeleton Saints

Sigrittrice Ulanitti: advisor and seneschal of the Imperial Authority; "the empress's sha-dog"; Beneditta's great-aunt

Stavio Jeudi: a bronze specialist of the Imperial Archives; married to Bijan del Tolube; of Ashtabari ancestry

Stellano Zezurin: a criminal of Caesura; of predominantly Borsyan ancestry

Tabith of the Copper: an Orozhandi saint whose bones were not safely translated; one of the wooden skeletons of the Chapel of the Skeleton Saints

Tafad Mazajin: Borsyan noble consul and former holder of the Borsyan ducal authority

Thunzi of the Iron: a sorcerer of mixed ancestry

Toya: a friend of Qalba One-Fox ul-Shandiian

Tunuk yula Manco: a bone specialist of the Imperial Archives; nest-child of Lord Obigen; of Alojan ancestry

Turon Kirazzi: Redolfo's younger brother; of Khirazji ancestry

Uruphi yula Manco: partner of the yula Manco nest; birth-mother of Tunuk; of Alojan ancestry

Vari yula Manco: partner of the yula Manco nest; nest-mother of Tunuk; of Alojan ancestry

Vigdza: an unsworn fabricator; of primarily Borsyan descent

Violaria Ulanitti: Iespero and Sestrida's daughter; killed by Appolino

Yakshooka: a Datongu household trickster god in the form of a birdman with one withered wing; worshipped to bring luck

Yanawa of the Gold: an Orozhandi saint whose bones are in the Chapel of the Skeleton Saints

Yinii Six-Owl ul-Benturan: ink specialist of the Imperial Archives; of Orozhandi ancestry; Dolitha's great-niece

Zara Kirazzi: current holder of the Khirazji ducal authority; Turon's daughter and Ibramo's cousin

Zobeii of the Gold: an Orozhandi saint whose bones are in the Chapel of the Skeleton Saints

Zoifia Kestustis: a bronze specialist of the Imperial Archives; of Borsyan ancestry

EMPIRE OF EXILES SUMMARY

Stavio Jeudi, Specialist Archivist, Bronze Collection, Imperial Archives

You want a story? I'm gonna tell you a story.

This starts in the summer, right at the end, when you can taste fall coming on, that chill on the breeze. It's been about a hundred years since we sealed the Salt Wall, putting those shape-changing monsters, the changeling horde, on the other side. It's been twenty-three years since anybody worried about Redolfo Kirazzi, the Usurper, that dashing duke with his Grave-Spurned Princess. The one who thought he could take the emperor's throne and wound up only taking a noose—everyone knows this.

But then, last summer, what happens? These Paremi scriveners show up—you know the types, all forms and cassocks and official seals for the courts—requesting artifacts that belonged to none other than—guess who?—Redolfo Kirazzi. And if you thought that was bad, one of those Paremi, a boy called Karimo, immediately turns berserk and kills the Alojan noble consul and then himself.

This would be the whole story, the whole scandal, except Karimo's got a friend—Quill—and he says, "There's no way my friend"—this crazy murderer, remember, who everyone saw *assassinate* this very important man, before cutting his own throat—"no way my friend would do this." Quill starts snooping. He tells the vigilants, he tells the archives, he tells the Paremi—all of them agree: this boy is a good friend, but he's making no fucking sense at all.

Except, blessed Noniva and all the little fishes, here's our Amadea, the heart of the Imperial Archives—Amadea remembers everything, and she knows there's a poison called the Venom of Changelings that can put a memory in your head. She's not going to tell anybody how she knows this, but I hear that, when she was a girl, she was close to Redolfo Kirazzi's son, Ibramo. She maybe saw things, maybe knew to worry about Redolfo Kirazzi's favorite poison? Maybe she's even been dosed with it—I don't know; it's rude to guess. But she sees that dead boy Karimo has a mark on him, I hear, like a black star on his shoulder where the venom goes in, and she knows what's happening: Quill's right; that boy didn't do it—someone *made* him.

And then there's the vigilant—Richa, he's called. He finds all the guests at that party, the one where the murder happened. And when he asks them about the murder, they all say the same things happened, in the same words exactly—like someone put those words in their heads. The empress's people want it all closed up, but this Richa, he knows something's not right: everybody got the venom that night.

And then there's Yinii, the ink specialist, but it's her business why she's helping that boy Quill. (Although you look at how she blushes when she talks about him, you'll know exactly what her business is. But I won't talk about that.)

Someone's a killer with a complicated plan, but the more they all look, the more it could be any of those people at that party: The Orozhandi merchant everyone knows deals in drugs. The angry old lord spitting bile about Alojans. The washed-up captain who betrayed the Usurper. The boy's sullen rival. The Paremi's mentor, who was keeping two books.

Quill finds in those books payments from someone called "the Shrike," and here's where it gets good: That's the name for Redolfo's changeling assassin, one nobody ever caught. The one who made the Venom of Changelings. They just took away all the memories of them with that poison and disappeared.

Then Quill's mentor turns up hanged, but everyone sees that star mark on him. The assassin's not finished, and here's where the troubles get worse, and people don't want to talk so much about what happened. I hear Yinii got the glass sorcerer, the one locked up in the Imperial Complex, to tell her all of Redolfo Kirazzi's companions. I hear Richa spat on the empress's great-aunt, her advisor Lady Sigrittrice, when she got him fired for doing his job. I hear, too, that Amadea got Ibramo Kirazzi, the empress's consort, to come and help her—although don't you believe anyone who says they're making a fool of his wife. Our Amadea's got more self-respect than that.

But what they do find out is someone's pretending to be Redolfo Kirazzi. And the one who's the Shrike? It's the old nobleman's wife, Lady Rosangerda Maschano, pretending to be a squawking hen all these days. She and the man pretending to be Redolfo—and I don't think this is actually Redolfo Kirazzi, mind; everybody saw him hang—they manage to kidnap Quill and tell Amadea and the consort-prince to bring all the things the Paremi were supposed to collect out to the old Kirazzi family lands.

This last part, it's hard to say what's true and what's gossip. I know a couple things. I don't know it all. I know that down in those Kirazzi lands, they found a tunnel that goes under the Salt Wall, back out to the old world. I know that the Shrike died, and the way Yinii won't talk about it, I think she had something to do with it, poor baby girl. I know there was a fire, and I hear there were changelings—I hear a dozen, I hear a hundred, but one is too many, if you ask me. And if you do ask me, I think that Redolfo Kirazzi everyone saw, well, maybe that was a changeling too.

What I know is that Rosangerda Maschano is dead. That Ibramo Kirazzi comes around the archives now asking for our Amadea, but so does that vigilant, and everyone's got a story about one or the other. That Quill left the Paremi, and he works at the archives now—lucky Yinii—but he knows that what his mentor was doing, it's not done, and it might mean a whole new coup.

And I hear, too, that Amadea and the empress had a chat after that, though that's between her and the empress just now; but if anybody knows that story, you come and tell me. I'll bet it's a good one.

I

THE HEART OF THE WORLD

Year Eight of the Reign of Emperor Clement
Unclaimed territory beyond the border of the Imperial Federation of Semillan
Protectorates

Two weeks from the Salt Wall, Redolfo Kirazzi, once Duke of Semilla, stops to consider a crumbling map. Two weeks of walking is enough time, enough space, that if Emperor Clement has discovered that the Redolfo Kirazzi hanged by this time for treason and sedition is *not* Khirazj's dashing duke but a shape-shifting changeling made to stand as his double—well, Redolfo doesn't think Clement is that clever, but Redolfo has enough of a head start to make sure it doesn't matter.

He has that two-week head start and a map from before the Salt Wall's sealing. He has four wineskins now filled with water, a sword and a knife and a coil of rope. He has four companions, among them his brother, his assassin, and his sorcerer—but really none of these, because he is also carrying a large quantity of the poison known as the Venom of Khirazj.

This he checks—he thinks there is enough left to lock two or three more changelings, to trap them in a single form and identity, to bind them to his wants. He's been lucky thus far—he's run across the creatures singly or in twos and threes. Maybe scouts, maybe outcasts—their encounters haven't been causes for conversation. He's taken over three, and with these new-made allies, he's left twice that many dead between the Salt Wall and here, and it's many days until winter, when the torpor that takes their kind will make them useless.

But he has no idea how many changelings might be between him and his goal. And it's many days until winter, when their numbers won't matter.

He lays the old map on the ground before him, its surface shiny against the dusty ground. The papyrus is thick and yellowed, the map inexact and written in ancient Khirazji, a language he has studied hard to reclaim. But if one wishes to traverse the lands beyond the Salt Wall, this is as good a guide as one can get.

"We are here," he says, and circles a place north of the isthmus that squeezes close before the once lonely and distant Empire of Semilla, the seas named unfamiliar things in glyphs above and below it. An entirely different world, he thinks, one that hasn't existed for centuries.

The fourth of his companions kneels down beside him. "What's that?" she asks, pointing at the center of the map, where proud gods have been inked over a thick river, binding reeds over a blue-domed city.

"That is Khirazj," he says. "The Heart of the World."

"Is it really?"

"Maybe once," he says. But mighty Khirazj was bled dry by the changeling horde, just as every land on this map was: the canyons of Orozhand, the Black Mother Forest of Borsya, the endless kingdoms of martial Bemina, and all the other birthplaces of the survivors who would become Semilla's protectorates. Diminished at the end of the world, but alive—the map is peppered with names he's seen only here, on *this* map, kingdoms and nations whose fate was to vanish utterly under the changeling menace.

"Is that where we're going?" the girl says.

"Would you like to see it?" he asks instead of answering.

"Yes," she says. She traces a finger up the river path, along the glyphs there. "Pa-de-mah-kee?"

"The river's name." The first king of Khirazj—tradition holds that every king and queen thereafter is the descendant of the river, that all the Dukes and Duchesses Kirazzi with their leashed authority are actually the children of gods. Redolfo smirks and thinks what they'll say when he returns, as if from the grave.

He hasn't got a plan—not yet—but he will. He might not have succeeded in seizing the throne of Semilla, his coup in the name of the emperor's niece crushed and his armies overtaken, but let no one ever say Redolfo Kirazzi was a man easily bested.

And let them not say Redolfo Kirazzi was an impetuous man either—he has time now to consider what it is he really wants. Is it the throne of Semilla? Or is it Khirazj? Or is it something much greater? What a gift Clement has given him, when you think about it, this time and this space.

And when you think, really think, could one not say Redolfo Kirazzi himself might be the Heart of the World, the axis it turns on, as much as anyone?

"Where *are* we going?" she asks. "You didn't say."

He searches the map to its limits: Orozhand, Borsya, Bemina, Semilla. The high mountains that come before Aloja. The roads that lead to iron-rich Min-Se and the glittering cities of the Datongu.

Unnamed, unknown nations, he thinks. *Changeling fortresses and monarchs.*

"Where would you go?" he murmurs.

The girl leans over the map, frowning, her hands tucked into her lap. "We should find more food. Water. More of that stuff that makes the changelings behave. They must have more of it out here than they do in there."

"Practical," he says, folding up the map. "Though not very imaginative." But he considers: the Venom of Khirazj and the Venom of Changelings, two things easier to obtain out here than within the walls of Semilla, and then...She's picked up the thread that leads through these lands to a purpose, a goal. What can he gain, after all, out here, beyond the Salt Wall in the graveyard of the world? What advantage can he seize that Clement cannot?

"A place to begin," he allows. "Through Orozhand first," he declares, and he smiles. "That's the clearest road. Would you like to see what remains of their saints? I find myself quite curious."

She strokes the inked trade road that passes through Orozhand. *The Hidden Kingdom. The Canyons of the Horned Ones*, the glyphs say. "I don't know about those," she says.

"Then your education continues," Redolfo says, rolling up the map.

CHAPTER ONE

Year Eight of the Reign of Empress Beneditta
An imperial relay station on the road south of Ragale, the Imperial Federa-
tion of Semillan Protectorates
(Twenty-three years later)

In the fading light of evening, Quill considered the array of charms spread out on the peddler's blanket: Iron thistle flowers. Iron long bones and arrows. Iron masks with serene, implacable faces. He pointed at one, a creature, its teeth bared in a horrible grin.

"What's that one?" he asked.

The peddler craned his neck to see. He was an elderly Orozhandi man with charms wrapping his down-curved dark horns nearly to the tips. His third eye sat half-open and weary at the edge of his white hairline, but his smile was wide and joyous, showing a gap in his lower teeth.

"Ah! It's called a 'jaguar,'" he said. "If you are Beminat, they're lucky. And iron, of course, so this one is lucky even if you're not Beminat!"

"Oh," Quill said. "I've read about those. It's like a cat?"

"A fierce cat," the man said merrily. "A *big* cat. It could maybe eat a changeling!"

For a century, the Salt Wall had stood, a barrier against the changeling threat that had destroyed the world, a monument to the magic of the sorcerers who had sacrificed themselves in its creation.

In those days, people had known that salt and iron were poison to the shape-changing creatures that might otherwise have replaced their loved ones, sown discord in their communities, brought down their civilizations. They had worn iron charms like these to prove their safety or to test a stranger's, but the accessory had fallen out of fashion in Quill's grandparents' youth.

How things had changed.

Several other travelers had stopped and purchased the hitherto unstylish iron charms as Quill carried in his and Richa's travel gear from the relay station's enclosed courtyard to the inn—one trip for the bags, and two for the crates full of documents he'd secreted out of the tower of Parem in Ragale a week ago. The documents might hold the secrets to what Primate Lamberto, his former mentor, had been doing when he agreed to assist not only the fabled changeling hunter of the Usurper's coup but a man claiming to be Redolfo Kirazzi himself, back from the grave.

A second coup, staged beyond the Salt Wall. This one riddled with changelings.

The Imperial Authority had quickly hidden everything they could about it, sworn Quill and the others to secrecy, and continued on as if it could be safely ignored.

And now people were buying iron charms again.

"I have amulets for the saints as well," the peddler said. "Do you need protection?"

Like you wouldn't believe, Quill thought. To be fair, though, nothing else had happened in the intervening months. They were approaching winter, the turn of the new year, and there had been no other attacks. No incidents of unexplained murders, no new breaches in the Salt Wall. The assassin they'd called "the Shrike" was dead, and so was the changeling pretending to be Redolfo Kirazzi, and Primate Lamberto besides. The tunnel beneath the Salt Wall they'd been intending to use had collapsed, its contents burned. The Imperial Authority was aware of everything that had happened—most everything.

But the Shrike's words to Quill before her death wouldn't let him relax: *I hope he never told you he was an innocent in this . . . Lamberto was never blackmailing me. I was paying him.*

Whatever was happening, whatever the primate had been hired to do, it wasn't finished. The risk was still there, the coup incomplete. Someone on the other side of the wall still held the reins.

Quill lingered over the rows of painted saints' medallions, some portraits of the Orozhandi sorcerers in life, some their posed skeletons. He recognized Saint Asla of the Salt, the Martyr of the Wall prominently among them, her hands spread to raise the salt out of the earth and the sea, by the strength of her affinity, her tiny beatific face still fleshed, her bare bones silvery. He wondered if Yinii would like one. Or, really, if she would like one from *him*.

"Do you make these yourself?" he asked.

"The saints' amulets yes," the peddler said. "I cast them of lead, paint them. The iron charms are the gifts and blessings of Thunzi of the Iron. I make a pilgrimage to the maqu'tajii once a year." He pressed his hands together in a fist and bowed against them, honoring the absent sorcerer.

Quill's Orozhandi had improved a little over the last two months. He knew enough to know "maqu'tajii" was the word used for sorcerers who weren't Orozhandi and therefore didn't *quite* fit into the connection the horned people felt their own sainted sorcerers made between their gods and their people. Holy enough to visit, to honor, to resell the tokens made from the magic of their affinity. But not saints.

"I'm seeing a girl who counts Saint Asla as her personal saint," he said to the peddler. Then: "Sort of. I've been away. And she's been busy. She works at the Imperial Archives. We both do, I suppose."

The peddler blinked up at him, bemused, as if he couldn't imagine what Quill meant. He reached over and picked up one of the amulets, laying it across his wrinkled palm. "This is Saint Hazaunu," he said. "Of the Wool. The guardian on the clifftop. The eye that watches the weft and the sentinel that guards the flock. A most holy lady.

"*This* is my saint," he added in a lowered voice.

Richa came up behind Quill, carrying the last of the boxes of Primate Lamberto's papers. He wore the deep-blue uniform of the Vigilant Kinship, the watchful order that kept safe the cities of Semilla from fire, crime, and destruction. The silver-gray fur of the long cloak's collar fluttered against his close-cropped dark hair and his tan cheeks as a cold autumn breeze snaked down the entryway to the courtyard.

"You all right?" Richa asked.

"Shopping. Do you want an amulet?" Quill asked.

Richa frowned at him, as puzzled as the peddler had been when Quill had brought up Yinii. "No, I'm set. We need to get these locked up," Richa said, lifting the box of papers. "Excuse us, esinor."

Quill rolled his eyes and bought the jaguar pendant from the man, then followed Richa into the inn that made up one wall of the relay station. The building was almost a small fortress, arranged around a central courtyard with a fountain at its center, a design formed in far-off ancient Khirazj. They dotted the network of roads that ran throughout the empire, improved by engineers brought by the Datongu and the Beminat when they'd fled to Semilla a hundred years before. The pale walls that rose up two stories to a red-tiled roof were Semilla itself's favored style, although the Ashtabari innkeeper had hung nets festooned with small charms from the corners, to bring luck and safety and good fortune.

After he and Richa deposited the last of the boxes in the relay station's storeroom, where they'd be locked up safe overnight, they collected their servings of pilaf studded with smoky meat, pistachios, and dried fruit.

"Haven't been here in a while," Quill said as he sat down.

"You stop at this station often?" Richa asked.

"I have," Quill said. "When I was traveling with Primate Lamberto and...Karimo." A flush of sorrow washed over him, but it was easier now to talk about his murdered friend. "But the primate hated staying in these station inns. We'd usually stop in one of the villages back toward Ragale if we were heading to the capital." Richa nodded, and Quill went on. "It's a nice one. Fountain and all. And the peddlers—I wonder if they sell much here?"

"That's for them to say," Richa said slowly.

"Do you think I ought to buy Yinii one of those amulets?" Quill asked as he scraped up the last of his supper. "There were some nice ones."

The older man sighed. "Does she need one?"

"Seems like a nice-enough present. I think. I don't actually know," Quill admitted. "It might be the kind of thing your aunt gives you when you take your oaths. Do you know?"

Richa prodded at his rice. "I don't."

Richa was many things, in Quill's estimation: he was a dedicated vigilant, caring about the safety of the city even when it went against his superiors; he was steady, thoughtful, and unruffled in a way that Quill envied sometimes; he was clever and good at figuring things out, people and problems.

He was also, however, a horrible traveling companion.

"You should get Amadea a gift," Quill said pointedly. "She likes those little animal figurines."

Mentioning the archivist superior had worked before to spur Richa into conversation, and Quill was pleased when Richa sat up, his mouth working a moment, before he said, "How are you liking working at the archives?"

Quill wrinkled his nose. "I barely have. The training was fine. It's not that complicated on paper. It'll be what crops up day to day that's tricky. Amadea said they're going to set me up with Tunuk when we get back, and I don't get the impression he likes me much."

"Give him a chance," Richa said. "You didn't meet under the best circumstances."

Quill looked down at his plate, a sudden plunging grief yanking on his chest. Karimo's death was a horrible thing to face, but in his madness, Karimo had killed Tunuk's nest-father Lord Obigen yula Manco.

"Fair," Quill said. He dragged his spoon through the dregs of the sauce. "It was sort of strange. Being back in Ragale. Being in the tower with all the Paremi and…not *being* one. Made me sort of wonder if I made the wrong decision rescinding my oath." He sat back and folded his arms. "Do you ever feel like that? Like you shouldn't have sworn to the Kinship?" When Richa only shook his head, his eyes on the pilaf, Quill pressed on. "How did you decide to join the Vigilant Kinship?"

Richa looked up, his expression…oddly still. "Why?"

"Making conversation?" Quill said. "We hardly talk while we're riding. I'm going mad. Give me this: ten minutes of talking. How did you come to take your oath with the Kinship?"

Richa drew a long breath through his nose, looking up over Quill's head, and for a moment, Quill wondered if he'd somehow hit on something Richa was more sensitive about than what was going on with Amadea, and Quill nearly apologized.

But then Richa looked down, smiled vaguely, and said, "It's not that interesting. I saw a need in the city, and I had a need for myself—I wanted a vocation, and that was something I cared about. Probably similar to you and the Paremi or the archives."

Quill made a face. "Not really. To begin with, my mother pointed me at the Paremi. Did you have family in the Kinship?"

"No." The older man stood, still smiling vaguely. "I'm going for a walk before I turn in. Feeling antsy."

Quill stood as well. "Mind if I come out with you? I think I do want that amulet after all."

They went back out, but the peddler was gone, the courtyard still and quiet but for the nickering of horses in the stable opposite the inn's entrance. Quill followed Richa to the gates and went up to the vigilants posted there, a trim dark-skinned woman pulling down the iron grate that barred the entrance and an Ashtabari man, his mottled green-and-gray tentacles coiled under him as he leaned on a spear.

"Do you know where the peddler who was selling amulets went?" Quill asked.

"The old man? He just left," the woman said. She nodded at the half-down gate. "You can probably catch him."

Quill frowned. "He doesn't live at the relay station?"

"Nah," the man says. "Just sells here." He nodded to Richa. "We're locking the gate so we can take our duty breaks. Pull the bell if no one's here when you get back."

"Much obliged," Richa said, ducking under the grating. Quill followed him, trailing several steps behind, until they were out on the wide road.

"If I don't see him, maybe I'll just walk with you," Quill said.

Richa stopped and turned, raising a hand. "Quill, I know you need to talk, but I . . . I am used to the peace of my own silence. I just want a walk."

"All right," Quill said. "I wasn't going to stop you."

Richa blew out another breath. "You didn't ask for my opinion, but we've been at this long enough that I think it needs to be said. You clearly miss Karimo. You need a friend. And, Quill, I think highly of you, but you and I are . . . in very different places in our lives. And even when I was twenty, I didn't really want to talk about what the first consuls were advocating for when they . . . did the thing you were talking about yesterday."

"All right," Quill said again. "We can talk about something else—"

"I need the quiet of my own head," Richa said, "and I'm sorry I'm not giving you what you need here, but it's not . . . if you want to talk about Karimo, I can talk about Karimo—I've lost people, and I know it's hard. But I'm not going to talk about what you think I should be saying to Amadea or what you want to buy Yinii, and I don't want to talk about *anything* right now, all right?"

It was more words than Richa had said to him in days. Quill stiffened, disliking how abruptly Richa had cut into something Quill himself hadn't been completely sure of. Disliking how sharp that hurt was, he took a step back, and Richa started to say something, maybe apologize.

Quill raised a hand. "That's fine. I'll just—"

Rising voices cut off Quill's reply. Both he and Richa turned toward the sound.

Down the road, out of the range of the relay station's lamplight, a tangled shadow writhed, like a many-armed monster. It took a moment for Quill's eyes to pick out the details of them in the shine of the moonlight: two people struggling, shouting.

And then Quill's heart nearly leapt from his chest as the moonlight caught the knife between the two.

Richa took off running, and what could Quill do but chase after him? A scream rang out, and the mass of shadows split into two—one falling and one running for the forest that lined the road.

"Get the vigilants!" Richa shouted back at Quill as he sped after the fleeing form.

But Quill was coming up to the fallen body—the peddler—and there was so much blood. He dropped down beside the old man, his hands going to the wound on the man's stomach, trying to hold the man's guts back.

Quill was kneeling on the road, but suddenly he was sure he was also in the yula Manco house, in the aftermath of Karimo's attack. The old man stared up at him, panting, his third, parietal eye wide, seeing the shape of Quill's body heat in the darkness.

"You must," the old man gasped. "You must..."

"Don't worry!" Quill said. "It's all right!" And in his mind, he was on the floor beside Karimo again, trying to put his throat back together, while a little part of him said, *That didn't work before. This isn't working now.*

Quill screamed for help. He must have. Where were the people in the relay station? Where was Richa? Where was the man with the knife?

"You have to...save her..." the peddler gasped.

"Who?" Quill gasped back. *Yinii*, he thought numbly. *Amadea. The empress. The Shrike.* "Who?" he managed around his panicking brain, his hands sunk into the wet of the man's gut. "*Who?*"

The man's day-eyes fluttered open, but when he looked at Quill, they did not focus. "In the woods," he said. "Upon the hill... Beyond the white rocks...You must protect her." He coughed, rackety and desperate, and blood spattered from his mouth, then poured. Quill automatically reached to push it back, to hold it in, and felt the man's last breath rattle across his hand.

Quill stood up. He couldn't catch his breath. He ran a bloodied hand through his hair, growing loose and shaggy since he'd begun the process to renounce his vows as a Paremi. Where was Richa? Where were the vigilants from the relay station?

Where was the woman he needed to protect?

Richa burst out of the same woods, furious and scowling, holding a small Borsyan cold-magic lamp in one hand. "Lost the bastard," he said. "Where are the vigilants?" He stopped, taking in Quill, the blood, the dead man on the road. "Shit," he said.

"We have to go," Quill said. "There's someone in the woods. A woman. That might be where the killer went. He said she's in the woods, up the hill, beyond the white rocks."

For a moment, the world felt too large, the sky unable to contain Quill to hold him down—the horror endless and the problem impossible and Richa was about to say, *Look, you've been through a lot. You're still figuring this out. It feels like Karimo, but do you really think a dying man raving about a woman in the woods makes sense? We should go back. We should wait for day. You should not be involved.*

But Richa cared beyond his basic duty, Richa wasn't ruffled by the unexpected, and Richa might not want to unburden himself to Quill, but he looked back toward the woods, scanning the tree line as if looking for a hint of a rise, and believed Quill. "Come on," he said, and plunged toward the woods.

The energy that surged in Quill to move, to do, to stop all this madness seemed to grip Richa just as strongly, and the younger man kept his eyes on the ghostlike patch of silvery fur as Richa moved ahead of him through the gloom and moonlight, along a path Quill couldn't see. In the woods, up a hill...

The white boulders were deep in the shadow of an ancient fir tree with deep, craggy bark, but even there they glowed faintly as if the moonlight sought them out. Richa stopped in the little clearing there, looking up the steep slope the boulders were set into.

Richa handed Quill the glowing orb. "Stay here."

He started to climb, scaling the smooth-sided rocks as if they were a ladder and moving up the bare earth slope beyond. Quill looked around, suddenly aware of the possibility of the man with the knife. He moved closer to the rocks, closer to Richa. Surely the vigilant, trained and dedicated to the protection of the Imperial Federation, had a knife on him? Quill only had a little blade for sharpening styli...

As he searched the woods, the rocks, the shadows, he found the gap between the rocks and the little cave beyond. *In the woods, upon the hill, beyond the white rocks...*

Quill squeezed through the gap, sweeping the light around the space beyond. The cold-magic lamp spread a thin bluish light around the small space. The ceiling had been dug out enough for Quill to straighten up, the beams of the tree's roots standing out here and there, and the peddler had dug into the hill, pounded the walls smooth.

There was a bed, a box full of dishes, a box full of battered books. A knife on hooks on the wall. A marked-up map. Portraits of saints everywhere. A cushion before the largest portrait of the saint, a quiet personal altar. The stink of a seldom-washed body.

There was no woman in the little dirt room.

Quill let out a breath. No rescue, no action—just standing in a dead man's home, all his things waiting for him to take them up again, the scent of his living fading already. The shock of Quill's adrenaline drained away, leaving him weak and grieving.

The portraits of the saints—fleshed and skeletal—stared down at him, and it took Quill a moment to realize they were all the same one. The woman with the shepherd's crook and the date palm. Saint Hazaunu of the Wool. In different hands and shifting styles, but the same woman. He approached the portrait over the little altar, stepping around the cushion. Her three black eyes regarded him solemnly.

This is my saint, the man had said. The one he'd chosen to venerate, to pray to for his own cares and worries. Quill swallowed and wondered if Saint Hazaunu knew, somewhere, somehow, that her follower had died. He turned away.

The ground beneath his foot gave a hollow *thump*.

Quill stepped back, shining the light downward. The ground was pounded dirt, but—he stomped against it again—here there was *something* beneath the dirt. A box, a chest, a wooden barrier—his imagination raced ahead, picturing some frightened hostage hiding beneath. He set aside the cold-magic light and started digging his bloodstained fingers into the dirt.

"Quill?" Richa shouted. "Quill?"

"In the cave! Between the rocks!" He found the wood quickly, swept it free to the edges. He took out the little penknife and fitted it into the uncovered groove, the grit of the dirt grinding the fine edge.

"It's all right," he said to the possible girl. "It's all right."

Richa came up behind him. "Did you find—"

Quill levered the penknife up against the edge of the box, snapping the blade but breaking the wood free. He grabbed the edge and pulled up, scattering more dirt across the floor, and looked down into the darkness he'd just revealed.

There was, indeed, someone in there.

Only they were very, very dead.

A skeleton lay curled on its side, its hands clasped before its face, as if sleeping. The bones of each browned finger glinted with caps of gold. The horn that curved away from the down-turned face sparkled with charms, and fine wires wrapped the arm bones, strung with pearls. Pillowed beneath its skull were pages of parchment intricate with layers and layers of writing.

The peddler's medallions flashed through Quill's thoughts again, the gem-encrusted faces in the Imperial Archives' Chapel of the Skeleton Saints.

In the woods, up the hill, beyond the white rocks, lay the lost bones of an Orozhandi saint.

CHAPTER TWO

Amadea Gintanas, archivist superior of the southern wing, sat in the prison tower of the imperial compound, reminding herself she was not twenty years away, young and fearful before the sorcerer known as Fastreda of the Glass—forcing herself to keep her attention on Fastreda Korotzma where she sat now, aged and isolated, tapping her glass leg against the chair and facing one of Amadea's specialists on the other side of the little table.

Fastreda's eyes glinted—one blue and whole, one paler and fashioned of glass. The scar that took the eye raked up her face from the middle of that cheek, full of crystals and ending in a tuft of spun glass that tangled in her red-blond curls.

"So," she said, her smile still cruel, still dangerous, as she poured coffee into tiny wooden cups, "do you have an answer for me this time, little shredfinch? How did I know I was a sorcerer?"

Yinii bowed her head, horn charms jingling as she brushed her clasped knuckles to the closed third eye on her brow. Her reddish hair had been braided into a knot at the nape of her neck, her dark blue archivist's tunic neatly pressed for the occasion.

"Maqu'tajii," she said. She looked so small, so delicate sitting opposite Fastreda—Amadea was abruptly aware Yinii was only a little older than Amadea herself had been, when she had been afraid and uncertain and used by powerful people like Fastreda.

But at the same time, Amadea thought of Yinii two months ago, caught in the spiral of her affinity, swathed in terrible power and endless ink. A specialist could speak to the worked material they held an affinity for, uncover flaws and histories and find ways to improve it. Amadea knew Yinii could date a scroll, could tell if fading ink could be protected, could identify writers by the faint trembling of the lines, could name the components—where the pigments had come from, what the solvent had been. She was a talented specialist and a very intelligent young woman. But an affinity strong enough to crumble wood into char, to pull water through stone, to dismember an enemy and distill her into gruesome ink...

How did you know you were a sorcerer?

"Oh no, little shredfinch," Fastreda had said when Yinii initially asked. "You must tell me the answer to that."

That first time Fastreda turned her question back to her, Yinii was startled—guessed without thinking.

"You couldn't control the spiral?" The pulling force of affinity magic, the dangerous tide that Amadea had to stay alert to, making certain her specialists weren't dragged into madness.

Fastreda snorted, waved that away. "Ah, I see you're just being nosy. No, goat-girl, there is no spiral for the sorcerer. You cannot control it any more than you can control the air around you, and it's only the weak who pretend otherwise. Go home. Think about this question."

Yinii returned to the archives, keeping to her rooms. Her hands—the touch of her affinity—she wrapped in cotton gloves. A few weeks later, she and Amadea returned. Fastreda poured the coffee, offered cakes, and asked again, "How did I know I was a sorcerer?"

"You could feel it, all the time. Calling," Yinii blurted. "It's supposed to come and go, but you heard it all the time."

Fastreda rolled her gaze toward Amadea. "This is not my responsibility, my sparrow. To hold your *specialists'* hands and tell them they are going to be all right because they enjoy their affinities. Perhaps you are no shredfinch. Go home."

Another month had passed, and that morning Yinii had come to Amadea in her office, where Amadea was fretting over letters from Ragale and the palace, and asked for a third time to see Fastreda.

Amadea was powerfully reminded of old Borsyan stories, tales from Fastreda's ancestors' homeland. The hero always gained his gifts from entering the Black Mother Forest, appeasing her crow-winged daughters and fulfilling their tests, and thereby bearing magic out of the strange, otherworldly wood. There were always three tests in those stories. Three tasks, three trials, three questions.

In the little wooden room in the tower of the Imperial Complex, Yinii lifted her head and tried a third answer: "You knew you were a sorcerer because the sand answered when you called the glass." Her voice was fragile, her little hands weaving together in anxious patterns. Amadea held her breath.

But Fastreda's disappointment pinched her face. She looked Yinii over, as if she were a dried-out joint of meat. "If you are this curious," she said, "there is an easy answer."

Yinii blinked up at her, her green eyes fearful and hopeful. "What is it?"

Fastreda held up a pinky finger. "Cut it off. Or a toe if you like. When it lands as only flesh, you'll know. Only sorcerers' bodies transmute."

Yinii made a soft sound of alarm.

"Fastreda," Amadea said sharply.

"What?"

"We've come to you for help," Amadea told the sorcerer sternly. "Frightening her is not helpful."

"What she is might be frightening," Fastreda said. "*You* know this."

Amadea made her face a mask to hide the thoughts that split her mind in two.

What she is might be frightening. You know this—because Amadea was an archivist superior, and how many specialists had she shepherded through their affinity magic, through the difficulties of its surges and droughts? Even if she had never worked with specialists whose powers approached the strength and reach that made someone a sorcerer, Amadea understood that if Yinii's abilities were that strong, it would not merely mean she was quicker at dating inks and identifying handwriting. The glass specialists in the archives could note inclusions and mineral stains, sense the marks of the furnaces and the molds—the best could re-fuse cracked artifacts.

Fastreda could stand on a beach and raise an army of glass soldiers if you asked nicely, reshape them as they shattered. If Yinii were a sorcerer, managing her affinity would only be the beginning.

But: *What she is might be frightening. You know this*—because Amadea had not always been an archivist superior, and when she'd known Fastreda of the Glass, it had been because she was a young girl held up by Redolfo Kirazzi as the true heir to the throne. She was dosed with memory-altering poisons, placed in danger, threatened and praised in turn. And when the coup had collapsed, when the Imperial Authority had spared her but made clear that she remained a danger and would not be allowed to imperil the empire again, Amadea had fled to the archives and remained hidden.

Until two months ago, when a changeling wearing Redolfo Kirazzi's face had lured her out, had promised her the world, had shown her the bodies of four changeling doubles, each wearing her face exactly.

What she is might be frightening—a lost princess…a hidden monster… something worse.

Did Fastreda know who Amadea really was? Amadea's memories rushed over clandestine meetings, Redolfo's inner circle, Fastreda Korotzma in conference by candlelight. She was as close to the Usurper as anyone alive. If Amadea asked, she might let something slip.

If Amadea asked, she might have to know the truth.

"What do you think, my sparrow?" Fastreda asked. "Is she something frightening? Or just a little…strong?"

"I think we should leave," Amadea said, standing. "Yinii?"

"No," Yinii said. "I want to ask something."

The Orozhandi girl raised her gaze from the table, the charms wired to the horns that curved back from her round face all tinkling as she moved. She drew a deep breath, her shoulders rising with the effort, and turned her green eyes on the sorcerer.

"Is it very terrible? Your power?"

Fastreda's sly look turned curious. "This is the wrong question. I cannot be more or less than the glass. That would mean I am not myself. What I was before it woke up…that is gone. The glass is mine until I am old and ready to be fed to the forest. And I, for one, would not trade it—though I suspect Her Imperial Majesty would love to return me to my prior state." She turned back to Amadea, her sharp smile returned. "Wouldn't that be so much easier?"

"I find," Amadea said, "that the idea of remaking a person for one's own convenience and preference turns my stomach. You shouldn't rewrite people."

"'Shouldn't,'" said Fastreda grimly, "is different than 'cannot.'" She said to Yinii, "Little shredfinch, you don't have much stomach today, for cakes or for talking. Why don't you go? Let me talk to my Amadea for a moment."

Amadea nodded when Yinii looked up at her. "I'll be quick," she promised, as the girl stood, made her obeisance. To the Orozhandi, after all, sorcerers were something holy. Fastreda smirked as she did, watching Yinii leave the room.

When the door closed, she spoke to Amadea. "You have not told me how your hunt for the Shrike went. You come, you go, but I find myself curious over and over. What was so important that you came to me, after all these years, my little sparrow, and you don't even tell me how you fared?"

"It didn't seem relevant."

"Nothing else on this side of the Wall or the other was enough to make you come and see me," Fastreda said. "So I am very invested. Did you catch her?"

Yinii's haunted look. Quill's halting retelling. *She took the Shrike apart. She just . . . set a hand on her, and then there was screaming and heat and then . . . ink. Just ink.*

"She's dead," Amadea said flatly.

Fastreda tilted her head. "I don't think that's all. You would have told me, if that were all. 'No, Fastreda, no friends are coming for you.' Who was she?"

"You knew her as Rosa del Milar then, but she was Lady Rosangerda Maschano." A prim noblewoman, a doting mother—but really the assassin who'd wielded the Venom of Changelings for Redolfo Kirazzi, erasing and revising memories.

Fastreda frowned. "Hmm. Maybe it will come back to me. What

was she doing? A foolish thing—sticking your head out of your hidey-hole."

Redolfo—or something like him, something from over the Salt Wall—murmuring in that dark cave: *I won't say that this was all for you—I wouldn't dream of it—but the plans did turn on you, on how to draw you out.*

Amadea folded her hands together, let her gaze drift across the room. *White icing. Blue eye. Red chair. Red jacket.* She took a long, slow breath, then nearly lied and told Fastreda she had no idea.

"Did you know about the tunnel?" she asked instead.

"Which tunnel?" Fastreda asked.

Amadea's pulse churned, Ibramo's assurances that there *were* no other tunnels a rope she clung to in the sudden storm of panic. "Under the Salt Wall. Near Sestina."

"Ah!" Fastreda nodded. "This makes sense. Redolfo...he was always so smug, so coy about how he got his poisons." She gave a little laugh. "I will tell you a secret. I thought the venom was a big man's gambit. A lie. I didn't believe in that poison, not until I realized someone had given it to me. That Shrike. Rosa."

"What tunnels did you mean, then?"

Fastreda waved this away. "Tunnels, tunnels—Redolfo had a hundred secret strongholds. Or at least more than I want to think about. I know they found some full of notes and coin and weapons. What was in this one? Just a dangerous door?"

Four bodies on the biers. Four women, with long dark hair, shafts of silver along their brows. Four arched noses, four pairs of eyes that weren't so wrinkled really. Four pairs of high cheekbones scattered with freckles she could never quite cover. Four pairs of lips she had been assured were her best feature. Four changelings wearing the form of Amadea Gintanas, hidden away for years and years. Waiting.

"It's gone now," Amadea said. "Collapsed."

"Probably best," Fastreda said.

Amadea studied her a moment. "Before, what you said about the empress remaking you, did you mean that the venom...? Could the Venom of Changelings make a specialist forget their gift? Could it...? If someone had given that to you..."

Fastreda's shard-sharp smile grew very slowly, her living eye as cold as the glass one. "I would cut my own throat first. And I'll bet the little shredfinch would, too."

When Amadea reached the entry courtyard, Yinii was standing beneath the bright-washed bricks of the tower, buttoning her cloak against the chilly autumn wind. She stared down at the stones and straightened her gloves with a distracted expression, a frown pulling her mouth and eyes, tightening the third eye nestled closed along her hairline.

Amadea sighed and pulled her own cloak back around her, thinking of Fastreda's cold eyes. She exchanged her shoes with the guard and paused beside Yinii, watching as she fastened the quartz charm back to one horn—the guards had held it when they entered, knowing it would trigger Fastreda's affinity.

"We don't have to come back," Amadea said. "If you'd rather."

"We don't have an answer," Yinii said.

"It's...not always a clear-cut thing. You aren't having problems now. You could take the gloves off—"

"No," Yinii interrupted.

Amadea reached out and took Yinii's arm, folding it around her own as they walked into the city. "I would not ask you to risk coming here if I were worried you weren't out of danger." She squeezed Yinii's arm. "You have always had a strong affinity. Stress makes affinities more erratic."

"Fastreda acts like there's an answer I'm missing."

"There is always the possibility that Fastreda isn't being entirely forthcoming."

"She's maqu'tajii," Yinii said hotly.

Amadea thought of the rows of skeletons in the chapel, the holy remains and relics of Orozhand's saints, and wondered if any of them had tormented innocent children in life like Fastreda had.

"I don't think we ought to have this argument again," Amadea said gently. Yinii only sighed.

Amadea squeezed her arm once more as they came out into the square the archives sat on—the building rose up five impressive stories. A colonnade of caryatids—ten figures for the ten nations that formed the empire after the Salt Wall was sealed; scholars and knowledge gods and noble rulers—framed a walkway on the second and third floors, and above them, the Datongu wisdom goddess, Aye-Nam-Wati, perched in marble on all the red-tiled corners of the roof.

Amadea felt a weight lift off her at the sight. Whatever dangers Fastreda posed—whatever still lurked beyond, in the hands of changelings or Redolfo Kirazzi—the archives remained a refuge.

"I had a letter from Quill this morning," Amadea said. "They should be arriving back soon. Yesterday was his hope, but travel can be unpredictable." Amadea watched her from the corner of one eye as they entered the archives' bright foyer. "I heard a rumor that you two were meant to sit down for a coffee before he left for Ragale."

Yinii touched the pink salt crystal on her horn. "Who said that?"

"Stavio, of course," Amadea said. The bronze specialist was entirely too invested in the budding romance. "Would you rather," she asked, trying to sound casual, "I keep Quill busy elsewhere?"

"No," Yinii said. "No, not...not that...only..." She sighed, her shoulders sagging. "I wish I knew the answer. Sorcerers don't go sit down for coffee."

"Well, that's silly," Amadea said. "Fastreda is delighted to have us for coffee."

"You know what I mean."

"Don't make decisions for an evening based on how your whole life might go," Amadea told Yinii. "You'll find you're often wrong."

"Is that the argument that lets you sneak off to spend evenings with the consort-prince?" Yinii asked snappishly.

Amadea started at the question. Yinii's cheeks were bright, her mouth a tight frown, and Amadea marveled that she'd misread their conversation so completely. "Meeting with Ibramo is entirely about the Wall and Fastreda—"

"Never mind," Yinii said, turning from her toward the stairs leading up, away from the rest of the archives. "I think I need sequestration."

The great opal doors to the archives parted, and two runners in turquoise uniforms, a boy and a girl, eeled through the crack, calling out over each other.

"Archivist Gintanas, you're wanted—"

"—in the mask vault, right away—"

"—the new generalist and the vigilant—"

"Richa and Quill are back?" Yinii asked.

"Yes, and they want Archivist Gintanas in the Bone Vault, and they can't find Archivist yula Manco—"

"Lady Sigrittrice is here!" the young boy shouted over his fellow runner. "She's here, and she's in the mask vault, and she only wants to talk to you, and she's been waiting a quarter hour."

Amadea's thoughts shrank down to a point. She drew a slow breath, looking over the runners' heads at the opal-patterned mural, at the gold-masked emperor split by the doors. What could the empress's great-aunt and closest advisor want with Amadea? In private?

She thought of their last conversation and knew it was nothing good.

"It sounds like Lady Sigrittrice has the advantage," she said lightly.

"I'll go meet Quill and Richa," Yinii offered, avoiding Amadea's gaze. "I'll tell them you'll be there soon."

"Thank you." Amadea dismissed the runners and made her way up to the Imperial Mask Vault, before stepping inside and locking the door behind her.

The masks of generations of Imperial Majesties looked down on Amadea Gintanas. Imperial gold, private green, invisible black, as well as the rarer masks: the red of war, the white of mourning, the blue of birth, the silver of death. She flicked her gaze up toward these last ones, a quartet waiting for the ends of the empress and her heirs. Her husband, the consort-prince.

An older woman stood beneath the wall of golden masks. Sigrittrice Ulanitti, the empress's great-aunt and closest advisor, wore a mask of her own, black as dark as her velvet dress to show she was not to be confronted, not to be noticed. Unless, of course, she told you to.

"Did you change your mind about killing me, esinora?" Amadea asked.

"If I had, you would be dead," Lady Sigrittrice said mildly.

Amadea kept her expression smooth as a mask on the wall. This was the third time she had faced Lady Sigrittrice alone. First, as a young girl in the palace of Sestina, fearful and grieving, facing punishment for having been used by the Usurper, Redolfo Kirazzi, in his attempted coup. She had pleaded then—just let her go, her and Redolfo's son, they wanted nothing to do with the Imperial Majesty, only each other. She had not known, not really, who she was or what more she could lose. But Sigrittrice had laid it all out in cut-glass clarity, how it would be best if Amadea let everything slip through her fingers. No one wanted to hang a teenaged girl, after all.

Then, only a few months ago, Amadea, a woman of a certain age who knew herself or thought she did, tucked into a tiny room with the Empress Beneditta and a secret that might unmake all her authority, in the wake of deaths and revelations that threatened chaos and ruin. Sigrittrice had intervened then as well, made it clear Amadea would not risk the empire once more—a word of this, and she would die.

This, the third meeting, Sigrittrice had entered Amadea's realm. When she had been spared, so long ago, Amadea had fled to the archives looking for a place to hide from the world, but twenty years later, it was her fortress and her armor.

Three tests, she thought. *Three trials*.

"Are you well, Archivist Gintanas?" Lady Sigrittrice asked. "No further enemies or conspiracies dogging you?"

"I have an unruly bone specialist, paper in alignment, and four apprentices I don't think will work out," she said glibly. "Otherwise, nothing you need to trouble yourself with." She paused a moment, thinking of what might have brought Lady Sigrittrice to her: a rumor too close to Amadea speaking the empress's secrets; something found in the charred remains of Redolfo Kirazzi's hoard; Ibramo.

Yinii, she thought, a sudden lump in her throat.

"Tell me why you're here, esinora," Amadea said. "Neither of us has time for games."

"You call it 'games,' I call it 'politeness.'" Lady Sigrittrice folded her hands against the black spread of her skirts. "I requested your presence because I require your help. I need you to stop me from doing what the empress has tasked me with."

Amadea frowned, considering the peculiar request, the traps that might lie in it. "I'm not sure how I can do that," she said slowly. "I can't rebuke the empress any more than you can."

"No one needs to rebuke anyone," Sigrittrice said. "What I require is *bureaucracy*." She paused, considering Amadea. "The empress has requested the Red Mask."

For a moment, Amadea couldn't make sense of what she'd said—she found herself casting back through her memories and searching the wall for a mask of imperial gold with carnelian accents, a mask of private green trimmed by a red ribbon. But no matter how she turned the statement, it remained simply as Sigrittrice had said it: *The empress has requested the Red Mask.*

Amadea glanced up at the wall where the Red Mask hung, shining with carmine lacquer, the deep black grooves of its carved cheeks powdery with stubborn dust. Full face, mostly human, the eyes shaded behind fine silk coverings, the mouth an expressionless line.

This was the mask Emperor Clement had donned when he rode against Redolfo Kirazzi and the Grave-Spurned Princess. It was the same mask Emperor Eschellado had worn when the changelings threatened the last of civilization and the Salt Wall had been made, sealing Semilla and her protectorates from the wider world.

The Red Mask was for war, and there was only one.

"Who are we at war with, esinora?" Amadea asked, her voice calm, her expression still.

"Do not pretend to be a fool, and I shall not treat you like one," Sigrittrice said. "Beneditta fears what lies over the Salt Wall. What might have infiltrated Semilla."

Amadea met her piercing gaze. "Redolfo Kirazzi."

"Redolfo Kirazzi is dead," Sigrittrice said, the weight of imperial authority behind her proclamation. "He was hanged by the neck twenty-three years ago. He is entombed at Sestina."

"And something wearing his face and speaking with his voice

came back over the Salt Wall to activate an assassin you couldn't find in those twenty-three years. A changeling cannot be that accurate without reference, and that changeling was working for *someone* who knows the recipes for the Venom of Changelings and the Venom of Khirazj."

Sigrittrice tilted her head. "You are lecturing *me* on the nature of the venoms?"

This was the secret Amadea had uncovered, the words she could never speak: the emperors and empresses of Semilla, every Ulanitti born, had changeling blood in their veins. Born to be molded into the perfect rulers, just and fair and dedicated to the good of the empire—but made that way only by their relation to the worst of civilization's enemies. Sigrittrice was not only the empress's advisor but the keeper of this knowledge and the knowledge of the twin poisons—the Venom of Changelings and the Venom of Khirazj— that molded and manipulated the minds of people and changelings, respectively, and shaped the Ulanittis into what they were.

Amadea brushed her sleeves reflexively as if she could dust the misstep from her. "No. I am merely suggesting that what happened...Have you exhumed the body?"

"And done what?" Sigrittrice said. "A changeling locked into a form looks like a dead man. A man dead twenty-three years looks like a pile of bones. Perhaps your bone specialist could tell the difference, but I think more than enough people know too much at this point, and I would not bring him into this. The Salt Wall is intact. The wall-walkers report only the usual numbers of changelings, distant scouts or travelers, perhaps. Who knows what the changelings are doing, but they aren't doing it in numbers, and they have no means to breach the Salt Wall. We are not at war."

Amadea understood. "But if the empress dons the Red Mask, we are. And then she must explain."

"She must," Sigrittrice agreed. "She is, in fact, eager to.

"Your little stunt during Lord Obigen's memorial gathering shook her," she went on more sharply. "She was never meant to know what she is. She clings to the threat of Redolfo Kirazzi, of what it might mean if he commands a changeling army somewhere out beyond the Wall—of what she must do to atone for the fact that she was born what she is."

She waited as if she expected Amadea to apologize. But Amadea would not apologize—she knew too well what it was to be molded into something other people wanted you to be. Redolfo had poisoned her with the Venom of Changelings, filled her with the memories of Lireana Ulanitti, the dead daughter of the old emperor.

Or maybe, a little voice in her head whispered, *the memories of an abbey brat.*

Amadea cast her gaze up over Sigrittrice's head, named the colors of the masks, their shapes: *Gold full, buccal black, green domino.* She had gone twenty-three years avoiding the question, so she could keep on going—in the end, who she was before the Usurper put her to use was irrelevant. Who she was now was what counted.

"My apologies, Lady Sigrittrice," Amadea said slowly. "I understand the empress's desires, but the Red Mask is regrettably due to be seen to. The wood is inclined to warp if not cared for."

Sigrittrice frowned. "That seems very easy to resolve."

Amadea crossed to the wall and pulled down the mask. She turned it to the side, where there was a chip in the lacquer, and flicked a piece off with her thumbnail. "No, you see, it's already been sent to the workrooms to repair damage to the lacquer. It will be ready soon enough."

At that, Sigrittrice's mouth quirked. "Perfect. You are a credit to this empire, Archivist Gintanas. Never let that change. For your sake and ours."

The threat was unmistakable. Amadea hesitated. "What if she's right?"

"What if the Salt Wall is made of flour?" Sigrittrice returned, striding toward the door. "Bring me proof, and I will worry then."

Amadea did not follow her but packed the Red Mask into one of the boxes meant for transporting the imperial masks safely and privately, folding the fine cloth over it. It wasn't a lie that it needed some care, but deep in Amadea's thoughts, she could not shake the feeling that she had made the wrong choice aiding Sigrittrice. Lady Sigrittrice was as loyal an advisor as the empress could hope for—there was no question she stood on the side of the Imperial Federation, by the design of her birth and by her temperament, too.

But Amadea's thoughts floated back to four changeling doubles lying in the tunnel beneath the Salt Wall. Four Amadeas—four *Lireanas* left sleeping, waiting, for Redolfo Kirazzi or his agents to return. She smoothed a hand over the Red Mask's covering. She hoped the empress's fears would not come to pass, she agreed with Sigrittrice that leaping after the changeling threat was premature... but she did not trust that the Red Mask would stay on the wall in the vault forever.

She left the vault, locking it behind her, and had only reached the ramp that wound down to the floor below when Quill rushed up to her, wild-eyed and out of breath. The young man's silky black hair had come loose from the knot he wore at the back of his neck, and his normally hearty cheer was gone.

"We have a very big problem," he said.

"You can't find Tunuk, I heard," Amadea said. "Why do you need him? Is it something in the files from Ragale?"

Quill shook his head. "We found something in the woods. I think we're in a whole different sort of trouble."

CHAPTER THREE

The saint looked at Yinii, its jaw open like a sigh, its three orbits dark voids trimmed with beaten gold. Horns curled down around the flare of cheekbones, their fine grooves caked with dirt, their ridges ornamented with charms. The wires that had held the bones together once were now corroded and failing—one hand lay in pieces, the gold-capped fingertips arrayed in a half circle around the tiny bones of the hand, the stump of the wrist.

Cut it off, Fastreda had said of Yinii's own fingers. *Only sorcerers' bodies transmute.*

Yinii flinched away from the damp bones, knotting her hands together and pressing her knuckles tight against one another. The bones *fizzed* with power, a feeling that wove in and out of the insistent whispering of the ink scattered around the bone-artifacts workroom. There was no pretending they weren't exactly what they looked like.

Exactly *who* they looked like.

"It *has* to be Saint Hazaunu," Quill said—again—his voice rough with fatigue. He stood on the opposite side of the table with Richa, both of them watching Amadea as she carefully examined the bones. When Yinii had come into the workroom, her heart had swooped at the sight of him, a feeling she had quickly tried to stifle—this wasn't the time, she hadn't figured anything out, Richa was *right there.* But then she had seen the skeleton, and Quill had run for Amadea, and the situation had pushed aside those petty little worries—what was a boy beside a lost saint?

Although the swoop in her chest kept returning. She touched Saint Asla's amulet again.

"You didn't see the place," Quill went on, "but it was done up like a shrine. I don't see how it could be anyone else. What do we do?"

"We slow down," Amadea said, leaning over the reddened bones. "Saint Hazaunu is in the chapel downstairs, and no one has reported any sort of theft in the chapel since before I took this post."

Yinii squeezed her folded hands together, focusing on the pressure against her own bones, instead of the tide of affinity magic pulling on her attention. *Saint Hazaunu*, she thought, the words to the prayer for the sorcerer's guidance. *Guardian on the clifftop, the eye that watches the weft, and the sentinel that guides the flock, grant me a measure of your vigilance, your compassion.*

The saint gaped at Yinii, as if appalled she could ask for anything right now, and a slithery, wicked sort of question slid through her thoughts: *What will you think when they pray to* you?

Yinii yanked her gaze up to the two men on the other side of the table, pushing the thought away. Richa shifted, folded his arms again. "Do you have another bone specialist who could examine them? Someone else who sees to the chapel?"

"Only Tunuk." Amadea straightened. "Where did you look for him?"

"All the bone workrooms," Quill said. "His apartment. The sequestration rooms."

"He doesn't use those," Amadea said. "Check Stavio and Bijan's apartment, the roof off the north side of the top floor, the west side of the sorting facilities, and if none of those, check the pancake shop down the street and send a runner to his parents' nest. But first: I need you to go to the wood workrooms on the first floor and ask for a specialist, one of the cedar-preference ones if possible, to come up here."

"Wood?" Richa asked.

"Why?" Quill said. And Yinii was surprised to realize they both had thought the bones were a true skeleton.

"It's a wooden skeleton," Amadea said patiently. "And if it's genuine, it's cedar."

"Why is there a wooden skeleton?" Richa asked.

"There are nineteen of them in the chapel," Yinii piped up. "We brought what we could, but not everything made it to Semilla before the Wall was sealed. Saint Hazaunu of the Wool's bones are believed to lie in Hanizan Canyon. Here she is the wooden replica crafted by Saint Qilbat of the Cedar." No less holy, no less revered for being what anyone not Orozhandi might think of as a placeholder.

Richa looked down at the skeleton. "And these are one of those replicas?"

Amadea drew a cloth up over the skeleton with a brisk sort of reverence. "These are wooden bones, regardless of whether they are in fact Saint Hazaunu." She hesitated. "They...seem sorcerer wrought. But a wood specialist would be able to say for certain." She nodded at Quill. "Hurry, please. I would like this sorted out before I have to decide whether Mireia needs to contact the rezas."

Yinii did not see how Amadea wouldn't need to bring this before the leaders of the Orozhandi protectorate. How the Vigilant Kinship had not already contacted the rezas.

Amadea brushed her hands together, dusted off her sleeves, a gesture that sent a trill of nerves through Yinii, and she reached up and tapped the saint's amulets dangling from her own horns as Amadea turned to her.

"Do you know by chance if we have any records of Saint Qilbat creating...practice replicas?" she asked. The question was calm, even, a curiosity—but Yinii could tell she was searching for an answer that wouldn't upend everything. An answer that meant there was only one catastrophe sitting in Amadea Gintanas's lap.

Yinii knew the book she needed—*Saints of the New World*—and knew already that it didn't say what Amadea wanted. *Where Saint Qilbat walked upon the land, the cedar trees followed, and so Orozhand came to Semilla.*

"They are a *miracle*," Yinii said. "She didn't practice."

"Maybe he carved it," Richa said. "The hermit."

"You carve wood," Amadea said. "Could you do that?"

He considered the bones, the graceful curve of the wrist, the subtle planes of the upper arm, the joints of the skull, the pinprick foramina—Yinii could not imagine a mere knife making these shapes.

"I concede the point," Richa said.

"Which brings us around to who the man who had them was," Amadea said. "And why someone killed him. Did you catch them?"

Richa shook his head. "Medium build, medium height. Not an Alojan or an Ashtabari, but other than that?" He shrugged. "It was dark, and they were hooded, and they got away from me. The vigilants who patrol the road will canvass for witnesses who might have seen someone lurking around beforehand. They'll be the ones to handle the murder."

Amadea's eyebrows rose. "You're not investigating it?"

"Not...officially." Richa cleared his throat. He looked up at Yinii, as if unsure of her presence there, fearful even. Yinii felt her cheeks grow hot—he was remembering what had happened in the tunnels, she was sure of it, and for a moment, that was all she could think of. The darkness, the assassin, and the susurrus of the ink becoming a roar.

The assassin had been about to kill Richa, her sword in hand, her arm pulled back. There was no other choice. Yinii threw herself into the full force of her affinity, dived down deep into the spiral of it, where there was only ink and no Yinii. She sensed no longer only the ink but what might become ink. She felt the waiting darkness in the Shrike's unburnt bones, saw the potential fluid in the slick fat of her skin, and pulled the ink into being.

And then she had come back.

And that...that was something. They said sorcerers lost themselves and lived in the spiral. That they could not differentiate between themselves and the worked material they had been born with an affinity for. Someone with the power of a specialist—like Yinii or Tunuk or any of the other archivists who had such an affinity—might fall into the spiral, growing too close to the magic, too powerful for a time and lose themself, but this was temporary. They were too weak to live in the spiral.

She thought of Tunuk, shivering with plaques of bone forming on his skin, trapping him in place. She thought of Zoifia, bronze

pouring out of her mouth, seeping molten over her skin. Bijan, his
eyes growing hard and red, his body growing still.

She thought of the feeling she had, even now, that she did not
know what would happen if she pushed toward that connection,
if she reached not for the ink she knew but instead for what might
become ink. It felt as if she might break through the skin of the
world.

Ink in her mouth, ink in her nose . . . Saint Hazaunu of the Wool, guard-
ian on the clifftop, how did you know you were a sorcerer?

Yinii clenched her hands together and sucked in air through her
nose. "Do you want me to leave?" she asked, meeting Richa's gaze.

"No," he said. "I think you should look at something I found."

He brought out a case from the table behind him, which he laid
down and opened beside the covered skeleton. He withdrew two
papers crumpled and worn and brambled with ink. "These were
underneath her. Can you read them?"

Layers and layers of writing covered the surfaces, the pages reused
several times without care for anyone coming afterward. Words
knotted over words knotted over words. The inks sang a strange
harmony—same hand, she guessed, different inks, different times.

"It looks like Orozhandi," Richa prompted. "On the edges here."

Yinii folded her hands together, studying it. She picked out *saint*
and *my task* and some numbers curling from the edges like runners
from plants seeking less crowded soil. She itched to touch it, to peel
the ink apart. It was more than she'd handled since the tunnel below
the Salt Wall . . .

Amadea took the pages from Richa instead, eyeing Yinii. "I
thought you weren't investigating this."

"Not the murder," he said. "Not technically. But the bones—"

"You have ink specialists connected to the Vigilant Kinship."

He shook his head. "Not ones who can untangle that mess. Not
ones who . . ." He glanced at Yinii again. *Not ones who can turn a per-*
son into ink if they're not careful, she imagined him saying.

But Richa turned back to the case and took out a rolled parchment, laying it out on the same corner of the worktable, beside the
wooden saint's head.

"Not ink specialists," he said carefully, "who know why *this* might be a very bad thing."

Yinii slid off her stool, creeping forward to look at what Richa had brought out. It was a map, old and faded, decorated around the edges with elaborate illustrations—and Khirazji glyphs.

Yinii traced the glyphs with her gaze, the ink a rich metallic one ringing with the memory of the deep earth, the illustrations around it done in a thin, watery paint that nearly noticed her, it was so close to being ink.

People who did not understand affinities sometimes asked Yinii what the difference was between paint and ink, and while she often found it easier to speak of solvents and carriers, of absorption and coating, the truth was...one was one thing, and the other wasn't. Ink knew it was ink. Paint knew it was paint.

A specialist knows they have an affinity, she thought, a curl of dread in her stomach. *A sorcerer knows they are a sorcerer.*

"Crafted for the Son of the River," Yinii read, pushing away from the thoughts again...before she realized Richa was really showing it to Amadea, waiting for *Amadea* to translate it. They were both looking at her now. "It's...it did belong to a Duke Kirazzi," she added quietly.

"The walls in that place were covered," Richa said, "but Quill's right—it was almost all portraits of the same saint. Except this. Which apparently was made for Redolfo Kirazzi."

"No," Amadea said, her eyes on the map, on the title bound in a knotwork of vines to emphasize it. "The style...it's older than that. But here's the Salt Wall, and it doesn't say 'Daughter of the River.' This would have been made for his grandfather, the second Duke Kirazzi." She gestured at Shadorma, high up on the coast, the rusty circle around it. "Why are these places circled?"

There were about a dozen marks across the map, encircling both large cities like Terzanelle and Shadorma and points in the middle of open country. Yinii peered closer, counting the circles.

"Targets for some aspect of the Usurper's coup?" Richa suggested.

"Ah, yes," Amadea said dryly. "The well-known strategic center of 'somewhere northwest of Bylina.'" She paused. "I shouldn't say that. He was very brilliant. I suspect he did find surprising and effective targets. Including ones he hadn't put to use yet."

"Alcaic," Yinii said, finding the spot they'd been talking of. They looked at her again, as if she were not supposed to be there, and she blushed. "It's... it's a village. In the mountains? Oluali of the Marble lives there. She's maqu'tajii. It's a map of sorcerers." She pointed at the circled locations one after another, naming not places but the people who lived there. "Oluali of the Marble, Thunzi of the Iron, Anarai of the Silver, Iosthe of the Wool, Ichenda of the Pottery... That one might be Ahkerfi of the Copper, but he doesn't have a fixed domicile..." She curled her finger back into her fist as she reached Arlabecca. "It's old. Older, I mean. Fastreda of the Glass isn't on it. And I don't know all of them."

"Why does the Duke Kirazzi have a map of sorcerers?" Richa said.

"He doesn't," Amadea said. "An Orozhandi man did. Which is not that odd." She pressed her hands together. "Right. Perhaps this all has a very simple answer. Perhaps it is just a... new problem we will have to manage alongside the primate's files."

A soft rapping came at the door, and a dark-skinned human woman peeked in. "Amadea? Did you need me?"

"Bucella," Amadea said warmly. "Thank you for coming so quickly."

Bucella del Vodopma was a young woman only a little older than Yinii. She was slim and small, with the deep-brown skin and tight black curls of her Beminat ancestors and large hazel eyes. She waved to Yinii as she came in, but then her gaze went to the table, and she froze.

Amadea introduced Bucella to Richa, but the wood specialist only had eyes for the bones on the table, covered by the sheet. "Did Quill tell you what we needed?" Amadea asked.

"He said... he said you found some wooden bones? Is it true?"

"They found *something*," Amadea said firmly. "Do you have the wood workroom's catalogues of the chapel with you?"

Bucella shook her head. "But we do a review once a year, and last time, the only things of note were some degradation on the adhesives

on Saints Maligar and Shaliath's ornamentation and no progress on
the spot of fungal damage previously noted in the ilium of Saint
Tabith. If I recall correctly. The adhesives were replaced," she added,
looking up at Amadea at last. "We weren't missing anyone."

"Wonderful," Amadea said. "We'll want to look at them anyway,
but can you go ahead and tell us everything you can about these?"
She pulled the sheet back, revealing the skeleton to the waist.

Bucella sucked in a breath. Yinii couldn't blame her. Even if she'd
known there were wooden bones beneath the sheet, it was another
thing to lay eyes on them.

Bucella came around the back of the table and reverently took the
skull in her bare hands. Her gaze grew glassy, distant. The wooden
bones trembled as her affinity touched them, as if the vital force of
the wood were still inside them, struggling to sprout.

"Cedar," she said, her voice husky. "Ninety-two years. This is
Qilbat's, absolutely Qilbat's. Never cut. Grown this way. It...
She's...oh..."

Bucella sucked in another breath as if she were breaking the surface of a pool and slipped her hands from beneath the skull in one
swift movement. She clasped them together and turned to Amadea.

"I would be willing to state," she said, her voice steady again,
"that these are unquestionably sorcerer wrought. They have the
same feel as the wooden bones created for the chapel by Saint Qilbat, although I haven't handled enough cedar-aligned sorcerers' creations to say they are her relics with perfect confidence." She rubbed
her hands together, sliding the palms over the backs of her hands.
"But it feels like hers," she said softly, reverently.

Amadea sighed, her mouth curved in a stubborn smile, but her
brow pinched. "Well. I suppose we need to contact the rezas, then.
Bucella, will you go get your catalogues for the chapel? I want to
make certain we have all our responsibilities covered."

Bucella nodded absently. "Do you think it's a new saint?"

"Do you remember the state of Saint Hazaunu in your last review
of the chapel?" Richa asked.

"No." She frowned. "But she's not one of ours. She's bone's."

A trill of worry went through Yinii—Saint Hazaunu of the Wool was most certainly one of the wooden saints. That wasn't even hard to find out. How did Bucella not know that?

"I think I would like to make sure of what we know before we start guessing what we don't," Amadea said. "Catalogues, please. Quickly."

Bucella left the Bone Vault, and Yinii hopped down from the work stool, hurrying to Amadea. "Saint Hazaunu is one of the replicas," Yinii hissed. "Why does she think otherwise?"

"Is there any *chance* you've misplaced a wooden skeleton?" Richa asked.

"No," Amadea said. "That would be…" She blew out a breath. "There's no record of a theft of that level, and if we're talking about a theft of that level, there is an excellent chance I'm the one who is going to be thrown out because of it."

She said it lightly, but it made Yinii sit up straight. "They can't do that."

"If we lost one of the saints, it will be a lucky thing if that's all that happens." Amadea crossed to the shelves beside the door, where a row of heavy leather-bound books rested. She counted down the row and pulled one down.

"What's that?" Richa asked, moving toward her.

"Catalogues for bone," she murmured. Her placid expression was slipping as she paged through the book. The Kirazzi map, the inked-up page, the bones that shouldn't be there—Amadea did not have the time or attention for a problem of this order.

Yinii felt the ink in the catalogues start to shiver, agitated by her nerves. Amadea looked up. "Yinii, why don't you go…take a walk?"

"I'm fine," Yinii said. "I can help." She pushed the ink away, as if it were a cat pressing demandingly against her legs. "Do you want me to look at that…palimpsest thing?" she asked Richa. "I could do that."

"No," Amadea said firmly. "That's a lot of ink, connected to a very stressful situation. You're not recovered yet, and you've already had a trying morning."

Yinii knotted her hands together, her jaw tight. Amadea was

trying to help. Amadea was trying to take care of her. Amadea was just doing what she always did, but *this* time, Yinii could see it was going to be more than she could manage. If the ink on the page found with the skeleton might tip Yinii into the spiral, what would one more insurmountable problem do to Amadea?

Yinii lifted her chin. "That's fair," she said. "So I will compromise by helping you with Tunuk and whatever is going on in his catalogues." That, at least, Amadea couldn't pretend she didn't need help with.

⊶ ⚎ ⊷

Tunuk yula Manco sat on the roof of the Imperial Archives, his back against the stone bulk of one of the corner plinths, his long inky-black legs stretched up the slope of terracotta tiles. He listened to the thrumming of the giant horned rabbit skull he held with both hands so that he did not have to think about the mysterious letter folded on his lap and everything else that was going wrong.

"Listening" was the wrong word, and really so was "thrumming"—when Yinii spoke of the ink, she talked of "feelings" and "scents" and "whispering," but to Tunuk, worked bone had a rhythm. A pulse—but he tried not to say "pulse" to other people when he talked about bone because they always made it ghoulish, thinking of blood and death and what the bone was before it was bone.

Clouds hung low in the sky, sluggish and pondering rain, but only drifting by. He leaned his head back, looking up past the statue of the snake-tailed wisdom goddess, Aye-Nam-Wati, that coiled upon the plinth behind him, regarding the city with beatific grace and shading him from the meager sun. It was quiet on the roof, without even birds to bother him. He watched the clouds and imagined them dropping down to the roof's level. Wrapped up in clouds and insulated from all the rest of the world—that sounded ideal right now...

He drew a sharp breath, as the memory of the spiral crept in, and pressed his thumb against the dull ache between his ribs, where a sword had pierced muscle and flesh months ago, so it sharpened, too, and focused. The pain drowned out the thrumming, but it also chased away the thoughts of bone spreading over his skin, sealing him in, cutting off all the messy, painful things hovering around him, demanding his attention and refusing to be solved.

The pain in his side was one thing—he'd almost died two months ago, an assassin's sword in his ribs, and at night it rose up again in his nightmares. Then there was his nest-father, Obigen, whom the assassin had killed—Tunuk kept forgetting he was dead, kept finding himself furiously angry when he remembered.

Stress made the alignment cycle worse, and while Tunuk was only now supposed to be coming into alignment, the peak strength of his powers, he'd felt the ache in his bones and shuddering in the artifacts early. Then—as if he hadn't had enough problems—Amadea had told him he needed a dedicated generalist.

"I thought we agreed Radir had to go," Tunuk had said.

"Radir *is* going," Amadea replied. "To ink. Quill is going to be your generalist as soon as he comes back from Ragale and is inducted."

Dread poured through Tunuk's long limbs. "The grinning Paremi? I don't want him!"

Amadea acknowledged this with a patient nod. "You need a generalist."

"Then find someone else!"

"There isn't anyone else," Amadea said. "Tunuk, I am not asking you to be anyone but yourself. But I want you to think about the fact I cannot keep a generalist in this position for more than a month or two. Quill likes you. He is happy to take the position. Please do not decide to change that before he begins."

Tunuk stormed away from Amadea, sought out Yinii in her library. But she wasn't there. Or in her rooms. Or in the chapel. He finally found her when he'd given up, coming in with her cloak all buttoned up, from who knew where.

"Amadea is assigning me Quill," he started, following her toward her rooms.

Yinii stopped walking, looked over at him, alarmed, and Tunuk felt gratified that Yinii appreciated how incredibly *bad* this situation was. But then she'd *blushed* and said, "So...he's staying?"

He could *not* complain about his generalist to Yinii anymore.

She will be even busier, he thought glumly. *You will only see her when she's ignoring you for that idiot Paremi.* Before, Yinii would often come down to talk to him, to confide in him, and they would go get pancakes at the shop down the street. She would tease him and listen to him complain about the pigeons and the sun and his generalist. She would worry about her reza or her family or her work, and he would tell her none of that mattered, they could fuck off. He would feel a little better, and so would she.

And then, the misadventure down by the Salt Wall. And then, the Paremi.

So Tunuk had declared he was taking a respite, a temporary leave from the archives.

"Your bones are all getting noisy," he told Amadea. "My injury is healed enough. I'm going to the seaside before I spiral out of alignment."

"Do you want some company?" Amadea asked. And Tunuk considered it—if Amadea were to come, that would be all right, or Yinii—but then he realized there was a good chance she meant sending Quill, and so he said no.

He wished he'd asked Yinii himself. There weren't a great many people Tunuk liked, and even fewer he wanted to tell anything so personal as *I'm still having nightmares about the assassin*, or *sometimes I miss Obigen so badly I don't even know who I am*, or *you are going to spend all your time with Quill, and I'm jealous.*

Actually he would never, ever say the last one. He didn't even like that he'd thought it. If he said that sort of thing in the nest, his parents and even siblings would leap on it and assume he was in love, finally, thank the stars and the moon above, Tunuk was finally normal, even if it was for a little three-eyed horned girl. And Tunuk would have to once more have the laborious conversation of *I don't feel that way about anyone, and I don't care if you don't understand. I don't care if you're disappointed. I don't care what they would have said in Aloja.*

Aloja was long gone—that was the truth Tunuk had grown up hearing, the root of his and every other Alojan child's cultural upbringing: *We left our gods on the mountains, our pasts, our careful charts of the future. They are lost and gone forever—all we have in this new world is* now.

Tunuk sighed. The shadow people had left their lands to the changelings, their high temples and steeply built roads, their elaborate hanging bridges, and their cliff-strung homes. But far, far from that land, *Aloja* chased him out into the daylight like a monster from a story.

This isn't how we do things, his mothers would say. *There aren't enough of us*, his fathers lamented. *This friend, that distant cousin has space in their nest. You should meet. You should talk. You shouldn't be alone.* If he were in love with some humans, some Orozhandi, some Ashtabari, they would understand, but this...did he not understand that *now* more than ever he should not be alone?

They would have been horrified he went to the seaside by himself. They would rail at Amadea. They would call in one of the assessment teams to make certain he wasn't going mad.

In the old stories, Alojans had a monster called the yinpay. The yinpay lived in the jungle shadows and oozed out in the night to prey on travelers. Not an animal, not a bandit—the yinpay was what happened to Alojans who "went into the jungle alone."

"What does *that* mean?" young Tunuk had asked the first time he'd heard the story. His elder siblings all looked at him with cocked heads, their eyes bright and glowing softly with puzzlement.

Mother Alzari, who'd been telling the story, waved this off. "It's not safe to be alone in the forest."

"Why?"

"It's better not to be alone in general," she'd said, as if that were enough. "But you understand, it's a different forest, a different place."

Tunuk did not believe in the yinpay—how a person walking in the woods by themselves, regardless of where those woods were, could be warped into a cannibalistic creature fully given over to shadows was too ludicrous to waste time on. But while it was a silly myth, it clung to his thoughts. This was what his parents feared—something in him was warping the longer he went without finding a nest full of lovers to settle himself with.

Even now, here, it was a transgression—being alone, wanting to be alone—whether Aloja was lost or not.

"But I'm not alone," he said to the skull in his lap. "You're here, aren't you?"

Biorni only *thrummed*.

He took the letter out from beneath Biorni—the final drop that had overflowed his cup. It had been cold by the sea, along the northern shore, west of Terzanelle, and Tunuk had gone hunting in the respite cabin's dusty corners for quilts to pile into his bed. He'd gone to the chest under the window and found, atop the colorful blankets, this letter.

The wounded jackal limps along a winding path, but it knows the one it hunts for.

Tunuk scowled down at the letter. It made no fucking sense, but also…he could not stop thinking of how it looked like Qalba's handwriting.

Qalba One-Fox ul-Shandiian, and her husband, Chizid del Hwana, had been the bone specialists when Tunuk, barely more than a child, came to the archives. They were patient and kind, and gentle with Tunuk—understanding of the *thrumming* and how you needed it, even when it was all around you some days and deafening. They had trained him in the ways of the archives and the ways of the bone affinity.

But while leaving the note was the sort of thing Qalba might have done—it wouldn't be the first obscure proverb she'd written for Tunuk—he hadn't seen her in longer than it had been since he'd gone on respite. It had been five or maybe even ten years since he'd been in that cabin, and the letter had not been there before. Maybe.

So was this letter a lost piece of Qalba? Or had he forgotten her handwriting, found some other specialist's note, and taken to carrying it around like a talisman? Or had Qalba returned, somehow, and left this for him?

Not that one, he thought, putting the letter away. They'd left, after all. They hadn't come back.

He picked up the horned rabbit skull, holding it even with his face. Maybe that was the part nobody told about the yinpay. Maybe it hadn't always been alone—maybe everyone had left it, and that was what made the difference.

"You're lucky, Biorni," he said to the skull. "Everyone you know is *definitely* dead. Except me, I suppose."

Below Tunuk's perch, a window creaked open, and a moment later, Quill's dark head popped over the roof line, his tapered eyes scanning the roof tiles. For a moment, Tunuk thought Quill might miss him, camouflaged against the shadow of Aye-Nam-Wati, but then Quill's eyes settled on Tunuk, and he burst out, "Lord on the Mountain, there you are! You have to come now."

"I'm sequestering," Tunuk said flatly. "Leave me alone."

"We have a bone emergency. Now," Quill said. There wasn't anything annoyingly cheerful in his voice, and a little tendril of panic curled up Tunuk's chest. Then Quill said, "It's Amadea asking, not me."

"Then maybe she should have come to yell at me," Tunuk spat, but he climbed to his feet, pretending he couldn't possibly care less. He slipped over the side of the roof and in through the window, avoiding Quill's gaze.

"I have been here for a decade and a half, and there has never once been a 'bone emergency,'" Tunuk said, starting down the hallway. "You don't have to exaggerate to feel important."

"There's a fucking Orozhandi skeleton saint in your workroom."

Tunuk stopped, glanced back over his shoulder at Quill. He looked a little wild-eyed, a little disheveled—but he wasn't joking.

"Why did you bring one of the saints up to my workroom?" Tunuk demanded.

"It's *not* one of the chapel saints," Quill hissed. "Richa and I found it. Out in the woods. In some peddler-hermit's...hovel-shrine thing." He blew out a breath. "Do you know which of them is Saint Hazaunu? Is she in the chapel?"

Tunuk froze. And for a moment, it was as if he were once more standing on that rise before the stream near Sestina, once more stabbed through the ribs, once more facing death out of nowhere, Tunuk, revealed as fragile and frangible as old forgotten bone.

Tunuk preferred to be alone, to not worry about who he was

relying on and who he was disappointing. But in that moment, knowing they had found Saint Hazaunu, he wished for Qalba and Chizid like he was fourteen all over again, thrust into the archives and absolutely lost. They could explain it. They could shield him. They could reassure him this would be all right.

But there was only Tunuk and the bones and the lie. He would have to manage alone.

"Tunuk?" Quill asked, frowning. "Are you all right?"

"Fine!" Tunuk heaved a loud sigh and handed Biorni roughly over to Quill. "I don't know why you need me when the catalogues are right there, but let's get this over with."

CHAPTER FOUR

Everything Richa had learned since they'd found the bones in that little hollow in the woods was beginning to settle together into concrete leads by the time Quill and Tunuk returned to the Bone Vault a little later.

Quill marched his charge through the door. "Found him."

The Alojan bone specialist was slouched over his folded arms, a rabbit skull tucked into the crook of one. His shadow-black face was sullen, his eyes dimmed and slitted. *Sulky?* Richa wondered. *Or guilty? And if guilty, of what?*

Amadea set the catalogue from the bone workroom on the table beside the tall shelves. "Good afternoon," she said. "We have a very big problem."

"I assumed," Tunuk said acidly. "Since he *dragged* me down here, shouting about bone emergencies."

The first thing Richa had realized: This was not going to be a small curiosity. There were no records of a theft of this scale from the archives, and so the wooden saint was not expected to be missing. Moreover, for the Orozhandi this would be nothing short of a crisis—what was this relic, and where had it come from? Why did the archives not know?

"They've found a replica skeleton," Amadea said. "Bucella feels confident it's sorcerer wrought and dated to the creation of the wooden saints. There's evidence that suggests it's Saint Hazaunu of the Wool. Did you notice anything odd about her?"

Tunuk folded his arms. "I don't really bother with the wooden saints."

The second thing, Richa thought, considering Tunuk, was that if this was a genuine relic—and given the cedar specialist's findings, and Yinii's insistence that there were no "practice miracles," he thought it wiser to assume it was nothing less—then someone had to have removed it from the archives secretly. Which suggested someone working inside the archives was involved.

"Your catalogue lists her as a replica," Amadea said.

"Because she is?"

"Not according to Bucella. Bucella says she can't ever remember working on Saint Hazaunu. That Saint Hazaunu is one of yours."

The third thing, right there—the person working from the inside would need to be someone with access to the chapel. And it wasn't the cedar specialist. There was no question in his mind that Bucella knew nothing about these bones before today. But Tunuk?

Tunuk looked down at the book, then up at Amadea. "All right. I guess there's a mistake in the catalogues." He set the rabbit skull down on the table beside the door, looking at last at the wooden bones laid out on his workspace. "Do you want me to redo my catalogues? Is that it?"

Tunuk was *lying*.

"I think," Richa said, "we should start by visiting the chapel. Seeing who or what exactly is in Saint Hazaunu's place."

Tunuk turned his glower on Richa, looking as if he were going to refuse. But then Amadea nodded. "Exactly my thought. Come along." And the whole band of them followed her, as if marching to war, down a narrow staircase into the Chapel of the Skeleton Saints.

Richa hadn't been in the chapel before—it was one of the holiest sites for the Orozhandi in Semilla, but Richa couldn't deny he'd always thought it would be... well, a little creepy.

Entering the chapel through the back door, seeing the rows and rows of decorated skeletons, articulated in lifelike poses—it *was* creepy. But there was also a reverence to the place that made him very aware that was only his opinion. The space felt like a cavern out of far-off Orozhand—black granite and red sandstone gleaming from a long vaulted ceiling down columns dividing alcoves full of skeletons. Smaller glass-topped cases divided the long hall of the chapel, more bones resting on shimmery fabric, as if they were too frail and tired to stand. At the end, near the small door, there was an altar before a mural of Saint Asla, the Martyr of the Wall, young and solemn as she sacrificed herself to make the Salt Wall. At the far side, two sets of heavy doors led out to the street.

There were faithful in the chapel this time of day, Orozhandi kneeling before Saint Asla's altar, genuflecting to the saints posed on the columns, tucked into the alcoves whispering their worries and their hopes. A few looked up as they passed through the chapel, but most did not.

Amadea pulled on a pair of white cotton gloves and took a ring of keys from one pocket as she strode across the chapel toward one of the alcoves. Tunuk sloped after her, flanked by Yinii and Quill, with Richa following. Once they were all four inside the empty alcove, Amadea pulled a curtain closed across the opening.

Three saints stood behind glass-fronted doors—one hung with a net of clay beads, one armored in copper, one swathed in a wool garment and holding a spindle—all of them sparkling with gems and precious metals.

"Saint Doba of the Pottery, Saint Tabith of the Copper, and Saint Hazaunu of the Wool," Amadea said, pointing at each. "They're all replicas according to the bone records."

Quill leaned forward, peering up into the face of Saint Hazaunu tucked into a wimple and framed with fine golden chains. "Are they all the same sort of wood as the one upstairs? It's brownish, but... yellower?"

Amadea did not answer but flipped through her keys, eyeing the skeleton on the right. She unlocked the case and stepped back, making a bow.

"Hazaunu Four-Hyena ul-Hanizan, honored guest of the Imperial Federation of Semillan Protectorates, I greet you, Your Holiness, and offer the welcome of Her Imperial Majesty and to renew the safety of the archives." Yinii mirrored her bow and then made another to the other skeletons in the alcove. Tunuk stood stiff and watchful.

Ritual complete, Amadea stepped into the case and carefully pulled back the woolen veil to study the skull and the bones of the shoulder. She pursed her lips and pulled the garment a little farther back. "Tunuk."

"It's bone," he said grimly. "I can tell from here. Do you want me to look her over and see what the cataloguing missed?"

"Can you tell us who it is?" Richa asked.

"It's a *skeleton*."

Amadea sighed heavily. "Tunuk."

"I'm answering the question," he said testily. "It's not a person, not anymore. It's just bones. I can't just"—he mimed setting his long midnight fingers over the skull's dome—" 'Oh yes, this is Eneyth Five-Bee-eater, mother of three and avid singer. She was killed by the blue death.' None of that's in her bones, so why would I know? And more particularly, she barely counts as 'worked.' She doesn't have a voice if the bone's not worked. It's just raw material."

Richa nodded slowly. "But you said 'her'? It's a woman?"

Tunuk stared back for a blank moment before his expression twisted into something scornful and annoyed. "No," he sneered. "The invented woman whose horned skull that *isn't* is a woman. Creative liberties."

Richa considered Tunuk, who stared back as if he didn't dare look away. That blank expression on Tunuk's soft, shadowy features made Richa think of a rabbit trying to hide by holding still. It was there and then gone, and for a moment, Richa found himself reflexively searching Tunuk's bare wrists and neck for a bruise that would indicate someone had injected him with the Venom of Changelings, had rewritten Tunuk's memories.

But that wasn't it, Richa thought.

It's a skeleton, Tunuk had said. *It's just bones.*

But he'd asked Amadea, *Do you want me to look her over and see what the cataloguing missed?* "Her"—not "it." This one was more than their bones. And then that pause.

You're lying, Richa thought, holding Tunuk's gaze again. "Well," he said, all affability and calm, "what *can* you tell me?"

Tunuk fidgeted a moment, as if he would refuse, but then he met Amadea's eyes and stilled. "Fine," he said, and stepped into the alcove to set a long-fingered hand against the skeleton's bared shoulder.

When Tunuk spoke, his voice took on the same distant husky sound Bucella's had when she'd used her affinity: "It's Orozhandi bone. An adult—the plates are all connecting. They didn't get out in the sun enough. Left femur's chipped from the wiring. It's been bone for...twelve years." He shook himself, pulled his hand away, and his voice was normal again when he said, "Maybe. I don't know. Again, it's barely worked. Probably older since the chapel's air is controlled."

"So not old enough to be the genuine Saint Hazaunu—who I understand died four hundred years ago—miraculously translated to the chapel. Got it." Richa would need to look into missing people, people maybe connected to the archives. Maybe connected to Tunuk. "How do you think she got in the saint's alcove?" he asked mildly.

"Miscreants picking locks?" Tunuk suggested.

"No record of a robbery," Richa said. "At least according to Archivist Gintanas here. Sounds like there are guards on the doors all day and night."

"Maybe it's a miracle," Tunuk drawled.

"What it is," Amadea said grimly, "is a problem we will need to involve the head archivist in." She rearranged the skeletal saint's dressings. "Now."

The younger archivists walked ahead, out of the alcove and toward the door, with Tunuk slumping along at the lead. Richa moved closer to Amadea as she tied back the curtain. She brushed a hand over her sleeves as if dusting them off, tugging the cuffs down as if they could be any straighter—*anxious*, he thought, as she brushed a hand over her skirts, smoothing the fabric over the curve of her hips.

"He's hiding something," she said. "This is a nightmare." She started after the three, too tense and too fast. Richa caught up to her, gently took hold of her arm to slow her down. She glanced at the Orozhandi at prayer...who were all watching now that an archivist superior was charging across the chapel.

"You were right before," Richa reminded her. "We don't know what this is. We don't know what happened."

She blew out a breath. "And we don't really have the time for this right now."

"Did something else happen this morning?" he asked, as he pulled open the door that led back up to the bone workroom.

"Besides you arriving with what sounds like a small mountain of material to go through?" she asked. "Let's just say Yinii's not the only one who had a difficult morning." She blew out another breath, slowed down a little more. "Lady Sigrittrice was here."

"Did they find another tunnel?"

"No," Amadea said. "And so far as she's concerned, the whole notion of Redolfo Kirazzi being on the other side of the Wall should be dropped, and if we don't drop it, she will make us." Every time she exhaled, it sounded like she was trying to blow out a candle. "I'm handling it."

"And this," Richa said, slowing down more. "And the files." They came out again into the bone workroom, crossing the workspace in time to see Tunuk scoop the horned rabbit skull he'd carried in and push through the door after Quill and Yinii. "Do you have any idea what Tunuk is acting so strange about?"

"No." She rubbed her forehead. "I can't even imagine where someone would have found those remains, let alone why they would have brought them here and...exchanged them? Maybe the original bones *were* stolen."

Richa hesitated at the door out into the wider archives. "Tunuk's a bone specialist. Can he skeletonize a corpse?"

"There's a colony of grave beetles in one of the smaller workrooms for preparing specimens," Amadea said, as if he'd been asking if she could do him a favor, and of course, it was that simple. Then she stopped. "You think someone *made* that skeleton? Here?"

"It's possible."

"Tunuk wouldn't do that."

Richa did not say what he thought of Tunuk—the young man was sullen, sharp-edged, and prone to lashing out. It didn't seem a far stretch to think his temper might have gotten the best of him at some point in the past. "Twelve years ago," Richa said, recalling what Tunuk had read in the bones. "You think that's accurate?"

"Why would he lie about that?" Amadea said, flustered.

"All right, let's say that's *not* wrong. That's not what he's hiding,"

Richa allowed, opening the door again and walking out onto the wide
iron mezzanine that looked over the archives' sorting facilities below.
The three younger archivists were far ahead now—he saw Yinii look
back at the far end of the mezzanine before following a hallway that
bent off to the left, toward the front offices of the archives.

"Let's say that person died twelve years ago," Richa went on.
"Was Tunuk here?"

Amadea tugged her sleeves again. "Yes. But he wasn't the only
bone specialist. There were two more, a married couple. Qalba
ul-Shandiian and Chizid del Hwana."

"Where are they now?" Richa asked.

Amadea shook her head. "I have no idea. If I recall correctly, they
rescinded their oaths."

"Does that happen often?"

"No," she answered. "But there will be records. They were both
specialists, so we would have tried to keep track in case they needed
intervention. But I was a generalist in the metallic workrooms at
that time. It wasn't my business why they left or if they were ever in
contact after that."

Richa ran a hand through his hair. "So, just to be clear, an Orozhandi woman disappeared along with her husband, and now a
female Orozhandi skeleton turns up where it's not supposed to be, in
the chapel the husband was in charge of caretaking?"

"He didn't say for certain it was a female skeleton," Amadea said.
"It's hard to tell for certain. And he might have just said 'her' because
he *thought* it was Saint Hazaunu—"

"But you noticed he switched," Richa said. Then: "He's hiding
something. Maybe he knows more than he's saying about that skeleton."

She drew another deep breath. "I can...I can ask Mireia for Qalba
and Chizid's files. See if there's any report of violence or...some-
thing untoward there. Saints," she cursed. "If that's why Tunuk..."
She heaved another breath.

They followed the hallway around to a door that opened out onto
the upper floors of the entry hall, where half a dozen doors lined
another mezzanine that looked down upon the wide marble-tiled
entry. The door to the head archivist's office stood open, Quill and

Yinii speaking to Mireia del Atsina, an older woman with a sharp nose and her silver hair in a crown of braids.

"I'm going to have to question him," he said quietly as they approached. "It really has to be at the Kinship Hall."

Amadea glanced sidelong at him. "What if he just tells you what he knows here? Now?"

Richa shook his head. "Still has to be official. Paremi seals and all that. Something like this? It's going to be a catastrophe if anything isn't done exactly right. And maybe even if it is."

She nodded. "I was supposed to meet with His Highness once you were back with the papers. But if Tunuk is going to be questioned... I'll just have to reorganize things."

Richa rubbed a hand against his neck. "Ah. How is the consort-prince?"

Quill rushed toward them, cutting off Amadea's answer. "Where's Tunuk?" he hissed.

"He was with you," Amadea said. She hurried toward Mireia's office as if she would find the Alojan bone specialist tucked inside, sulking in a chair.

Quill leapt in front of her. "He passed us. I thought he went on to Mireia, but she hasn't seen him." He glanced at Richa, then said, "I think he ran off."

Amadea cursed under her breath. "You have to find him. I have to talk to the head archivist and work out what we need to do to rectify this, so it needs to be you. This isn't what I had in mind when I said I would assign you to be his generalist, but—"

"But who plans for this?" Quill said grimly. "Is he acting odd? He seems odd."

"He..." Amadea faltered. "Find out, please. And keep him calm. He's a lot closer to his alignment than he's pretending."

Quill nodded and sprinted back to Yinii.

Amadea turned to Richa, tugging on her left sleeve. "I will bring him to the Kinship Hall as soon as I can."

She was tense again, so he said, "It will be all right. If you can send me those files about the bone specialists at the Kinship Hall, I can get out of your hair and stop making trouble."

Amadea gave a soft laugh, and the tension slipped off her a little. "You are by far," she said, "the least troubling thing about my day."

He felt a little of his own tension slip at that. He leaned in, smiling, and said quietly, "If it gets any worse, you stick a note in those files on the former bone specialists, and I'll come back with very important evidence we *must* discuss over wine."

She gave him a curious look, a little surprised, a little pleased. "I'd like that. Though I do hope it doesn't get any worse."

He collected the document cases from the Bone Vault and took his leave of the archives, crossing Arlabecca back toward the Kinship Hall. He ought to be puzzling over the murder and the missing skeleton, but his thoughts turned around Amadea Gintanas.

Richa was not about to take Quill's advice or even seek it out. She was lovely, funny and smart, and sharp in ways he loved discovering—but she held him at a distance. He wasn't even sure she knew she was doing it. He wasn't sure how much of that was related to the consort-prince who she claimed was a "childhood acquaintance" but who looked at her like she was water in the desert.

Richa wasn't an idiot—not anymore, anyway. He wasn't going to pine after someone he couldn't have, someone he wasn't sure wanted him back. But more and more, the distance fell away. And Amadea Gintanas didn't seem like such a foolish person to be attracted to.

Maybe he would bring her that wine.

He nearly turned toward home but knew he ought to register the map and the palimpsest as evidence and see what exactly the state of his desk was after a few weeks away.

The great statue of Vigilant Mother Ayemi, founder of the Order of the Vigilant Kinship, stared down the long hall at him as he entered, and Richa gave the venerable lady a cheeky nod. Mother Ayemi had been a jaguar-knight from Bemina, a powerful tactical warrior who had bent her talents to organizing this force of peacekeepers and firewatchers. He liked the statue—he liked the fact Mother Ayemi looked as though if someone had told her to stop what she was doing, she would have given them a moment to realize how stupid they sounded and continued on with her business.

"Richa!" The imperial liaison, Hulvia Manche, called to him

from down the hall. The Ashtabari woman still wore her cloak, her black hair curling down over her shoulders as she slid across the floor on dappled tentacles. "Where the fuck have you been?"

"Technically, I'm still on leave," he said. "What's wrong?"

"What's wrong," a new voice said, "is that you fled a crime scene with evidence and no statement given."

Behind Hulvia, another vigilant stood. She was half-Orozhandi, half-human, her hooded black eyes set below a tawny forehead marked by a swell of bone where her third eye would have developed. Her dark hair was slicked back in a severe knot between the curls of her horns. She did not wear charms like Yinii's, only a row of silver loops down each ridged horn. She wore the uniform of the Vigilant Kinship, each silver button shining, each crease as sharp as chipped stone.

Hulvia gave him a look full of warning. "This is Salva Nine-Scorpion Gaitha-hyu from the road cohort."

"Vigilant Gaitha-hyu, please," she said. "I need you to give a sworn statement about the murder you witnessed."

"Now?" Richa said.

"Yesterday, when it happened, would have been preferable, but Vigilant del Anthal was convinced to let you flee back to the city, leaving me to chase you and your companion down. I have a Paremi waiting. Let's go."

Richa handed the two document cases to Hulvia. "Can you get these into the evidence vault?"

"Do I look like your cadet?" Hulvia demanded, but she took the cases and dropped her voice. "Are you in trouble?"

"*She* certainly thinks so," he answered just as quietly, and followed the vigilant from the road cohort up the stairs to the interview rooms. He'd used this one a thousand times before, his body now rebelling as he sat not in the vigilant's chair but the witness's seat facing it. The Paremi in his scarlet robes, a young Alojan man sitting at the desk to the side, prepared his stylus.

"Richa Langyun," the scrivener read out. "Order of the Vigilant Kinship of Mother Ayemi."

"Correct," Richa said.

"Begin," the scrivener said, and set his stylus to the page.

Vigilant Gaitha-hyu wasted no time at all. "You were a witness to a murder outside the relay station at the fifty-mile marker north of Arlabecca yesterday. Please describe what you saw."

Richa cleared his throat and shot a glance at the Paremi before speaking. "I was traveling with a Paremi, Sesquillio Seupu-lai, as his escort from Ragale. We arrived just before sundown. I'd secured lodgings and a meal and stabled the horses. I was going out for a walk when I saw two persons struggling on the opposite side of the road—"

"How far away?"

"Forty feet," he guessed. "It was dark by then. They were out of the reach of the relay station's lights, and the moon was behind the trees where they were. One of them was Orozhandi, and one had a hood up—so I can tell you they weren't Ashtabari or Alojan. That's as close as I could get to a description. Taller than the victim, not quite as tall as me. The hooded one pulled a knife and stabbed the Orozhandi before I could reach them, then took off. I gave pursuit."

"You saw a person pull a knife in low light forty feet away."

"Yes," Richa said mildly, "and if I wasn't sure, I saw the dead man after. It was definitely a knife."

The scrivener's stylus scratched along. Came to a stop. Vigilant Gaitha-hyu was watching Richa silently.

"You didn't catch up to the aggressor?"

"No," Richa said. "They ran into the trees—it was dark, and I didn't get my lamp going quickly enough to see where they were headed. I tried to follow—"

"You returned to the victim," she interrupted, "where your companion was waiting. And then you both fled the scene."

Richa frowned at her. "'Fled' is a bit heavy of a word there. Do you think I stabbed him?"

She held his gaze, implacable. "The Vigilant Mother teaches that we leave no path untested," she said. "You fled the scene."

"The victim said we needed to protect someone. 'Save her,'" he explained. "He gave directions to the hollow—"

"Which you managed to follow, in the dark."

"With the lamp that I'd gotten working," Richa said. "Quill found the cave and then the skeleton. Which we realized—"

"And what else?" she asked.

"Excuse me?"

"What else was in the dwelling?"

"A lot of depictions of an Orozhandi saint," Richa said. "I didn't go through it all. As you said, it's outside my jurisdiction." He studied her a moment. "I don't even know the dead man's name."

"It sounds as if no one did. They just called him 'the old man,'" she said, studying him right back. "But someone very specifically targeted him. You left off the map you took from the scene."

Richa cursed to himself. "I brought it to the Imperial Archives to be dated and translated. It looked old and out of place. I gave it back to Vigilant Manche to be deposited. It should be downstairs now. It's just a sorcerer map."

"You took," she said, "a map, the wooden bones, and two unidentified documents to the Imperial Archives."

"I had," he retorted, "the local vigilant's agreement that this was the best course of action. The archives verified the bones," he added. "I expect the rezas will be much happier they're where they're meant to be instead of in the evidence vault."

She stared at him, her face like a mask. He had to admit, she was very good at that. "You were disciplined nearly two months ago for disobedience."

Richa glanced at the Paremi. "Did you read the entirety of that notation?"

"I did," she said. "It's missing quite a bit of information."

Richa bit back a curse. It would be—the Imperial Authority still hoped they could keep everything that had happened a secret. He thought of what Amadea had said about Lady Sigrittrice still on the alert for any hint they were talking about what had happened and decided against telling Salva anything.

"My oath was reasserted," he began. "The Kinship felt that information—"

"And before?" she interrupted.

"Before what?"

"Before you joined the Kinship."

Richa straightened. *How did you come to take your oath with the Kinship?* Quill had asked, and Richa wasn't getting into it then, and he certainly wasn't now. "Before I joined the Kinship is before I joined the Kinship. As the Vigilant Mother says, 'All willing to wash the stains from their weapons are welcome to the Kinship's fire.' What are you getting at?"

She waited a long moment before saying, "Stellano Zezurin."

It didn't hurt like it used to, hearing his name. Instead, it made Richa angry—swift and sudden and sucking as the tide. He could picture Stellano—his yellow hair, his crooked tooth, his teasing smile. Riling up the dog. Complaining about Richa's muddy boots. That stupid trick he used to do, flipping a blade over his fingers— how many times had he nicked that third finger? How many times had he asked Richa to kiss it?

He stood up. "Fuck off."

"We're not finished, Vigilant."

"Yes, we are," he said. "The Vigilant Mother teaches us to pass a cold hearth by, and my past is just that."

"And a cold hearth may be a banked fire," she said. "I would hope you'd ask the same questions in my place."

"I have not spoken to Stellano Zezurin in fifteen years," Richa said hotly. "I have not been to Caesura in a decade. I have been dedicated to this order as much as any other person—"

"And you still own a set of lockpicks," she said. "Much like those that seem to have been used on the entrance to the former Maschano mansion during the investigation that saw you reprimanded. You stole for Stellano Zezurin—"

"If you don't even know the fucking situation," Richa interrupted, "then I'll thank you to leave my past out of this."

Salva sat back, her brows raised. As if his outburst said more than enough—it probably did, he thought.

"So you didn't kill the peddler," she said, almost conversational. "Did he?"

"Did who?"

"Stellano Zezurin. He's pretty distinctive looking, but I suppose a man in a hood could be anybody. Was that the plan?"

Richa suddenly felt light-headed and leaned on the chair he'd vacated. It felt impossible, as if when Richa had cut that part of his life away, it should have died, all of it. He thought of the killer, the hooded figure, and tried to fit Stellano's trim form into the shape of them—but he couldn't remember enough. "Stellano Zezurin doesn't work in Arlabecca or north of it."

"And what do you base that on?" she asked. "If you haven't spoken to your former lover in fifteen years?"

Richa squeezed the back of the chair, willing his anger to stay down, willing his thoughts off the way she said "former" as if it were a joke they were sharing. "I'm finished."

She gestured to the Paremi to stop recording, then stood. "Let me put it to you this way, Vigilant. Regardless of anything else, Esinor Zezurin is in a great deal of trouble. Now here you are, stealing from a murder victim, refusing to give your testimony in good time, and happening to have...let's agree to say, deeper entanglements with Stellano Zezurin at the same time, which I might add, are not in your records with the Kinship? And we look to your recently spotted record? All these gaps? This hearth isn't cold, if you ask me. So you can tell me what's going on, or I will do my diligence and find out."

Richa did not respond; he did not trust himself to utter a single word. He turned and walked from the room, telling himself he was leaving all his past behind him in that room as he crossed the threshold.

CHAPTER FIVE

Tunuk hunched into his cloak against the damp autumn wind, Biorni tucked under one arm. Dry leaves from distant trees skittered over the cobblestones as he hurried through the city, clinging to the one clue he had and trying not to think about what was happening behind him in the archives and how much *more* was going wrong.

He could picture it, perfectly—that vigilant ready to hear the worst, Quill full of Tunuk's many flaws and indiscretions, Amadea...He couldn't imagine what Amadea might say, but he could imagine her disappointed expression. How stiff she would be when she told the rezas.

It's not my fault, he wanted to howl.

But that was a lie—or at least part of a lie.

The wind whipped around the corner, where the tall buildings funneled it down the hill, along the aqueduct. Tunuk pulled his cloak more tightly around his long body, steeling himself. *Get in, get the letters, get out.*

He repeated the words until he reached the door of his parents' nest-house. Tunuk laid a hand on the door and closed his eyes, trying to probe through the wood and the air behind it, into the house beyond for any sense of bones that might be waiting to become something, but whoever was home was too far away.

"Get in, get the letters, get out," he muttered, and rapped on the door.

Alzari, one of his nest-mothers, opened the door, and her huge eyes flared bright with surprise. "Tunuk!" she cried. Her long arms wound around him in an embrace as she pulled him into the house. "Oh, Tunuk! Child, come in. What are you doing here? Uruphi! Kulum! Tunuk is here!... What is that?"

"A skull. I just need some things from the crèche," he said, shifting Biorni to the side and returning the embrace. She smelled of fennel and apples, as if she'd come from cooking, and he was loath to let go of her.

"Of course, of course," Alzari said, still holding him tight. "And then you'll stay for a meal. Should I tell the young ones you're spending the night? They'll be so glad to see their older brother!"

"Alzari, don't get their hopes up," a woman said. Two more Alojans, long inky shadows in the high-ceilinged hall, came toward them—his birth mother, Uruphi, and one of his fathers, Kulum. He'd no more than hugged Kulum, but the entryway was full of bodies.

There were his eight parents, plus two siblings still in the crèche, and all of them were suddenly very eager to see Tunuk. His minesht, his nest-mothers—Alzari, Senca, and Vari—fussed over his injury, and was anyone tending to it? His zheru, his fathers—Kulum and Bayan—and his zhum, his nest-father—Jinjir—picked at his cloak and the quality and how was he not frozen to the bone?

The little ones, Conzi and Duwan, hugged him shyly, and Tunuk found himself looking over their heads without thinking, braced for Obigen, his other nest-father, and his criticisms.

He found Uruphi's gaze, and remembered Obigen was dead, and felt that flood of anger—at Obigen, at his murderer, at himself for not remembering.

The other one wasn't lucky, the assassin's voice whispered in his memories, his injury aching where the same blade that had killed his nest-father had sought to end Tunuk. He had seven parents now.

Uruphi, his gedet, his mother-who-bore-him, watched with a worried expression while her partners fussed over Tunuk. She was taller even than Tunuk, the skin across her cheeks and chest a warmer sort of black, like the shadow of a firelight, her large glowing eyes faintly green. A dip-dyed shawl in shades of red wrapped her long body over a shiny black tunic. The thrum of her bones felt soothing, a sense he had known before he had a name for it, even as her expression made him brace.

He stared up at the plastered ceiling, its high curved shape reminding him suddenly of the vaulted ceiling of the chapel, and his stomach twisted tighter.

Once everyone had hugged him and prodded him and asked if he was bringing anyone else home for the meal they had all decided he'd agreed to stay for already, Tunuk was left at last standing beneath the high-vaulted ceiling of the hallway with only Uruphi.

"What do you need from the crèche?" Uruphi asked.

"Just some notes I left here," he said. "It's nothing interesting."

"You don't look like a person with nothing interesting on his mind," she said. "Do you want to tell me what's going on?"

Tunuk hunched down into his shoulders, feeling the prickle of his bones resonating to his affinity. "What?" he said irritably. "That I still keep things here that I don't want cluttering up my rooms at the archives? I think you know that."

They started up the curving ramp that wound around the house to the second story, the passage decorated with Alojan-style knot-work hangings that draped from the center of the arched ceiling and down both walls. In the knots were words, Tunuk knew, but he'd forgotten most of them—he thought he could remember the shape of "mountain" and "moon" and "serpent." A few of his sisters made them now, and they probably could have read these, although he wondered how many of their customers knew what their walls said.

You could probably knot together some of Zoifia's idiotic adventure chap-books and sell it as a traditional epic, he thought. *Rafiel del Sladio and the Yinpay.*

"You haven't been home since Obigen's memorial," Uruphi said quietly. "I find it curious that you've come now."

Tunuk started to answer that this had not been so long, but Uruphi interrupted. "A month and a half," she said. "We bound up his bones a month and a half ago. So I would say that's been longer than I'd like."

Tunuk wrapped his arms around himself, his bones and his

mother's growing noisy in their thrumming—live bone was chaotic, arrhythmic. It made his teeth ache and his skin itch. A bad sign.

"My apologies. I've been recovering."

"I suppose we all have." They came to the bend of the house that
wrapped around into the crèche room. Uruphi stopped and folded
her hands, studying her son. "I know you did not love Obigen so
well as your other fathers. He came late to the nest, and you were
misaligned stars, the two of you. But he did care for you—whatever
he said, it was with the aim of making you better."

"'A lost cause,'" Tunuk spat. "Funny way to make someone
better."

"I believe he said you were determined to make yourself a lost
cause," Uruphi said dryly. "Which is unkind, but different."

"I don't know why you're still arguing for him," he said. "He's
dead. He can't very well lose face with me. Unless you *agree* with
him, of course, in which case using a dead man as a puppet isn't very
sporting."

His anger made his affinity suddenly lurch—the spiral catching hold
of him, the pull on the skin of his left forearm where a bone plaque
was trying to form. He pressed his hand down on it hard, digging his
hands into the flesh—a very present pain worse than the bone.

Uruphi stared at his hand on his arm. "I see."

Tunuk scowled at her. "I'm just here for letters. You can go."

Uruphi sighed. "Please stay for a meal at least. You have some of
us very worried. It would help to see you alive and reasonably well."
She looked at his arm again, then turned and headed back down the
stairs. Tunuk checked his arm—no plaques—and continued with
his errand.

The crèche room held a series of small alcoves off a larger space.
Most of Tunuk's siblings were grown and off in their own nests of
partners, having their own crèches of children. Duwan and Conzi's
alcoves were easy to spot, a riot of keepsakes and crafts, toys, and
clothes spilling out of their two side-by-side alcoves. Between the
two was a nest of blankets and mats, a sleeping space for them both.
Tunuk studied it a moment, remembering sleeping this way with his
siblings, all tangled up and content.

Focus, he told himself. *Get in, get the letters, get out.*

At the end of the room, the alcove that had been his was dusty and disused, old trunks and unworn clothes waiting for him to return. Shelves lined the back wall, full of books he had wanted to keep close but not to read again, as well as little treasures he hadn't known how to part with: a little rag-pulp changeling mask, an iron whistle shaped like a skull, a little mouse jaw. He climbed up onto the platform where his sleeping mat had gone and felt behind the shelves there, careful not to spill books into the mess of his old belongings, and found the case.

It was a flat case meant for holding papers—inside was mostly schoolwork he'd been proud of, letters from grandparents in far-off nests whom he never spoke to anymore, a leaflet about joining the Vigilant Kinship that he could not remember taking or keeping...

And there at the back, three letters he hadn't known what to do with. He laid these out on his folded legs, almost afraid to read them. If there weren't any answers in them, then Tunuk did not know what to do.

He picked up the first, written in Chizid's strongly slanting hand:

Tunuk, I am very sorry that I have to leave you now. There is a little danger, and it's best if none of it stays in the archives. You will be safe there and hopefully everything will be back to normal soon. It is better if you say nothing about it, but I could not leave without word. I hope this is not too confusing for you—please understand it should never have gone this way. We meant to keep you from harm and this is the best way to do so at the moment.

Tunuk read it and reread it. A little danger—*We meant to keep you from harm.* A lot of vagueness—*say nothing about it; it should not have gone this way.* This was a problem he'd always had talking to Chizid. His mind would go so quickly that he forgot to say the words out loud. *Would you get it? Do we have one out? Are they ready?* And Qalba would chuckle and shake her head and fill in what her husband had forgotten to say.

But there was no Qalba here to interpret for Tunuk. There was nothing in the note to explain what had happened. If he gave it to the vigilants now, it would show there had been *something*, some secret, some problem, perhaps, with the skeleton.

We—Tunuk kept his eyes on that word, reasserting that it was there. Chizid had said "we," but he'd said it in the past tense. Not *we mean to keep you from harm*, not *we will keep you from harm*. Did that mean there was no "we" once he'd written the letter?

He thought of Qalba, her crooked smile painted that particular shade of orange she favored. He thought of her weeping and shouting at Chizid that night—*You don't understand! I can't just cut him off!*

Tunuk felt sure *he* did not understand at all.

The second letter was shorter, the same slanting hand:

Tunuk, this is goodbye. I wish it had not come to this, but there's no other way to be sure everyone is safe. Her name is Hazaunu. I won't ask you to pray for us, but if you could ask the priest at the temple on the corner, I would be grateful. Goodbye.

That, at least, had nouns Tunuk could use. Hazaunu was named—it wasn't an admission he'd tampered with the skeleton, but it was something. Tunuk didn't know which temple on which corner Chizid had meant—Arlabecca had a temple every few streets, and most Alojans went to none of them, as the mountains and the gods in them remained far over the Salt Wall. But if Tunuk asked? If he just…went into the temples and asked? Would they remember a man twelve years before, desperate about…something?

The third was the shortest. It was not from Chizid.

Lah-aada, lah-diiqad, hiimqoqim yaa b'eh bimehem'ooqaliithem, hiimqoqim yaa b'eh naaqitajiihem qitsilii.

You will know them by the power of their gifts, by the relics of their affinity. He had recognized the Orozhandi and asked Yinii once what it meant, and she—not suspecting the story behind it, the lost bone specialists, the fight, the mistake of the skeleton—had told him it was a proverb from a very old holy book, attributed to a saint called

Alsama, and the Orozhandi argued whether it referred to sorcerers or affinity magic or even changelings.

Under it was written: *Tunuk, keep the bones safe.*

He had found it after they were gone, tucked into a stack of letters he'd been neglecting. It was Qalba's handwriting, Qalba's sort of message, but there had been no way to know for certain when he'd received it or what she'd meant when she sent it. He'd tucked it away here and put it out of mind.

He took out the letter from the seaside cabin and set it alongside the older one. Most of it was in Orozhandi script—and he could recognize the handwriting in that worse than he could recognize Alojan knotwork. But the five words along the bottom...they looked similar, he thought.

You could ask Yinii, he thought. *Then you'd know. You'd know if she's come back.*

He thought of the bones standing in the alcove, no longer a person, just a message he couldn't decipher. *The saints just need a little extra care*, Chizid had said, pulling the curtain close. *Little privacy. Don't worry. I've got her.*

Who is "her," Chizid? Tunuk thought.

An unwelcome voice rang out from the doorway: "A best evening and may the stars align beneficently, sapa. Thank you once more for your hospitality."

"A pleasure as always, apprentice," Uruphi said to Quill. "Best of luck with our wayward son."

Tunuk shoved the letters back into the case with a curse. He'd only just managed to extricate himself from the alcove when Quill appeared, blocking the exit.

"Yinii's downstairs," he said. "Do you want to tell me what's going on? Or should I get her?"

"No and no," Tunuk said, striding forward as if he were going to bowl Quill over. "Glad we had this chat."

Quill stepped *into* Tunuk's stride, forcing him to skip back. "It's about the skeleton," Quill said. Tunuk glared at him, but then Quill added, "Twelve years ago, you said. You would have been an apprentice. This is about your mentor."

Tunuk felt his skin heat across his chest. He narrowed his eyes at Quill. "Did Amadea tell you that?"

"No, I just did the sums. And then you were here." He shrugged. "Twelve years ago, you would have just been a kid."

"That is indeed how time works, now go away."

"We're supposed to take you back to the archives. The vigilants want to talk to you. Did you come here to find some evidence it was your mentor? Is that it?"

"Leave me alone," Tunuk said, moving to pass around Quill again. "You don't understand."

Quill laughed, so bitter it caught Tunuk midstride. "You think I don't understand? Your mentor did something. I'm guessing they meant a great deal to you, otherwise you would have pointed a finger right from the start. You don't think *I* know what that's like? To face that someone you looked up to might be a villain?"

Tunuk hesitated, ashamed. Quill had come to the archives when his superior's attempts to blackmail an assassin had led to first the death of Quill's best friend and then the superior himself. And then all the bribes, all the influences, all the darkness that had been covered by the man's office in life had poured out.

Tunuk hadn't thought much of the man—what kind of idiot thought he could get away with blackmailing Redolfo Kirazzi's favorite assassin and not catch a sword? But...

"Fine," Tunuk said. "Maybe you understand a little. Except mine wasn't a villain. Weren't villains." *You don't know that*, he told himself.

Quill looked up at him, studying Tunuk with an intensity that made him feel itchy and unsettled. Quill's buried bones gave off a ghostly hum as Tunuk's anxiety rose.

"Amadea doesn't know any of this, does she?" Quill asked.

No—the answer heaved itself up out of Tunuk's very marrow. *No, I can't tell Amadea, because telling Amadea means she will know I've been lying and how badly I've been lying and...*

"Come on," Quill said. "We're getting coffee. There's a place under the aqueduct that's not too busy. You can explain what's going on, and we'll figure out what to do."

"You're not my type," Tunuk snapped. "Go get coffee with Yinii."

"Hilarious. You need to tell me what's going on if I'm going to help."

"If you're going to tell Amadea, you mean."

Quill blinked at him. "If you haven't told Amadea, I'm assuming there's a reason. So tell me the reason."

"If I haven't told Amadea, what makes you think I want to tell you?"

"I don't think you want to tell me," Quill said very reasonably. "But I think you should. I understand a little, remember. And I want to figure this out too."

Four letters, a little danger, a lot of questions—and no answers that led back to Tunuk managing on his own, not really. And Quill did know a little what it was like, having someone you trusted keep secrets from you, secrets that left you in danger.

"Plus," Quill added, "Bayan and Vari right now are interrogating Yinii about which other nests they should send dinner invitations to, so if we leave now, you can decide whether you want to be ambushed with potential lovers over dinner or not."

Tunuk heaved another sigh. "They are going to think we are seeing one another. All three of us."

"I can't speak for Yinii, but if it gets them off your back a little, I certainly don't mind. *We* know we're not."

"We're *not*," Tunuk added thunderously. He clutched the case close to his chest and stormed past Quill. "You're buying the coffee."

The coffeehouse Quill led them to wasn't one Tunuk had been to before, and he wondered when it had tucked itself into the bottom floor of this apartment building only a few blocks from the house he'd grown up in. The walls were painted heavily blue around the little alcove they'd found a table in, the memory of other colors concealed in its thickness.

Tunuk perched on a too-small chair, his back to the wall, contemplating the delicate cup of coffee before him, the pale brown patch of foam on its surface. He imagined it a skull, half-flattened, then revised that to—what was less obvious? A flower? A wilting flower? Then with annoyance called it a skull, half-flattened—it was only himself that might call him ghoulish for it. Biorni, set before him like a guard animal, had probably already made everyone else's minds up.

Yinii hardly touched her cup, her green eyes darting from Tunuk to the steam wafting up from her coffee to Quill, the whites of her day-eyes flashing like an animal signaling danger.

Quill just watched him impassively. Sipping his own coffee. Waiting and waiting. Tunuk had been expecting—hoping really—that Quill would start talking, start trying to fill up the quiet. *What were you getting from your parents' house?* and *Are you in danger?* and *Lord on the Mountain, Tunuk, why didn't you tell me?* If he did, then Tunuk could just snatch up his words and throw them back like sharp rocks.

"Do you need another coffee?" Yinii asked at last. "I could get it."

"I don't know why we're *here*," Tunuk spat. "The coffee's awful, and the chairs are ugly."

"It was close," Quill said. "Which means no one else from the archives is likely to be here." Quill waited another long moment, the laughter of the trio at the table beyond him filling the silence. Tunuk glowered back, and then Quill said mildly, "Do you want us to guess?"

Yes, Tunuk thought. *Guess and tell me what might be true. Tell me what makes sense.*

Chizid killed Qalba, his thoughts whispered. *They fought, and he killed her, and that's been her looking down at you all this time.*

Yinii pressed her mouth into a tense line and looked at Quill. "You don't have to tell us, but...are you in trouble?"

Tunuk drank his coffee down, all in one gulp. "I don't need help," he said. "I...know what to do."

"No, you don't," Quill said. "Honestly, what are you afraid we're going to do? Laugh? Not believe you? Tell Amadea?"

"We could tell Amadea," Yinii offered.

"I don't want you to tell Amadea." Tunuk scowled down at the coffee cup, looking for signs in the grounds clinging to the sides. "I lied to her."

"Yes," Quill said slowly. "But...you do that all the time. 'I was in my workroom the whole time.' 'I didn't put the skull on Radir's chair.'"

"'No one told me about the change of forms,'" Yinii added.

Tunuk scowled at the coffee. "Not like this."

Sometimes, Tunuk thought of the yinpay with a savage kind of joy—*Fine, I'm a monster, an ending. That means you'll let me be.* If there was something wrong with him, let it be wrong; at least everyone understood where he belonged—alone in the dark jungle.

But then...Amadea would be there. And he couldn't say he was alone and abandoned—not entirely—because Amadea would not leave him. She would let him have his space, she would see the truth behind his little lies, but she would pull him out of the shadowy jungle and onto the paths, into the fresh air. She would remind him he did not hate everyone, and it was worth seeing what else he might be before he, too, became bone.

"Tunuk," Quill said, "you can tell us. You can tell me. This is my job now."

Tunuk folded his arms around his chest. Quill was not Amadea. But he was trying. And Yinii had never been anything but kind to him.

They weren't going to leave Tunuk alone, in the dark.

"I lied," Tunuk said again. "I knew the skeleton was...wrong. I've been lying on the catalogues since they became mine."

Yinii made a little noise in the back of her throat, and Quill sucked in a breath. "Who...?" He caught himself, put on an expression that was *all* Amadea. "That's a very heavy secret to carry."

Tunuk made a face. "I don't *know* who it is."

"But you have a guess," Yinii finished. "Don't you?"

Tunuk blew out a breath. "Look, I was young—very young. An apprentice. Fourteen, almost fifteen. There were two bone specialists then: Chizid and Qalba. So I had two mentors, two guides." He looked at Yinii. "They were gone, before you came."

It wasn't the story they were asking for, but it was what poured out of Tunuk. "And that doesn't mean much to you," he said to Quill, "but you need to understand how *rare* bone-speaking's become. The affinity doesn't come up much—we don't work bone the way we used to—and when it does... You *saw* Zoifia lose her fucking mind over some bronze statues when you first came here?"

The bronze specialist spiraling, losing control of her abilities, melting pins and nails and chains and statuary into a flood of bronze that threatened to drown her. Tunuk shuddered, remembering the tug of the spiral, the times he'd lost his own fucking mind. He looked at Yinii, and she reached over to take his hand. He moved it before she could, tucking his hands beneath his thighs, his eyes on the coffee.

"She can't be around bronze when she's in alignment," he said. "We're all a little dangerous around our materials in alignment. But it's worse when you have something that can be *unworked* too. Zoifia only reacts to bronze—not tin or copper. But a salt specialist in alignment can't manage by the seaside, and a wool specialist will suffer on a sheep farm.

"When I come into alignment, the raw materials for my affinity are under the skin of every person in this city. You cannot imagine what that's like, how *loud* it is, how much it rattles your nerves. My fathers are fond of telling me that in the old world, we had rituals and processes for the bone speakers, for making sure they weren't alone and yet they weren't ready to tear out their own teeth, but nobody knows them here. It's too rare."

"So... all three of you were at one another's throats four times a year?" Quill asked, puzzled. "Like Stavio and Zoifia?"

Tunuk shook his head. "That's *metallics*. And Chizid and Qalba weren't like that at all. They were married, you know—I don't know of a lot of specialists who marry someone with the same affinity. It seems like it would be overwhelming, but they... fit together, I suppose." He nodded at Yinii. "Qalba was Orozhandi—they're good about making peace with the spiral. And bone's one of the organic affinities—it doesn't cycle predictably. Each specialist has a different alignment period. So they were there to help.

"They liked me," he said softly, remembering how, for the first time, his stormy moods, his ghoulish humor hadn't been *too much*. They'd understood what lurked underneath, even when Tunuk hadn't, and Chizid had said all the right things to Tunuk's parents, and Qalba had shown him the best places to tuck himself away when the spiral felt too close. The window that led to the roof. The west side of the sorting facility away from all the worktables. The cabin by the seaside.

He thought of the letter—maybe it was Qalba's. Maybe it meant she had come back, sometime in the last few years, left that for him to find. *The wounded jackal limps along a winding path, but it knows the one it hunts for.* Maybe it just meant they had always planned to come back, that they *were* coming back.

But: *Tunuk, this is goodbye. I wish it had not come to this . . .*

Grief swelled up in his chest, and he blurted out, "Something happened."

Quill studied him a moment, then said the words Tunuk couldn't. "Do you think the skeleton is Qalba?"

"No," Tunuk said. Lied. Because he wasn't deluded—Qalba had vanished, and those bones had appeared. He spent ages trying to convince himself to check; he never dared—until the vigilant had forced him.

Yinii watched him warily. "Could you tell? When you touched the bones?"

"I didn't . . . I didn't really read them," Tunuk said. "I got scared."

"You think it's her," Quill said.

"Chizid wouldn't have done that," Tunuk said. "He wasn't an angry man." *Except the once.* "And I got a note from Qalba after she disappeared." *Unsigned, undated.* "He *wouldn't* have killed her."

Quill nodded. "But he did something with the skeleton."

"Maybe," Tunuk allowed. He studied the coffee cup, the grounds sliding down the side of the cup. "He was working on one of them in that niche right before he left. And then . . . Saint Hazaunu was different."

Yinii wove her fingers together, tapping them nervously. "*How* did no one from the wood room notice? They have to do the catalogues too. Surely they know which saints are the replicas!"

"Luck," Tunuk spat. The first cataloguing that had come up after Chizid had vanished, Tunuk had been a nervous wreck, teetering on the edge of a spiral for a month. "The cedar specialist in charge of the wooden relics had an apoplectic attack and retired just before it would have come out. Bucella took over, and I guess their catalogues had been adjusted too. Nobody noticed, and nobody brought it up. And nobody was Orozhandi, so, no, they didn't know which ones were the replicas." He blew out a breath. "I told Bucella she'd heard wrong. That it wasn't nineteen wooden saints, it was only eighteen."

Yinii let out an involuntary little noise of horror, and Tunuk locked his gaze on the cup again.

"'Adjusted,'" Quill repeated. He raked a hand through his hair. "All right. So who might know what happened? Besides Chizid and Qalba."

Tunuk thought of the strange letter from the cabin and fidgeted. "Nobody."

"Look, someone *has* to know something. Otherwise, you're going to end up in an imperial prison."

"No, I won't. Amadea wouldn't let that happen."

"Tunuk," Yinii said. "They have to tell the rezas. If they find out you knew and you didn't say anything, *maybe* you won't be blamed. But then *Amadea* will."

Tunuk made himself fold his arms over his chest and said, "Well, if all of Stavio's gossip has any basis in reality, I assume at that point the consort-prince will step in." *When has Stavio's gossip ever been something to trust?* he thought, panic swirling in his chest.

Quill sighed. "All right, setting aside imperial prisons and whose fault this might be . . . don't you want to know what happened? Who that *is*?"

If it's Qalba, he didn't say. Tunuk considered the cryptic note from the seaside, riding in his pocket, but left it—he could almost hear Quill saying, *Where did you find it?* and *Why would anyone leave a note there?* and *What is this supposed to mean?* and finally *Tunuk, I think you're imagining things.*

He could hear Yinii telling him sadly, *This isn't hers. This is just some archivist, writing poetry. I can hear the bad rhymes they didn't use.*

Tunuk scowled. "I'm not a monster. I care who it is."

"So who else might Chizid and Qalba have talked to?" Quill asked. "Who else might know what happened before they left?"

Tunuk pinched the edge of his coffee cup, felt the faint *shush* of bone ash in the ceramic, like a ghost haunting an old house, and it made his bones whisper back, busy on the edge of alignment.

"There was the generalist," Tunuk said finally. "Per. He was friendly with them and...not gossipy like Stavio, but nosy. Chizid had a half brother he was close with, Gunarro. They went out often and took me once or twice. Qalba had a friend called Toya who was around a lot. He was older, maybe an uncle." He exhaled hard, his chest tight. "There...there was a girl too. A first cousin of Qalba's, once removed. Oshanna something. Ul-Shandiian. She was a little older than me, and she'd sometimes visit Qalba and come bother me. Qalba would make me take her out for pancakes and listen to her brag."

"Oh. I think I know her," Yinii offered. "She's...she's the reza ul-Shandiian's daughter. One of his advisors now."

"Well, she was a smug and preening little know-it-all at sixteen, so that tracks," Tunuk said.

"You already said she was ul-Shandiian," Yinii said, taking a sip of her coffee, and that little bit of venom surprised Tunuk so much he barked out a laugh.

"I could probably talk to her," Yinii offered. "She might see me since...well, there's a lot of arguing about the new reza ul-Benturan. Would that help?"

Quill frowned pensively at his own cup, rapping his knuckles against the wooden table. The boisterous trio of humans behind Quill got up and left. "I think that's a good idea. Do you know where the others live?" he asked Tunuk.

"Gunarro," Tunuk said. "But not Toya. He always came to the archives. And Per...Mireia probably has some sort of address for him in the personnel files."

"That's easy enough. We have to go back to the archives anyway."

"After dinner," Tunuk said, dreading it.

Quill shrugged. "We could just...not. What happens if you don't come home for dinner?"

Tunuk sighed. What had Uruphi said? *You have some of us very worried. It would help to see you alive and reasonably well.* "It's just a stupid dinner."

Quill hesitated as if he were going to say something more, and Tunuk braced, ready to retort, but in the end, Quill just shrugged and stood up. "We can walk you back."

"We'll stay if you want," Yinii offered. But by the way her gaze kept darting to the pockets of his uniform where he was carrying the notes, he knew she needed to go home, to rest, to not trouble herself with eight nosy Alojan parents.

Seven, he reminded himself.

"You should go back to the archives," he said. "You look so tired. You could sequester."

"I'll walk him back," Quill offered. Yinii looked from one young man to the other, and Tunuk sighed. He stormed from the coffeehouse, not wanting to watch the spectacle of them trying to negotiate a goodbye.

Quill caught up quickly. As they walked back to Tunuk's childhood home, he found himself wondering what Quill had stopped himself from saying. *Be more grateful for what you have? Be nicer to your mother? It must be hard having so many parents?* Tunuk's bones kept buzzing, and he found himself composing arguments to all of these, uttering none of them. If Quill wasn't going to speak first, Tunuk wasn't going to either.

When they came around the corner, Quill stopped, blocking the way. Tunuk braced—first for a fight... then with the sudden realization that Quill had been there, in the house, when Obigen and Karimo had died, and it was rather callous and *ghoulish* even that Tunuk didn't remember that, didn't insist Quill go back to the archives instead of walking him home.

But then he followed Quill's gaze up to the house, where Alzari and Uruphi were talking to a vigilant. A vigilant and a hospitaller from the House of Unified Wisdom in the Necessary Arts. His mothers looked tense, worried. There was a transport wagon behind the vigilants.

"Are your parents all right?" Quill asked. "That looks like an assessment pair."

"It is," Tunuk said.

Biorni's jaw chattered in his hands.

Uruphi looked around the street, then gestured the assessment pair into the house. He remembered his birth mother watching him as he pressed the plaques back, and panic started rising in his chest. "They called them for me." They had done it before, deciding something was going very wrong with Tunuk—and it had been days and days of questions and isolation and judgment, and everything got worse.

Quill looked up at him. "Do you *need* assessment? Can you just tell them you're fine?"

"They don't *listen*," Tunuk said, the words slipping out without any chance for him to hide them. He didn't have time to go through their questions—not now, not again. This was what the archives were supposed to prevent, but he couldn't go back to the archives, not without knowing what had happened, who had stolen the bones. Who was the skeleton in the chapel. He could see Amadea's disappointed face, see the vigilants' skepticism. Not talking to the vigilants would make him look guilty. Except right now, without any sense of an answer, would talking to them make him look just as guilty?

He couldn't think. Couldn't figure out what to say. Everything was thrumming, the pulse of bones in Quill and the vigilant and the hospitaller and his mothers, people in the houses, and Biorni, chattering so hard now he had to dig his fingers in to hold on. *You have some of us very worried.*

"I don't have time for this," Tunuk blurted. He felt the thrumming coming from deep in him, the chaotic rhythm of his bones reaching toward those others. The skull in his hands matched it, and the crackling of the network of bone spreading echoed through him. "They're not going to listen, and the vigilants will decide something happened that didn't and—ow!"

A plaque of bone erupted from his wrist, crept over his forearm. Alojan bone, black as a crow feather, curled along its edges as it spread. Tunuk grabbed his wrist and felt the spiral licking at his thoughts. *Hide, smother, shelter.*

Quill yanked Biorni away from him. He grabbed Tunuk's arm and pulled him back the way they'd come. "Tunuk, are you with me? Are you all right?"

"No!" he spat. He hooked his fingertips over the plaque of bone, but it was rooted in him, still clinging. Still thrumming against his heartbeat. "I can't. I can't do this. I can't."

"Don't, then," Quill said. "New plan. You're going to calm down. I'm going to find somewhere to stay. We're not going to your parents' house or the archives right now."

"How?" Tunuk said. "My parents and Amadea know everywhere I go! And I didn't exactly walk out with a pocketful of metas for an inn—no, that's worse, they'll check the inns. Ow!" The bone plaque spread further. It would keep going, would overtake his pulse, would swallow him whole.

You'll be safe then, a dim part of him thought. *Safe and alone. No one but the bones.* He squeezed his eyes shut, his thoughts buzzing, pulsing. *Is it better to lock yourself in a carapace of bone or become the yinpay?* he wondered giddily.

"Stay with me, Tunuk," Quill said. He was sounding a little hysterical too. "I'm not going to let them take you, but you have to stay out of the spiral. We're going to fix this. We're going to find the answer." He stopped hauling on Tunuk.

Tunuk opened his eyes. They were standing at the edge of one of the city's rivers, but in his agitation, he couldn't remember the name. Quill was looking back the way they came, breathing a little hard.

"What am I supposed to do?" Tunuk said, hating how small his voice sounded.

Quill turned to face Tunuk with a glint in the dark center of his eyes. "Wait. I know where they won't find us. Can you pretend to be a postulant Paremi for the night?"

⊷ ≍✦≍ ↦

The files for Chizid del Hwana and Qalba One-Fox ul-Shandiian had arrived by courier from the archives, just as Richa ran out of things to keep himself busy with. So, instead of bringing them to his desk to review, he tucked them under his arm and went home.

He stopped to buy dinner from the Alojan flatbread vendor next to his apartment, the fluffy disks wrapped around unctuous chunks of meat, chopped onions, and fragrant herbs. He ate it one-handed as he climbed the stairs to his apartment, the juice dripping down his knuckles, held carefully away from the files.

Salva Nine-Scorpion Gaitha-hyu might be the one in charge of investigating the murder of the peddler, but the wooden bones and the skeleton in the chapel weren't a matter for the road cohort. This case he *could* claim, he could solve, and in doing so, perhaps he could solve the murder so clearly connected to this decade-old theft and avoid the question of Stellano.

Richa unlocked the door with a hand wiped clean on his trousers. The room beyond wasn't large, but it was worlds better than what he'd had before he joined the Kinship. He'd filled the space as efficiently as possible: a narrow bed that doubled as seating beside a table he could work on documents on; a set of shelves on one and a half walls to hold books, clothes, dishes, and some of his favorite carvings; a basin and worktable near the door, plus some water jugs; a big window overlooking the city, with a little row of plants before it; and an altar.

He dropped the documents on the table and washed his hands in the basin. Then he fished in his pocket and took out a coin for each of the Datongu household gods on the altar: One for Yakshooka, the trickster birdman with one withered wing who guarded his luck. One for the Golden Innocent—a cheap big-eyed plaster statue of a boy with one finger in his mouth—for the protection of his home. And the third for a little figurine of the Beminat honored-spirit Ninaoku, a red-furred dog with a lit torch in its mouth that was meant to symbolize ingenuity and piety, but which Richa usually asked to keep the house from burning down.

He'd bought it in a shop down by the West River when he'd first come to Arlabecca, not really understanding what it was meant to depict. The Beminat told stories of the god of storms sending the gift of fire down in the jaws of his faithful pet, when the sun god had declared humans could have no flames.

To Richa, it had simply looked like the dog he'd had growing up, and he took it as a sign that Egillio approved, from wherever dogs went when they were dead, that he had gotten out of Caesura.

Today, the dog was lying on its side, tipped over on the altar, and Richa frowned. Not an auspicious state. He'd probably knocked it over as he rushed out the door to head to Ragale. But just to be certain, he looked around the room, making sure everything else was as he'd left it.

He was long past the stage of setting up traps and tells—a cup of water easily spilled, a spread of flour easily disturbed—he hadn't been robbed once since he'd moved to Arlabecca, outside of other cadets borrowing his things unasked. But there were places he knew to look—were the baskets on the shelves pulled out, were the drawers ajar, were there things out that shouldn't have been out?

Just the dog lying sideways on the altar.

You're being jumpy, he told himself as he righted it, and added two coins to the stack in apology for the ill treatment. He scratched the little statue dog's head with one fingernail and said a little prayer for continued protection before sitting down with the files.

He untied the twine Amadea had bound around the leather envelope layer and unfolded the waxed paper. On top of the pages were two notes in her spiky handwriting:

Under loan to Richa Langyun, Vigilant Kinship, authorized by Amadea Gintanas, archivist superior.

Original copies. Must be returned with all pages intact.

And

Mireia and I are still in conference planning how best to inform the Orozhandi, so I cannot escape. Another time. Get some rest before you read these.

Richa smiled and shook his head. He moved some pillows around and lay down to read.

Chizid del Hwana had come to the archives thirty years prior at the age of fifteen. A bone specialist of high capability with "a sub-affinity for avian bones." His parents were Kuali, though his mother had died when he was eight, and his father had married a Borsyan woman. One half brother with no affinities. The only notes about problems related to the sort of youthful indiscretions Richa regularly wrote cadets up for—showing up to work while hungover on too much sap wine, scuffling over personal matters, losing pieces of uniform. Chizid had been sequestered once, early on, and once shortly before his retirement date. There were notes that he had taken ten respites over his twenty years at the archives. A letter was tucked in the same leather envelope and agreed with what Amadea had guessed: he and Qalba rescinded their oaths and wished to live outside the order. It didn't mention where they'd retired to. There was a receipt that mentioned the last disbursement of Chizid's stipend going to the half brother in Arlabecca.

Qalba One-Fox ul-Shandiian had come to the archives at the advanced age of twenty-three. Her affinity was described as "middling" but with a clear specialization toward sentient remains that seemed to be highly valuable. There was a letter of recommendation from the ul-Shandiian reza that praised her ingenuity and her cleverness and said, very much without saying, that Qalba One-Fox had been a troublesome young woman to the reza ul-Shandiian, but that stopped now, if she knew what was good for her. And Qalba seemed to very much know what was good for her—she had been sequestered three times with the note beside each that it had been voluntary, taken thirteen respites of a week or so, and had not a single disciplinary note to her name.

She and Chizid had married four years after she came to the archives, and both collections included a note about combining their living arrangements and stipends. There was a note regarding her retirement in the letter from her husband. The final disbursement had been sent to the ul-Shandiian clan, who had not responded to requests for information about her current residence.

It was as if they had both vanished twelve years ago.

Twelve years ago. The age Tunuk had estimated for the Orozhandi skeleton.

Richa went over the notes again, puzzling over what might lead him from the Chapel of the Skeleton Saints to a hermit's hideaway on the northern road. There was nothing obvious, nothing immediate. But two people didn't just vanish any more than a wooden skeleton became bone.

Had he been right, and the skeleton was Qalba's? There was nothing that suggested Chizid del Hwana might murder his wife—or anyone else. Had something in Qalba's misspent youth caught up to her? There was nothing that suggested it was anything worse than dabbling with sandsmut and stillwax and leaving rude graffiti on buildings.

Were they changelings all along? he wondered a little wildly. How many changelings could hide inside the Salt Wall?

His thoughts slid back to Stellano, to Vigilant Gaitha-hyu's intimations. What would be worse? A changeling in his shape or Stellano himself dogging Richa's footsteps?

You were always a coward, Stellano snarled in his memory. *Always ready to betray me. You loved him better than me, all this time—that's the real cruelty.* The flash of the knife.

He stared up at the ceiling and blew out a breath.

You are not in Caesura anymore, he told himself. *You are not that man anymore.* Even if Stellano was circling him—and why would he? It had been fifteen years—Richa was a vigilant with his Kinship beside him. And the archives.

He imagined Amadea's expression if she caught him not quite going to sleep, her files a mess, and he smiled to himself, putting them back on the table...then picking up the first page to read one more time.

He dozed, chasing threads—bird bones and ul-Shandiian, respite sites and dogs, the trouble a young person could get up to, Stellano Zezurin and Amadea Gintanas.

II

THE GHOST OF A PROMISE

Sometime in summer, the reign of Emperor Clement
Benturan Canyon, Orozhand

Orozhand tucks itself into the rocks near the Red Desert, the canyons coiled like serpents around the water that bubbles up from beneath. The cities are a maze, canyon after canyon wind-scoured through and chiseled into the red layers of rock. The girl looks up their sheer sides, across massive murals flaking from the rock, to the ribbon of cerulean sky above.

"The Hidden Kingdom," Redolfo says. He looks over at her. "Well. Not so hidden. The changelings found it surely enough."

The remnants of the Orozhandi of a century ago litter the canyons. Broken wagons and fallen tools. Tatters of cloth and bits of pottery. Faded murals line the high stone walls, painted figures of horned people, gods, demons, saints. Doors to cave houses hang open, the belongings that were left behind desiccating in the dark.

Once, the girl spots a giant horned rabbit ducking into a disused cave, and one of the changelings catches it, roasts it on the fire along with a handful of lizards and roots.

"Why are we here?" the girl asks, cracking the rabbit's bones to eat the marrow.

"Paying our respects," Redolfo says, and she knows this is not the answer. The changelings are sent to scour the caves, looking for something. They return with small game, rusty knives held in heavy cloths, water urns filled from the clever system of ducts and fountains built into the rock.

"It's such a strange place to live," the girl says.

"Not every land has the gift of the river," Redolfo says, watching the entrance to the cave they've settled into, and it takes her a moment to realize he means Khirazj and Pademaki. He means himself. But then he turns to her and adds, "The roads east lead to all sorts of places—and more importantly all sorts of goods. The water comes up from the ground in this place, so travelers would have been happy to stop. And the canyons are defensible—even the Beminat couldn't have taken the canyons easily."

"But the changelings did," the girl says. She frowns at the fire. "Why aren't they here?"

Redolfo cocks his head. "Who says they aren't?"

That, she realizes, is what the others are hunting for. His little army has swelled to a dozen, and he's growing smug with the success. So long as they keep encountering scouts and small groups, that number will keep growing.

The girl has learned to hide her fear. Or perhaps the fear has been burned out of her. She isn't sure. The changelings do not frighten her—the locked ones, that is. The assassin, the brother, the sorcerer—she remembers these people in their own flesh, and some of them were frightening, but the ones who travel with them are only pale shadows of the originals.

The fresher ones she feels sorry for, like birds caught in traps. She has seen them as the wild things they are inside, made dull and distracted by Redolfo's clever magics.

The ones who appear out of the darkness, trying out faces and voices...those still frighten her a little, if she's being honest.

And Redolfo—Redolfo she is afraid of, down to her bones, though not for reasons she can articulate. She feels like a bird, too, clutched in his palm, held so carefully, but so easy to crush.

The sorcerer returns with two of the newer changelings carrying a box between them. An inlay of shimmery stones describes a pair of three-eyed horned men, a huge goatlike creature with long horns, a diamond-patterned snake. They set the box before Redolfo.

"You were right," the sorcerer says, sounding disgusted. "As always."

Redolfo smiles to himself and opens the box, which is packed with bundles the size and shape of two apples stacked. The girl peers over Redolfo's arm as he pulls the broken bark-paper back to reveal a lumpy brick of yellow and a faint smell of old eggs.

"More than enough," Redolfo says. He needs it to make the potion that locks the changelings, she knows. That must be why they came here.

The sorcerer offers up a case as well, the kit of a healer. Redolfo picks through this, tossing aside what hasn't weathered the century and keeping what has. The fire crackles, the chimney hole sucks away the smoke, and the girl curls up tight, missing home. The fields around Sestina, the smell of pistachio flowers, the sound of the little creeks burbling through the landscape, Ibramo's face—how quickly will these memories fade as they leave Semilla behind? They already have a wavery, indistinct quality that makes her think of the air above the fire.

The changeling who looks like Redolfo's brother comes back next, the three changelings he's brought with him bearing bones and jewels. The girl peers at these, the promised saints, but if there is any power in these dead things, she can't sense it.

Still, as Redolfo picks through the bones, she asks, "Do you know that one's name?"

"It's not important," he says, adding finger and foot bones to a small pouch.

"Why are you taking those?"

"Do you imagine the saint still needs them? I have my reasons." There's an edge to his voice, and she doesn't ask any more. When he finishes with the bones, he goes back to the sulfur in the box, breaking off a small piece and bringing it to the workspace he's assembled near the entrance to the cave.

The girl curls up tighter, feeling the rabbit meat leaping in her stomach.

The assassin returns late into the night, this time with an unconscious changeling hanging slack between her assistants. The girl looks away—they hurt her eyes when they're like this, fizzing between forms, unstable and unsettled.

"It's a strong one," the assassin says, her smirk a perfect ghost of the original's. The changeling looks almost dead.

"Good," Redolfo says. He holds up one of the metal syringes, shaking it as he turns to the girl. "Lira?"

The girl looks up. There are two names he calls her, and that's the *serious* one. "Yes?"

"Come here."

She feels the echo of other needles in her arms and has to rub the discomfort away as she stands and crosses the cave. That fear she thought was gone comes shuddering up through her, and it's all she can do to look Redolfo in the face, to not stare at the syringe in his hand.

He holds it out to her. "Do you know how to use this?"

The girl frowns. This isn't how it goes. "You put it in my arm?"

"Not this one." He molds her hands around the syringe, turning her toward the half-dead changeling. "You're going to lock a changeling."

Her stomach lurches again, the wrongness of what he's asking reverberating through all her being. The syringe is warm in her hand, and her eyes ache trying to resolve the changeling into a familiar shape. She wants it to get up. She wants it to run.

Redolfo takes his hands off hers, sets them firmly on her shoulders. "Who do you want it to be?"

She can feel the three old changelings staring at her—the assassin, the sorcerer, and the brother—waiting for an answer, or maybe waiting for her to decide if she can.

They'll have to kill it if you don't, she thinks. Then: *It might kill you if you don't.*

Redolfo squeezes her shoulders. "Come on now, Lira. There are no wrong answers."

The way he says it means there are countless wrong answers. The girl sifts through them.

Ibramo—if Ibramo were here, the world would not feel so endless, so unsafe. But as soon as the want forms, she discards it. She wants Ibramo, her friend—she does not want his ghost, his echo. It feels wrong to make a copy of him, and she realizes this is one person even Redolfo has not duplicated. A wrong answer, most definitely.

She thinks of the day-sisters, the ones from the abbey at Gintanas— wrong answer. That's too close to her split memories, to suggesting she's not Lira, and Redolfo doesn't like it when she gets the story wrong. She thinks of Lireana's sisters, the young princesses long dead—wrong answer. They would be children, and what use is a child out here? She thinks of Beneditta, the heir who's her own age, a friend in this strange place—wrong answer. There are so many ways to use that sort of double that Redolfo will say she has wasted this one. Maybe he'll even take it from her. She thinks of guards and nurses; dukes, duchesses, and attendants; merchants and orphans and soldiers—they all blur into nonsense, the fitful, fizzing incompleteness of a changeling in flux. Her mother, her father, her grandmother, the emperor—

Herself? She pictures a face, almost like hers: *A better me.* And with that thought comes an anger, a despair so intense she wants to scream it out from her body, to shed it in one powerful sound.

Redolfo shoves her forward. "Well?"

What is the opposite of that rage? A new face rises up—rosy and still somehow incomplete. A baby, her brother. Prince Melosino. Dead in the cradle when the Fratricide came. She has the memories of that unfinished rosy face, a little loaf of blankets, a promise he would be something more, one day. When people mourned Melosino, she heard them mourn his future mostly. They said all the things he could have been because he hadn't had the chance to be anything yet.

It reminds her suddenly, painfully of the changelings. Endless possibilities. Something out of nothing. She pulls on those memories, and they slide up out of the darkness—imagining the baby as a little boy she could have played with, and then imagining the little boy as a laughing young man. Imagining him riding, his dark hair shining, a dark beard patching his cheeks. A whole person who never was whom she still mourned, a decade later, because she believed in him.

A person who could still be.

The changeling hangs between its captors, so close to its death. She sets the needle against its arm and tells it the story of its rebirth.

CHAPTER SIX

The chapter house of the Order of the Scriveners of Parem was not a comfortable place to sleep, but it wasn't too far from the yula Manco house, which meant not too long for Tunuk to walk while fighting back a spiral. No one would think to look for Tunuk there—few enough people would think to look for Quill there, seeing as how his oath was technically undone. And it gave Quill a chance to visit with the ashes of his best friend, resting in the columbarium of the chapter house.

It wasn't easy to talk the prelate into letting them stay, but Quill opened with the possibility that he would end his so-called "sabbatical" not by completing the renunciation of his vows and swearing new vows as an imperial archivist but by returning, chastened, to the Paremi. From there he leaned on the prelate's constant need of new dedicants—Tunuk did not paint the most convincing picture of a would-be scrivener, scowling at everything around him as the prelate fretted. And Quill closed by bringing up that perhaps he should be consulting with his mother on this, especially if the prelate wasn't going to be open to counseling him.

In the end they were given a closet of a room and a frenetic speech on the virtues of the order before the prelate had to run off to attend other duties.

Keeping the horned rabbit skull with him, Quill scribbled a carefully vague note to Amadea and another to Yinii, then passed them off to a scrivener headed out for the evening. He paused, considering the ebb and flow of scriveners from the chapter house, the familiarity of it.

The hollow feeling that watching them left.

He missed this, but did he only miss it because he knew it? Because he'd been sure about what he was doing, who he was following? Did he miss it because he missed having a scrivener's common connection, that friendship among peers?

"You clearly miss Karimo," Richa had said. "You need a friend." Maybe he was only lonely, only feeling out of step with his days. He still hadn't worked properly in the archives, and it felt like he never would. The generalists had spent the weeks he'd been trained showing him forms, ledgers, manuals on what signs of a spiral looked like and where the various emergency items he might need were located—and then running off to do their proper jobs.

You're good at talking to people, Karimo had said to him before. Quill liked the details, he liked the history, but the thing that made him think he could fit into the Imperial Archives was that he was good at talking to people—and the specialists needed that.

He thought of Tunuk, alone in the bone workrooms, abandoned by his mentors, maybe because they just tired of the archives, maybe because of something far more sinister. He doubted very much that Tunuk was going to be his friend...but if he could help Tunuk through this, it would mean he hadn't made a mistake choosing the archives.

When he returned to the room, Tunuk had pulled the blanket and pillows off the bed, winding them into a nest that he wedged in the narrow space between the bed and beneath the desk. He almost melted into the shadows there. He scratched at the shiny black plaque of bone that had spread over his skin. A piece flaked off and clinked to the floor, crumbling into dust a few moments after it fell.

"Is it all right if Biorni's in here?" Quill said. "Is he going to make you spiral?"

"No. Why is the prelate afraid you'll tell your mother he's a git?" Tunuk asked, not looking at Quill.

He set the rabbit skull at the foot of the bed. "You know how, when we first met, you didn't want to discuss who your nest-father was? It's like that."

"Your mother is a self-absorbed eel of a politician?" Tunuk poked at another bone fragment on his arm, wincing as if it hurt.

"Not exactly." Quill climbed up onto the bed over the footboard, pulling off his cloak and spreading it out like a blanket. He sighed. "My mother is Khoma Seupu-lai."

Tunuk's eyes glowed in the shadowy space, and they narrowed. "Why do I know that name?"

"Probably because Lord Obigen was your nest-father," Quill said. "She's an advisor to the Duke Minseno in Hyangga. She deals with the noble consuls *a lot.*"

Tunuk tilted his head, puzzled. "And you're an itinerant scribe?"

"Until I get to be an apprentice generalist," Quill said. And then he added, "My mother doesn't actually know that yet. She's not going to like it."

"I don't see how it's *worse* than being an itinerant scribe, really."

"Because being a scribe would have been a very traditional and well-established calling for the third son of a dignitary of Min-Se. And forsaking your oath—whatever that is—is not."

"Especially when you're romancing an Orozhandi girl."

Quill scrunched his face up. "First off, I don't know that I'm romancing *anybody*. Second, maybe that's an Alojan thing, but my mother wouldn't care what protectorate any girl I like is from, so long as there's a chance of grandchildren. I think she's got the paper horses ready to burn at the first whiff of a grandchild—no, actually, scratch that. I think she might strangle an actual horse, like the old days. She wouldn't care about dark eyes or whatever. She's half natal Semillan herself."

Tunuk pulled himself out of the shadowy corner, leaning on the bed. "Wait. What do you mean you're not romancing anybody? What happened with Yinii?"

Quill considered him. Tunuk and Yinii were close friends. Was it unfair to put him in the middle of things? "It's nothing," he said.

Tunuk opted to put himself in the middle. "Did you break Yinii's heart?" he demanded, furious.

"How can I break her heart when I can't even get her to have coffee with me?" Quill replied. "I've asked her plenty, and she always says, 'Another time.' And it's obviously not the coffee."

Tunuk blinked at him a moment. "What did you do? She's

ridiculous about you for some reason. Moping all the time you were gone. Avoiding me."

Quill frowned. "She's avoiding you? I don't think that's about me. Or if it is, something is really odd with her. Or maybe, is she worrying about you? What with…" He gestured at Tunuk's ribs, the slow-healing wound. "She was really upset after…but then I guess she wouldn't be avoiding you."

Tunuk fidgeted. "It's probably something to do with the new reza," he blustered. "She would get tangled up in ul-Benturan's stupid rules and arguments again." Tunuk fell silent for a long moment, though Quill could see the glow of his eyes watching him, as if Tunuk had melted into a shadow himself. Quill waited, letting Tunuk sort out what he needed to say.

"This isn't…" He stopped, began again. "What happens if this doesn't work? If no one remembers what happened?"

"I will bring you pancakes in prison," Quill said lightly. "Or we…steal a boat and learn to sail up the coast."

Tunuk huffed. "I hate the water."

"Then we're going to try the investigation plan first. Good night."

Quill slept fitfully, waking at last when the first gray light of dawn slid beneath the door. Tunuk was still folded up in his blanket nest and snoring faintly as Quill got up, straightened his clothes, and slipped out, pausing to rinse his mouth in the fountain and grab a bowl of rice porridge from the Paremi doling out breakfast. He went down to the basement storage rooms and riffled through some of the records there for an hour, until he found the first of Tunuk's names: Per del Huigas. The former generalist lived in an apartment building on the outskirts of the city and, according to the records, always paid his taxes on time. If they didn't have to go back to the archives, that might be easier on Tunuk.

If Tunuk's memory of Gunarro's address was right, they could easily visit both today. He thought about looking for Toya, but with only a first name, they'd never track him down—something to ask Per and Gunarro about.

When he was finished, he went to the columbarium at the back of the building.

The columbarium of the Arlabecca Paremi had been designed to mimic a library, the ashes of former scribes shelved in place of scrolls. Quill made his way down the long passages and up a flight of stairs to the corner he had selected months ago and the urn that held the ashes of his best friend, killed in the machinations of Redolfo Kirazzi and the Shrike.

"Hey, Karimo," he said softly, touching the lid of the urn with careful fingertips. He crouched down on the floor beside the urns. "Sorry I haven't visited. I had to go to Ragale and..."

But then he stopped. Everything he thought about saying seemed strangely profane: The dead peddler. The bones. Lying to the Paremi in Ragale to get the files. Lying to the prelate to keep Tunuk away from the vigilants. He felt suddenly as if he wasn't a person Karimo would even recognize anymore—maybe he wasn't someone Karimo would even respect, as sure as his friend had been about the rightness of the law—and the thought shook loose a tumble of panic in Quill's chest.

"I'm trying to fix things," he said softly. "They might be too big to fix—I can't tell yet. And more things keep happening—I can't stay on top of them all." He rubbed his thumb over the edge of the niche. "But this one...I don't know. I have a new friend, and he's in trouble. And I keep thinking...I keep thinking I couldn't save you, but maybe I can save him."

It felt foolish, saying it out loud. What threatened Tunuk wasn't as dire as what had taken Karimo away. So far as he knew. But deep down, it felt the same—something too big to wrap his mind around threatened someone he cared at least a little about, and if he looked away, it might take them from him.

A long shadow fell over him, too long to be anyone but Tunuk. Quill kept his eyes on the urn and sighed. "I'm almost done."

But Tunuk only waited.

Quill pressed his forehead to the urn, then stood and dusted off his knees. He wiped at his eyes. "All right," he said. "Let's...Did you get breakfast?"

Tunuk shifted awkwardly, folding his long arms across his chest. "Look, I heard...You don't have to pretend we're friends. Everyone hates being my generalist. It's very normal."

Quill frowned and only then realized what he'd said. *I have a new friend, and he's in trouble.* Maybe he was wrong about Tunuk.

"If you want me to hate you," Quill said, "there's a pretty high bar right now. And since I already said I don't think you murdered anyone, I don't think you're getting past it."

Tunuk huffed a sigh, but he unfolded his arms, as if he didn't need the barrier anymore. "Come on. If I stay here much longer, your prelate will measure me for vestments."

<hr />

Amadea kept her eyes locked on the oryx statue that perched on the table up against the wall opposite her. The paper behind it was garish, gold leaf on a crowded field of painted flowers, and if she looked too closely at it, she felt the memories crowd in, of Redolfo Kirazzi's study, of the birds flocking the dark wallpaper there as she sat on the sofa, not looking at her arm, not looking at the needle full of the Venom of Changelings that rewrote her memories.

"As we all appreciate," Mireia del Atsina was saying from beside Amadea, "this is a delicate matter. The recovered bones are being preserved, as that is our first priority. But, of course, the archives wish to assuage any concerns that the reza ul-Hanizan might have about the disposition of their saint's relics."

It was not the leader of the ul-Hanizan clan who sat opposite the archivists but his grandson. Nanqii Four-Oryx ul-Hanizan was, so far as Amadea had gathered, a merchant of some sort and, according to Mireia, the surest and quickest way to speak to the actual reza, Bishamar Twelve-Spider.

"I'm sure you do." Nanqii ul-Hanizan set his fingertips together, considering the two of them. He was only a little older than Amadea, though his hair was long and silvery, a shade peculiar to the Orozhandi who descended from the easternmost of their canyon cities. His clothes matched the garishness of the room—a fuchsia shirt, a cream brocade vest, an over-robe of green velvet with a feathered collar. Ostentatious, superficial—a camouflage, she thought, for the very calculating man it wrapped.

"You're very quiet, Archivist…" Nanqii smiled curiously at her. "What was your name again, esinora?"

"Gintanas," she said politely. "You have a very interesting sculpture collection, esinor. Does the reza have an interest in art? Perhaps he would appreciate a tour of the archives' facilities." The simplest concession she knew—*Let them see what we do, let them marvel at what we protect, let them understand how what we shelter is the memories of ten nations.*

Nanqii smiled at her. "Bishamar Twelve-Spider has an interest in everything."

"Not enough to come down from Maqama," Mireia said a little tartly.

"The reza doesn't come down from Maqama for anyone less than the empress," Nanqii replied, still looking at Amadea. "And though I will concede a lost saint does manage to trump the empress, he's not had time to make the journey."

"But you'll tell him," Amadea asked. "You'll encourage him to step in?"

"I don't think I need to," Nanqii said, all innocence. "The word is, as they say, spreading quickly. I heard the rumor myself last night. Though I do think Grandfather will be pleased that you came to ul-Hanizan first. She is, after all, our saint."

Amadea squeezed her hands together, focusing on her breath. Rumors were dangerous—Mireia's careful plan to reassure the leaders of the Orozhandi clans and the Imperial Authority aside could come apart so easily if undermined by tales racing around Arlabecca of a lost saint, an unidentified skeleton.

You don't have time for this, she thought, the crates of documents waiting in her office heavy on her mind. She'd managed to read and sort a dozen files that morning before she'd had to accompany Mireia out into the city. There had been no obvious pattern, no clear treason—there were letters and requests and court filings, but it would take time to find their meaning. She hadn't wanted to leave.

"If there's any justice in the world, you're going to take over for me one day," Mireia had said as they crossed the city. "Which means you need some training on the part where we have to make accommodating noises at the ducal authorities and their relations. Besides, the chapel's in your wing. Whatever happened, you have to convince them you're the one to resolve it."

It was too close to the problem of Redolfo Kirazzi—*you're the only one who knows everything; you're the only one who can possibly fix it*—and Amadea's chest kept closing around her breath.

Bronze oryx, she told herself, naming the objects. *Turquoise sofa. Fuchsia shirt.*

Nanqii Four-Oryx was smiling at her. "I'm glad you came as well, Archivist Gintanas. You're the one Bishamar Twelve-Spider will want to speak to, should he decide to involve himself. And if he does not, then you and I shall . . . simply become better acquainted."

Amadea met his flirtation with a bland smile—the only way to possibly complicate this further, saints and devils. "I am grateful for ul-Hanizan's trust," she said politely.

"You seem very trustworthy."

"Can we assume," Mireia interrupted, "that ul-Hanizan will agree to the necessary reviews of the chapel and its inhabitants and the required time to assess the situation? Since we're"—she paused for the barest breath—"trustworthy in your eyes?"

Nanqii turned lazily to Mireia. "I'm not such a fool as to make promises for Bishamar Twelve-Spider. He hasn't led the ul-Hanizan clan for over thirty-five years by being easily predicted and substituted. I'll send a message right away. And we will wait." He smiled again at Amadea. "Perhaps you could stay for lunch."

The lacquered double doors that led into the salon broke open with a cacophony of voices. The servant who had led Amadea and Mireia into the garish room, a young man with Minseon features, rushed in ahead of a half dozen Orozhandi led by a sharp-featured woman with fury in her eyes, her horns glittering with a multitude of enameled charms.

"So," she said, as if she were pronouncing doom upon them all, "it's true."

"A good morning to you as well, Manith," Nanqii said lazily. "We were just discussing lunch."

"The archives have misplaced one of the holy relics," said a bearded man with an aquamarine the size of a cuckoo's egg hanging from his left horn. "One of the saints was removed from the chapel yesterday, and ul-Liphiltan demands to know what is going on!"

"As does ul-Tahnaz," chimed in an elderly woman at the back.

Mireia stood, turning to face them all. "I have made requests to discuss this matter with each of the rezas or their representatives. Which includes several of those present. We have indeed located a relic of one of the saints that was previously thought to be in the chapel. We are determining"—she raised her voice over the sudden swell of argument—"what has happened and what must be done, but the first matter is that Saint Hazaunu of the Wool has been located and is being examined for damage, and steps have been taken toward her preservation. I trust you all understand why we came to ul-Hanizan first."

A youngish woman with red hair stepped around the angry speakers. She had large dark eyes that seemed very intense as she asked, "The reza ul-Shandiian wishes to convey his...concerns."

Mireia's jaw tightened, and Amadea racked her brain for a memory of the reza ul-Shandiian. Middle-aged, graying hair, the loudest voice in a group—the older rezas, she knew, found him difficult, the younger ones drifting in his wake. She wondered how the absence of the reza ul-Benturan, who had stepped down after her injury and not been replaced yet, had shifted the balance and did not have to wait long to get an answer.

"Dushar Six-Agamid didn't respond to my request for a meeting," Mireia said. "That would have been an ideal time to express his concerns."

The woman nodded in a slightly embarrassed way. "He learned you'd chosen to sit down with ul-Hanizan first."

"And why not?" Nanqii asked sharply. "Hazaunu Four-Hyena is a saint of *our* canyon."

The ul-Shandiian woman pursed her mouth. "With respect, esinor, you are not a reza, and yet you were given primacy. *This* is Dushar Six-Agamid's concern."

"And yet he sends you to do his dirty business stirring up everyone else."

"It's *all* our concern," Manith interjected. "You are not a reza, you are not *respectful*—who are you to give promises and assurances?"

Nanqii stood, his eyes still on the ul-Shandiian woman. "Oshanna, go tell your grandfather to take it up with the reza ul-Hanizan if he doesn't like my being his representative. And, Manith, if you want Bishamar Twelve-Spider to take ul-Chavresh seriously, maybe start by deciding what you hope to achieve before you start shouting."

The sharp-faced woman's third eye flashed open in surprise as she drew back. Then her expression tightened as she said, "Ul-Chavresh intends to call the empress and the noble consuls into an emergency session."

Amadea froze, and beside her Mireia went rigid.

"That seems premature," she began.

"Is it?" Manith demanded. "The archives have failed in their sacred duty and made a game of politics out of resolving it— ul-Chavresh feels the ducal authority is in dispute with the Imperial Authority, and this is how we solve that." She cut a glance over at Oshanna ul-Shandiian. "And ul-Shandiian agrees."

Oshanna said nothing, only flicked her gaze from Nanqii to Manith to the suddenly shouting representatives of the other clans, as if gauging where the shift of power fell now. The others started shouting demands and adding their own calls for a meeting of the noble consuls.

Amadea looked up at Mireia—a meeting of the noble consuls was serious. They were the connection between the Imperial Authority and the ducal authority of the protectorates. If the Orozhandi protectorate's leaders felt the empress and her agents were no longer working in their favor—

"If this matter is meant to go to the noble consuls," Mireia said over the din, "then we shall prepare and see your rezas there. Please convey to them my apologies for this matter from the archives and my wishes for a speedy resolution." She turned to Amadea, her temper simmering, and nodded once. "Thank you for your hospitality, Esinor ul-Hanizan. We'll let ourselves out."

Amadea pulled her cloak close around her as they left the manor, the chill air not enough to cool the panic flooding up inside her. "This is very bad," she said to Mireia.

"Chances are it boils up into a lot of mess and quiets down in a week," the head archivist said. "They have a right to be angry, but what's the goal? Probably reduced funding—not that *less* money ever helped us have *more* security—but we'll take what lumps we must and get on with it." She scowled at Amadea. "Did you find Tunuk?"

Amadea blew out a breath. "Quill's bringing him back. He had an episode." She'd gotten a note from Quill as she and Mireia had left the archives that morning.

I have Tunuk. We're both safe. He saw someone looking for him and started to spiral, so we're going to look for information that exonerates him. I have this.

It did not reassure her. Who was "someone"? The Imperial Authority? The vigilants? Changelings sent by Redolfo Kirazzi? Quill had left out where they were staying too, which made her think it *was* the vigilants and that he expected Richa to come to her asking where Tunuk had gone. There wasn't any other reason to hide where they were from her. And if he was afraid of the vigilants, then what had he *done*?

They reached the square before the Imperial Archives, the last stretch before Amadea was back safe inside her refuge again. As they crossed, Mireia asked, "What was all that with the ul-Hanizan fellow? Do you know him?"

"Not a bit," Amadea said. "Though clearly he'd like to rectify that."

"Hmm. Well, if he keeps that up and starts trying to get up your skirts, hold him off until this noble consuls nonsense is settled, or it'll add more fuel to whatever fire Dushar ul-Shandiian's stoking behind his granddaughter's back."

"I beg your pardon!"

Mireia snorted as they reached the archives' steps. "Don't act as if you've never sipped the kaibo. Just because you're too busy now doesn't mean I don't remember *someone* having quite the churn of young men stay over when she was my generalist. Begging me not to note the times she didn't have permission to do any such thing."

There had been a stretch of her past when Amadea had wanted more than anything to establish *Amadea*. To be someone without the Usurper's promises of a throne, without Ibramo, who she could never, ever have. It was easy to find handsome, charming young men, even outside the archives where she *never* dabbled. She had been lonely and eager, but every time she had gone cold with the realization that it could not last. She could never let any of them find out who she really was.

At some point, the knowledge it was risky and it would have to end had more weight than the need and the desire and the loneliness. At some point, it was easier to make herself busy with the archives.

Amadea sighed as they entered the archives, the great marble entry hall opening before them, the interior doors to the archives proper gleaming with their opal mosaics. "I covered for you and Circia when you weren't supposed to have her more or less living in your rooms, so that was more of a trade. I don't have any intention of indulging him, before or after the noble consuls' meeting. What do we need to…do…"

Amadea's voice fell away. Because standing in the middle of the entry hall, wearing a midnight-black mask, was the consort-prince, Ibramo Kirazzi.

How could something so familiar hit her with such a shock? Ibramo had been her constant companion for nearly a decade, her first love, her first lover. She knew the shape of his face, the arch of his nose, the dark brown of his skin, and the warmth of his gaze better than her own breath in some ways…and yet seeing him suddenly was like being struck from above.

Twenty years apart will do that, she told herself.

Mireia cut a severe look back at Amadea. The black mask meant privacy, meant the wearer wasn't meant to be acknowledged or noticed unless they invited it, but it was a difficult taboo to navigate when, for example, the empress's husband, in all his fine brocade and fur cloak, was standing between you and your office.

"We'll discuss when I get confirmation the noble consuls have agreed to the meeting," Mireia said to her, as if Ibramo weren't standing there. "In the meantime, I wouldn't strike the ul-Hanizan boy's name from your lists. There are certainly less suitable options out there." She moved past the consort-prince and up the staircase that led to her office.

Amadea glanced back at the archivist sitting reception duty, a young Ashtabari woman watching wide-eyed, as she twirled a curl of brown hair in one finger, her tentacles winding curiously up the sides of the desk.

"Good morning," Ibramo said softly. "Could we discuss our previous business, ah, elsewhere?"

Amadea nodded once, then beckoned him toward the opal-decorated doors into the archives, not wanting to give the watching archivist any more fodder for gossip.

She led him down along a side hallway, into one of the galleries not yet opened for the public that day, an exhibit of furniture pieces from ancient Semillan reclining thrones, to Minseon scribing desks meant to be folded up onto saddles, to an enormous Beminat map table.

"Did you find something?" she asked, when she was sure they were alone.

"They've swept from Gintanas to Ghazal this time," he said, keeping pace beside her. "There's no sign of another breach, but..."

"But it's hard to be certain," Amadea said. Who knew where the entry points might be hidden? No one had known about the tunnel under the Wall near Gintanas Abbey, after all.

They stopped beside the map table, their eyes on inlaid wood pieced together to mark the many territories of Bemina's vast empire under the jaguar-lords. Amadea could not have imagined the words that managed to convince a court to haul that heavy piece north across the desert with changelings on their heels, as beautiful as it was. But it was their best record of Bemina's many kingdoms and the only record of several of their lost neighbors—Manchebar, Zifar, the Ballyat. Nations and peoples that had disappeared in the wake of the changelings.

"What happened?" he asked. "What necessitates the noble consuls?"

"It's...it's not related."

"Are you sure?"

Panic flared in the base of her chest—the Kirazzi map, the murder while retrieving the primate's files—before she shook her head, her eyes still on the map table. "As sure as I can be. Unless your father was trafficking stolen saints?"

Ibramo paused. "Not that I'm aware of. Why would someone do that?"

"I have no idea." But the chances there was a mistake, a misunderstanding had all slipped away like fishes darting out of the shadow of this greater problem. She told him about the documents now waiting in her office, the sheer quantity of them and the lack of any guiding clue. She told him about the wooden bones, the unknown skeleton, and now the angry Orozhandi and the noble consuls.

"I don't know what to do," Amadea confessed. "I can't even guess how this happened, I can't find my archivist who might know, and I am so worried that while I'm dealing with this lost relic, everything from before is happening again." And she meant all of it—the changeling horde, Redolfo Kirazzi's coup, the chaos and uncertainty that came after, the danger of being pulled into the middle of all these politics. "I can hardly sleep for worrying." And abruptly, absurdly, she thought of Richa tired and drawn and still going, still searching for answers. She brushed her sleeves off and dared a glance up at Ibramo.

Ibramo took her hand recklessly, and—just has recklessly—she let him, folded her fingers around his. "I know," he whispered. "Me too. But we're in this together now. That counts for something."

She swallowed against the words she wanted to say. "Are you going back to Sestina to keep searching?"

"No," he said. "I...I'm needed here." He gave a short, bitter laugh. "I hate going back there. Full of memories. I find I walk into a room, and I'm a child all over again. And I have to pretend it doesn't happen. I have to keep the mask in place."

She drew a slow breath, shutting her eyes even as the words dragged up another memory, ragged and piecemeal:

Redolfo, resplendent in green and gold, considering her as she sat on the sofa with the rose-patterned cushions. The sharp stab of the needle in her arm. "All right, Lira. Say it again," he intones, and she hears her own voice reciting, "In the mornings in the abbey, they wake us up with the sun and give us raisin cakes to eat. They stick to the roof of my mouth, and they taste like fennel."

"Good, now say the other."

"In the morning, a woman would come in with hot water and flatbreads soft as pillows. Sometimes Katucia or Violaria would be in my bed already, and the woman wouldn't scold us until Nurse came in."

Amadea rubbed her forehead, feeling the pinch of stress there. She remembered reciting both lives, both ordinary histories. They wouldn't untangle. Had that been his plan? Obfuscate everything? Sometimes it felt as if she were remembering, and sometimes it felt as if she were watching at a distance, and everything held a strange surrealness.

Except...Ibramo. When she remembered Ibramo, it was different, clearer. *Realer.* She might have been under the Venom of Changelings' effect then, too, but it didn't matter who she'd been or who she'd become—she was just a girl alone with a boy, pretending nothing else was going on.

"I'm sorry," she said. "I know how that feels."

"It's not all bad, I suppose," he said. "We met there, didn't we?"

"Yes." Amid the blur, that moment stood bright. She'd been in the gardens, placed beneath a pistachio tree, its twisted limbs all in flower, when Redolfo brought his son to meet her. No one said it was a test, but she sensed by then, everything was a sort of test.

"You've heard the rumor that one of the princesses survived, Ibramo?" Redolfo had said. She could still feel his eyes on her when she remembered it, his gaze as heavy as a sword laid upon her shoulder. Amadea had held perfectly still, her hands folded, her gaze on the gangly young boy before her, both of them dressed in stiff brocades, both of them perfectly still. She met his eyes and in that moment knew this boy understood, as much as anyone could understand, how frightened she was and how much she could not afford to be frightened.

Ibramo's gaze flicked to his father, as if gauging his response. He stepped forward, examining Amadea's face. Then he said, "She doesn't look like a princess."

Later, he would tell her he'd been told to say that, to see whether she'd absorbed those lessons, those sessions of poison and repetition, reshaping her into what Redolfo needed her to be. Later, Ibramo would be sorry and embarrassed and guilty.

In that moment, though, Amadea only tilted her head, only asked, "You can't have met very many princesses. What should they look like?" The only answer to what had seemed a silly question at the time.

Redolfo had chuckled. "You see? She has it naturally. That is all the difference."

"I remember that day," she said to Ibramo, looking at their still-joined hands. "In the garden."

"By the fountain," he added.

Amadea laughed herself now. "No, not that garden. The smaller one with the tree in the corner. The one we climbed up to see the bird nest in that spring your father left."

Ibramo blinked at her a moment, a moment puzzled and even... afraid.

Amadea's heart caught, and she squeezed his hand. "Maybe one of us... It's the venom," she said.

"Maybe." He looked down at her hand in his, lifted it to his chest. "I should go. I want to stay, but—"

"You should go," Amadea agreed. This was already too dangerous, too foolish. She took her hand back before he could dare any further. "I'm sorry," she added. "I didn't mean to—"

"It's fine," Ibramo assured her. "I... I will let you know when I hear back. Unless you'd rather I didn't?"

She should tell him not to come. She should tell him to send a message. She should insist he summon her to the Imperial Complex where what was transpiring between the consort-prince and the archivist superior would be plain and open.

She should not be anywhere at all with him when the memory that he'd kissed her, there under the Salt Wall where they'd found the changeling doubles, was so present in her thoughts and so very dangerous.

"It's fine," she said, repeating his assurance. "Here's hoping your scouts continue to find only packed earth." If the problem of the skeletons was going to be pressing, then perhaps Redolfo Kirazzi could stay settled and firmly beyond the edges of the empire, the changelings kept back by the chill of winter and the safety of the Salt Wall.

CHAPTER SEVEN

Yinii stopped at the corner of the street that led up to Nanqii ul-Hanizan's manor, turning to face her unwanted shadow.

"Radir," she said, firmly but quietly so the passersby didn't over-hear, "go back to the archives. I don't need a generalist right now."

Radir regarded her skeptically as people wrapped in their cloaks strolled past. He was a human man, only a little older than her, with medium-brown skin and dark curls that fell over his large black eyes. Yinii could recite all the things Tunuk had claimed made Radir a terrible generalist—he was nosy, he talked too much, he couldn't sort out non-bone from bone in smaller artifacts—but she only agreed with one: he was very afraid of the spiral.

"Your eyes are still darker," he said stubbornly.

Yinii took a deep breath, pressing down her irritation. "Do you think maybe you don't remember exactly what color my eyes are?"

"I think I remember what happened an hour ago," he returned, and Yinii flushed.

She had quickly discovered after waking that Quill and Tunuk hadn't returned. Neither was in his rooms, so she went to ask Amadea if she knew where they were.

Amadea wasn't in her office either. Just the files from Ragale spread over her desk. Yinii took off her gloves and brushed her fingers over the text and felt vine-char black vibrating with the rough memory of a reed stylus, the sort carried in a scribe's kit. She touched the signature of Primate Lamberto and felt a different reed pen—the way the ink had gone down on the page, each fiber's drag and scratch.

She was sorting the stack by pen before she realized she was doing it—more filings, more requests. The shushing of the ink wrapped Yinii in a comfortable cocoon.

Yinii frowned. It didn't seem like the way you'd commit treason—if you were going to commit treason. But then, these might be the only records they could get from Ragale. She moved to the next stack, picking up the file, reading the words on the page, trying to fit the pen to one of the file types:

The named parties request the transfer of the imperial ward, Iosthe del Sepharin, from Endecha to more secure holdings at Sestina for her safety and the safety of those caring for her. The quantity of the material her affinity magic spawns from is too great in Endecha.

Imperial ward. Affinity magic.

It was a transportation order for a sorcerer.

None of the eleven sorcerers in Semilla were saints—they were not Orozhandi, so they could not be. But still they bore the blessings of the Gods Above and Below. To move one around like a criminal when she'd done nothing felt blasphemous.

No, Yinii thought, *not blasphemous. Terrifying.*

The chorus of inks swelled into a roar, her hands black with the flood of Primate Lamberto's missives. The desk beneath her hands felt suddenly alive, shivering with carbon, if only she let it burn.

And that was when Radir had found her.

"I just got a little worked up," she said again as she started walking. *Iosthe of the Wool*, she thought like a chant to the strike of her feet. *The named parties request the transfer of the imperial ward Iosthe del Sepharin.* She couldn't stop thinking about how Iosthe herself had not been among the "named parties."

"You broke into Amadea's office and pulled the ink off a crate of documents," Radir corrected, still following her. "Protocol says you're not supposed to be alone and in contact with your affinity material the first month after an irregular alignment."

"I'm not in contact with my affinity material," Yinii said. "And it's been *two* months."

And if you do spiral again, a little part of her thought, *the Imperial Authority won't just send you to the sequestration rooms.*

Somewhere in those stacks and stacks of files there would be the sort of sequestration order they wrote for sorcerers—a place, a list of limitations, warnings, maybe even sedation requirements. She thought of Fastreda, locked away from the glass, locked away from anything she might turn into glass. Away from anyone who might bring her affinity to her.

Fastreda had done terrible things, though. She should be an outlier.

Yinii thought of the stories of how sorcerers had been treated in other lands—weapons in Min-Se, sacrifices in Datong, prisoners in Bemina, outcasts in al-Kual. A Semillan sorcerer was lucky by those standards. They belonged to the Imperial Authority. For their own safety.

"You were in sequestration last week," Radir reminded her.

"Because I was tired, not because I was spiraling."

"And I had to call your name three times to get your attention," Radir went on. "*And* let's go back to the cloud of ink you made. And I think your eyes are darker."

"When it's bad enough for the ink to change my eye color, they'll be solid black," Yinii said. "There won't be a question. I'm fine. You don't have to—"

She broke off as she spotted Amadea and Mireia coming up the street, deep in conversation. Yinii darted around an ornamental tree, bare-branched with autumn's passing and surrounded by dark-leaved shrubs, and turned away to face the houses on that side of the street. Radir came to stand beside her.

"You're also hiding from Amadea," he noted.

"That's not because of the ink. It's because of..." She caught herself. "It's not related."

"Are you going to tell me what you're doing?" When she didn't say anything, he asked, "Is it about changelings?"

That startled Yinii. "Why... why would you think that?"

Radir leveled a skeptical look at her. "I mean, everyone's gossiping about those murders involving the Venom of Changelings.

Maybe because of actual changelings." He fished a pendant out of his robes, an iron mask with hollow eyes, holding it out on his palm and then squeezing it tight, as if demonstrating that *he* wasn't one of the shape-shifting monsters. "Have you not seen vendors selling these everywhere?"

"No," Yinii said. She reached up to touch the pink salt crystal that hung on her left horn, an amulet of Saint Asla that had replaced the one Amadea had lost in the tunnels beneath the Salt Wall. "It's... about the chapel. The missing saint. Tunuk...he needs some help figuring out what happened. And I know someone he thinks could help, so I'm going to talk to her. That's it."

Radir made a face. "Why did you think you couldn't tell me you were helping Tunuk? He hates me—I don't hate him." He looked up at the building they were pretending to admire. "I do actually care that he's all right, even if he made me crazy."

Affinity magic ebbed and flowed, a specialist's closeness to their material shifting on a schedule unique to that material and sometimes even that specialist. When the specialist was out of alignment with their affinity, the power pulled away, a distant tide, and limited what the specialist could do. When they were in alignment, however, the magic surged, and the specialist became capable of much stronger—albeit still narrowly focused—magic. They also sometimes lost their grip on reality.

That was where the generalists came in—they took on tasks of the archives, but their primary purpose was to keep the specialists grounded. Which they couldn't do when their specialists wouldn't let them, Yinii supposed.

"I just have to ask someone he knew when he was apprentice what they remember about his mentors," she said. "I might not even find her here."

"What's she look like?"

"She's Orozhandi. Red hair. Maybe...a little older than you?" Yinii tried to remember the last time she'd seen Oshanna Eleven-Sand Iris ul-Shandiian—it would have been one of the times her great-aunt the former reza ul-Benturan visited. "She's tall. And she has...Her eyes always make me think of a hawk."

"Intense," Radir commented, looking back over his shoulder. "Is she good-looking?"

Yinii flushed again. "I don't know, and anyway, what happened to that girl from the Golden Oblates you were seeing?"

Before Radir could answer, she saw a cluster of Orozhandi passing up the street and, trailing the group of them, Oshanna ul-Shandiian, deep in thought. Yinii glanced back the way Amadea and Mireia had walked, making sure they were out of sight before she darted out into the street.

"Esinora!" Yinii called. "Esinora ul-Shandiian?"

The red-haired woman turned, frowning, as Yinii ran up to her and made a hasty bow.

"Esinora, I'm Yinii Six-Owl ul-Benturan. I'm Dolitha Sixteen-Tamarisk's grandniece?"

Oshanna took in her uniform, her gloved hands, and offered her own tentative bow. "Atnashingyii," she said, using the honorific for someone with affinity magic.

Yinii bowed over her clasped palms again. "I was hoping I could speak to you for a moment. About the Imperial Archives?"

Oshanna's expression tightened, her third eye flinching. "This is about Saint Hazaunu, I assume. I'm afraid your superiors already had their say. There will be a meeting of the noble consuls."

Dread scaled Yinii's throat. "They *what*?"

"It's out of my hands," Oshanna said. She looked up past Yinii and frowned again. Radir jogged up behind her. "I'm sorry I can't do anything for you. The reza is expecting me back with an answer."

"That wasn't what I wanted to ask," Yinii said. "Or, well, it's related, but... Tunuk thought I should talk to you about what might have happened to Saint Hazaunu? Originally?"

"Tunuk? I'm sorry I don't..." Oshanna looked down at Yinii's uniform, the chain of silver hanging from shoulder to shoulder, and recognition lit her face. "Oh. The ... apprentice. The Alojan? Saints, I haven't thought of him in years. I hope he's well. What does he think I might know?"

Yinii folded her hands together, tapping her knuckles and trying to think of how to ask, *Do you know why someone would have stolen the wooden bones twelve years ago?* "Just, did you remember anything? He's worried. Were you close?"

She smiled. "Forced proximity. I was underfoot, I suppose. I don't know that he liked my company all that much. He was at a... prickly age."

"Still is," Radir chimed in.

Oshanna glanced at him, still evidently unsure of how to address him when he hadn't introduced himself. "Yes... well. He was the apprentice to my father's cousin. We talked sometimes when I visited. He was funny. A little melancholy. But I think we got along all right."

"Your father's cousin was Qalba One-Fox," Yinii said. "Do you know anything about where she might be?"

That startled Oshanna. "No. She... Well, it's... It's a matter for the clan."

The misstep tangled Yinii's tongue. "Of course. I—I didn't mean to pry. This has all brought up some... puzzles, and as I said, Tunuk is just worried. Did you visit often?"

Oshanna shrugged. "What's 'often'? I suppose more than most people. Aunt Qalba was always kind to me, and she and my father were close at the time. Obviously, things are different now, what with..." She cleared her throat. "It's not something I really want to talk about in the middle of the street." She looked once more over at Radir, her bright black eyes seeming to stare right through him. *I don't want to discuss this with an audience,* they seemed to say.

"Perhaps I could come by the ul-Shandiian manor?" Yinii said. Then, mustering her courage: "Perhaps tomorrow afternoon."

Oshanna hesitated, her eyes flicking from Yinii to Radir. Then she sighed. "I should warn you: the reza ul-Shandiian is going to want me to ask you about the ul-Benturan reza proceedings. But... it might be good to talk about the old days. Would you bring Tunuk?"

"I'll have to check with him," Yinii said. "But that would be lovely." She made arrangements to come by the next afternoon, and Oshanna continued on her way.

"Do you actually think Tunuk is going to want to go with you?" Radir asked, watching Oshanna go.

"No." Yinii sighed. But it didn't matter—with or without him, she would go and find out what had happened. She would help Tunuk and Quill and really Amadea too, so that there was one fewer thing. And she would not spiral in the process. She would calm down and not need sequestration, not need to worry about sorcerers being remanded. She could do this.

⁎⁎⁎

Per del Huigas's apartment was on the third floor of a five-story building, one of the huge edifices that took up an entire block on the outskirts of Arlabecca. As they climbed staircases up narrow hallways, Quill could sense the tension winding Tunuk's long frame tighter, hunching the Alojan over into himself.

"How are you doing?" Quill asked lightly, as they reached Per's floor. Biorni was tucked deep in a borrowed satchel, where it hopefully wouldn't trigger anything. "Do you feel like you're close to spiraling?"

"No," Tunuk snapped. He rubbed his arm where the bone plaques had risen on his skin.

"Is that...?" Quill considered Tunuk's arm. "Is that the only thing that happens? Not that it's not plenty," he added, "I just know... Well, I saw Zoifia spiral. And Yinii."

"And you want to know if I'm going to pull out your bones?" Tunuk asked witheringly. "You're still using them, so they're not worked material. I can't *do* anything with them. Honestly. Which is the door we need?"

"But you... make bone on yourself?"

"You should read up on organic affinities before you try to manage them," Tunuk said, striding past him. "It hurts and it's awful, and spiraling's a lot easier when there's worked bone around I can repurpose, not just Biorni. But that's what it does. What is the number?"

"Thirty-seven," Quill said, hurrying to catch up.

Quill knocked on the door when they found it tucked around the far side of the building.

"Who is it?" a man's gravelly voice called back.

"Good morning," Quill answered through the closed door. "My name is Quill. I'm from the Imperial Archives. I have some questions about the Bone Vault."

"Haven't worked there in a decade," the man said back. "Clever thing to know, though, if you were trying to pull one over on me."

Tunuk sighed. "Per, it's Tunuk. He wants to ask about Chizid and Qalba."

A pause. The door opened a handspan, and a human face peered out—a man, balding, with short white hair around his brown-skinned face, and small beetle-black eyes. "Tunuk?" he said, sounding baffled. "Huh. Wow. You got taller?"

"Not really," Tunuk said. "Can we come in?"

Per hesitated. "You got iron to show? Just...you know. In case."

Quill pulled an amulet out from his shirt and showed it against the palm of his hand. When Per looked expectantly at Tunuk, he huffed and grabbed the pendant, shoving it toward Per. "Not a changeling!" he spat. "Open the door."

Per shrugged and pulled the door open to reveal a sitting room arranged around a pair of windows that looked out over the road south of Arlabecca, winding between the low hills. There was a cluster of upholstered green chairs and a Borsyan cold-magic panel set to heat the space, a wooden table for two with a plate of bread on it, and a worktable with some more foodstuffs, jars of oil, and salt. A darkened doorway led off to the left, a bedroom.

Per beckoned them to the chairs by the heating panel, the faint bluish glow of the cold-magic on the back casting an eerie light against the wall. "Don't have much to offer you," Per said. "Some dhoro? It's a little early for dhoro."

Tunuk lowered himself into one of the chairs, his knees up around his shoulders. "The cursed sun just came up," he said. "It's too early for dhoro."

Per shrugged. "So who are you?" he asked Quill. "And why do you want to know about Qalba and Chizid?"

Quill smiled. "I think I'm your successor."

Per's sparse eyebrows rose. "Bone has a dedicated generalist again? Huh. Congratulations, Tunuk. It's hard to find someone who can manage it," Per confided to Quill. "Some people get squeamish about skeletons. Or the bone spiral. But I always said I'll take bone over those maniacs with the metallic affinities. Every month, losing their minds, throwing punches. Throwing artifacts." He shook his head. "Such a mess."

"Sounds like Chizid and Qalba were pretty easy to work with," Quill said.

"Mostly," Per said. He nodded at Tunuk. "This one was a handful, but most novice specialists are. You have any of those yet?"

"Not yet," Quill said.

"Hmm, well, bone's a fading art. That's how you lose an affinity."

"We wanted to ask about how Chizid and Qalba left."

Per shifted in his chair, his gaze on Quill suddenly suspicious. "What do you want to know about that for?"

Quill glanced at Tunuk, weighing how much to tell Per. It seemed best to start with "an irregularity in the catalogues" and go on—

"There's a skeleton in the archives that doesn't belong," Tunuk said flatly. "And someone stole a wooden saint's bones. And it probably happened around then, but as I'm the only one from that set left in the archives, they're going to throw me in imperial prison for murder if I don't have a different answer."

Per stared at Tunuk for a moment. "Maybe it's not too early for dhoro," he said, heaving himself out of the chair and crossing to the kitchen.

"Lord on the Mountain, Tunuk!" Quill whispered.

"We will be here forever if you don't get to the point."

Per came back with three small ceramic cups painted vibrant green and a bottle of heady groundnut liquor. He poured a little for himself and drank it down before filling all three cups again.

"We're just trying to figure out what might have happened," Quill said. "It's all a bit mysterious. But it seems like the skeletons might have been exchanged around the time Chizid and Qalba left the archives. And since no one can contact them..." Quill shrugged. "It's not usual that archivists rescind their oaths."

"No," Per said. "Not specialists anyway. Specialists *fit* in the archives when they can't in other places, so long as they can manage the spiral. Generalists, they aren't tied so close to the work. And it can be a lot of work. You can burn yourself out trying to keep *them* from burning out, you know?"

"I can see that." Quill took a polite sip of the dhoro. The harsh alcohol etched up the back of his throat, filling his nose with the scent of groundnuts and burnt sugar. "Strong stuff," he managed.

"Good stuff," Per said. Then: "They were fighting. I remember that."

Beside Quill, Tunuk went suddenly rigid.

Per didn't seem to notice but rubbed his bristly chin. "Yeah," he said. "That was when they had the big shouting match in the Bone Vault. I got out of there when it boiled over, so I couldn't tell you how it ended exactly, but given the run-up . . . well, it wasn't a *new* kind of fight, you know? Even if it was the first any of us had heard about it."

"What were they arguing about?" Quill asked. *Was it enough to kill over?* Why hadn't Tunuk mentioned they were fighting?

Per gave Quill a knowing sort of look. "What do you think? A man."

Quill frowned. "Which of them was having an affair?"

"Qalba. Maybe," Per said. "Or maybe Chizid just thought she was."

And then he kills her, Quill thought. *Puts her skeleton on display and discards the wooden bones, so no one will ever find her.* It fit together, horribly together. People did terrible things for what they thought was love.

Except . . . why the wooden bones? Why not trade out an actual skeleton for an actual skeleton? Or if you were going to murder and de-flesh someone and you worked in a room full of bones in various states of preservation and categorization, why not just stick them in a box? Why not just throw the body over the Salt Wall? Or into the sea?

Tunuk just sat motionless, glowering at Per with his arms folded.

"Did Chizid ever strike you as someone who'd resort to violence?" Quill asked.

Per frowned at him, then looked over at Tunuk as if confused why the Alojan had left Quill to come to such a strange conclusion. "Chizid? No. Not at all. Mild as milk. That might have been the only time I even heard him raise his voice. Mind, it was . . . a lot of shouting. When I came back, Qalba was weeping so hard she'd vomited, and Chizid had left. But the next time I saw them, they were right back to usual. Sweet as bean cakes. Like nothing had happened."

Quill took another careful sip of the dhoro, trying to find a path forward from here.

"Do you remember the man's name?" Tunuk suddenly asked. "Who they were fighting about?" Then he added, "Was it Toya?"

Per wrinkled his nose and shook his head. "No, pretty sure Chizid knew Toya came along with Qalba in all things." He turned to Quill. "Toya was an old friend of hers, but he'd taken a blow to the head or something. Wasn't entirely there. Had visions and such, and Qalba was real protective of him. You got Toya with Qalba, and you got the ul-Shandiians. She was close with her family."

"Do you mean Oshanna?" Quill asked.

Per squinted. "That's the girl, right? The one who came with Nimar?"

Now Tunuk was making a face. "Who's Nimar?"

"Brother or cousin or something?" Per shrugged. "Qalba's, I mean. Like I said, she was close with them. I can't remember all of them, but Nimar Eight-Myrrh was the one who brought a kid."

"Did the ul-Shandiians mind Qalba had married a non-Orozhandi?" Quill asked.

"I don't think they liked it," Per said. "But, you know: atnash-ingyii. She can talk to the bones, so she can do what she likes."

"Do you think it was true?" Quill asked. "That she was having an affair?"

Per shrugged. "Dunno. Like I said, they seemed happy. But then that fight . . . Oh! I do remember something else. In that fight, Chizid said he'd kill him. Whoever 'him' was. They didn't make *that* clear."

Tunuk suddenly sat up much straighter, his hands on his knees.

"You're sure?" Quill asked.

Per set his drink down, staring up at the ceiling again. "Yeah. He said, 'He's going to ruin you,' and 'I'll kill him if it comes to that.' That's how I knew it was over a man. Like I said, he was a quiet type. So, if he was threatening to kill somebody, I have to

assume something serious was going on." He looked over at Tunuk.
"I would have sworn you were there for that. I have a feeling like
I thought I should get you out of there, but I couldn't for some
reason."

"You probably just remember me because we were both there all
the time," Tunuk said flatly.

Liar, Quill thought, staring at Tunuk. How much had he not told
Quill?

"Do you remember anything about the skeletons?" Quill asked
Per. "Any work done in the chapel around the time they left?"

"Not especially," Per said, waving in a vague gesture. "It all sort
of blurs together. We did work on them sometimes. Usually simple
things like adhesives failing. Checking bones for critters and things.
I can't recall what Chizid and Qalba were working on then."

"What about after Qalba left, but before Chizid did?"

But here again, Per's memory failed. "I was just glad everything
had calmed down. Qalba going on respite was a normal thing."

"You saw her leave?" Quill asked.

"Yeah, I think so." Per scratched at his bristly chin again. "Early
one morning, I came in as she was going out. She had on that orange
cape she liked so much. She gave me a hug." He picked up the dhoro
again. "That would have been the last time I saw her. Didn't know
it at the time, obviously. I got a letter but never saw either of them
again."

"You got a letter from them?" Quill said. "What did it say?"

"Just that they were sorry they had to leave. Things weren't working out, and they decided they'd be happier outside the archives. No
address or anything. I figured they were trying to save their marriage, you know. And they'd send word when they were settled. But
no. I didn't stay on too much longer than that," he added. He gave
Tunuk a wan smile. "Sort of left you in the lurch, I suspect. But I
wasn't the right generalist for you, kid."

"No," Tunuk agreed.

They chatted a little longer, extending the visit enough to feel
polite, but Quill was distracted, fitting together what Per had said
and what Tunuk had known. There were still strange gaps, strange

inconsistencies. When they left at last, climbing the steep road out-side Per's apartment back toward the center of the city and their next stop, Quill hurried to match Tunuk's long strides.

"You didn't tell me they were fighting."

"They *fought*," Tunuk corrected. "Singular. It was... the only time."

"But you heard it?"

"Some of it," Tunuk admitted. Then: "I panicked and hid in one of the back workrooms and waited for it to end."

"And you didn't think that bore mentioning? Lord on the Mountain, Tunuk, I thought you wanted to figure out what happened."

"I didn't think it mattered. They didn't fight, not most of the time, and—"

"And this one time you remember them fighting in front of you—because *fighting* and *fighting in front of someone else* are different things—it led to the bones of Saint Hazaunu being stolen, some-one's skeleton being hidden in the chapel, and Qalba and Chizid disappearing. That seems worth mentioning."

They cut across the West River, around the edge of the livestock markets. Quill pulled his shirt up over his nose to keep the scent of pig shit down, but it didn't help. They stopped speaking until they crossed the river again, up into the craftwork district near the College of the Five Forests, the long, low building's red-tiled roof ornamented with stylized tentacle curls and zigzag corners, where the wind shifted, bringing instead the smell of wood shavings and winter as they climbed toward the older part of Arlabecca.

Quill took a deep breath. "Does what Per said match at least? That they were fighting about a man?"

Tunuk shook his head. "I...I heard Qalba say something like, 'What do you want me to do? I can't just stop talking to him,' before I hid. I never heard him threaten someone. And...when I came out, Chizid *was* gone and she *was* upset. She threw up, she was sobbing. She told me it was nothing, that they were just having some prob-lems," he added. "And I don't believe she had a secret lover on the side. She wasn't like that."

Quill thought of Primate Lamberto—his outward propriety, his secret treachery. "People can hide things. They can surprise you."

"Not like that," Tunuk insisted. He made a face. "I also don't think she was that close with her family, but maybe that's just a cultural difference. Maybe *he* thinks it's close if your one cousin visits... I guess maybe *two* cousins, but I don't remember Nimar. Anyway, maybe Per thinks that's close, but if my family held me off that much, I'd assume they were all dead. So maybe he's wrong about the lover too, or maybe he can't tell the difference between a lover and a person you exchange comments about the weather with."

"Tunuk, I can't help you if you're not ready to find out things you don't want to be true."

Tunuk stopped in the middle of the street, turning on Quill with sudden menace in his lanky frame. "Just because," he said acidly, "your mentor and your friend turned out to be keeping secrets from you—just because you were disappointed in the truth, doesn't mean everyone has the same story."

Quill took a step back. "Hiding things and lying isn't going to change what happened."

"And neither is telling a story you think makes sense before you get all the facts," Tunuk shot back. "Come on, let's find something to eat before we look for Gunarro."

CHAPTER EIGHT

Richa arrived at the Kinship Hall the morning after he read the archives' files, a little late, a little tired, but ready to work. Despite the chill of winter on the air, the sun was bright, the streets were tidy, and Richa's path was clear.

Salva Gaitha-hyu would keep investigating the murder of the peddler and whatever was going on with Stellano—there wasn't anything he could or *should* do to stop that. But the theft of the wooden bones and the skeleton in the archives were squarely in his own jurisdiction. One led to the other, but if he could figure out who had stolen the bones and why, and who was dead in the archives, it might leave all the questions about Stellano on the other side of the Wall, so to speak.

So he'd start with who had stolen the wooden bones.

Amadea had said there were no thefts from the chapel in all the time she'd worked in the archives. Clearly, the wooden skeleton proved her wrong—but Richa wondered. In his experience, if someone was stealing one thing, they were stealing more—once you knew what you were doing, it was easy to keep going, easy to tell yourself the risk wasn't getting higher, and hard to convince anyone who knew you could get them things that you wouldn't anymore. If you stopped, in his experience, you were dead, or you'd made a huge, fundamental change—and he had two people who fit one of those categories in Chizid and Qalba. And that still left whoever they might have been stealing for.

So: Were there *any* reported thefts from the Imperial Archives over the last, say, fifteen years?

He avoided his desk and went down to the Kinship's records room, where he asked the attendant for all reported thefts from the Imperial Archives, plus any reports related to the disappearances of Chizid del Hwana or Qalba ul-Shandiian. He went and bought a bowl of onion noodles from the stand down the street and reread the files Amadea had sent, careful to keep broth off them. By the time he was done, the records attendant had a meager stack for him to peruse.

There were nine reported thefts in the last fifteen years, which tracked with Richa's assumptions. The Imperial Archives made a tempting target, but the layers of protection and the density of archivists meant it would never be easy. You might be able to snatch something from the chaos of the sorting rooms or the neglected corners of this workroom or that, but you'd never get in or out easily.

Unless, he thought, reading through the files, *you worked there.*

Two of the thefts were marked as resolved. A gold specialist had put a necklace in her pocket and forgotten she'd done so. The vigilants had been called, and she'd assisted enthusiastically with the search, only to realize it had been in her work apron all along. The other was a proclamation by the then Duchess Qualli, which had been misfiled upon its return after one of the Kuali rededication discussions that year. Frantic panicking, and then it was just on the wrong shelf.

Two more had been generalists trying to make some money selling shiny, arguably unimportant things. Both had been apprehended, discharged from their duties, and sentenced to make restitution. One artifact, a ring, had been recovered. The other, a pearl-encrusted hair stick, had not.

Five thefts were still outstanding, and in four of these, there was a strange pattern: a four-inch-high icon of a Khirazji sea god, made of salt, crafted by the sorcerer Djudura of the Salt, pre-Sealing; one wooden lion piece from a throw-board game, grown by Isecco of the Acacia, pre-Sealing; three pea-sized sapphires, created by Aungwi of the Corundum, pre-Sealing; and one miniature ceramic sculpture of a hand, a practice work by Ichenda of the Pottery, post-Sealing.

Four sorcerer-wrought artifacts stolen from the Imperial Archives, all small enough to slip into a pocket. The report dates ranged all over the place—fourteen years ago for the salt icon, three years ago for the sapphires. Richa checked that one again. The archivist who had filed the report was one he knew still worked in the archives, under Amadea: Bijan del Tolube.

He sat back, considering the theft reports. It was a beginning, but where did it lead? What made a person steal sorcerer-wrought artifacts? Was there a market for that sort of thing?

If there was, he thought begrudgingly, Stellano probably had tapped it—and there again was the memory of Stellano, edging around the archives, where he had no business being. Richa rubbed his eyes. *You haven't thought about him in ages, stop it.*

The sorcerers listed in the reports weren't Orozhandi—the names were Khirazji, Semillan, Datongu, Beminat. Not saints' relics. And while there was a pattern, he had to admit, the pattern didn't immediately lead to the theft of a full wooden skeleton from a visible, public space.

And it didn't suggest who had died twelve years ago and been left in the bones' place.

He scrubbed his hands over his face. *Back to the archives*, he thought. *Ask about these thefts and then pin Tunuk down and find out what on this side of the Wall and the other he knows.*

"Here you are." Hulvia slid around the door into the records room. "Richa, what in the fuck is going on? That road cohort vigilant's been elbow deep in your files all day."

Richa tapped the records back into a neat stack, considering the hour, the archives, where Amadea might be now. "It's nothing."

"It's a lot of work for nothing."

"It definitely has nothing to do with the Imperial Authority," he said pointedly.

"Then good, because I'm asking as your friend, not as the imperial liaison." She yanked one of the Ashtabari-style leaning chairs away from the wall and settled opposite him, her chest propped on the curved surface. "You have to tell me if you went corrupt," she said solemnly. "I got sacked for you."

"For all of two weeks," he said. "And you were demoted, not discharged."

"Richa."

He sighed. "It's *nothing*. I've kept my oath. She's got a suspect who happens to be someone I crossed paths with a long time ago. Before I joined the Kinship."

Hulvia frowned. "Like in Caesura? Don't make that face. You don't talk about it, but you *talk* like it. You have more of an accent than you think."

Richa folded his arms, suddenly very aware of the way his mouth shaped the words, as he said, "Yeah, well. There you go. We all know how Caesura is. She's just being thorough. It's not interesting."

Hulvia snorted. "I sort of assume if you've got anything interesting in your past, it's a one-and-only situation. I can't even imagine you without your oath."

"Isn't that most of us, though?" But even as he said it, he knew it was a lie—he knew enough about Hulvia, had gleaned enough about her to picture her in perfect detail before the Kinship—Tornada family with some wealth, some prestige; splashy debut, maybe some marriage prospects, probably her choice of orders, but stubborn as a cat about it. He felt as if he could guess at Salva Gaitha-hyu, too—smart, observant, one Orozhandi parent, one maybe Minseon, two worlds, two sets of rules, so don't ever mess up, and don't let anyone who does slide...

He hoped no one saw through him that easily.

"Well," Hulvia said, eyeing the documents he'd stacked under one hand. "If you need to talk..."

"I'll let you know," he said, scooping up the files and returning to the records attendant, trying not to think about what would happen if Salva's intimations spread.

Quill and Tunuk found a stall selling Khirazji rakharakh—chickpea crepes that cost all of Quill's coin and were bitter with cumin seed and blackened in spots. Quill started to argue with the vendor that they were burnt, but Tunuk was too hungry to care. He took the folded-up crepe and shoved it in his mouth. Quill sighed and took his own crepe, dragging Tunuk to sit down beside a yellow brick building where the wind couldn't gust at them. He unfolded his own rakharakh, carefully pulling off the burnt parts with a wrinkled nose.

"Give them to me," Tunuk said. "I'm starving."

"*Please* don't talk with your mouth full," Quill said, handing him shreds of burnt crepe. "It's really gross."

Tunuk obliged, keeping to his own thoughts. What Per had described didn't contradict his own memories...not exactly. But at the same time, it was so different. They'd had a fight. They had made amends. He tried to remember Nimar Eight-Myrrh or any ul-Shandiian but Oshanna, any sense that Qalba was close with the clan. He tried to remember what Qalba had said, or Chizid—either of them saying something that made him think there was another man.

But the memories wouldn't come, washed away by time, or maybe they were wrong? He was sure Oshanna had come alone—he only remembered being sent off with her. He was sure Qalba wouldn't have loved anyone but Chizid.

In fact, it had been a point of contention among his parents.

"I'll just say it," Father Bayan had declared after Tunuk had brought Chizid and Qalba home for dinner, "I know that's how they do things, but it's not natural. And I don't know that it's good for Tunuk to be around that all day."

"Do you think monogamy is *catching*?" Tunuk sneered.

"It's a bit obsessive," Mother Alzari said. "All your love and attention on one person? And then your home—so empty!"

"You have such a hard time anyway, sweetie," Mother Vari said, patting his hand.

"I don't think the issue is the humans," Obigen said. "If Tunuk became a bit obsessive about someone, wouldn't that be an improvement?"

Tunuk scoffed. "Don't you have some senator whose apples need polishing?"

"Tunuk!" Uruphi had said, and he had fallen silent. "Leave the boy *alone*, Obigen. He is *happy* for once. You cannot make a nest of sadness."

Against the yellow brick wall, Tunuk pulled his knees close. Quill sat against him, side by side, and...it wasn't awful, that closeness. It was nice. Not that he was going to say anything—people absolutely got the wrong impression when he said things like that.

"I'm glad you're helping me," he said instead.

Quill chuckled. "You feel better now you're full?"

"No," Tunuk said. Then: "I didn't tell you something else. I found another letter from Qalba. Maybe. While I was on respite." He wiped his greasy hands on his tunic and pulled the letter out of his pocket, holding it open for Quill to read. "It wasn't there before."

"'The wounded jackal limps along a winding path, but it knows the one it hunts for'?" Quill read. "That sounds kind of ominous."

"Who leaves an ominous letter in a chest of blankets?" Tunuk demanded.

"Who leaves any kind of letter in a chest of blankets? Did you show it to Yinii?"

Tunuk put it back in his pocket. "I haven't had the chance."

Quill made a dubious face. "Whatever she tells you...it's already true, you know? Maybe Qalba wrote it and maybe she didn't. Maybe it's old or maybe..." He trailed off. "You didn't really check the bones before," he said. "The ones that were left in Saint Hazaunu's place."

"Are you my generalist or not?" Tunuk asked. "I almost spiraled yesterday. I shouldn't be doing that."

"That's not it, though, is it?" Quill said. "You're afraid it's her."

Tunuk scowled down at the ground. "Eat faster."

It began to rain as they walked toward Gunarro's house on the other side of the city. Downslope of the wealthy parts of the city, down where the tradespeople worked, where the houses climbed up one another's walls and slumped into tenements. Tunuk pulled his cloak more tightly around his long body and paused, getting his bearings. He didn't come to this part of Arlabecca often.

Not anymore, he thought. Twelve years ago, he'd known where to go, who to ask for information or goods. Which doors led to a good place to rest or eat or listen. He turned a corner, and suddenly it was as if his bones all remembered being a gangly youth, and he was looking for Chizid, his teeth bright, his eyes crinkling as he beckoned Tunuk into a shop that sold "the best stick-fried eel." For Qalba, with her horns fringed in bone tokens, her smile patient and painted that particular shade of orange that always, always made Tunuk think of her now.

They crossed the river—he remembered the bridge, carved with triangular spirals, and the fact that if he turned two roads down, he would come to the house of Chizid's brother, Gunarro, and if he kept going straight, he would come to his place of work. One of these would hopefully hold the secrets they needed, the ones that made everything work together and meant Chizid and Qalba were...

They're not alive, he told himself. *And they were probably villains. The note is from some other archivist. It means nothing.*

Quill grabbed his arm. "Tunuk," he whispered, "we're in the fucking Hawk's Nest."

Marked on the doors and the window shutters all down the street were stylized birds of prey in paint and chalk and scratched wood. The faces that looked out over the street were pale, with thick blond curls—all very interested in Quill and Tunuk, all very clearly of Borsyan descent. Tunuk drew himself up to his full height and glared at the watchers. They stared back, unconcerned.

Of all the protectorates, Borsya's children were the most unsettled. In the old days, Borsya had kept to itself, always within the boundaries of their ancient forest, always close to the center, the source of the strange magic they'd carried all the way to Semilla, the cold-magic that the fabricators built minor marvels from. To rule in old Borsya, so far as Tunuk understood it, you proved you were strong and blessed by the Black Mother Forest...and then you took down the formerly strong, blessed man who was in your way. The laws of Semilla didn't let them kill their dukes—the Duke Borcia was replaced by a vote in these days—but there were those who wished for the old ways and, beyond that, those who chafed at the rule of an empress who did nothing to earn her throne—at least her father, Clement, had defended his rule in war twice over.

The whole business gave Tunuk a headache. "I've been here before. They're not going to bother you. Anyway, they're not all separatists. They're just loud about being Borsyan."

Two roads down, Tunuk stopped and frowned at the street. It didn't look familiar anymore, and he nearly turned around to go wait at the Temple of the Black Mother Forest.

"Is Gunarro a separatist?" Quill asked. "If you're making me go to a fucking separatist's house—"

"He's a *fabricator*," Tunuk said. "He works at the Temple of the Black Mother Forest, and I'm pretty certain most all of them follow the Duke Borcia, whoever that is, if only because it's not very politically expedient to piss off the ducal authority that runs your order. So he's only as separatist as all Borsyans are *a little* separatist. Now calm down, or you have to leave."

"Huh," Quill said, catching up. "I've never met a fabricator actually. What kind of things does he make?"

"We're not friends," Tunuk said. "I didn't ask."

"Do you actually think all Borsyans are a little separatist? That doesn't seem accurate. What about Zoifia?"

"Zoifia's a bronze archivist. Until strongmen come in metallic form, she's not going to care about politics." He stalked down the narrow street, annoyed at Quill's constant commentary. Annoyed at himself for being annoyed. Behind the doors, he could feel the vague hum of bones like the echoes of a plucked harp string, the edge of a spiral.

He counted the doors, until they reached the one with a rusty charm in the shape of a Kuali wind god's open-mouthed face nailed to the doorframe. This was it.

"We should make a plan," Quill said.

"Plan is we knock, then talk, then go," Tunuk said, rapping on the door.

The door opened, and there was Gunarro, older and squinting at the two young men in front of his door. He had Chizid's wide nose and the same dark brown eyes. His skin was paler than his half brother's, but with the same reddish undertones that made Tunuk think of the red clay the Kuali wrapped their dead's bones in. His hair was yellow, not quite as pale as the Borsyans' who'd leaned out the windows, curly and bound back at the nape of his neck. He wore a leather apron emblazoned with the Brotherhood of the Black Mother Forest's eagle and tongs.

"Can I help you?" he asked, suspicious.

"I'm a friend of your half brother's," Tunuk said, before Quill could give another long-winded introduction. "Or...I was. I came here with Chizid before. I'm Tunuk. He's Quill."

Gunarro's squint tightened. "You're...the apprentice, right? I..." He glanced past them, up the street. "I have an appointment to keep, so—"

"This should be quick," Quill assured him.

"It's about Chizid?" Gunarro looked down the street again and seemed to come to a decision. "Fine, come in. But it does have to be quick."

The house was not built for an Alojan. Tunuk had to stoop over to fit beneath the low plaster ceiling. He found a chair quickly and settled into it, his knees up around his shoulders. Quill's gaze darted around the room, probably looking for signs of a conspiracy, an uprising of Borsyan separatists in the making.

Gunarro shut the door behind them. "Did you find him?" he asked. "Is that what this is?"

"Irregularities with the catalogue," Quill said, swift and neutral.

"You think he stole something," Gunarro interpreted.

Quill laughed once, and there was something false and hearty to it that made Tunuk's bones itch. "I wish. It's a lot more technical and boring," he lied. "And before we dive into trying to untangle it, we figured it would be faster to see if anyone had had word of your brother."

"Half brother," Tunuk corrected. He didn't know why some humans were so bad about being specific about the kinship names they'd chosen for themselves. He leaned toward Gunarro and added, "Someone stole a skeleton."

Gunarro stared at Quill, then at Tunuk. "I haven't talked to Chizid since he said he was leaving. He didn't tell me where he was going, mind, so I can't help with that... She stole a skeleton? Really? Is that why they ran?"

"They left to go on respite," Quill said. "Something bone specialists do a lot."

Gunarro laughed in a brittle sort of way. "Yeah, you don't believe that, and neither do I. Otherwise, wouldn't he have come back? Wouldn't Qalba have come back?"

Tunuk looked away, a peal of grief ringing in his chest. They would have come back. They always came back. That was the reason they were probably dead.

He remembered the first time he'd needed a respite in the archives.

He'd felt the spiral coming on, the way ghostly notes shivered from the bone flutes when he passed. The way he felt like the skulls were about to speak. The way his skin started to itch like something might be growing on it. He knew he was encouraged to leave the archives when this happened, but...he was so afraid. Wanting to be alone and really *being* alone were different things.

Qalba noticed first, when the flutes started to moan. "Tunuk, shashkii," she said, taking his arm and looking over the faint lines of scratches, "have you ever been to the seaside?"

"No," he said. "I'm fine here."

She screwed up her face, skeptical and silly, and Tunuk darkened with embarrassment. "Well, the archives keep a place," she said. "Chizid and I go all the time. Nice and quiet. Good bathing. You can even fish from the shore if you want."

"Fish have bones."

Qalba chuckled. "That they do, although they're not much for working. They sort of... *bubble*. What do you think, Chizid? Do you feel like a respite?"

Chizid looked up from his work, blinking owlishly at Qalba still holding Tunuk's arm. He seemed to understand at once. "Now?"

Qalba shook her head fondly. "Give me a day to pack and arrange things, you goose."

The little house by the seashore was far enough from any city that Tunuk thought this was truly what it meant to be alone. He spent the days walking up and down the seashore, the sound of the waves soothing his nerves where the bones thrummed against them. When he came back to the house and its merry fire, Chizid showed him how to carve driftwood into little humeri and femurs, tibias and ulnae. Qalba tucked herself close against him, her arm around his shoulders as they sat by the fire cooking fish and roots on skewers, dusted with Kuali-style spices, and Tunuk felt so happy.

"Maybe we don't have to go back," he said one day, in the middle of the trip. "Maybe we could just stay here."

Chizid sighed, looking out at the endless sea, the ocean that stretched into the unknowable. "That sounds nice sometimes. But you'll want to go back."

"What if I don't?" Tunuk demanded.

"Then I suppose you won't," Chizid said. "But we'd miss you, kiddo. And I think you'd miss the work."

Tunuk fidgeted, watching the sea instead of Chizid. "I'd miss you too," he said finally.

They had always come back, the tide returning to the shore. Until the day they hadn't.

Tunuk brought his attention back to Gunarro, to the low-ceilinged house deep in the Hawk's Nest. Something the human had said caught his attention. "You think Qalba stole the skeleton?"

Gunarro shrugged. "I mean, whatever happened, I assumed that woman was behind it."

" 'That woman'?"

"Well, it wasn't Chizid," Gunarro said. "Not alone. Can't imagine him making trouble."

"Did you help him leave the city?" Quill asked.

"So what if I did?" Gunarro said. "He's my brother."

"What did he tell you?" Quill asked.

"That…that he needed to leave, and he didn't think he could come back. I got the impression he'd gotten on the wrong side of someone powerful, but he wouldn't say who. Or how, before you ask. I didn't get involved. I didn't want to know."

Quill shot Tunuk a look. "Who would he have gotten on the wrong side of?"

"I didn't ask," Gunarro said. "Look. You're not idiots, I don't think. I live where I live, and it means *sometimes* you have to deal with someone who's out of favor, do you understand what I mean? And Chizid, being not an idiot either, came to me. So I filled in what he wasn't saying, made sure he had a knife he knew how to use, and arranged a way out of the city for him a week later. That's it. I never heard anything else, and I don't know what he was doing. That was intentional. I'm sorry I can't help you find him."

It wasn't enough to be sorry, Tunuk thought. This was going nowhere; he had no answers, only reminders of everything he'd lost—everything he didn't *know*. Qalba stealing? Chizid stabbing someone? Neither of them returning, when they always came back?

"What about Toya?" Quill asked.

That surprised Gunarro. "You know Toya?"

A banging on the door interrupted their conversation. Gunarro shot to his feet, moving toward the door, but it opened before he reached it.

The woman who stepped inside was tall and broad-shouldered, with a wide curved nose, pale skin and paler frizzy hair peeking out from under a hooded cloak. She pushed the hood back and stared at Tunuk with puzzlement in her bright brown eyes.

"Vigdza, I'm sorry," Gunarro said. "They just showed up."

"Well, it sounds as if you're finished then." The man came in behind her, his voice teasing in a way that hid an edge Tunuk didn't like. He was Borsyan as well, although with the sort of ancestors who had taken the curl from his yellow hair and left some warmth in his pale skin. He had a strong, striking face that made Tunuk very aware of what his skull must be shaped like, and he wore a long yellow coat embroidered along the bottom with stylized spirals, thistles, and red-winged birds. "Vigdza says you can solve this." He held out a leather bag with something the size of Biorni in it. "Quietly."

Gunarro glanced back at Tunuk. "Yeah, just...a moment." He ushered Tunuk and Quill toward the door. When they were near to it, he stopped and added, "The friend you mentioned. I might be able to help you there. But...come back tomorrow. I have a lot of work to catch up on."

"Thank you for your time," Quill said, nearly leaping out the door.

Fucking separatist drama, Tunuk thought, hating that Quill had been right. He glowered at the intruders as if he could frighten them off, make them think of nightmares and other ghoulish things. The man watched back, amused, and tapped a finger to his lips. Tunuk broke his gaze and stormed toward the door.

He glanced back once as he exited, in time to see the object revealed from its covering: a nest of glass bottles and copper wire and stitched and pitch-smeared leather tubes, all surrounding a thin glass globe, like a cold-lamp's. A fabricator's work, meant to channel the energies of the cold-magic, the pieces of the Borsyan Black Mother Forest that powered minor marvels.

"Who made this?" he heard Gunarro ask, and then the door slammed shut.

Quill stood in the middle of the street, looking furious. "That right there is why we should have a plan." Tunuk started walking again, but Quill caught up quickly. "Did you hear what he said? Chizid had a knife."

"So do you," Tunuk said.

"He said he was going to kill someone. Do you know who?"

Tunuk stopped and scowled up at the cloudy sky. He thought back to those days before Chizid and Qalba had left, but the more he tried, the more his mind filled with the memories of the seashore, the spot where he found the note, the wish it was all going to be fine. He tried to picture Chizid with a knife—Chizid angry, Chizid shouting, Qalba almost screaming back, *I can't just end it! I can't just cut him off!* He squeezed his eyes shut.

It's gone too far, he remembered Chizid saying, the words sliding around, refusing to settle. *It's too far gone.*

What is "it," Chizid? he thought.

"I don't know," he said at last. "They wouldn't have told me something like that."

"Well, we found some things out. Let's go back and see whether Yinii had any luck."

Tunuk's arms started itching. "I can't go back to the archives. We don't know anything useful. The vigilants—"

"We'll wait until late and go in through the back before they lock the chapel," Quill said. "Up through the Bone Vault, then over to the dormitories. You can stay in mine if you're afraid Amadea will find you in yours. Or I guess if sleeping under a table was fine last night, Yinii would probably let you sleep in her library." Quill tilted his head. "Did you never have to sneak in after curfew before?"

Tunuk hunched his cloak higher, uncomfortably aware of how small his world really was—the workroom, his apartment, his parents', sometimes the pancake shop. He'd never had to sneak in because he didn't really go out.

"I'm fine in the Bone Vault," he blustered. "Come on, before the rain gets any worse."

⊷—⥲⬧⥲—⊶

Yinii's thoughts were full of sorcerers late into the evening, steeping in her calming tea and knotting around her fingers as she braided her hair. *How did you know you were a sorcerer?* And then: *How did they decide she wasn't safe?* She sat down on the bed, staring at the empty bookshelf opposite her—she'd put everything inked in Bijan and Stavio's apartment for the time being—tying off the braid of auburn hair and itching for ink.

But it wasn't her books she was thinking about just then. It wasn't even the files in Amadea's office, although she kept wondering about the sequestration protocol and what would happen to Iosthe of the Wool. No, she was thinking of the black, black pages Richa had offered her. The palimpsests of Saint Hazaunu, as she had begun thinking of them.

That was how she could actually help, if she could just be sure she wouldn't lose her grip on her affinity again. If she could know what the consequences were.

If you are this curious, there is an easy answer, Fastreda had said. She imagined cutting off her finger, the splatter of ink hitting the ground—and shuddered. She just wanted her affinity back in her own hands.

Richa would let you see the palimpsests, she thought, remembering how Richa had given Stavio the bronze goblets to examine even though he'd been midspiral, when he'd thought that clue would lead to Lord Obigen's murderer. *Richa is the opposite of Radir,* she thought. *He doesn't know to fear the spiral.*

But then she remembered the look he'd given her over the wooden bones, as if he could no longer look at her without thinking of her spiral beneath the Salt Wall. She didn't know, really, what Richa would do. Unless she asked.

A frantic rapping came at her door, scattering all her thoughts. She pulled her dressing gown on and opened the door, letting Quill and Tunuk spill into her room.

"What—" she started.

Tunuk shut the door behind him and laid a finger to his lips before pressing his ear to the wood.

Amadea, Quill mouthed.

"What are you doing in here?" Yinii whispered. She was suddenly very aware of the cramped space of her room, the peculiarity of her empty bookshelves, the *proximity of her bed.*

Quill, she realized, was in her room, standing right next to her bed, smiling at her with that incredibly distracting dimple, and Yinii did not think she could blush any harder if she'd tried. All her thoughts of ink and sorcerers wrote themselves larger, more frantic on her mind as the urge to solve this, right now, so she could know whether she could even let herself daydream about him being in here, with her, with the bed—

She pushed Quill toward the chair beside her desk, trying to clear her thoughts—but he was already looking everywhere.

"Do you not have any books?" he asked. "I sort of assumed."

Tunuk shushed him, waving at him to be quiet. A moment later he straightened. "I think she left."

"Why are you hiding from Amadea?" Yinii asked, still whispering.

"Because I don't want to go to *prison*?" Tunuk hissed. "You *know* she'll tell the vigilant I'm here, and we didn't find out what really happened!"

"You just have to give a statement," Yinii started.

"And say what? 'Yes, I knew there was a dead person in the chapel, and I didn't tell anyone because I was fourteen and I didn't know what to do'?"

Yinii hesitated. "Yes?"

"We found out a few things," Quill said. He described their visits to Per and Gunarro, the things they'd said, and their plan to go back to Gunarro at least. "He said he knew something about Toya, whom we can't find. It sounds like it's very possible one or both of them were stealing artifacts, *and* we have someone else to look for—Qalba's lover."

Tunuk balled his fists, looming over them both. "She didn't have a lover, and they wouldn't have stolen anything."

Quill caught Yinii's eye, as if to say, *This is not going well.* Yinii took a pair of pillows off the bed and put them on the floor for Tunuk. "Sit down," she said. "Did you find out where Toya might be?"

"No," Tunuk said gloomily. "Did you?"

"I only managed to talk to Oshanna for a little bit. She agreed to meet me tomorrow. She...she asked if you'd come too?"

Tunuk made a face. "What? Why?"

"Because...weren't you friends?"

"No, we were agemates who were stuck in the same space occasionally," he said, as if this could not be plainer. "Did she say we were friends?"

"Sort of," Yinii said. "I mean, she wanted to see you." She sat on the foot of her bed, making a triangle of the three of them. "I think she might know something about where Qalba is."

Tunuk straightened. "What? Why? What did she say?"

"She didn't *say*," Yinii said. "But...the way she reacted—"

"Why didn't you *ask* her?"

"Because Radir was there, and she didn't want to talk in front of him," Yinii said.

"Why the fuck was Radir with you?" Tunuk demanded. "This isn't his business!"

"Because," Yinii said, her temper slipping, "he caught me in Amadea's office pulling ink off papers, and he was sure I was about to spiral! Honestly, Tunuk, I had a really bad day, and I'm trying to help you, even though I'm rotten at this! You could be a little nicer!"

Tunuk went silent at that, clutching his forearms. He looked down, his eyes dimming. "Sorry," he muttered.

"Were they the...Ragale papers?" Quill asked.

Yinii met his gaze, unsure of what was all right to say in front of Tunuk and what they were trying to protect him from. He knew a little of what had happened under the Salt Wall, but not everything. Amadea was very adamant they shouldn't tell anyone *everything*.

Yinii had argued—they were in this together—but then...she'd seen the transfer order.

"When you were with the Paremi," she asked Quill, "did you ever write a transfer order for a sorcerer? Or...I don't know what sequestration orders are called for them."

"'Isolation mandate,' I think," Quill said. "But no. That's not really common. The sorcerers are pretty much where they need to be."

"Who...?" Yinii touched the amulet of Saint Asla and tried again. "Who signs those? The one I found...The sorcerer didn't sign it. She didn't agree."

Quill shrugged. "Usually a noble consul, since it sort of falls between the Imperial Authority and the ducal authority. And one of the people under the Imperial Authority who's responsible for them. Sorcerers have to have at least three people checking in, if I remember right. But again," he added, "it's eleven people in the whole empire. It doesn't come up, and nobody's usually very bothered about them."

"Lucky them," Tunuk said.

A hot flush of anger raced up Yinii's neck, and she felt her affinity roll out from her like hundreds of seeking vines. She pulled it back. "They get locked up and can't make any choices for themselves," she said. "Fastreda sits in that tower—"

"Fastreda literally raised an army for a coup and killed hundreds of people," Tunuk said. "I think *that's* the reason she's locked up in a tower."

"And what about the rest of them?" Yinii demanded. "Does Iosthe of the Wool deserve to be taken from up north in Endecha all the way down to Sestina because someone who *isn't* her thinks she's a danger to herself?"

Quill and Tunuk were both looking at Yinii as if *she* might be a danger to herself, as if nothing she'd just said made any sense at all. The whole room felt as if it were pressing on her, and she stared hard at her own hands, not letting her attention slide to the char hiding in the wooden furniture, the linen sheets, the solvents buried in—

"Yinii!" Amadea's voice called as she knocked. "Yinii, are you in?"

Tunuk shot to his feet. *Say no*, he mouthed.

But Yinii had already stood, bumping the bed into the wall with an audible *thunk*. "Yes!" she said. "One...moment." Tunuk darted across the narrow room, tucking himself into the corner behind the door, indistinguishable from the shadows, as Yinii yanked the door open.

Amadea smiled down at her, her brown eyes tired. Yinii didn't think she'd been the only one to have a very long day. "Good evening," Amadea said. "Can I come in?"

"Um," Yinii managed. "Why?"

Amadea leaned forward enough to see Quill sitting at Yinii's desk. He waved at her. "Ah," Amadea said. She looked back at Yinii as if assessing.

"Um," Yinii said again.

Amadea's gaze swept over her head, across the room. "I was going to talk to you about what Radir told me. That you were in my office, taking ink off the documents. I wanted to make sure you're all right, first of all."

"I'm fine," Yinii said. "Radir...helped. But it wasn't as bad as he thought."

Amadea nodded in a way that made Yinii think she didn't believe her. "Did you find anything?"

The named parties request the transfer of the imperial ward, Iosthe del Sepharin...

"Not really," Yinii said.

Amadea smiled tightly again. "It does seem like it will need more focused attention. Unfortunately, not something we have time for at the moment. You're sure you're all right? No spiraling?"

Yinii nodded.

"Good. Then, Tunuk?" Amadea called. "Either you're under the bed or behind the door, and you need to come out, or I'm going to have to haul you out."

A moment passed, then Tunuk slid out from behind the door, his shoulders hunched up to his ears. Amadea stepped inside and closed the door behind her. Yinii backed up onto the bed again—this was more people than had ever been in her room.

Amadea reached out and took Tunuk's arm, looking over his long wrist, the meat of his forearm. "What happened?"

"Nothing," Tunuk said. "I had errands."

Amadea turned back to Quill, her eyebrows raised.

Quill shrugged. "Errands," he confirmed.

"Did you forget you sent me a note about Tunuk spiraling and looking for information to exonerate him?" Amadea asked tartly. "Errands, indeed." She smoothed a hand over Tunuk's wrist, as if to assure them both there was no bone growing there, and let go of him. "You knew about the bones, didn't you?"

Tunuk folded his arms. "Maybe."

"Was it Chizid and Qalba?" When Tunuk didn't answer, she went on. "Tomorrow morning, I have to go with Mireia to the noble consuls' meeting—"

"Tomorrow?" Yinii interrupted, at the same time Tunuk cried, "Why are they involved?"

"I have to go with Mireia," Amadea repeated more loudly, "to defend the archives' handling of this, so I would appreciate you *not* leaving again, and then after I'm finished, I'm going down to the Kinship Hall with you to tell them what you know. I promise this isn't going to end with you in prison."

"You can't promise that," Tunuk said in a small voice. And while Yinii wanted to believe Amadea—no one could possibly think Tunuk was a killer or an artifact thief—she also knew if the noble consuls had been called that the rezas were not patient, and the severity of these crimes wouldn't be ignored. Someone would pay, and it *might* be Tunuk.

Amadea touched his shoulder. "This is my job, Tunuk. I will not let them take you. But you can't keep hiding. You can't keep lying, especially not to the Kinship. Do not leave the archives."

"We're trying to find out what happened," Yinii said. "We could meet you—"

"No. Leave it to the Kinship." Amadea sighed and looked around at the three of them. "I'll wish you all a good night. Please get some sleep."

She left, closing the door behind her, and once more Yinii felt a sudden anger rise in her, a sudden yearning for the ink as if something inside her had turned voracious. *Stay here, stay inside, it's for your own good.* The room felt tiny, collapsing.

"Well..." Quill said slowly.

Yinii turned. "You have a meeting planned already, right? You should just go while she's at the noble consuls' meeting. She won't know."

Tunuk's eyes widened. "_You're_ telling me to ignore Amadea? Are you well?"

"She can't actually _make_ you do anything," Yinii said. "And she's going to do what she can to protect you, but...she's not infallible. Something happened. We should find out what. You should go meet with Gunarro. Find out what he knows. See if you can find Toya. I'll go meet with Oshanna like I planned, after the noble consuls' meeting, and I'll ask her about him, too.

"And I'll meet you at the Kinship Hall after," she added, thinking of the inky page Richa had taken back with him and how that ink would feel peeled apart in layers. "So Amadea can't be _that_ mad."

"She probably will be," Tunuk said.

"Then...let her," Yinii said. "We can go to the Kinship Hall after."

Quill's smile hitched in a crooked way, flashing a dimple. "Sounds like a plan."

And a plan, Yinii thought, pleased, was all they could really ask for, when everything was so difficult to predict.

III

A FALLEN GIANT

Sometime in autumn
Near the borders of Khirazj

The changelings begin to have trouble waking as the trip
northward brings them into autumn's reach. The nights are
cold and crisp, the mornings damp and chilly, and Melosino lies as
if dead beside the girl who is not really his sister until the sun burns
off the scraps of fog.

"They don't like the cold," Redolfo tells the girl grimly.

"How cold will it get?" she asks.

He does not answer—she wonders if he knows—and they press
on anyway, aimed at Khirazj. The Heart of the World. And each
morning the changelings are slower to wake, each night they are
sooner to fall, and each day the slow building of their torpor shows
in the way their answers stall, their actions slip.

When one morning frost sparkles on the grass, the sentries are
all still. Redolfo's fury is a quiet thing, and the girl watches at a distance, stirring up the fire as he feeds that anger back into his own
thoughts, putting it to use.

"We will have to store them," he says at last. "For the season."

"Won't that be dangerous?" the girl asks. "What if we're attacked?"

"Who's going to attack us?" he replies. "Winter does not discriminate."

They hunt for caves high up in the mountains the road hugs, following paths along cliffs decorated with more paintings—more long-horned goats and horned rabbits, but coiling snakes and long-legged water birds too. Hands, on one cave wall, revealed by the halo of paint around them, as if someone set their palm against the stone and sprayed the bright white paint against it. She sets her hand into the blank space where some other person once did.

A shadow falls across her: Melosino, come to stand behind her. She looks, automatically, toward Redolfo, but he isn't watching. He doesn't like the changeling she made.

"I think you frighten him a little," Melosino told her, a few nights before, huddled near her by the fire. The changeling keeps trying to act like the brother she imagined it into being, and the girl isn't sure how to respond. She wants to weep, she's so glad to have Melosino back, but she worries at what she's done. She thinks about telling the changeling what it really is, but then she imagines how it might make the poison stop working or make the changeling slip out of this form into that shimmering, shivering shape that makes her eyes hurt. That wouldn't be better, would it?

Still, she finds herself caring about Melosino and thinking too much about what it means to be oneself. She's not sure if she's been allowed that herself, even as she wishes she could give it to her changeling-brother.

"What do you think is up here?" he asks. "What is he looking for?"

"A place for the winter," she says. "Don't worry."

They find a cave the right size to hold them all, and two days later, it's cold enough the changelings do not wake. Melosino is curled beside the girl, as stiff as a corpse, and it throws wild memories through her that she shies away from. She has nothing to leave him, no token of her return, and this feels wrong. She presses her hand to the ashes of the fire and leaves the mark on the stone beside him.

Redolfo does not linger—they will not stay with the changelings for the winter; why would they? Khirazj is so close, and they will be faster now, the two of them, winter or not.

Redolfo Kirazzi has told the girl about the land of his ancestors in countless stories—mighty Khirazj, gift of the river. The gleaming steles, the golden domes, the barge-temples, and the fertile fields. The kings and queens, sons and daughters of the river, ruling absolute and inviolable from painted palace-temples. This would have been his birthright, had the changelings not come: a king of the River Kingdom—birthplace of the sun, wealthiest of the nations of the world, wise beyond measure.

But as the old road, broken by time and weather and—who knows?—the feet of changeling merchants traveling to and fro, dips toward the border and the first city comes into view, the girl is startled.

It is just a city—just pale brick and shining roofs—like the body of a giant lying stretched beside the road. Not the wonderland he'd conjured of gold and power. Not the shell of an empire waiting for its favored son to return and bring it back to life.

The story is wrong, she thinks, and she's afraid what that will mean.

"Who lives here?" the girl asks. She points across at the spirals of smoke rising from the town. "Is it changelings?"

"Not in winter," Redolfo says. This is a surprise. "Let's go introduce ourselves."

The girl expects to creep around the city, to watch and assess and choose the path that gives them the advantage, but Redolfo walks straight up the broken road, unconcerned. She follows after, watching for archers, watching for bandits, watching for changelings... but she reminds herself it's too cold for those.

These are people, she realizes. People who survived.

Redolfo puts an arm around her, keeps her walking beside him. "Do you know the story of the two brothers?" he asks.

"No," the girl says, watching the empty city gate. The sun is high, the shadow of the wall obscuring what lies inside it, but she thinks there's movement. She thinks *someone* is watching back.

"Once there were two brothers who lived beside the river," Redolfo says, his voice proud, almost defiant. "Mazu and Ifa. Both were virtuous and hardworking, wise and patient, all the things the gods hold dear, and at their birth, the wisdom spirits blessed them both: they would be beloved all their days.

"The elder brother, Mazu, praised the gods in all his works, made offerings, and worked hard at the land. His days were full of toil and sweat. Some years the land flourished, and some years the land faltered, but Mazu always thanked the gods for their blessings.

"The younger brother, Ifa, went down to the city, smug in his blessings. He demanded the best things and dealt with the wealthiest of merchants. Soon he was rich in gold and wheat, with a beautiful house overlooking the river and a wife so clever and lovely she was like a daughter of Alletet come to earth."

The girl frowns up at him. "Is that backward? Shouldn't the hardworking brother have been blessed?"

Redolfo gives her a dangerous look. "I'm not finished.

"Ifa was wealthy and prosperous, yes, but he claimed all the success as his own and gave no thought to the gods who had blessed him. He devoured the offerings, stayed home on feast days, and dedicated no prayers in the temple.

"Until one day," Redolfo says, "when Ifa was in his splendid home, and the river heard his boasting and became furious. Pademaki, the source, the waters of life, drew the waters up their banks like a great tidal wave off the sea and swept Ifa, his home, and all his wealth off the earth."

The girl looks back at the gate, at the body that has stepped into the light—a man, a *huge* man, carrying a curved pair of swords. And then two more, a man and a woman, all in armor. Redolfo squeezes her shoulders against him, holding her in place as they keep walking toward the city.

"Mazu wept at the loss of his brother but did not curse the gods. He begged them to return his brother to him, offering to sacrifice their generous blessings to cement it. The gods heard him and granted his request, putting the brother's seven souls into the body of a donkey, with seven holy marks on it. The queen regnant heard of this donkey and wished to acquire it, but when she arrived herself to demand the deal, she fell hopelessly in love with Mazu instead and wed him before the week was out. Thus was Mazu's piety rewarded. Do you understand?"

The girl feels the story sliding in her head like wet stones in a box. It doesn't want to fit. It doesn't make sense. "There are people there," she warns him. "With weapons."

Redolfo's gaze is pinned to the city. "When you are blessed by the gods," he says, "you cannot doubt their hand. You are meant for greatness, and greatness will come on you eventually."

The girl shuts her eyes as he drags her on, visions of the temple at Gintanas in her head, her former life or maybe not. Services with the day-sisters and working in the garden and the taste of raisin cakes that were always too dry to swallow without a mug of cold water. She's not sure she believes in the gods these days—can they follow her out here, among the wilds? Do they care? If they care, why have they let any of this happen, the world's bones lying bare out here, the forgotten footholds of people long gone?

She doesn't believe in the gods...but she thinks, out here, so far away from everything else, she might believe in Redolfo. She is afraid of him, she is angry at him, she is still hurting deep down from being cast aside. But there is not, she thinks, anyone else on either side of the Salt Wall she might trust to bring her to safety.

The man at the gates shouts something at them, and it takes a moment for her mind to pluck the words from the sounds. *Where is your iron?* He's speaking Khirazji, his accent odd and his words in strange places, but she understands him enough.

Redolfo grins and draws his sword, calls back in the same language, more or less. *Will steel do if the mountains have blown their cold breath across it?*

The people look at each other, puzzled, and she wonders if his words sound as strange to them. *Who are you?* the woman asks. *Where have you come from?*

The girl thinks in that moment that Redolfo will tell them his name, his birthright, demand their fealty, but she doesn't understand how power comes to certain men. It isn't time for that.

Very far, he says. *Beyond the wall of salt. Can we join you for the season? We are in a strange land, but we have much to offer.*

The people exchange words she can't hear. The gesture at Redolfo and the girl to wait, to stay where they are, and the smaller man goes back into the city, presumably to get someone in charge.

Redolfo looks down at her and smiles with a cruelty she hopes is meant for someone else, somewhere else. "And when you slight someone greater than you," he adds, "vengeance may be slow, but it will be complete. That is what the story means. We will succeed." He squeezes her shoulders. "I will still succeed."

The girl looks up at the spirals of smoke and thinks of Melosino, inert beside a cold campfire in the mountains. None of this feels like success, but then, perhaps the story hasn't ended. And if it is foolish to doubt a god, then what is it to doubt Redolfo Kirazzi?

CHAPTER NINE

Tего is going to be an unmothered spectacle of shit," Mireia muttered as she and Amadea stood outside the Court of the Noble Consuls the next day, watching the representatives and their attendants file in. They had been waiting almost an hour by this point, far longer than Amadea had been prepared to be sitting in the Imperial Complex.

Red dress. Black envelope. Gold earring.

When the Salt Wall had been sealed and the empire formed, each protectorate had been given a certain amount of self-governance—the ducal authorities. The former rulers of the nine nations that had come to Semilla were styled as dukes and duchesses or formed councils to share that authority, as the Orozhandi had. The ducal authority was a cultural one, people looking to their kings and queens and rezas, but Semilla retained its overarching control—the Imperial Authority. There were customs and laws, after all, that the ducal authorities could not enforce—witness, for example, the Pashuntana's attempt to enslave the Ashtabari, leading to their ejection from the empire.

To bridge the two, the noble consuls were elected—members of the Imperial Authority meant to represent their protectorates' interests to the empress and advise her in ways that preserved the separation of the two authorities. It was one more piece in the complex workings of the empire.

"At least they didn't insist on calling up the whole damn senate," Mireia muttered as the newly established Alojan noble consul, Lord

Obigen's replacement, sprinted for the doors, chased by her attendants. She stopped and raised elongated arms to adjust her robes, the glittering chain net that adorned her bald head. Even in the well-lit hallway, she looked like a living shadow.

"Saints and devils, whose daughter is that?" Mireia whispered as the Alojan noble consul ducked beneath a raised doorframe still slightly too low for her enormous height. "She's entirely too young to be a noble consul."

Amadea thought of Tunuk and blew out a breath. She'd told him to stay put. Quill was watching him. She had to trust he would be all right. For the moment, anyway.

A man's deep voice interrupted her distraction. "Archivists." The Borsyan noble consul stood before them, a broad-shouldered man of about Amadea's age, his silvering blond curls and beard cut to frame his angular face above a brocade coat in geometric patterns.

"Lord Tafad," Mireia said curtly.

"I hope this is not a waste of everyone's time?" he said.

"Of course not," Mireia said. "The rezas have every right to ask for a ruling."

On the other side of the stream of people, the Orozhandi waited. Amadea found Manith pacing restlessly back and forth before the elderly reza ul-Chavresh. She spotted the ul-Tahnaz representative who had backed Manith's call and what had to be her sister or cousin, wearing the reza ul-Tahnaz's elaborate embroidered shawl. She saw ul-Nymand, ul-Liphiltan, two members of ul-Benturan...

Blue horn charm. Green tunic. Silver hair.

Nanqii ul-Hanizan stood a little apart from the other representatives, studying her with a faint smile. Today he wore lavender and deep blue in sheer layers that shifted and shimmered and reminded her of a clear sky at dusk. She met his gaze frankly and offered a polite nod. The smile spread in a suggestive way.

Oshanna ul-Shandiian came in and spoke to him briefly, her expression grim and fierce in a way that made Amadea unsettled. She did not think the woman was inclined to be on the side of Manith and the others, but her reza was a different matter.

"Honestly," Mireia muttered as Lord Tafad strode away, "what does he think I'm going to say? 'This is officially an unmothered spectacle of shit'? I wish the Borsyans would vote *him* out of the chair like they did when he was Duke Borcia." She scowled after the man. "Probably would end up duke again as soon as he did, my luck."

"Neither the reza ul-Shandiian nor the reza ul-Hanizan are here," Amadea murmured to Mireia. "Is that bad?"

Mireia snorted. "It means they're going to *do* something, although little telling what. From Bishamar Twelve-Spider, I would expect him to speak up directly before a decision gets made. From Dushar Six-Agamid...I'm expecting theatrics." The Orozhandi began filing in, and Mireia nodded. "We go in after. You don't have to speak, but I trust you to jump in if you've got something to say."

The Court of the Noble Consuls was a large square room, its walls paneled in carved wood painted with a dark blue stain and huge silver mirrors, its floor a mosaic of dark wood and gilded tiles. Five of the noble consuls sat on each side of the room, facing a row of four daises ringed by wooden railings. Mireia and Amadea were led into the one at the far right, while Manith ul-Chavresh and Oshanna ul-Shandiian stepped into the far left.

Opposite the entrance on a throne of dark wood sat Empress Beneditta. She wore a wide skirt paneled in orange and cream and a short blouse, with a pale shawl wrapped around her shoulders and over her dark hair. Her face was covered from forehead to mouth in a mask of imperial gold. The mask was flat, undecorated, and the eyeholes were dark slits—the effect was eerie and distant.

Beneditta, pulling the mask from her face, slamming it on the table. "Hold my hand and pretend you are my sweet cousin come to life again."

Amadea looked down at the intricate floor, trying to steady her breath. She glanced up at Ibramo sitting in a smaller chair beside the empress's dais and saw Lady Sigrittrice appear out of the shadows between them. Watching Amadea. Amadea nodded politely to her and turned away.

The Orozhandi noble consul, a middle-aged man with reddish hair and darker skin, wearing three pink crystals on his left horn, rose to his feet. "Your Imperial Majesty. My fellow noble consuls.

Thank you for coming with such brief notice to the requests of Orozhand for deliberation. The complaint is very severe, I am afraid."

He looked to Beneditta, waiting for her to speak the words that
began the meeting, but the empress said nothing, and the mask
betrayed nothing. She turned her head slowly, as if taking in the
room one face at a time.

"Your Imperial Majesty?" the Orozhandi noble consul said. "May
we begin?"

Beneditta stopped her slow sweep of the room, turning her masked
face toward the Orozhandi noble consul. For a long moment, she
said nothing.

"Your...Majesty?"

Beneditta made a curt gesture. "Begin."

"Then, with Your Imperial Majesty's permission and the grace of
my fellow noble consuls, I will direct your attention to the complain-
ants, Manith Ten-Bee-eater ul-Chavresh, who has registered this
issue under the authority of the reza ul-Chavresh, Jautha Fourteen-
Horse, and Oshanna Eleven-Sand Iris ul-Shandiian, who has registered this issue under the authority of the reza ul-Shandiian, Dushar
Six-Agamid."

Oshanna offered a bow over her pressed hands to the noble consul and to the empress. Manith did the same but glowered over at
Mireia and Amadea before speaking in a loud, clear voice.

"Ul-Chavresh requested this meeting," Manith began, "on behalf
of the Orozhandi. The Imperial Authority has failed in their duty to
us, and we demand to be made whole."

The empress tilted her head, merely watching Manith through the
eyeholes of her mask. Oshanna frowned, and Manith's gaze flicked to
the Orozhandi noble consul, and he nodded minutely. Amadea squeezed
the railing in both fists. What was happening with the empress?

"We...we agreed," Manith began again, "in the Accords of the
Protectorates that the bones of our saints would be cared for by the
specialists of the Imperial Archives in the hope that their gifts would
preserve the integrity of the saints and their relics. We sanctified the
chapel and lent our funds and protection to its upkeep. But it has
been uncovered that the bones of Saint Hazaunu of the Wool, the

wooden relics crafted in her memory by Saint Qilbat of the Cedar, were stolen, and the archives were none the wiser!"

"A question," the young Alojan noble consul piped up. "Are the wooden relics covered under the same agreements and protections as the actual remains of the saints? Or is it a separate discussion?"

The Orozhandi all muttered to one another, some glaring at the Alojan noble consul. Oshanna spoke up. "The wooden bones *are* the remains of Saint Hazaunu, so far as we are concerned, esinora. The differentiation is not necessary and not, to be clear, welcome."

Manith hissed something at Oshanna in Orozhandi that Amadea missed. The Alojan noble consul darkened in abashment, and Oshanna continued. "Obviously something has gone amiss in the archives' duties. The ducal authority feels this is a clear breach of the accord of the protectorates and demands restitutions be made."

At this, Nanqii stood and stepped into one of the center daises. "The ducal authority is not in agreement. I am Nanqii Four-Oryx ul-Hanizan. I speak for the ul-Hanizan reza, Bishamar Twelve-Spider. We would move to address this issue at a later date. It's not even clear what's occurred."

"I think you'll find it hard to argue that a breach hasn't occurred," Oshanna said, her words calm but her eyes burning brightly.

"So clear," Nanqii said, "that your reza did not bother to attend this emergency meeting himself?"

Oshanna hesitated. "He is delayed."

"So this meeting *had* to happen this day, everyone together, right now," Nanqii drawled, as he turned toward the noble consuls, "and could not wait for Dushar Six-Agamid, who seems to be leading this complaint?" Again, Manith glowered and looked as if she might interrupt, but Nanqii forged on. "I fail to follow the logic. I move to disregard ul-Shandiian's request, as I have been directed by the reza ul-Hanizan to do because he knew he would not be able to arrive at these proceedings."

"A question." The Beminat noble consul spoke up. She was an older woman, her hair a dense cloud of gray curls around her dark brown face, her gown a brilliant pink. "Before we get into the procedural chaos of when the rezas would like to exercise their ducal authority, could we hear the Imperial Archives' response? Did this happen, Head Archivist?"

Mireia cleared her throat. "It is the case that an inconsistency of records has been determined. The extent of the issue is still being explored."

"Were the bones of this saint misplaced?" the Beminat noble consul asked.

Mireia paused. "Again, the extent of the issue is still being determined. But our preliminary findings...It appears the bones were indeed removed from the archives and a different skeleton was put in their place."

Another murmur ran through the room. The Beminat noble consul raised her brow. "Has the culprit been determined?"

"That is a question for the Vigilant Kinship and the Imperial Authority, esinora," Mireia said. "Our task is to secure the bones and make certain any damage is addressed and they are preserved once more. We will also attempt to determine if any of that damage suggests a date of the theft and if there are security issues with the archives."

"A question!" Lord Tafad boomed. "You have no records of any theft occurring from the chapel? How is that possible?"

"That is something else we will attempt to determine," Mireia said. "No theft was observed before now."

"You were already sworn to preserve and protect the saints!" Manith burst out. "Your bone specialist had the responsibility— hand *him* to the vigilants, and we'll find out everything we need!"

Nanqii shrugged. "Ul-Hanizan will offer no complaints about letting the Vigilant Kinship do their jobs. But this meeting remains unneeded."

"This makes sense to me," Lord Tafad said, raking a hand through his beard. "No one can even clearly state what occurred, so how are we supposed to determine fault?"

Amadea looked over at Beneditta. She seemed to be staring out the window again, utterly disconnected from the tension in the room. Beside her, Sigrittrice was taut as a wire, her gaze sliding from Beneditta, over to the Orozhandi—

RELICS OF RUIN 151

The door opened, taking everyone's attention for a moment. A gray-haired Orozhandi man entered, his horns ornamented to their tips, his suit a modern cut in a pristine white wool. The embroidered cape he wore flashed bright geometric patterns as he removed it, handing it to Oshanna as he took her place at the stand. The Orozhandi who had been arguing subsided, watching this man.

"I am Dushar Six-Agamid ul-Shandiian," the man said. "Reza of ul-Shandiian and bearer of that ducal authority."

"Reza ul-Shandiian," the Orozhandi noble consul said, sounding nervous. "You honor us with your presence."

"For a matter this serious, how could I not attend?" Dushar said.

"Your representative has already described ul-Shandiian's complaint," the noble consul went on. "Would you add anything to it?"

Dushar turned to consider first Mireia on the end, then Nanqii between them. "Has she declared our demands for restitution?"

"We haven't gotten to that part yet," the Beminat noble consul said. "We're still determining if ul-Shandiian has grounds to make the complaint when the ducal authority isn't in agreement—"

"Which I don't see it has," the Borsyan noble consul interrupted. "I side with ul-Hanizan in this."

Dushar looked over at the human man with narrowed eyes, the lid of his dark-eye tensing in sync. "Lord Tafad," he said, with a false graciousness that made Amadea think they'd fought before. "Whether you feel the Imperial Archives have failed in their duty or not, ul-Shandiian will take action. We intend to demand the rezas unite and use the ducal authority to reclaim Orozhand's gifts. We would reclaim the saint's bones."

Amadea sucked in a breath of surprise. It had always been within the ducal authority of each protectorate's power to reclaim the treasures they had entrusted to the Imperial Authority's order of archivists and specialists. The dukes and duchesses requested artifacts all the time—to use in rituals, to check records, to simply show off.

But the saints were different—the chapel was different. The chapel was itself a holy site, its care divided between the archives and the Orozhandi ducal authority. The cavern-towns of Maqama had no facility for Saint Hazaunu's wooden bones, and Amadea could imagine the wood specialists' protests at their removal to the high humidity of that area.

They have the right, she told herself, trying to gauge what would need to be done to make certain the wooden bones were safe, either in the chapel or in Maqama.

"Saint Hazaunu of the Wool is ul-Hanizan's saint," Nanqii said dismissively. "And ul-Hanizan is not interested in making demands for her to leave the sanctity of the chapel."

"The ducal authority in total has responsibility to the saints," the ul-Shandiian reza said. "So please convey to Bishamar Twelve-Spider, whenever he decides to rise from his bed, that it is not solely ul-Hanizan's place to make the request."

Nanqii turned to Reza Dushar. "Reza, are you implying ul-Shandiian means to seize the bones of one of ul-Hanizan's saints without the agreement of the reza ul-Hanizan?"

"No," Dushar said mildly. "We intend to demand the return of *all* the saints' bones."

A murmur ran through the assembled court, the noble consuls all stunned from their boredom.

Mireia cursed under her breath. "Unmothered spectacle of shit."

"The chapel is purpose-built to house and protect the saints," Amadea called out, not waiting for the notice of the consuls. "I don't doubt they would be welcome in Maqama, but I can give you moisture levels and temperature ranges, I can show you the reports my cedar and bone specialists produce to track any signs of—"

"Your bone specialist," the reza ul-Shandiian interrupted, "who failed to protect the relics of Saint Hazaunu? Who, from what I have gathered, may in fact be the villain who stole them?"

"We are still looking into what happened," Amadea said. "Archivist yula Manco has been a valuable member of the archives and an excellent steward of the Orozhandi saints. There is no evidence he had anything to do with this."

"Yes, yula Manco," the reza said. "The son of the late Lord Obigen, I believe. Architect of the 'second wall'? Is it a family trait to threaten our sacred relics?"

"Nest-child, Reza," the Alojan noble consul piped up. "Correct-
ness is appreciated, I understand."

Dushar waved a hand apologetically at the noble consul, but when
he spoke next, there was nothing apologetic in his tone.

"You ask us to trust our most sacred relics to the Imperial Authority, when they cannot protect them"—he flung a hand toward
Mireia and Amadea—"and when that same authority was happily
entertaining a plan by the Alojans to knock down our most sacred
site and disturb the sanctity of Saint Asla and the martyrs? I question whether the Imperial Authority has Orozhand's best interests in
mind at all."

At that, the court went silent as a tomb.

Beneditta turned her masked face from the windows, the flat,
featureless plane of the golden mask gleaming in the sunlight that
shone in. "You question my authority?" she asked, her quiet voice
hard.

Dushar ul-Shandiian paused. The empress's presence in these
meetings was largely ceremonial, her lines pre-established—the
noble consuls existed to be the layer between her and the ducal
authorities. And while the Imperial Authority of the empress held
primacy over the empire, it was not done for her to imply it gave her
sway over the protectorates this way.

But then, it was not done to question her dedication to the empire
either.

"Your pardon, Your Imperial Majesty," Dushar said, an edge of
acid to his voice. "I did not mean to repeat past challenges to the
current line's claim."

Amadea caught her breath, a sudden panic seizing her. Dushar
naming the cause of the Kirazzi coup, implying it was still alive—
this was everything she'd hidden from, everything she needed to
protect against. Ibramo's head turned incautiously toward Amadea,
his eyes bright with alarm in his mask.

Beneditta closed her hands around the arms of her throne, shifting forward as if to stand.

Sigrittrice lunged toward her, setting a hand on Beneditta's
shoulder, her voice fast and loud as she said, "I think I speak for

the empress when I say this meeting was called too quickly and we do not have enough information to act. I will therefore, under her authority, suggest we adjourn. The archives have one month to draft a report on what exactly failed within the current system and detail how it will be rectified, as well as provide a full catalogue of the chapel and the status of all the saints and their relics. Perhaps, given the conflict, it would be wise to name a neutral party to take custody of the wooden bones—"

"Ul-Hanizan will be given custody. I declare it so," Beneditta said, her gaze still on Dushar. She stood, speaking low and angrily to Sigrittrice, and swept out the back of the room, which fell to whispering.

"Saints and devils and all the little fishes," Mireia muttered. "What was that?"

"I don't know," Amadea said.

Sigrittrice rubbed her temple behind the curve of her own golden mask before seeking out Amadea and beckoning her with a curt gesture.

"I seem to be summoned. I will see you back at the archives. If you can tell Bucella to start preparing Saint Hazaunu for translation, I'll get the cataloguing requests started this afternoon." She winced. "After I take Tunuk to the Kinship Hall."

"If you're not attending the Imperial Authority, you're going to be preparing the bones," Mireia said. "You're not going to the Kinship Hall."

Amadea crossed the room to where Sigrittrice stood beside the door hidden in the paneled wall. Ibramo hovered nervously beside the dais—Amadea didn't dare look over at him.

"Archivist Gintanas," Sigrittrice said brusquely, "the empress wishes to speak to you. About a mask request."

"Of course, Your Ladyship," Amadea said carefully. "I will do whatever I can."

"Within reason," Sigrittrice said.

Beneditta stood in the small antechamber, wringing her hands beside a burbling wall fountain. Amadea dipped into a curtsy, and when she stood, Beneditta had removed the golden mask, staring back at Amadea barefaced. Amadea's eyes went to the fountain—the empress was always masked. Gold for authority, green for personal matters, even black for privacy, but when the mask was removed... there were no clear rules for how she must be treated, because it wasn't meant to happen.

"Give me the Red Mask," Beneditta said, leaping past any questions of how Amadea should address her. "Please."

"I can't," Amadea said. "It's being repaired."

Beneditta shook her head. "We're at war with or without it. I understand that. But if I have the mask, then it will be clear to everyone else, you see? They need the symbols, the clarity of it."

"It will take a few weeks to finish," Amadea said, apologetic. "Could you use that time to prepare?"

"I am already behind," Beneditta said. "Gritta doesn't... She says the threat is ended, that it was a fluke, but if one changeling managed to make it over the Wall, there could be thousands of them in Semilla, waiting to rise up. And if they know... if they discover..." She reached up to touch her bare face, an almost self-conscious gesture. "Everything is at stake," she whispered. "And now all this? Give me the mask, broken or not. Please."

Amadea pursed her mouth, stopping herself from replying too quickly. The empress had a point: Something terrible was brewing, and if the people discovered that Beneditta—that every Ulanitti— was part changeling, the Imperial Authority would lose its ability to weather this storm. If Beneditta came out strong, if she pointed them at the actual threat, if she made good use of the authority the Accords of the Protectorates afforded the empress—they would stand a chance.

And here Beneditta was, not ordering Amadea's compliance, not demanding her fealty: asking. All Amadea could think of was that moment, three months prior, when Beneditta, faced with the truth of what she was, had asked Amadea to hold her hand. Amadea nearly agreed to procure the mask.

But Amadea could see why Sigrittrice was worried. Sigrittrice might not believe there was a threat worthy of the Red Mask, but Amadea could agree that threat did not exist within the Salt Wall.

And without knowing what precisely the threat beyond the Wall was, there was no good to be done in declaring the Imperial Federation and its protectorates at war.

Beneditta needed evidence.

Amadea reached out and took Beneditta's hand between her own, risking impropriety in the face of her missing mask. "Dita," she said, daring familiarity, "if you had proof of...something, of a growing coup, wouldn't that help more than donning the Red Mask? You could get the noble consuls on your side, and then the ducal authorities, the senate. The people."

"It's the authority of the empress to..." Beneditta trailed off, pursing her mouth. "Yes. Probably." She withdrew her hand, rubbing the wrist absently. "I have not managed to regain the loyalty my father and my uncle lost. If they think I am going mad like the Fratricide, then..." She stopped herself, stiffening at the mention of Appolino Ulanitti, the prince who'd murdered Emperor Iespero, his consort, and their four children, including Lireana.

Unless, a voice whispered through Amadea's thoughts. She brushed it aside. Beneditta was watching her, as if trying to gauge her reaction. As if she could see whose face peeked out—Amadea Gintanas's or Lireana Ulanitti's. Amadea swallowed.

"I don't think you're going mad, Your Majesty," she said. "But I do think you are under a great deal of strain, and this isn't a situation that will solve itself in one fell swoop. In the meantime...the empire needs you."

Beneditta shook her head absently. "It seems so little of this will matter if Redolfo Kirazzi has sent changelings to sabotage me."

"But if we are talking about the simple problems of an empire," Amadea said, "then misinterpreting the sabotage will make it worse. You're watching. Your agents are watching—Lady Sigrittrice, the consort-prince. Have they found anything?"

"No," Beneditta spat. "But that doesn't mean there's nothing to find."

"It doesn't," Amadea said. She hesitated. "Is there someone, some advisor you could discuss this with?"

"No one wants to believe what we're dealing with. No one

wants to connect all these signs." Beneditta paused. "This theft, this saint—what if it's connected?"

Amadea thought of the Kirazzi map, the unidentified peddler—it felt like it ought to fit...and yet... "There's no reason to think that. This is just a...well, not an ordinary problem of the archives but not a problem of the empire."

Beneditta huffed out a breath and shut her eyes. "This is what you do, isn't it? For the archives. People think it's all adjusting cold-magic and filing reports, but you handle the people. You get them to sort out their problems. Get them to talk."

Amadea looked away. "Apologies, Your Majesty. I thought I was helping."

"I didn't say you weren't." Beneditta picked up the discarded mask, considering the curved interior of it. "My agents, as you put it, tell me Ibramo has been visiting the archives repeatedly of late."

Amadea nodded, remembering the feeling of Ibramo's hand folding around her own, remembering the frantic kiss in the tunnel beneath the Salt Wall, those too-close moments in the galleries. *We're in this together*, he'd said, *that counts for something.*

"Yes," Amadea said. "He said he's looking for possible tunnels beneath the Salt Wall. I showed him a map."

Beneditta's mouth was small, tight, and her eyes didn't leave the mask's curved interior. "Has he found anything?"

Amadea held her expression very still. Was Ibramo not telling Beneditta what his search was turning up? "He didn't say," she lied. "I think...I think the possibility of his father's crimes being unfinished has shaken him."

Beneditta sighed but said nothing. At last, she slipped the mask on, her features vanishing into its blunt golden countenance. "You may go," she said.

Amadea curtsied and moved toward the door that led to the Court of the Noble Consuls, but then Beneditta called her back. "Archivist Gintanas?" she said, all formality again. "Should I call for you again...to discuss...without the mask...?" She cleared her throat.

Amadea hesitated. For all it was not done for the empress to address her subjects unmasked and open, for all Beneditta's attention stirred a worry deep within Amadea that she might be treading too close to the life that had put both her and the empire itself into danger... Amadea could see Beneditta desperately needed a friend.

"Of course, Your Majesty," Amadea said. "Whenever you wish."

She passed through the door and the court beyond, the large room empty but for a few aides still chatting as they gathered their superiors' belongings. She felt their gazes flick uneasily over her as she collected her cloak, as if the empress's demands might have left marks upon Amadea that spelled out the origins of her outburst.

Amadea ignored them, drawing a long, slow, steadying breath. If there was anything she could offer Beneditta, either to soothe her worries or direct her attention, it would lie in the primate's files. It had to.

And if Ibramo knew anything he wasn't telling the empress...

She took out the small notepad she kept always in her pocket and wrote a note: *To His Highness, Consort-Prince Ibramo, may I request your audience soon? I have more information on that which you requested. I am the empire's humble dedicant, Archivist Superior Amadea Gintanas.* She folded it neatly and brought it to the guard standing before the noble consuls' chamber, trying not to read anything into the fine expressions of their face when she declared it for Ibramo. She left the court and made her way down the hallways of the Imperial Complex, back toward the exit.

Blue flowers, she thought, anchoring her mind on those things she could see. *Bronze vase. Paper scroll. Silver hair—*

"Archivist Gintanas?" Nanqii ul-Hanizan was waiting at the end of the hallway, perched on a plush bench. "I was wondering where you'd gone. May I walk you out?"

Amadea blinked at him, too full of unsolvable problems to recognize such a simple question. "Walk me out?"

"Yes," he said, standing. "From the palace? I assume you weren't planning to take up residence?"

Amadea gave a polite laugh. "Apologies. As you can imagine, I have a great deal on my mind."

"The reza ul-Shandiian does have quite the ability to infuriate a whole room of people all at once." He took her by the arm, and they began walking out of the Imperial Complex. "And now it seems I need to make space in my home for a literal saint."

"He has concerns that merit attention," Amadea said, "and the Imperial Archives are grateful for the opportunity to address them."

"Which will matter not at all to Dushar, I suspect." His eyes danced as he grinned at her. "Don't worry, I can say that, you can't. I understand."

She smiled but kept her voice polite as she said, "The archives appreciate ul-Hanizan's forbearance. We're doing our best."

Outside, people bustled through the streets, clutching their cloaks close against the brisk autumn wind. Amadea buttoned hers one-handed as Nanqii led her along the winding road down the hill.

"I suppose someone will need to come assess your facilities," Amadea said.

He leaned in just a little bit. "Well, you can do that, can't you?" he said. "Come for dinner. Assess my facilities and...talk awhile."

"As pleasant as I'm sure that would be," Amadea said, "I refer you back to the many things on my mind. I'm afraid I have to return to the archives. I'll make sure you have a specialist and support to approve your vault before the end of the day."

Nanqii's voice did not shed its teasing tones as he said, "Would it change your mind if I told you this dinner comes with a very compelling final course?"

"I'm sure you promise that to all your dalliances," Amadea returned. "But alas, duty calls."

He was so close now that he spoke softly into her ear as he said, "You don't remember me, do you? I suppose I should have expected that."

Ah. *Quite a churn of young men*—it hadn't been so many, really. Not so many she would have forgotten...Had she forgotten? She looked askance at Nanqii ul-Hanizan, considering his face, the softness of his smirk. He was handsome—she wouldn't have minded his company in another place and time. Maybe she hadn't?

"Esinor, if this was all an attempt to renew an assignation..." she began.

"My, but you do continue to return to the topic of my bed," he said, that teasing tone returned. "You were a child. I was hardly more than one myself."

Dread unfolded in Amadea's chest. "A child?" she managed.

"Oh yes. I was sent to spy for my grandfather," he said softly. "In the Usurper's palace. To procure things for the Usurper and see which way the wind blew the chaff. And you, I think, were Lireana. You were the Grave-Spurned Princess."

CHAPTER TEN

There was no degree of stillness, of coolness that could make Amadea vanish from Nanqii's sight. She froze, nevertheless, her breath trapped in her lungs, her mind spinning out of control. Her memories flooded with people at Sestina, Terzanelle, Shadorma, more, searching for a pale-haired horned man among them, until she felt as if she *were* standing before that ever-changing crowd.

"I don't know who that is," she managed to say, her voice careful but too flat, a hard board across the roiling fear that surged in her. She turned from him, searching the crowd for things she could anchor her thoughts on. *Green cloak. Fur hat. Red skirt.*

"Don't you?" She could feel Nanqii's gaze on her face. "That seems odd. She was infamous. Redolfo's pretender. Lireana Ulanitti back from the dead, demanding her father's throne. *Beneditta's* throne," he added. He moved around her so that she had to look him in the eye. "Seems to me, even if you aren't her, surely you would know who the Grave-Spurned Princess is. And how she vanished after the coup was crushed."

The memories swelled and threatened to split her mind in two. She felt as if she watched herself from outside once more—an expression like glass, hard and cold and full of nothing at all. *Redolfo in a dark room, Fastreda beside him playing with the remnants of a glass, a petitioner— she couldn't fit a face to them. But she could feel Redolfo behind her—*

"Are you with me, esinora?" Nanqii asked.

She turned away, looked at the bookshop they were passing, counted the spines on the shelf beside the door. *Eight. Nine. Ten. Eleven.*

"It sounds to me as if you're confessing to treason, esinor," she said. "But that would be foolish."

"Very foolish," Nanqii agreed. He tilted his head, his charms clinking. "Does the empress know?"

"The empress is privy to all the records of the Usurper's coup and the trials that followed," Amadea said. "She is aware of plenty."

"My, my, that's almost a threat," Nanqii said.

"And what is it you're doing?" Amadea returned.

"You wound me, esinora," Nanqii said. "This isn't a threat. It's an overture. Beginning with the trade I'm offering."

That was worse. "What? Has Bishamar Twelve-Spider finally decided to sign on for the coup? My apologies, the Usurper isn't taking any more alliances."

Or is he? a little voice in her whispered. *Out beyond the Salt Wall, still planning, still preparing . . .*

Nanqii shrugged. "What can we do but respond to the moment? I wouldn't suggest the Usurper is looking, only that not everyone who sided with him was punished, and I think that puts the empire in a perilous position."

Amadea's cheeks burned as she thought of herself. There had been no trial for the Grave-Spurned Princess, only years of arguing and debating and negotiating what was to be done with her, while she hid in Sestina, trapped and spinning solutions with Ibramo that would never come to pass.

"The empress is secure," she said.

"Do you really think that? Esinora, are you aware that today's . . . performance by the empress is only the latest in a series of worrying events? Rumors abound. Memories of the Fratricide. You know Vigilant Langyun. Do you know what his last case uncovered? The murder of Lord Obigen? Did he tell you the tool used?"

Amadea hesitated. "The Venom of Changelings."

"Redolfo Kirazzi's apocryphal mind-control poison," Nanqii agreed. "I was at the party where Obigen was killed—maybe Richa told you that—which means I was dosed by Rosangerda Maschano with the Venom of Changelings. And what I remember is the empress being there . . . but then she wasn't. And I'm not the only one that's true of. I think the empress was there, and she was dosed too. The Imperial Authority insists that's not true, that this was part of Lady Maschano's plans, putting the empress in all our thoughts."

"That is how it works," Amadea murmured. *The needle goes into her arm with a pop, and she clutches the slick skin of the pillow tighter...*

"You'd know better than I would," Nanqii said. He lowered his voice. "In fact, if anyone can tell if the empress is under the effects of a mind-control poison, it seems as if it should be you."

"She's not," Amadea said. *Not like you think*, she added to herself, thinking of the great lie the whole empire rested on: the empress could not be controlled like a normal person, thank the gods in every gate, but because the empress was part changeling, she was already under control.

"I can't say what's more comforting," Nanqii replied. "Our empress compromised or our empress in full possession of her faculties lashing out at the ducal authorities, the noble consuls? But that's only the beginning. There are rumors of a final stand near Sestina, a fire, a collapse in the tombs. Ibramo Kirazzi out of favor. Soldiers aren't supposed to talk, but suddenly, I see a lot more iron talismans among the peddlers. Changelings in the shadows. People testing the iron like the old days.

"And now...a missing saint," he went on, watching her closely. "And ul-Shandiian demanding the whole chapel. The empress threatening the ducal authority. Something is brewing, Archivist Gintanas. All I'm asking for is a meeting. You and the reza ul-Hanizan, and myself. Sit down. Make your case. Perhaps you can reassure us all the empress is in her right mind, that she has you to lean on. Or"—he drew the word out—"that you are a viable alternative if a regime change is required. A regent for the crown prince if you wish. And in exchange...I will tell you who may deserve closer scrutiny. For the good of the empire."

"I think, for the good of the empire, we shouldn't even be discussing this."

"Discussing isn't deciding," Nanqii said. "And you haven't heard what I'm offering in exchange."

"There is nothing—" she began.

"Did you know Bishamar Twelve-Spider was a friend of Redolfo Kirazzi?" Nanqii interjected. "Do you know that before they fell out, he had...an awareness of this plan to find one of the lost princesses?" He leaned forward. "Did you know they say Bishamar was the one who found Lireana Ulanitti?"

All of Amadea's buzzing, stuttering memories froze, her breath caught in her mouth. *Redolfo Kirazzi, his eyes shining. "We found you in Sestina. They will be so grateful to have you back." Hope blooming warm in her chest, a safety she hadn't thought to imagine before—*

"No," she said.

Nanqii held her gaze. "It's a terrible thing," he said. "Not knowing where you came from."

"I do know," she said—she lied. "I was given to the abbey at Gintanas."

"Then you should have absolutely no fear of what Bishamar Twelve-Spider can tell you," Nanqii said. "And it would be wise to have him on your side, to be clear. Especially with Dushar Six-Agamid turned against you."

Amadea drew a long, slow breath, pushing off the memories that threatened to wrench her from the present. She was *here* and *now*, and there was no hiding from Nanqii's accusation, his offer. She'd been caught off guard and hadn't deflected the way she should have—but then, it had been so long since someone had noticed any likeness and so recent that she'd said the words out loud herself: *I was the Grave-Spurned Princess.*

But one thing she knew for certain, standing in the middle of this square, surrounded by dozens of people who had no idea what was happening: if she made this agreement, it was the first step on the same path Redolfo had charted for her years and years ago. To admit to Lireana, to admit there was still a question in anyone's mind about Beneditta's legitimacy, was to pull bricks loose in the foundation of the empire.

And now was not the time for that.

"I will meet with Bishamar Twelve-Spider," she said. "But I will tell you again: whatever you think I am, I am only an archivist superior. I am not the person you're looking for."

He leaned in once more, conspiratorial as he said, "If I were you, I wouldn't assume what the reza ul-Hanizan is looking for." He straightened and smiled. "Do you like eel? My cook mentioned he got a lovely fresh pot of them this morning, and he does a dish somewhere between a Semillan curry and a Beminat green sauce that is a revelation with eel."

⊶ ⚏ ⊷

Light spilled across Richa's face, jerking him from an uneasy sleep. "There you are," he heard Hulvia say. "What are you doing sleeping in the duty room? It's past midday."

Richa's thoughts pulled back together. He sat up, his back stiff, his muscles protesting, and stretched. "I took an overnight firewatch shift," he said, his voice snagging in his dry throat. "Did you bring coffee?"

"No, get it yourself. Why are you taking firewatch? That's cadet work."

Richa pulled on his shirt, deciding whether to ignore the question. The night before, he'd cleared off the worst of the files his desk had collected while he'd been in Ragale and learned that the best the Kinship's ink-readers could glean from the peddler's palimpsests was that there were indeed years' worth of writing layered on top of one another.

Stymied, he headed home with a copy of the peddler's map and the notes he'd taken on the archives' thefts and a half bottle of wine. He'd been thinking about whether he ought to have taken all three of these things back to Amadea as he laid the coins on the altar like usual—

And found again, the dog icon tipped over.

"I couldn't sleep," Richa lied to Hulvia. "Why are you hunting me down in the duty room?"

"I thought you'd want to know your chaos with the archives skeletons just got a lot more chaotic," she said. "The Orozhandi called the noble consuls to a meeting, none of the rezas are happy with the archives, but they can't agree on what to do, and now there's a whole riptide rolling through them, because guess who the empress decreed is the proper neutral party to hold on to the wooden saint?"

Richa sighed. "Us. I'll get a vault cleared."

"Wrong!" Hulvia said with a vicious glee. "Nanqii Four-Fucking-Oryx ul-Hanizan."

"What? Why?"

"Far as I can tell, she's spitting mad at the reza ul-Shandiian who wants the bones—all the bones—moved to Maqama. So this is what he gets, and it's the archives' problem whether it's reasonable. They're supposed to transfer them *today*, which I don't know how they're going to manage. Anyway, the Imperial Authority will provide an honor guard, but rules are the Kinship sends four as well. Pick out some cadets who clean up nice and make sure the mortuary is ready for the imposter skeleton."

Richa gave her a sarcastic salute and finished pulling the rest of his uniform on, mustering his energy, dwelling on the dog.

Maybe it was the door sticking, he thought. Maybe it was his neighbors downstairs slamming a door, rattling the wall and knocking over the icon.

Maybe someone was poking around his apartment.

He had done a slow circuit of the room, looking for things out of place, trying to remember if he'd folded the blanket that way, if he'd set the pitcher down like that. If the knife had been on the top of the table, not back in the box where he usually kept it.

The knife was what made him lose his nerve, lying clean on the cutting board. It was an old blade, one of the only things he'd brought with him from Caesura, but it still kept an edge. The handle was polished horn, the grip worn smooth from years of use. But... he hadn't used it yesterday.

He'd bought food off the vendor last night and stopped at a coffeehouse that morning, so there'd been nothing he'd needed to cut up. Had it been there since the night before, or earlier?

He couldn't remember. And he couldn't shake the knowledge that it was the only thing he could think of in the whole apartment that he'd had in Caesura, and Salva Gaitha-hyu was implying Stellano had been in the relay station. And his dog icon kept falling over.

Richa checked the lock on the door—the best he could find, built around a sliver of cold-magic that should shut the whole thing down if someone tried to work picks in them and wasn't very, very skilled. Nothing. The door was fine. The window faced the street and was too high to get to without attracting a lot of attention. He was safe. Stellano wasn't here.

But the apartment had felt like a changeling of itself, and rather than sleep there, Richa had locked it back up and retreated to the Kinship Hall and the duty room and a very long night that bled into a restless morning.

He got up and came out into the main duty room, where he called up six older cadets and sent them to get dress uniforms for the translation of the saint. He then went downstairs to where the cells and vaults and mortuary room were and let the vigilants on duty know the unidentified skeleton from the chapel was coming and needed to be stored as evidence. Then he pulled his cloak on and headed to the archives.

Vigilant Gaitha-hyu's accusations still rattled Richa. He hadn't thought about Stellano in years—at first by sheer force of will and then, eventually, by hard-won habit. He could remember the streets of Caesura and the rooms he'd lived in and Egillio curled by the door without the memory of Stellano intruding. But now Stellano was seeping up through the surface of his mind, like smoke oozing out of a house you hadn't yet realized was burning down.

When he thought about those years in Caesura, it sometimes felt like he was thinking about a different man—a kid, really. That other self was quick and impulsive and very good at pretending he wasn't scared out of his mind. He was too eager for someone else to have the answers and too full of bravado to understand that need was in him, that lodestone heart always pulling toward someone who had it figured out.

He didn't think, looking back, fifteen years on, that Stellano had figured anything out, but saints and devils, Richa could admit even now that he had been good at pretending. Confident, careless—the way Stellano moved through the world, you would be excused for thinking it just naturally bent out of his way. And after enough years of that confidence, well, maybe it started to be true: you did not fuck with Stellano Zezurin.

That hadn't been how it started. Stellano had been just a kid once too. He liked to show off, to be the center of things—in fact, if Richa didn't ask him how his day was, Stellano would inevitably wilt at being ignored, curling up around Richa's dog and burying his face in Egillio's red fur. He liked to share his successes and be the one who knew where pitfalls were waiting for the young thieves of Caesura—the ones Stellano liked, anyway. He was magnetic to them, amassing a small army of worshipful urchins eager to hear his teachings, when other thieves stayed territorial.

"Good updraft carries all birds alike," Stellano used to say. "If there's enough of us, the vigilants can't track us all. Besides, look at their little faces—how could you not help them learn a trade?"

More and more, though, Richa was the only one Stellano was willing to be weak in front of—with those other thieves, the ones who wanted to claim he was working their territory, he was terrifying.

"Don't worry about it, Pigeon," he'd say, planting a quick kiss on Richa before he left for the night. "You hate blood."

He still told Richa exactly what he'd done those nights. He was sullen if Richa didn't ask.

And when he started branching out, started dealing with those other thieves—suddenly, Richa was crossing lines to ask where he was, what he'd been doing. When he asked who was that person he'd seen Stellano talking to, where had he been all night, why was there blood on his cuffs—Stellano shut him out, called him jealous. Turned vicious.

He held Richa at arm's length while he made friends with all the monsters.

And then, when it had come down to it, Stellano had crossed every line, broken every promise in one bloody night, and turned on Richa when he hadn't thanked him.

Richa put Stellano out of mind as he reached the archives and saw Amadea returning just ahead of him. Her uniform was different—formal for court, he thought. A cape-like jacket cut high in the front and flowing long over skirts whose hems were stiff with embroidery, elaborate letters of many languages interlocked into one puzzle-like promise: *What is past is our duty and our honor.*

He sprinted to catch up to her, reaching the door alongside her. "Good morning," he said.

Amadea looked up at him, and a smile papered over the worry in her expression. "Good *afternoon*," she corrected. "Long night?"

"Fires don't put themselves out," he said. "I'm going to ask if you have a minute, but I've already heard you probably don't?"

She sighed. "No. Tunuk came back, by the way. I was planning to bring him to you around now. But they want the bones moved today."

"To Nanqii ul-Hanizan's house," he said. "What a fellow for the empress to make a point on."

Amadea tilted her head, looking concerned. "Do you know him?"

"Yeah, we've crossed paths," Richa said. "He sells a lot of things. Rumor is substances the Imperial Authority prefers he wouldn't. But we never catch him with it, and he knows it. Plus, do you know he's Bishamar Twelve-Spider's grandson?"

Amadea nodded, her gaze drifting past him around the room. "I'm supposed to have dinner with him after I review their vault."

An odd pang went through Richa. "With *Nanqii*?"

"And hopefully the reza."

Which was unsettling in a very different way, Richa thought—you didn't just *talk* to Bishamar Twelve-Spider—but it soothed that odd worry. *You're being an idiot*, he thought.

"Mireia wants me to do more of the political side of the archives' work," Amadea went on, "to prepare to succeed her, but..." She glanced around the hall again, empty but for the archivist at the reception desk. "I'm not sure I can handle one more problem," she confessed. "And he is most certainly going to be a problem. And then I think none of this might even matter! What's happening out there might make all of it moot."

Richa thought of the camp in the forest, the other side of the Salt Wall. "Did you look through those files?"

"I haven't had the time," she said. "What I found was just... bureaucracy."

"Sounds like the Paremi."

"Ibramo says they haven't found any other entry points," she went on. "Lady Sigrittrice is sure there's nothing to be found. But the empress is talking like we're about to have a war, and—"

"Slow down," he said. "It is a lot. But it's not all on you. The Imperial Authority is 'the Imperial Authority' for a reason. I'm with you on going through the files for evidence, but what's on the other side of the Wall is not either of our responsibility."

Doubt etched itself in her lovely features, but she smiled still, as if she appreciated the effort, and he decided to stop being quite such an idiot.

"How about this?" he said. "After you have dinner with Nanqii, I will take you out for a coffee, and we can talk about the files and maybe what I found out about someone stealing from the archives."

She frowned. "Someone's stealing from the archives?"

"Previously," he said. "And I need to talk to Archivist del Tolube. But . . . can I meet you at Nanqii's? When you're done?"

Amadea blinked at him, clearly surprised, but then a small smile curved her lips. "All right," she said decisively. "I tell them all the time to take breaks. This . . . this will be good."

"Perfect," he said, matching her smile.

The doors to the archives opened, the great opal mosaics depicting representatives of the protectorates defending the empire against the changeling threat splitting as Yinii exited, dressed to go out. She saw Amadea, and a sudden guilty look washed over her face.

"Yinii," Amadea said pleasantly, "would you go get Tunuk before you go out? Unless you're in a hurry?" *Where are you going?* She didn't say.

"He's . . . he went out. But he'll come back," Yinii added quickly. "They said they were going back to talk to Chizid's brother and then the Kinship Hall right after."

"And when was that?" Amadea asked.

Yinii wove her fingers together, flustered.

"If they go to the Kinship Hall, someone will come find me," Richa said. "And if they don't, I'll find them. For now, I found something I wanted to follow up on. Bijan reported some stolen sapphires three years ago. I'm wondering if our thief started small."

"Oh!" Yinii said.

"I don't know if that's a good idea," Amadea said. "Bijan's still... not happy about what you did to Stavio. In the coffee shop."

Right—Richa had convinced one of the bronze specialists, who was in alignment at the time and not meant to be handling bronze, to look at some evidence for him and wound up finding out *why* specialists in alignment weren't meant to handle their affinity materials. Bijan must have been the frantic man who'd come in with Amadea when she'd realized what Richa had done.

"I do think he was angrier at Stavio," Yinii offered.

"He's allowed to be angry at me," Richa said. "I messed up. But this might be important. It might lead to the skeleton theft."

"I'll take him," Yinii offered.

Amadea's gaze flicked to Yinii's gloved hands. "You don't need—"

"I can keep her away from the ink," Richa said. "Go do your work."

Reluctantly Amadea left. When she'd gone, Yinii said, "You know it's not... it's not about keeping me away from ink."

"Fair," Richa said. "I wouldn't make a good generalist, I'm thinking." He offered her a friendly smile. "It's funny you call them that."

"It's because they can go to any of the collections," Yinii said. "They're not bound by an affinity."

"But they have a specialty," he countered. "At least, I think Ama—Archivist Gintanas's specialty is you all."

"Sometimes." She fidgeted with the gloves she wore. "Um, Bijan's workroom is this way."

She didn't say much as she led him into the archives, up the iron stairs and along the open walkways that looked over the sorting facilities. Archivists in blue robes and leather aprons passed them, carrying heavy ledgers and crates of materials, greeting Yinii with nods as they passed, and looking curiously at Richa.

On the highest floor, on the southern side of the building, Yinii pulled open a door and led him into a room shaped like a long triangle. Tall windows along the outside wall let in plenty of light, which winked and glittered on an array of small items on a velvet-covered worktable.

A compact dark-skinned man, his hair in braids tight against his scalp, Bijan del Tolube stood bent over this treasure, tweezers in one hand, a pick in the other. Cold-magic lamps had been propped close on either side of him, and magnifying lenses distorted his eyes. His soft smile, however, suggested for all his gaze was locked on the project before him, he had one ear on the raucous conversation.

"So then this man, he's so upset. He's screaming—screaming his head off," Stavio Jeudi, one of the bronze archivists, said, his mottled tentacles waving lazily around him in a halo. He was perched on an Ashtabari-style leaning stool, his broad chest resting fully against it. "'Ah, my gods! Ah, my saints and devils! Ah, I've been poisoned! Curse on your clan, curse on your children, curse, curse, curse!'"

Near him, a young blond woman perched on a smaller work-table with her knees crossed up under her. Zoifia Kestustis, Richa remembered. Another of Amadea's bronze specialists. She looked up and spotted Yinii, giving the other woman a small wave and a raised eyebrow.

"But then my grandfather, he just looks at him like this—" Stavio leveled a fierce dark glare over his bent nose at Zoifia. From the waist up, the Ashtabari archivist might have been mistaken for a handsome, well-muscled, and slightly thick human, olive-skinned and crowned with shining black curls. But from the waist down, his body split into eight thick tentacles dappled green and brown.

"He looks at this man, this olozo," Stavio went on, "and he says, just like this, cold as iron, he says: 'The only curse on you is the one coming up on your bowels. Nobody brought cakes. You ate the soap.'"

Zoifia burst into a cackle of laughter. "That did *not* happen!"

"It's true," Stavio protested. "I was there."

"He ate a cake of soap without realizing it was soap?" Zoifia said skeptically. "What do Ashtabari make soap out of? Honey and groundnuts?"

"Sorcha!" Stavio spat, but he chuckled too. "I tell you it happened."

"Can we come in?" Yinii called.

Stavio turned. "Hey, odidunu, what are you..." He trailed off, his eyes finding Richa. Stavio turned to Bijan, alert.

"I had some questions for Archivist del Tolube," Richa said.

Bijan jerked up, startled from his work. He pulled the goggles off and blinked his brown eyes exaggeratedly, clearing them. Something lay in pieces on the board before him, beads laid in lines and broken shards of wood laid out in the shape of a rough triangle...

And Richa realized what Bijan was working on: those were the pieces of the broken and burned Flail of Khirazj. The last he had seen the ancient artifact, a changeling wearing Redolfo Kirazzi's face had taken it, dying in the tunnel that Yinii soon set ablaze and partially brought down.

"I can't believe they recovered it," Richa said.

Bijan was regarding him, his expression cold. "Does Amadea know you're here this time?"

"Bedo," Stavio said cajolingly. He slid off the stool and came to stand next to his husband. "You're not still mad about *that*."

Bijan turned back to Stavio, pushing a lock of his loose hair behind one ear. "He put you into danger."

"It wasn't so bad," Stavio said. "I mean, you're not mad at *me*, right? And that was a lot of me doing something dangerous. This isn't dangerous." He frowned at Richa. "It's not, is it?"

"It's about some missing sapphires," Richa said. "You reported the theft of three stones created by Aungwi of the Corundum three years back."

Bijan folded his arms. "I told the vigilants what I knew when I reported them missing."

"You were thorough," Richa agreed. "With the span of time they could have gone missing in, it's hard to pinpoint who took them."

"Yeah, well, there's only one of me," Bijan said. "Which the vigilant at the time seemed to think meant I was the one who took them. As if there aren't a hundred more valuable stones in this room. As if *I* can't tell which they are."

Richa leaned on the table edge. "Let's assume for a moment that it's not about the *sapphires*," he said. "Let's assume that whoever stole the gems stole them because they were *sorcerer wrought*. Is there any reason you can think of that they would do that?"

Bijan regarded him, puzzled. "No. I assume some generalist or support worker just thought they wouldn't be missed."

"Is that truer of those stones than any other ones?" Richa said. "Like you said, there's a hundred more valuable stones. So why those three? What's different about sorcerer-wrought artifacts?" When Bijan shook his head, Richa tried a different approach. "You can tell when a gem is sorcerer wrought instead of naturally occurring, right?"

Zoifia snorted again.

"Of course," Bijan said.

"Everyone can," Stavio added. "Everyone with an affinity can tell something's sorcerer wrought in their own material, I mean."

"Why?" Richa asked. "What's different about them?"

Bijan exchanged a glance with Stavio. "It's...Look, gemstones have a...structure to them. They're crystals, and the...Imagine it's a tiny house. The bricks all line up in a certain way for a certain kind of gem. And you know what the bricks are made of. So, the same way you can look at a building and say, 'Yes, that's from Old Semilla,' or 'That one had a Datongu-inspired builder,' I can tell whether the gemstones are corundum. There will be other minerals in them, that's what makes the colors different and really determines..."

Stavio made a small sound in the back of his throat, and Bijan started again. "Never mind, that part doesn't matter. The paint on the house changes depending on where you build it. The roof might be different. Even if the houses are all in the same place, they're just a little different."

"I can't tell if this is a terrible story or a very smart example," Stavio said.

"Terrible," Zoifia piped up.

"Both of you hush," Bijan said. "Sorcerer-wrought gems... they're...too perfect? All the bricks in the house are exactly straight, all the mortar is perfectly smooth. The paint is immaculate. No matter where that house is, it stands out because a house isn't *supposed* to be like that. But more than that..." He looked at Stavio again, searching for words. "They do the thing."

"They do the thing," Stavio agreed.

Richa shook his head. "Which means?"

"You're not going to understand it," Zoifia said.

"Sorcerer-wrought stuff is like a tiny spiral," Stavio said.

"I wouldn't say that," Bijan interjected.

"Shush, it's my turn to tell a terrible story," Stavio said. "Like this: Like you hear a song? You hear a song, you can't see who's singing it, and maybe it's the song your granny used to sing to you. Something special that makes you feel at home and safe. But the one singing it, they have the key just a little off. Maybe they sing it too slow. It's something you want and something you want to fix, both at the same time. Because it's not quite right. But all you can do is listen."

"That I will agree with," Bijan said. "That's a really good way to describe it."

Richa considered the broken Flail of Khirazj. "Do they have... some of that affinity magic in them, then?"

All three specialists looked at Richa, confused. "How can a *thing* have an affinity?" Stavio asked.

"It feels similar," Yinii said. Richa turned to look at her. The girl had a somber, haunted sort of look, staring at the fragmented Flail of Khirazj. "If you're around a sorcerer, it can...it can sort of feel like you're standing at the edge of a spiral. Like if you weren't careful, you could just fall into it. And sorcerer-wrought things...Stavio's right, they're like a tiny spiral. But they can't affect other objects. I don't think."

She looked up and flushed—all three specialists had transferred their stare from Richa to Yinii, alarm in their expressions. "I just... It's sort of like that," Yinii managed.

"Did you spiral again?" Zoifia demanded, climbing off the table.

Stavio pushed past Richa, coming around the table to press a hand to Yinii's cheek. "You're kinda clammy. What's the vigilant making you do?"

"Stop it!" Yinii shouted, swatting Stavio's hand away. "I'm *fine*, and all he did was ask me to walk him up here."

Richa searched her, trying to see what the others were seeing. She looked tired, distracted, as if she had at least three other things on her mind, but she needed a nap first.

But something had triggered alarm in the other specialists.

"You're not in alignment," Zoifia said. "Why are you spiraling? Is it Quill? I bet it's Quill. I bet he's actually horrible at this—"

"Will you stop it, you sorcha?" Stavio said. Then: "Let her tell it."

"*Both* of you stop it," Bijan said. "Yinii, you do look a little peaked. Where's Radir?"

She did look peaked, but Richa had to assume people shouting questions at her wasn't helping. "I wasn't done asking questions," he said. "Those stones aren't the only unresolved theft of a small sorcerer-wrought artifact. There are three others. If there's *any* reason you can think of that might explain why someone would steal those specific items, I am very curious."

The three of them looked from one to the other, as if the answer lay in one of their minds. Bijan at last turned back to Richa. "You might," he said, "ask someone from the Kuali protectorate. Someone who, you know, follows the old ways," he amended, which made Richa guess at least some of Bijan's family had been from al-Kual. "Sorcerer-wrought stuff is supposed to be lucky, how they tell it. Maybe someone's stealing it for that reason."

"Interesting," Richa said. Very interesting—Chizid del Hwana had been Kuali *and* in the archives. Was there anything in his life that had warranted accumulating that much luck? Something where that luck's failure might have led to murder? "I'll have to look into that."

"Why would they *bother*?" Zoifia said. "You can just *buy* sorcerer-wrought junk from sorcerers. I think you're just looking for a weirdo. Someone who collects stuff. We get a lot of those." She turned back to Yinii. "You should go up to sequestration to wait for Radir. I'll take you."

"Actually, Yinii, I got a little turned around, and I know Amadea wanted you to run that errand," Richa said. "Do you think you could walk me out now?"

She looked up at him, her eyes bright with gratitude, and nodded quickly.

"I'll be in touch if I find anything out," Richa said to the others. "Thank you for your time."

As he followed Yinii out of the room, he heard Stavio's muttered voice. "Maybe it's Radir. Tunuk spiraled with Radir."

"Shush," Bijan said, as the door closed behind Richa. "You know it's not that."

Richa wondered how much they knew. How much of what had

happened in the tunnel below the Salt Wall had been shared by the archives' protocol, how much had raced through the workrooms as gossip. How much was written on Yinii's tense expression.

Yinii had said everything was fine... but even looking at the way the girl held herself, he knew that was a lie. She looked as if she were twisted tight around her own spine like a rope wound around a spike.

What was she? Seventeen? Eighteen? Gods, at that age he'd been so deep into trouble he couldn't even tell how it was wearing on him. Him and Stellano and a burgeoning flock of little thieves hanging on his every word. They were going to make something of themselves, even if Caesura was fighting them every step—but somehow, Richa had known even then, deep down, for him it wasn't going anywhere good.

But now you're here, he thought. And how much of Stellano and Caesura and all the dark days were necessary to that? He didn't like to dwell on it.

"It will be all right," he offered to Yinii. "Whatever it is."

She looked back over her shoulder as she descended the next staircase, utterly confused. "If... you don't know what it is, how can you say that?"

"Because it's usually true," he said. "You just keep looking forward. Keep moving. This will all be behind you someday."

Yinii regarded him, still puzzled. "It's what happened in the tunnel. That's what I'm worried about. Do you still think I should 'keep looking forward'?"

Richa hesitated, remembering Yinii's fathomless black eyes, the screams of the Shrike as she'd broken the assassin apart. "Yes. Yes, I do. It was one moment. One bad day. You can leave that behind."

"Or it's just in you forever."

"I don't believe that," Richa said, and he found that he meant it, even though a flicker of worry rose up in him—for her, for himself. "Do you believe that?"

Yinii stared at him a moment longer, then went back to walking. "I don't know."

For a strange moment, Richa thought about telling her everything: about who he'd been in Caesura, about Stellano, about Salva's implications, and about the fact he did sometimes still use his lock-picks. But just as swiftly, he buried the thoughts. It was the past, as good as dead. This girl didn't need his problems. No one did.

"Well," he said, as they came through the doors to the entry hall again, "you're the only person who is really going to know *you*. But I have some faith that you're surrounded by people right now who would tell you if there was something about you that was danger-ous or bad. I mean, we just left a room of your friends who were all ready to do everything they could think of to make sure you were safe."

"Including lock me up?"

Richa frowned. "Is that something you're worried about?"

Yinii sighed. "No. Sorry." She turned to face him. "You have that ink page still? The palimpsest from the peddler?"

"I do," Richa said carefully.

"I'm not in alignment. I could look at it," she offered. "I have to meet someone, but I could come by afterward. To the Kinship Hall."

"I feel like Archivist Gintanas would have an opinion about that."

"Do you have another plan?" she asked bluntly. And he didn't. Not a one. The pages were unreadable tangles of ink, and no one in the Kinship could pull it apart. When he didn't say anything, Yinii nodded. "All right. Then I will come to the Kinship Hall tonight," she said, and left him standing on the archives' steps.

CHAPTER ELEVEN

The manor owned by the ul-Shandiian clan was an old, pre-Sealing building, lichen-stained pilasters topped with mask-and-wheat-sheaf capitals in the old Semillan style still visible behind the red saints'-skull-adorned banners that signaled the current residence of the reza ul-Shandiian. The interior was more traditional: Murals on the walls, wool carpets on the stone floor. Cold-magic lamps turned down low as one passed deeper into the building. It was a handsome house, Yinii thought, and it did nothing to calm her nerves.

Oshanna met Yinii in a small sitting room near the back of the house, a pot of coffee and a plate of cakes with almonds pressed into the tops waiting for them. She offered the proper greetings and smiled when Yinii entered, but it didn't seem to meet her glittering dark eyes.

"I'm sorry Tunuk couldn't come," Yinii said.

"It's all right," Oshanna said. "Has ul-Benturan heard about the noble consuls' meeting yet?"

"I heard from my superior," Yinii said. "I can only imagine what Reza Dolitha would have to say."

"Yes, well, the reza ul-Shandiian is not pleased, as you can guess." Oshanna sipped her coffee. "He's been under a lot of stress."

Yinii took her own cup, looking around the room, wondering where to start. Her thoughts wouldn't settle—the peddler's palimpsest, the sorcerer transfers, the wooden bones—so she took a moment to admire the room. Dark walls and a bright woolen rug patterned with flowers. High-backed couches around a low wooden table. A red-tiled hearth with a low crackling fire in it. A small altar to the side, four white candles on a bed of grain.

"Oh!" Yinii said. "Has someone died?"

Oshanna glanced at the altar. "Yes—well, not exactly. It's a memorial. An anniversary. My father's actually. I build it every year around Sixteen-Spider. Usually I try to go back to Maqama, but this year, it won't be possible." She sighed. "I miss him very much, but the world keeps turning."

Nimar Eight-Myrrh, Yinii recalled. Qalba's cousin who'd brought Oshanna to the Bone Vault. Dushar's son.

Yinii wondered why it was tucked away in this little room, a memorial for the reza's son, but she knew better than to ask such a personal question. "I'm sorry," she said.

Oshanna nodded in thanks. "You had questions about Aunt Qalba."

"Yes, if it's not too much. I . . . Tunuk . . ."

"Who can't come on his own." She smiled wryly, her eyes down as she plucked a cake from the plate. "I suppose there are too many bad feelings tangled up in these memories."

What had Tunuk said? *A smug and preening little know-it-all at six-teen.* That didn't sound like Oshanna, and it didn't sound as if Tunuk remembered her fondly at all—although Yinii wondered if Tunuk spoke of *anyone* fondly. How might he describe Yinii if she weren't there?

No, she told herself. She knew Tunuk was prickly, but he was fiercely loyal. Still, Oshanna seemed careful and thoughtful now, perhaps a little sad, and Yinii found herself wondering how much Tunuk had changed in the same time. How much they might all change, having gone through grief and come out the other side.

"Tunuk is just trying to figure out what happened. He remembers the bones of Saint Hazaunu being different, but not why or how."

Oshanna's auburn brows rose, her dark-eye blinking open in surprise. "Tunuk knew? He didn't tell anyone?"

Yinii cursed to herself, her panic coiling around the utter lack of ink in the room. "He . . . did. Although, it was . . . It's complicated. I don't think it was malicious. I think he assumed Qalba and Chizid might have taken them, and they would be back." She cleared her throat. "Do you know where they went?"

Oshanna studied her. Her eyes had such an unexpected sharpness to them, a feeling that you were being judged, and may the God Above and God Below and all the saints plead mercy for you. "No," Oshanna said finally. "If you asked Dushar Six-Agamid, he would tell you Qalba isn't a member of this clan anymore. If she wanted to remain, she would have come to us instead of disappearing a decade ago."

"Do you know why she disappeared?"

Oshanna looked up, that wry smile still not reaching her eyes. "I was hardly more than a child. Not someone anyone bothers telling things to."

Yinii shifted on the couch, her skirts sliding against the slick fabric. "Someone...someone mentioned Qalba having an affair. Maybe with someone dangerous."

At that, Oshanna looked surprised. She said nothing for a long moment, picking up her coffee again and sipping, before saying slowly, "I wouldn't have said so. She was very in love with her dark-blind husband."

"But?" Yinii prompted.

Oshanna considered her coffee, rather than Yinii. "There was a man."

When she didn't continue, Yinii guessed, "Toya?"

That made Oshanna look up. "Toya? Toya One-Saint?"

"I think so," Yinii said, tucking the man's birthday name away. "Tunuk mentioned him. That he was close to Qalba. That...he doesn't know where Toya is now."

"Toya One-Saint wasn't Qalba's lover," Oshanna said firmly. "He was just a...an addled man living in penitence for unforgivable sins. He is anathema in this house."

That surprised Yinii—a declaration of anathema, of something so far from correct that it must be swept from the eyes of the gods, was severe. What had he done?

She wished Tunuk were there—Tunuk would just have *asked* that unutterable question and damned the consequences. But Yinii, still tangled in what she could and could not say, only managed, "Oh. Then . . . who was the man?"

Oshanna stared at her, then broke her gaze to glance at the door, as if making certain no one was listening. "It was another darkblind man. A Borsyan. I remember him being in the archives once, when we visited, but Uncle Chizid was gone. Stellano Zezurin, he called himself." She turned back to Yinii, studying her. "Does that name mean anything to you? Does Tunuk remember it?"

Yinii shook her head. "He didn't mention."

"He seemed dangerous," Oshanna went on. "Though, at that age, most men seemed a little dangerous to me. But if I were going to look into something . . . bad that happened in the archives twelve years ago, I would consider looking into him."

"Thank you," Yinii said. It was something—something concrete. She could even ask Richa about it when she went to the Kinship Hall that evening.

"You are . . . blessed with the ink, atnashingyii?" Oshanna asked. "Is that right?"

Now Yinii was the one surprised. "Yes. I've been a specialist at the archives for five years."

"If I showed you something, could you tell me who wrote it?"

"Oh, um, it's more complicated than that? I can tell you where the ink came from, when it was made, and when it was written. Although if I can look at samples of writing from the same person, I can often tell—the pen and their mood at the time sometimes affects it, though, so when I haven't tested a lot of their writing, I have less confidence."

Oshanna nodded. "Wait here?"

She returned with a letter, its envelopment battered and badly damaged. The note inside was stained and torn, but Yinii could feel the ink whispering along her nerves, songs of a far-off kiln, a far-away fire, built of unfamiliar wood.

"My grandfather," Oshanna said, "would probably prefer I leave this to rot and name it anathema. But I think the clan is owed an explanation, and I don't know another way to secure it. I want to know if it's authentic, but I would ask for your discretion. It is ul-Shandiian's to deal with."

Yinii didn't bother to tell her that she could already feel so much from the ink, just being in the same room. It was pre-Sealing—she knew that char, that wood from old letters, and nothing like it grew on this side of the Wall. "Of course. Do you have a cloth to lay it out on?"

"I don't," Oshanna said, and thrust the letter into Yinii's hands.

Yinii took it gingerly—a paper specialist would need to evaluate the state of the bark paper it had been written on—and laid it on her lap. She took off her gloves and set her fingertips to the writing even as she read the words.

The ink was as strange as she'd suspected, with all the substance of an ancient document. She felt the ghosts of the trees in the char—slow-growing, hardy-wooded things—and the scrape of a kiln, but . . . none of these felt older than a year.

Uncle Dushar, please forgive the abruptness and strangeness of this letter. The bees must return to the nest when the wasps begin to swarm . . .

The ink started to loop around her fingers, words sliding under her nails, and she pulled her hands free, staring at the text.

"What is this?" she asked.

"You tell me," Oshanna said in a too-light voice. So Yinii read:

Uncle Dushar, please forgive the abruptness and strangeness of this letter. The bees must return to the nest when the wasps begin to swarm. I know I am likely as not anathema in your house and after all that has happened you won't want to hear from me. But I am out of resources and what is happening right now is much more serious than anything I have done to you. We are in danger, but I fear you are in greater danger. I hesitate to give specifics in case this letter is intercepted, but if you will agree to hear me, please will you have someone raise the flag of the reza ul-Shandiian over a ship in the harbor of Terzanelle and hang a green-glass lantern from the prow, and I will come to you. I will accept any punishment, if you will hear me out.
—Qalba One-Fox

"Is it real?" Oshanna asked. Then: "Is it her?"

"I . . . I don't know if this is Qalba's letter," Yinii said, still staring at the text, everything she knew about what might be happening on the other side of the Salt Wall grasping at the hints in this letter. Had Qalba fled *beyond the Salt Wall*? Did this mean she knew what it was that Redolfo Kirazzi was preparing? The ink started to shiver and hiss, peeled up by Yinii's nerves. She dropped the letter on the table and pulled on her gloves.

"I don't know if this is your cousin's letter," Yinii said. "I would need more samples to authenticate it. But . . . it does come from over the Wall. And it can't be more than a few months old. How . . . how did it get to the reza?"

"Over the Wall?" Oshanna said, her composure shattered. "Hai allainaa! How?"

"I . . . I don't know," Yinii said. "I can just . . . The char in the ink. It comes from a tree that, so far as I know, grows in Bemina. Not here. Someone used it in a fire and scraped the char from the kiln's roof. Probably the summer before last, but the seasons can be different once you start crossing the continent—"

"You think Qalba escaped over the Wall," Oshanna said, "and has returned to the port of Terzanelle. With . . . what? News of the changelings' expansion plans?"

Yinii's stomach flipped, and she reached up to touch the amulet of Saint Asla hanging from her horn. "I hope not. What does the reza think?"

"The reza thinks it's a hoax," Oshanna said, picking up the damaged envelopment and tucking the letter back inside. "Which seems both more likely and entirely unbelievable, doesn't it?"

"I suppose," Yinii managed.

Footsteps echoed in the hallway, and a man's voice called, "Oshanna! Where are you?"

Oshanna tucked the letter into a pocket. "Here, Babadi. I have a guest."

Dushar Six-Agamid swept into the room, bright as the sun in a suit of white wool. He held up a piece of paper. "Another of them. Pinned up by the corner of the fence. I'm taking it to the vigilants this time."

The ink bubbled with anger, thick with pigment, a slurry in alcohol. Even without touching it, Yinii could feel *rage*.

"'The saint's wrath calls the storm. The vulture is landed in the old cave,'" Dushar read. "It's a threat—"

"Babadi!" Oshanna said again, flushing at her grandfather's insistence on ignoring her. "We have a *guest*. This is Yinii Six-Owl ul-Benturan, atnashingyii."

Dushar Six-Agamid re-formed like a cloud of ink settling back onto a parchment, his spitting rage folded into the poised, shrewd expression of an Orozhandi reza. "Atnashingyii," he said, with an imperceptible bow that Yinii returned more fully. "You're from the archives."

"Yes," Yinii said. "Ink. I—"

"Your superiors sent you?" he said. "To make up for their shocking lack of decency?"

"Reza," Oshanna said, more sharply. "Please. I invited her. She is ul-Benturan. Dolitha Sixteen-Tamarisk's great-niece." She met Yinii's gaze. "We struck up a conversation and chose to continue it here." No mention of Qalba, the wooden bones, or Tunuk, and given Dushar's anger, Yinii was grateful.

Dushar's fury shifted, a new mask in its place. "I see. I already gave my condolences to Dolitha. She will be a difficult reza to replace. But I assume the discussions are fruitful?"

Yinii smiled uneasily—she honestly had no idea. "All things in their season."

Dushar smiled at her. "One hopes the season will turn soon. Dolitha would not have stood for this madness, giving ul-Hanizan the wooden bones of Saint Hazaunu."

Yinii swallowed. "Is...is that who you think is threatening you?"

Once more, Dushar seemed to shift, the calculations of a complicated mind brushing up under the surface of his features so a hundred thoughts seemed to shape themselves there in flickers of movement as he pondered.

"This isn't a problem for ul-Benturan," he said at last, a stern and kindly uncle. "Nor for the archives."

"Indeed," Oshanna said. "I'll show her out. The day is racing from us."

The clouds had thickened while they were inside, the sun behind them dipping low so that its golden light peeked beneath them. At the door, Oshanna paused.

"I hope that was all you needed. He doesn't like to talk about Qalba, so if there's more, I can't discuss it. Or really...well, it's a complicated time we're living in, just now."

"Of course," Yinii said, thinking Oshanna had no idea how complicated. "And you were very helpful. Thank you."

"Thank you as well."

Yinii started to go, but the twisting in her stomach tightened, and she turned back. "Oshanna? I know you don't want to discuss the letter. But...if something might be happening over the Salt Wall? You should show it to the Imperial Authority."

Oshanna drew a deep breath, considering the banner undulating against the side of the building. "That will be for the reza to decide," she said. "But knowing what you've said about the ink...I will take it up with him. Thank you again."

⚊ ⚌◆⚌ ⚊

Amadea waited in Nanqii ul-Hanizan's extravagant dining room, contemplating the influences of a tapestry depicting what seemed to be the snake-tailed Datongu wisdom goddess in a provocative pose around a fig tree, something that had never grown anywhere near ancient Datong's humid climate. She made herself tabulate color usage, weaving patterns, jumbled symbology—anything to keep her nerves steady and her mind off what Bishamar Twelve-Spider might be about to tell her.

The vault Nanqii had available to store the wooden bones of Saint Hazaunu was actually a wine cellar, but with the addition of a pair of cold-magic panels to take the humidity down, Amadea had approved it, with the condition of a specialist making regular assessments. She'd been shown to the dining room and told Nanqii would be there shortly.

That had been at least half an hour ago.

You should leave, she told herself once again, but once again she did not. She kept herself from fantasizing about what Bishamar could tell her about her past—how the plan was always to have a likely looking pretender, she thought firmly, before pushing away the imaginings again—and instead she wondered how long the translation of Saint Hazaunu would take.

When she'd left the archives, still in her formal robes but with her archivists' disbursements sorted and a stack of the primate's files weighing down her satchel, the procession had been forming in the entry hall. Six imperial soldiers of Orozhandi descent, gold patches pasted around their left eyes; six vigilants in fine dress uniforms, of polished silver and dark blue wool. A pair of veiled Orozhandi priests—one in the starry veil of the God Above, one with the gem-studded collar of the God Below—and their assistants giving directions. Bucella and a pair of generalists from wood perched anxiously on the stairs, ready to be told who to escort to the relics. Amadea had not paused, late as she was running, to ask about specifics, and she was regretting it as she sat waiting at the long table.

The weaving technique is Ronqu, she told herself, her eyes on the weight of the threads of the weft. *The dye is modern—Khirazji and Kuali techniques to get that orange.* It was a thing of many parts, yet wholly itself. Which admittedly was rather tacky.

The door opened at last, but it wasn't Nanqii who followed the servant in.

Bishamar Twelve-Spider had been the reza ul-Hanizan for nearly forty years, guiding the clan through six Imperial Authorities and two wars. He had been a man in his prime when he'd been elected to the leadership, and now his body was bent, his movements slow, his horns spiraling back into themselves and heavy with charms. But the eyes that regarded Amadea in a deeply wrinkled brown face were shrewd and sharp and curious.

She stood as he entered, trying instinctively to remember him from the days of the coup and failing. The reza ul-Hanizan looked her over once before starting toward the table, leaning heavily on a cane. "Does my grandson owe you money?"

"No, esinor," she said.

"Do you owe *him* money?" he asked, pulling out the seat at the head before the servant who had followed him in could do it.

"No, esinor. My name is Amadea Gintanas. He said . . . he said he had information for me. That you had information for me."

"That seems incautious," he commented. "For both of you."

"Did he tell you what he said to me?" Amadea asked.

"No," Bishamar said. "He wanted me to wait. I have to guess by your uniform that it has to do with the Imperial Archives. You're the one mixed up in this mess with the saint's lost bones, and since you're here, I'm going to assume you're also the archivist Beneditta took into her confidence today. Are you the one who convinced her to send Saint Hazaunu to us?"

Amadea might not have known Bishamar Twelve-Spider, but she knew his reputation: A calculating man, a sharp-eyed man. A gatherer of information. She felt as if he were looping ropes around her, building a trap.

"That was the empress's decision," she said. "I assumed it had to do with what would make Dushar ul-Shandiian mad."

At that, Bishamar laughed once. "I am sure it made him furious, and just as sure he would never admit such, the preening shit-lizard."

Nanqii swept into the room then, accompanied by another servant bearing a platter with bowls of soup. "My dear Archivist Gintanas, I'm so sorry to have kept you waiting." He clasped her hands as before, his eyes dancing, before bowing to the reza and taking the seat on the long side of the table between them.

The bowls were thin porcelain, edged with gold, the soup a cream of groundnut sprinkled with tarragon. Nanqii said nothing about his earlier revelation, only gestured at her to eat.

"How long," Bishamar asked, "is Saint Hazaunu to be our guest?"

"A month," Amadea said. "Possibly less."

Bishamar made a small disgusted noise. "Nanqii, shashkii, tomorrow move some of this gaudy mess into that wine cellar. Dushar and his crows will be here next, saying we've stuck the saint in a closet."

"We rather have, Babadi," Nanqii said.

Bishamar sniffed and scraped his soup bowl. "The saint doesn't care."

"Are you not devout, esinor?" Amadea asked.

Bishamar eyed her. He reached up and tapped a charm on his left horn—a crossed crook and spindle. The sigil of Saint Hazaunu of the Wool. "She is my canyon saint," he said. "But let's not be children, Archivist. The bones are a symbol, when one gets down to it. They are not the saint. The saint is gone—all of them, really, are gone. Hazaunu persists in her wisdom, and that is far more precious than some worm-eaten relics."

"Babadi," Nanqii cautioned. "She's going to think we can't be trusted with the saint now."

"No," Amadea said, holding Bishamar's gaze. "I think you understand best that they're a symbol of something more than the saint. That you are holding them for a reason beyond their basic protection."

"What a wise sentiment," Nanqii said. "Did you like the soup?"

She took a last spoonful, her expression still, imagining herself from outside, looking through the door to the room where the servants entered to exchange plates. Calm, still, unflappable. *Gold frame. Fuchsia rug. Green chair.*

"It's very pleasant, esinor. My compliments to your cook," she said. "Is our business waiting on anything in particular?"

Nanqii smiled at her. "I promised you eel." His eyes flicked to the human servant depositing a plate of roasted eels in a gingery bright green sauce before Amadea in place of her soup bowl. "Araldore, could you ensure us the utmost privacy?"

The man nodded and, with a careful, courteous disinterest, looked at neither Bishamar nor Nanqii nor Amadea as he left and shut the doors behind him.

Bishamar raised a shaggy eyebrow. "I won't guess, shashkii," he said, picking up his spoon. "Save your dramatics for someone else."

"My apologies," Nanqii said, a touch of acid in his tone. "I thought presenting you with Redolfo Kirazzi's Grave-Spurned Princess deserved to be a *little* dramatic."

Bishamar stopped, a curl of eel poised before his mouth, and looked at Amadea so intently she felt as if her skin were peeling back, exposing the heart of her. She made herself rigid, her face a mask of calm. Bishamar's dark-eye opened briefly, studying the invisible warmth of her.

Then Bishamar returned to his eel, chewed the bite thoroughly, and said, "Which one?"

For a moment, Amadea thought she hadn't heard him right, and her mind scrabbled at words he might have said, might have meant, only none of them fit. *Redolfo Kirazzi's Grave-Spurned Princess. Which one?*

It was Nanqii who replied, "What do you mean, 'which one'? There was only one."

"No." Bishamar held Amadea's gaze. "There were three. Which were you?"

"I . . ." Amadea felt as if she'd slid into a world where she couldn't quite speak the language, some lost nation over the Wall where it was almost familiar and yet broken on some fundamental axis. "I don't know how to answer that," she admitted.

"Lireana would," Bishamar said, and returned to the eel.

Amadea's thoughts spun, her memories folding over one another. What would convince Bishamar? How could Bishamar say there were *three* Grave-Spurned Princesses? What would even differentiate them? Gintanas? Sestina? For a moment, she panicked—everything might be a lie, poured into her mind like the venoms, stories and stories and stories, so she replaced a lost Lireana, somehow, at the end of the coup . . .

No, she told herself. She thought of the changeling doubles in the tunnel below the Wall. The duplicates ready if she died. Those had *her* face, not some stranger's. But she'd been so young when she'd come to Sestina, and so many enemies circled Redolfo—she could imagine there being a period of testing, obscuring, of crafting the *right* Lireana. What if he'd kept more than one of them ready? Memories where she saw herself, heard herself at a distance. Had that even *been* her?

No, she told herself. *Ibramo remembers you.*

Red walls. Striped rug. Black eyes.

"I was the one standing on the field when Fastreda of the Glass was hit by imperial cannons," she said crisply. "She screamed first, and then she laughed, because that part of her became glass. Fastreda," she added, "knows me. If you want that confirmation. As does the empress, though you can imagine she doesn't like it brought up. If Redolfo Kirazzi had other girls he presented as the lost princess, that has nothing to do with me. And knowing the Usurper, it does not surprise me he kept alternates. If I had died, he wouldn't have stopped. I was the one who persisted. I was the one he went to war for. Will that do it?"

Bishamar raised his scraggly eyebrows and glanced at Nanqii. "Interesting."

"I wanted her to come talk to you, Babadi. I wanted to discuss..." He trailed away, wise enough to mark the hard look in Bishamar Twelve-Spider's gaze. "The conversation we had at Salt-Sealing," Nanqii finished.

"And what do *you* want?" Bishamar said, returning to Amadea.

Silver hair, blue tablecloth, green eels. She picked up her fork and lifted a curl of eel meat from the lauded sauce to give herself a moment. "Answers. I was told you were the one who recovered Lireana," she said. "Although, given there were three, I assume I know the rest."

"Do you?"

"It's a clever plan," she said. "Find a girl who looks vaguely like the dead princess. Convince her she is by any means necessary. And given Redolfo Kirazzi is who he is, it stands to reason he would be prepared with...extras."

The changelings under the tunnel, the Amadeas still sleeping. She made herself eat, named the flavors in her mouth—*ginger, garlic, bitter, brine*—

"I assume the archives employ you for your attention to detail, not your ability to fill in gaps," Bishamar said. "This began because the princess survived."

He watched her with that steady, bright gaze.

She made herself chew, feeling as if she would choke on the eel, feeling as if she would shout, *No, she didn't, she couldn't have.*

"The Fratricide happened," he said. "Appolino's men left the guards who'd surrendered to bury the imperial family that very night. But one of the girls wasn't dead, only badly injured. I found a guard who said his companion smuggled her out, took her to safety. I tracked them to Gintanas Abbey, which, as you can imagine, has a surfeit of dark-haired girls and an oath to never speak of their origins, since all are Alletet's now. I winnowed it down to the most likely few."

Amadea forced the bite of eel down, pressed her hands to the tablecloth. "And you told Redolfo?"

"We discussed the matter," Bishamar said. "We were concerned— all the ducal authorities were very concerned in the days following the Fratricide. None of this was what we'd agreed to."

"Were you part of the plan to put forward a pretender?" Amadea asked.

"No. If we'd clearly found the princess, then of course, I would have wanted to see her reclaim the throne, and of course, I would have wanted to be sure she had good, thoughtful advisors by her side. But we only found possibilities. And then Clement took the reins, killed Appolino, gained us peace again. Why trouble the waters after that?"

Amadea's thoughts were being pulled apart like carded wool— three girls in Gintanas. She found her memories scrambling after glimpses of other faces, other selves, other dark-haired girls. She remembered vaguely other children in the abbey, before Sestina, but after...

Redolfo, flail in hand, looming, looming. Lireana on the floor, on the carpet, the good Alojan carpet, and she's both a million miles away and close enough to hear the beads clink together as the flail swings—

After, there were no other dark-haired girls, but sometimes she felt like she wasn't in her own head in her memories. After, sometimes she felt as if she were watching her life happen to someone else. Sometimes a mind did that, she knew, because the truth was too much, the memories too painful.

But if there were others...

"You knew Redolfo had taken the three girls," Amadea said. "So I think you troubled yourself a little."

Bishamar picked up his wineglass. "Like I said, all I wanted was peace again. I knew Redolfo had taken one of them. He brought her to me, claiming she was Lireana. You look a bit alike, but she had a little mole on her cheek, just under her eye. I had her assassinated. After that, we didn't talk so much, he and I."

Horror washed hot over Amadea's nerves. "You killed her? A little girl?"

"A little problem," Bishamar Twelve-Spider corrected. "And I know you don't feel lucky when someone dies instead of you, but you ought to praise the saints this time. That's how I found out he'd spread his risks around—'Lireana' didn't disappear. He just got a lot more careful after that." He studied her, and she made certain there was nothing at all for him to see there, even though she wanted to scream in his face.

"Now, I hear we have a new little problem. I hear the empress is taking up the recent tradition of Ulanittis going mad. And this... this is something I could see myself bargaining a solution to."

"Rumors," Amadea said firmly. "The empress is fine. She cares deeply about the empire."

"So did her uncle," Bishamar said. "But I won't lecture *you* about the Fratricide. One way or the other, I think you know it well."

A memory flickered in Amadea's mind, one she hadn't known she had until she'd spoken with Beneditta after Lord Obigen's memorial: a man, *Appolino*, sunk deep in gloomy thought beside a fireplace, something grim and determined taking hold of him.

That's what happened with Appolino, Sigrittrice had confessed. *I chose the wrong time. He didn't take it well. He tried to strip away the locking. He went mad of it and decided he had to cleanse Semilla. That that was what was best and most just for the people.*

Orange knots, Amadea told herself. *Black coffee. Gray suit. Your little stunt at Obigen's memorial.* Amadea shoved the thought away. "She is not Appolino. There are factors at play that are—"

"The Venom of Changelings?" Bishamar interrupted. "I don't know how Sigrittrice thought that would stay a secret for long. Though obviously *you* were allowed to know, which is interesting. And the cracks were showing long before this." He leaned forward, his hands on his knees. "What I am seeking, what Nanqii has taken into his own hands, are contingencies. What I want is to know this empire isn't going to shatter on its own best intentions. What I wished for is a *reserve*."

Amadea's thoughts slipped: *"This could all be yours," Redolfo says.*

"The empress *has* an heir," she said. "Prince Micheleo will take the throne if she's unable to maintain her rule."

"The boy is fifteen. His horns are still soft."

"Then Consort-Prince Ibramo will stand as his regent."

"You think this country will accept Redolfo Kirazzi's son pulling the strings of government? You think Lady Gritta will allow that?" Bishamar's dark-eye opened again, regarding something in her she could never see. "What do you do at the archives? Sort things? Dust?"

"I oversee the southern wing," Amadea said. "I manage the generalists and specialists and keep things running."

"Busy," Bishamar said. "Little miniature empire you have there."

"No," Amadea said. "It's just a vocation."

"And yet you're not dusting or filing or getting those specialists their meals. You're in charge of things. Quite a lot of things. And you're helping the empress with *her* oaths. Why didn't you stop Redolfo?"

Amadea blinked at him, off-balance a moment. "Because . . . I was a child."

"Children ruin things all the time. They're very good at it. Why did you go along?"

Because he was terrifying, she wanted to say. *Because he was magnificent.*

"Because I believed him," she said quietly.

He nodded. "You may be Lireana, you may not be. Sometimes a thing becomes a symbol of more than it ever was. You could serve if the circumstances demanded."

"You want me to be your puppet. I think you can appreciate that isn't an agreement I'm interested in again."

"That's not what he meant," Nanqii started.

Bishamar cut him off with a curt gesture. "I speak for myself, shashkii. Let us hope you are correct. Beneditta is only at the beginning of a long and stable rule that will continue long after I've died. Appolino's madness is a fluke—a hiccup in the history of the Ulanittis and their wise and just guidance of this peninsula. Let us hope that between Lady Sigrittrice, Ibramo Kirazzi, and perhaps even yourself, Archivist Gintanas, that Beneditta has the allies to keep her serving and the Gods Above and Below bless us, every one.

"But," he went on, "if I am right, if she falters, if she endangers this empire, then you are my reserve. You will come when I name you. You will *believe* you are Lireana again, for the good of the empire. For the good of my people."

Amadea held that gaze, felt it calculating her worth, her mettle. In her mind, Redolfo murmured, *I made you, I can destroy you just as easily.* If the empire were collapsing...what was she made for but to solve problems?

She suppressed a shudder. "It will not come to that, esinor. I won't let it come to that," she said, standing and picking up her bag. "I would thank you both for your time, but I think we would all consider this appointment wasted."

"Fair enough," Bishamar Twelve-Spider called as she left. "There's another of you, after all."

Amadea looked back at him. "If there is," she said, "then you don't know what happened to her. Because if your grandson could surprise you with me, then for all you know, she is dead."

And that was certainly the case, she thought as she strode back through the house, panic pooling in her. There had been three. She was the only one left.

Or maybe not, and that was worse, somehow, that anyone else was out there, sitting with this constant strangeness, this bone-deep loneliness. The question of who she was—it only got more confusing. Was she a convenient orphan? A lost princess? Or the receptacle for the memories of both, mixed and mingled to create a more perfect pretender, to prevent any disruption to Redolfo Kirazzi's complex and devious plans?

You are Amadea Gintanas, she told herself, as the man by the door fetched her cloak. *You are a solver of problems. You are not a tool.* Not the Grave-Spurned Princess. Not Lireana.

A bowl of salt. A drop of blood. A little patience—she could know the answer. An Ulanitti's blood burned green like a changeling's. She could know.

Nanqii caught up to her at the door, plucking her cape from the man as he offered it and settling it around her shoulders. "I'm very sorry you're leaving," he said, low and in her ear. "I was quite looking forward to dessert."

Amadea yanked away from him. "If you tell anyone—"

"Why would I tell anyone?" he asked. "I'm not in the business of sowing unnecessary chaos."

"What else would happen if you put me forward?" she demanded, fastening her cloak.

"I think you are too modest, esinora," Nanqii said with a sudden solemnity. "And don't misunderstand me: We're not looking to replicate Redolfo's mistakes. He and I care about this empire just as you do. I see the cracks in the foundation. I hear the flood rising in the far-off canyons. And I think you do as well."

"And I think you mistake a flood's roar for the first rains," she said. "I'll agree there are uncertain times ahead of us, but I won't agree things are so desperate you should look to treason. Saint Hazaunu's bones should be here soon. I trust you'll manage."

"I usually do." He opened the door to outside, where the storm clouds hung heavy. Richa was sitting on a bench on the opposite side of the street. He waved at her and came to his feet. "Ah, you have another engagement. How interesting."

"Good day, esinor."

Nanqii caught her by the elbow, his expression solemn once again. "Perhaps you're right and what I'm hearing is only the rain," he said. "But the rain brings the flood, and if I'm wrong, I'll be glad. If you're wrong, you can't say the same. Have a pleasant evening, Archivist Gintanas. Stay dry."

CHAPTER TWELVE

Gunarro wasn't home the next day, so Tunuk led Quill up the street, out of the Hawk's Nest, to where the Temple of the Black Mother Forest stood.

"What do you think he knows about Toya?" Quill asked as they climbed the hill out of the neighborhood below.

"I have no idea," Tunuk admitted. What did he himself even know about Toya? He could picture him still: a round-faced Orozhandi man, enameled charms all along his horns, his hands folded on the curve of his belly. Toya, smiling blithely as he had tea with Qalba. Toya, with Qalba comforting him as he wept, Tunuk not knowing the cause. Toya weeping, and Chizid explaining Qalba would be back soon. Toya, praying fervently to saint after saint, and Qalba saying, *Let him be, shashkii. He's got a heavy heart.*

"It's going to be something," Quill said. "He wouldn't call us back for nothing."

"If he has, I want to go get a large amount of sap wine before we go to the Kinship Hall."

The temple had the shape of an eroding hill, a pile of domed brick buildings sloping upward from the squat workshop halls along each side to the polished bronze peak of the central tower. Cast statues of crow-winged women hung off protruding squared corners, and the dark mouth of the entrance was framed with stylized trees, and it felt like walking into that mythic forest passing between them and through the lightless corridor behind, until they came out into the entry hall, a long space full of light and statues of muscular Borsyan heroes.

There was a short line of people requesting fabricator work before Tunuk reached the desk and asked for Gunarro del Hwana. The man behind the desk looked momentarily confused, then seemed to realize who Tunuk meant. He gestured to a row of chairs below a statue of a bearded human holding a dead eagle by the talons and a bare branch of wood.

"I'm worried about Yinii," Quill said abruptly. "Did it seem odd to you that she just . . . told us we should ignore Amadea? I mean, I was going to suggest it—"

"*So* odd," Tunuk said, glad Quill had broached it. "Something must have happened. She would never have suggested that before."

"She didn't tell you anything's bothering her?"

"I told you, she's avoiding me."

Quill peered at him. "Is she avoiding you? Or are you avoiding her?"

"I . . ." Tunuk turned back to the statue opposite, a very hairy-looking human man strangling a vulture. "It's complicated."

"All right, well, maybe we should ask her why she's avoiding both of us, because something's clearly bothering her. You're her best friend, so if she's not telling you, it might be serious."

Tunuk wrapped his arms around himself. What a friend he'd been—sulking over Yinii ignoring him when something might be very wrong with her. "We should talk to her," he agreed in a small voice.

Gunarro came out soon after that, looking as though he'd hardly slept. "I was wondering who was asking for me with my father's name," he said. "Come back to my workshop; this has to be quick."

Gunarro's workshop was a cell of a room, every wall filled with pieces of the mechanisms used to channel the cold-magic: vines of copper tubing, leather hoses, glass globes and vials, sheets of metal, and more valves than Tunuk could understand the purpose of. It was like seeing a corpse laid out in pieces, and only his imagination could guess what it was when it was whole.

On the table to the side sat the object Gunarro had been passed the day before, by the tall woman and the man with the yellow coat—the tangle of tubing and vials around a thin glass globe.

Tunuk stepped a little closer to it and saw the cold-magic within it, an oddly shaped chunk of what looked like wood glowing faintly blue.

"Sorry," Gunarro said, closing the door and stepping between them and the object. "Forgot to take care of this." He grabbed a wrench that ended in a loop of leather and used it to twist off the globe. He muttered a little prayer over the cold-magic, that piece of the Black Mother Forest carried out of Borsya, and set it in a silver box waiting beside the contraption.

"New device?" Quill asked.

"Don't worry about it. It doesn't work." Gunarro put the whole thing back into the bag that sat beside it. "Someone thought they were being clever."

"Better than the alternative," Quill said.

"You said you knew something about Toya," Tunuk said. "You can tell us, and then we can leave."

"Right." Gunarro blew out a breath. "Look, I don't want to speak ill of the dead...assuming she's dead...but...Do you know what Qalba did before she was in the archives?"

Tunuk shrugged. What did any of them do? "Be annoyed at your noisy skeletons?"

Gunarro cut his eyes to the door before saying, "The first time I met her friend Toya, he told me how they met. Because...it's odd, right? He's almost old enough to be her father, and they're friends?"

"Not that odd," Quill said.

"They were related," Tunuk said. "Clans are huge."

"Maybe," Gunarro said. "But that's not what he told me. I asked him how they knew each other, and he said, 'From when we served the Duke Kirazzi.' Like it was nothing."

"Very dramatic," Tunuk sneered. "You don't think perhaps he meant Duke Turon? The duchess's father?"

"I assumed that too. But when I asked what he did for the duke, he got upset." Gunarro dropped his voice further. "He said, 'I don't remember anymore. I made things for the coup.' And that's when Qalba found us and shut him up."

Tunuk's bones were like ice in his limbs. Toya, smiling. Toya, weeping. *Let him be, shashkii. He's got a heavy heart.* "He couldn't have," Tunuk said. "He . . . he just wasn't capable."

Gunarro shrugged. "Maybe. Maybe something happened. You take a blow to the head the wrong way, and your brain changes. I've seen it happen. Or maybe he was faking all of it to escape execution."

"Or maybe he's telling stories," Tunuk said, throwing his shoulders back to fight the tightness in his chest. "Qalba wouldn't do that."

Gunarro gave him a skeptical look. "You were a kid. You don't know what she'd have done. I wasn't there, obviously, to catch her doing who knows what for the Usurper. But I know Qalba shut Toya up very quickly when he started chatting about his dear friend Redolfo Kirazzi. And I know my brother was suddenly in need of a knife not long after." He glanced at the door again. "Look, I have another appointment . . ."

"Do you know where Toya might be?" Quill asked. "Where he might have gone after Chizid and Qalba left?"

Gunarro pulled open the door. "That's probably a question for Qalba's family, not Chizid's. I hope your problems sort out and none of this . . . Well, I hope it has nothing to do with the Usurper."

Tunuk stormed down the hall. "Well, that was a waste of time. So glad I flouted Amadea for horseshit nonsense."

"What?" Quill said. "That was extremely useful!"

Tunuk stopped and turned to face him. "It was a bunch of nonsense. Qalba didn't work for the Usurper. She wouldn't have."

"She might have," Quill said. "He's right, you don't know—"

"I do know!" Tunuk snapped. "She's not a villain, she's not a monster."

"But somebody probably killed her, and if that person—"

"You don't know that!"

"No, because you won't *actually* look at that skeleton!" Quill said. "Look, I get it. Do you think I don't get it? The world is falling apart, and here's someone you cared about who could have been *fine* if they weren't keeping secrets. Someone you just want to be alive and all right, and all the signs are pointing to *neither*. Right now, I see two options: either she wasn't bad, but somewhere she'd made the kind of friends who meant having a screaming match in the Bone Vault and Chizid needing a knife. Or she wasn't who you thought she was."

Tunuk pulled himself up straight, his fists balled, frustration and shame flooding under his skin in a wash of cold. "You don't know *anything*," he snarled. "We don't know anything. If you think I'm going to go to the Kinship and tell them a story that makes all this simple, makes it all match up to *your* problems—"

"I don't think that."

"Then what the fuck do you *want*?"

"Read the fucking bones," Quill said. "Do what only you can do. Find out what the fuck we're missing, and stop acting like you can hide from it."

Tunuk turned away and nearly walked into a woman striding down the hall, carrying a bulky canvas tool bag. Quill stepped close to Tunuk to let her pass. As she did, Tunuk recognized her: Vigdza, the woman who'd visited Gunarro the day before.

"Fucking separatists," Tunuk said under his breath. "It's kind of rich, isn't it? Calling Qalba a friend of the Usurper and helping separatists."

"I guess," Quill said.

Hurt and furious, Tunuk slipped past Quill. "Come on, be quiet, and let's see what they're talking about."

Tunuk ignored Quill's hissed protest and pressed close beside the entrance to Gunarro's workshop, listening to the voices that carried through the closed door.

"It *looks* like it should do what you say," Gunarro said, "but I put cold-magic in it. It doesn't *build* enough. It's too steady."

"Never mind," she said. "I know why it doesn't work."

"All right. Glad I could help. Next time solve it yourself first?" A pause. "What is that? A wooden tooth?"

"Don't ask stupid questions," the woman said. Tunuk heard a clicking sound, the slap of something leather.

And then he heard Gunarro suck in a breath. "Take it out."

More clicks, more snapping. "That's it. It surges."

"What the..." Gunarro breathed. "You're not going to...Vigdza, that's incredibly dangerous. And what is that—"

"Do you think I don't know that? This is why I asked. I can't tell him what to do if I don't know what we're dealing with. I can't convince her to back off if I don't know the stakes. I'm doing what I can—"

"Of course," Gunarro said. "Of course."

A pause. "You should leave. You have somewhere outside the city you can visit?"

"Vigdza—"

"I don't want this coming back to you, all right? Give me a month. Go visit the sea. Come on, let's go now."

Quill yanked hard on Tunuk's arm, pulling him away from the wall. He jerked his thumb toward the exit, and reluctantly Tunuk followed. Outside, the storm clouds were low and ominous, the sun only a trim of golden-red light along their bellies.

"Did you hear them?" Tunuk whispered.

"I heard a bunch of suspect fabricator talk," Quill said. "I told you, I don't want to get involved with separatists."

"She had a wooden tooth," Tunuk said.

"And?"

"And the wooden bones!"

"Are in the archives," Quill finished. "Why would she have Saint Hazaunu's tooth?" He pulled his collar up around his ears. "Are you worried about telling Richa what we found?"

"Which is what?" Tunuk said. "A bunch of half stories and misre-memberings and lies?"

Quill counted on his fingers. "Qalba worked for the Usurper. Chizid was ready to kill someone. They had a big fight—"

"What part of this is about stealing the bones?" Tunuk said. "None of it. It's all gossip. This was wasted—except now—"

Vigdza and Gunarro came out of the temple then, hurrying across the square. She had her bulky bag and the sack from Gunarro tucked close against her beneath her long black cloak. Tunuk stepped backward, into the shadow of the building, watching them.

"Lord on the Mountain, leave them alone," Quill said.

Gunarro and Vigdza stopped beside the street Quill and Tunuk had come up. They spoke a little more, and then Vigdza dug into her bag, the shapes of tools and parts pressing against the canvas as she did. She pulled out a sack, and a small explosion of wrenches came with it. He heard her curse and saw her hand the bag—coins, Tunuk guessed—to Gunarro as they both picked up the fallen tools. Then she embraced him briefly and took off down the street, while Gunarro headed west . . . away from his house.

"Huh," Quill said. "I guess he's leaving town. Fucking separatists."

But Tunuk wasn't watching Gunarro. He was staring at a small twisted handle of wood that had come out of the bag and bounced away from the other tools. He started toward it.

"We don't have to go back that way," Quill said.

Tunuk ignored him, made for the piece of wood. It lay caught between two cobblestones where they gapped a little wider than the rest, but once he could see it clearly, he knew this was no tool. The serpentine curve, the ruffle of the articular capsules—it was a clavicle, probably a human's or an Orozhandi's by the size and the curve of the acromial region.

Only it didn't have the faint hum of unworked bone. It was silent.

No, he thought. Not silent. Not quite. Something in it pulled at him like a thread wrapped around his nerves, an insistent vibration that reminded him of nothing so much as the spiral edging up on him.

"What are you doing?" Quill asked, catching up to him.

Tunuk plucked the clavicle from the crack and thrust it at Quill. "She has a fucking saint. I *told* you." He looked down the street she'd left by. "Come on. We need to figure out where she went."

Tunuk started down the road toward the Hawk's Nest. He could see the woman ahead of him, walking quickly. She turned a corner, moving at an angle to where he knew Gunarro's house was, her gaze sweeping the road as she walked. She did not see Tunuk keeping to the shadows.

But she did seem to see Quill.

She pulled her cloak close and started to run, one arm snaked over the bulk of her bag. Tunuk reached back and grabbed Quill by the arm and pulled him as he ran toward the woman. She turned back down a meandering street. Deeper into the Hawk's Nest.

The sky opened up, the rain coming down in sheets, pouring into the collar of Tunuk's cloak and blurring his view of the woman. She was fast, but Tunuk was seven feet tall, and much of that was legs. They were nearly back to the bridge with the triangle spirals—he could just see it through the haze of the rain. He was gaining—and then Quill wrenched free, unable to keep up, and Tunuk looked back once to make sure he was all right.

When he turned back, the woman had vanished.

Tunuk left Quill and raced ahead. There was an alley there; she'd been nearly even with it. She must have taken the turning—

The alley stretched on, empty, so far away the next street was only a sliver. She was gone, and with her the hope of handing the vigilants something else to pursue.

Quill came hobbling up beside him, panting.

"I lost her," Tunuk said. "How did I lose her?"

"Did you lose the bone?" Quill asked. Tunuk held it up, still clasped in his left hand. "Good," Quill said. "We need to take *that* to Richa, right now. We can send the vigilants to look for her after."

⋯ ⊷≣⊶ ⋯

By the time Amadea sat down at the coffee shop Richa had chosen, she felt as if she were going to smother under the swarm of worries about Nanqii and Redolfo, Bishamar and Beneditta, Dushar ul-Shandiian and the chapel itself. *A masterful respite*, she thought wryly.

What would she say to one of her specialists? *There is nothing you can do in this moment to fix any of it.* She could not take away what Nanqii had learned. She could not make Beneditta not afraid. She could not soothe the Orozhandi ducal authority or convince Dushar ul-Shandiian specifically that the archives were the best carers for the skeleton saints or trust that Bishamar Twelve-Spider wasn't looking to repeat the Usurper's mistakes. *You need to take care of yourself.*

She wondered if that sounded as flimsy to the archivists as it did to her now.

She settled down at a table beneath a fresco of musicians and dancers, tucking the satchel with the suspicious files into her lap, while Richa spoke to the proprietor, a dark-skinned woman with long reddened braids, the "Corolia" whose name graced the sign. She waved him off, and Richa returned to the table balancing two cups of dark coffee, little confections perched on their saucers.

"She'll be over when she has a moment, and I can ask her questions about sorcerer-artifacts then," he said, setting one cup in front of Amadea before sitting down. He glanced up at the fresco and cleared his throat. "So I should have mentioned—should have remembered, really—that we've been here before."

"You mean when you coerced my specialist into working with his affinity material at the height of his alignment?" she said dryly. "Easy to forget."

Richa winced. "Well, I will be grateful Stavio has forgiven me even if you and Bijan haven't. I'm still sorry."

Amadea smiled and reached for the coffee, one hand still hugging the satchel of papers against her waist. "It was Stavio's fault more than yours, and now you know better. Plus, you bought me coffee." She took a sip—bright and fruity and gently roasted—and sighed, focused on the flavor and not on the many worries. "Do you come here much?"

"Yeah, I live nearby," he said. He plucked up the little square of candy—a brittle crisp with burnt sugar and fat with nuts and flecked with spice—and popped it in his mouth. "Mm. Got a kick to it, that one."

Amadea took a bite of hers—pistachio and peppercorn and fennel seeds in a brittle that stuck to her teeth. She shifted the satchel onto the table so she could cover her mouth and dislodge a bit of the sticky candy from a molar. "That's very nice."

Richa nodded at the bag. "You brought the files?"

"Yes," she said, breathing the word out in another sigh. "Some of them. I can't imagine the Paremi would approve, but—"

"I think the approval of the Paremi slipped our grasps a long, long time ago." He nodded at the satchel again. "Do you want to look through them together?"

She did. She very much did. "I thought this was meant to be a respite."

"Mm, is this not a respite for you?" He smiled. "You're not in your office."

"My office is ... comfortable."

"Is the coffee as good?"

"No," she admitted. "But I do keep a bottle of kaibo in the desk drawer."

He chuckled. "This is not the admission of someone who is good at taking a break."

Amadea huffed out a reluctant laugh. "If that isn't the bramble calling the rose thorny! Did you not sleep in the Kinship Hall last night?"

"Yeah, it's almost as if I know your type."

"Married to the oath," she said.

"I prefer 'haven't found something I care about as much as the oath.'"

"Oh, so you do know my type."

Richa met her eyes, a soft, curious smile on his face, and something in her shifted, a sense she'd stumbled off the path. Or perhaps that she'd stumbled onto a new one...

I made you, Redolfo's voice murmured through her memories. *I can destroy you just as easily.* Nothing had changed—if anything, her situation had gotten worse since she'd met with Bishamar. She couldn't let anyone else know. If she'd been one of her specialists, she'd have had a firm conversation about making good choices and setting expectations.

But the words she needed to say wouldn't come out.

Richa only smiled and reached out, pulling open the satchel and spreading the first dozen pages out of the stack in a fan that he claimed, and the moment passed safely by.

Perusing Primate Lamberto's files felt like chasing down a ghost. So much of it was only official language, the ritual of law, but here and there, Amadea found glimpses of the man who'd done the writing—a bit of sarcasm in a demand for clarification on Tornada's docking taxes, a sharpness in a demand for restitution from the Borsyan ducal authority that had gone unanswered, a noticeable lack of any teeth in the filing of an amendment to a lord from Isecca's will.

After a while, Richa sighed and rubbed his face. "I might need another coffee."

"They're rather dense," Amadea said, skimming an order for the transfer of a sorcerer called Oluali of the Marble from a village called Alcaic, in the administrative area of the Borsyan ducal authority's seat in Bylina, to Sestina. "And we still don't know what we're looking for or even if Primate Lamberto did anything we can find in public filings."

Richa slouched in his chair, picked up his empty coffee cup, and scowled at it. "What do you think it would look like? This something suspicious."

Amadea considered, setting the transfer order back on the pile. "Perhaps...land acquisition? Ibramo says there aren't any other tunnels, but perhaps there's one he can't find?"

Richa nodded, staring up at the ceiling. "Or...an elevation? Someone placed in the Paremi hierarchy out of order?"

"These wills," Amadea said. "If they were...directing funds to somewhere unexpected, it might be a sign of...well, of what the empress is afraid of."

Richa sighed in a way that said he understood exactly the implications—someone inside the Salt Wall preparing where Redolfo Kirazzi could not.

Corolia came over to the table then, her gaze flicking to Amadea. She pulled a little charm from around her neck—a dark iron square—and displayed it against her palm in a practiced flash. Richa introduced Amadea, and Corolia pulled up a chair.

"I have no idea," she said, "what you think I'm going to tell you that you couldn't just sort out for yourself, but ask your questions. You want to buy iap'mut?" she asked, folding a soft click into the center of the word. When Richa looked at her, puzzled, she said, "The sorcerer stuff. Good-luck charms. They're called iap'mut."

"Got it," Richa said. "Yeah. I'm looking into some thefts from the Imperial Archives. Of...iap'mut. They're all sorcerer wrought and not, at a glance, especially valuable in raw materials. But small—you can stick them in a pocket. So one of the archivists mentioned the good-luck charms."

Corolia tilted her head, eyeing him skeptically. "Are you asking if I know someone who stole from the archives?"

"No, I'm asking if you know if that's something people do. Might do."

"Fools, maybe. You can find iap'mut everywhere. In Arlabecca, you don't even have to wait for a peddler to come by—Eizem del Dolatemse up by the chapel of Noniva has a shop and he sells relics from at least four sorcerers..." She hesitated. "Although when did this happen?"

"Not sure," Richa said. "Obviously things are busy in there. The thefts were reported between fourteen and three years ago."

Corolia shook her head. "No, then. That's not for good luck. That's just some idiot thief courting worse luck."

Amadea spoke up. "What difference does the time of the theft make?"

"Not much," Corolia admitted. "I still think it would be a stupid thing to do, stealing artifacts when it's not like you have to go quest across the desert to find a sorcerer to give you iap'mut nowadays. It's just that lately... Well, there's a sorcerer. Iosthe of the Wool, right? She's in Endecha, up near Ragale? She sells iap'mut—or I guess bestows them for a donation, if you want to be proper about it." She held up a wrist where a winding chain made a bracelet half the length of her forearm, and with one finger, she lifted an intricate fox made of felted wool, hanging by its curled tail. "This is one of hers. My husband's mother got it when I was pregnant with my older daughter."

"That's kind," Richa said.

"Very handy too," Corolia said. "Slipped out like a plum from a skin. My husband's mother got it from Eizem, like I said, but that's the thing. I heard lately he doesn't have much to sell. Particularly from Iosthe."

Amadea frowned. "Is she not creating anymore?"

"No. Someone's buying it all—at least that's what I hear. Has been for months. So if this had been a week back, I might say all right, you have some young idiot in a panic, grabbing what they think won't be missed because their flow's late, or there's a position they're trying for or a girl they want to court, and there's no iap'mut to be had." She picked up their cups. "But that's not your problem. Your problem's just a thief."

"A thief who steals almost worthless items," Richa said. "I don't believe it."

"That's nice, Richa," Corolia said. "I'm closing, and the coffee's all drunk. You can go home and be disbelieving there. Come back tomorrow morning when Eizem gets his coffee and get an expert's opinion about why this is a stupid thing to steal."

Amadea fastened her cape back on and bundled the papers together in their leather envelopment, following Richa back out into the street. The sky was thick with clouds now, heavy and menacing, and a drizzle of rain made the air thick and cool.

Richa glanced back at the shop, where Corolia was pulling curtains closed and locking windows. "Well, that was absolutely useless."

"The company was all right," Amadea said, and he smiled at her.

"I'll walk you back," he offered. Then: "Unless...you wanted some kaibo."

"Maybe. Do you have better kaibo than I have in my desk drawer?"

"I don't know. I haven't drunk your kaibo." She looked askance at him, assessing if he'd meant the clumsy euphemism. But he regarded her seriously, no sign of the joke, and there was something rough in his voice when he said, "The company's better."

A warmth spread through the base of Amadea's belly, and any thought she was imagining this, that she was fooling herself, melted with it. "It...it's been a long time. Since I had company."

"Yeah," he said. "Me too. Hard to find something you care about more than the oath."

Redolfo. Bishamar. The Grave-Spurned Princess. "It's not just that," she said.

The rain began with a patter to come down in earnest, the rattle of fat drops hitting the cobbled road and roofs, swelling into a roar as the skies opened up. An autumn cloudburst poured down, sweeping over the city.

Amadea pulled her cloak over the satchel, curling her body protectively around the files, and tried to hurry out of the rain. Richa's arm went around her, stopping her and rushing her toward the farther side of the street at an angle—she couldn't see where they were going, only that suddenly the rain was off her, still coming down in sheets just beyond the arch of the doorway they were pulled into. Amadea's hair had come half out of its bun, soaked with rain in only those few minutes.

"Saints and devils," Richa cursed. He dragged a hand through his hair, flicking water behind him. "Welcome to winter. Did the papers get wet?"

"I don't think so." She tried to wrestle the satchel around, succeeding in dragging her soaked cloak with her. She cursed quietly, trying to push it back and managed to knock the comb free of her hair so it bounced on the stones below. Richa ducked to scoop it up. She cursed a little louder.

"Here." He reached up and unhooked the row of small round buttons on the top of her shoulder, unfastening each as easily as popping peas from their shells. Amadea caught her breath as he peeled the sopping garment from her. She could feel the warmth of him, on the other side of the bag she still cradled, and she heard his soft intake of breath.

Redolfo. Bishamar. The Grave-Spurned Princess. They all seemed... so very far away just now.

There had been a churn of young men once upon a time, and it was easy to not care, to move through the dance between one partner and the next, eyes on a future where everything didn't hurt so much. Amadea at seventeen, grasping at lovers, grasping at futures, never finding what she wanted, growing to understand she'd never have it.

Amadea, eyeing forty, silver in her hairline, understood the future was a fickle partner, not for her to seize, only for her to move along with step by step. The past, a jealous guardian always circling her, tripping up her steps. But the present? The present she could be greedy for. The present could be hers; Richa could be hers. For now. For a moment.

Now, she reminded herself, moving toward him. *Not then.* Amadea, not Lireana.

"You live near here?" she asked.

"Yeah. Upstairs," he said. "I *might* have some kaibo."

"I might not care about kaibo." Which earned her a lopsided smile.

The rain kept roaring as she followed him up the stairs, her thoughts on one step, then the next—the present, not the future, not the past. He opened a door to a small apartment, tidier than she'd expected if she were being honest, the space used carefully and thoroughly. Richa paused beside a little household altar, laying coins before a trio of Datongu deities with a casualness that said he did this every time he came in. His gaze swept the room, a quick assessment as he laid her wet cloak over a chair—

He stopped, staring across the little room. Across the table beside the cushioned bench, to a strange object, a nest of copper tubes and leather stitching wrapped around a glass globe.

Panic filled her chest, poured down from nowhere she could name.

Richa carefully crossed to the thing. He tapped the glass globe. "What is this?"

She couldn't tear her eyes away from the thing on the table. There was something brown and lumpy in the glass globe, and she had the sense this made everything worse but not why.

Lira, don't touch it, she heard Redolfo say.

"We have to go," Amadea said, her voice fracturing on her suddenly tight throat. That thing was bad. This was bad.

"Someone's been in here," Richa said.

She was not supposed to be here. They were not supposed to touch that—

Duke Borcia won't play, Redolfo had said, and she remembered her hands clutching heavy skirts, fidgeting with the fabric. *So your task is greater than ever. And this is all you have?*

And someone had died, she thought. Because of that thing.

"No purpose to Terzanelle any longer." Redolfo's voice is full of disgust. "Ul-Shandiian's pride is boundless but his sense less so. Clean it up."

"Richa," she said. "We have to go. Now."

He looked at her, baffled. There was a piece of paper in his hand. "Yeah," he said, walking back toward her. "I think it's time to bring this—"

"No, *now!*" The panic in her chest was a fire, burning away her breath. She yanked the door open. She shoved him through, hurrying him down the stairs, feeling as though the fire were behind her too, as if there were no amount of space she could put between her and that stone room that would be safe.

Stone room? a little part of her asked. That was a different place, a different time, a different danger—she couldn't get her thoughts back together.

They didn't stop until they had gone around the corner, under the eaves of the Church of Noniva, with their curling, tentacular carvings.

"I think I've had an intruder," Richa started. But then he frowned, took her by the shoulders. "What's going on? You're shaking."

She shook her head—she couldn't explain. "I don't know," she managed, fighting to keep the plaintiveness from her voice. "What was that?"

"Your guess is as good as mine," he admitted. He opened one hand, a paper clutched in it. "This was with it. I don't know what it is either."

The rain had smeared the writing, but Amadea could make out a single line: *The blasphemous are cast into the desert, their lying tongues bereft of water, and only the mercy of the vultures is theirs.*

Amadea started to ask who would have left such a thing, but then the roaring of the rain was drowned out by a greater sound, and a wave of wind and stones swept away all her senses. Richa pulled her close, and close against the wall of the Church of Noniva, as the front of his apartment building exploded.

IV

LACUNAE

Spring
Beyond Khirazj

Picture the map, as the girl does now, the world spread out in a neat square. Here is Khirazj, the Heart of the World. There is Semilla, once irrelevant, then everything. And now, here is the girl and Redolfo and humans who are not quite Khirazji and the changelings—beyond even Khirazj, in a lacuna of history, a land whose bones stick up from the plain, broken and abandoned. A fallen wall like a great beast's jaw. A tilting column like a snapped-off rib. The scatter of tiles, a skull smashed to fragments among the blue-blossoming weeds.

Winter was swift and lonesome, for her at least. Redolfo never claimed his birthright—not in words—but the river's gift felt ever present as he convinced these survivors to his side. The girl remains an oddity, one they eye as suspiciously as they do changelings.

She had believed they would forge on through Khirazj, up the river, seeking others. But the river receded into the horizon weeks ago, replaced by a disappointment rising out of the girl, bubbles racing out of water. Anticipation fills her, fizzing up against her skull,

Redolfo's promised triumph always just out of reach, just beyond her understanding. Redolfo's plan is always further than she can see. If it does not lie in Khirazj, then where? When?

She knows better than to ask.

As the air grows warm and wet, they cross the great plain of dead nations. Camp comes together under a lone arch of red stone, the mouth of a building long decayed away. The girl huddles beside Melosino for comfort more than warmth, eyeing the carvings of horned women with scorpions' tails that crawl up the solitary pillar.

"Are they real?" she asks him softly.

"I've never seen one," he says. Then: "I don't think."

Before winter, she had been wary of him. After, he woke, smiling to see her, when the lonesomeness of the village in winter had left her feeling so hollow. Now they are as close as her imaginings that fateful night.

She didn't make him quite right. There is no way to speak all the truth of a person into a changeling while the Venom of Khirazj takes hold—she knows now that the changelings' minds pull the stories you give them together, much as people's minds pull together the lies borne by the Venom of Changelings into true.

But Melosino seems to feel the gaps, to note what's missing, and the girl knows what this feels like. The edges of some other self are in her, and she doesn't know when she will brush against them or how they will cut her.

She remembers Ibramo, the first time she met him, a gangly boy in clothes as fine as her own. She remembers how the dress itched. How she was afraid to move. How the fountain splashed. She remembers Redolfo's hand pushing her forward, his voice saying, *You've heard the rumor that one of the princesses survived, Ibramo?*

She doesn't look like a princess, Ibramo said. And the girl remembers freezing, trying to guess what she did wrong, what she forgot. The ache of her cheeks, the swirl of her memories. Maybe she isn't a princess, or maybe being a princess is something Ibramo Kirazzi doesn't understand, but in that moment, the girl felt sure the most likely thing was that she failed a test.

This, she tells Melosino, was when she stopped thinking of her name.

She wishes these days, she could take it all back, leave Melosino to his wildness and unformed state. She wishes she could have such a state too—to be something that could remake itself as it wished.

When she looks away from Melosino, Redolfo is watching her.

"Why did the changelings raze everything here?" she asks, trying to be bold. "Did they not want this city?"

"This wasn't the changelings," Redolfo says. "This was Khirazj and Bemina. A long time before changelings—did you think they invented war?"

"No," the girl says, although she must admit, she never thought of it. Changelings *mean* destruction—what else could it be? The fire pops and flares as a vein of sap opens to the flames. There are two dozen trapped changelings now, sitting around them in the firelight. Watching. The humans have come to trust Redolfo has them in hand, but they never sit too close.

"This place I know," Redolfo says, "because it was lost so long ago. Isn't that funny? The ones who fell to the changelings, those we forgot easily. The ones we triumphed over? We carry them on.

"This was Yojiath," he says, gesturing into the darkness where the insects buzz. "And Khirazj took it for its copper mines. And then in the First Sickness, when the civil wars happened, Bemina took it from us for the same reason."

"Monstrous," Melosino murmurs.

"What happened to the people?" the girl asks.

Redolfo shrugs. "What always happens to people. They died or they moved or they changed. But they're gone now." His gaze moves to Melosino, and the girl feels an odd flare of protectiveness.

"Lira," Redolfo says, "come. Let me show you the carvings on the other side."

He will show her no carvings. The girl is sure of that as she rises. Melosino regards her with worried eyes, but she gestures at him to stay, to wait. She follows Redolfo out into the darkness.

Around the edge of the great gate, only the half-moon's light reaches them. Redolfo looks up at the carvings, indistinct, as he says, "You need to do something about your changeling."

"I did it wrong," she says, lowering her gaze.

"No," he allows. "That one's...difficult. Some of them have been. Willful. They require extra measures."

The girl's heart twists, that deep despair wrung from it. Extra measures. More poison. More *tell me again*. More memories she can't fit together. It's never enough; she's never enough.

Redolfo, still not looking at her, reaches into his jacket and takes out one of the syringes. "Here. Do it again. Tell it to be more... peaceful. More accepting. It needs to not notice the cracks."

She takes the syringe, weighs it in her hand. "Is that how the other one works?" she asks. "The other venom?"

"Lira." Redolfo turns to face her. "Go take care of this."

The girl walks back to the changeling with her maybe-brother's face, something congealing out of the cold despair. She remembers the needle going in—so many times. She remembers the words— her words? Perhaps. She knows the edges, the cracks, the lacunae that glow with the absence of memory—is noticing it why she's not the right one? Or is noticing why she's the one who's here, now, beyond any map? Are these the reasons she's the one who's survived?

Melosino watches her as she approaches. *The changeling*, she reminds herself. It's the enemy, a tool. It's destruction if she lets it be itself.

But it looks up at her, genuine worry in her brother's dark eyes.

"Are you all right?" he asks. "Did he hurt you?"

"No," she says, and kneels down in front of him. If she doesn't do it, Redolfo will know. If she doesn't do it *now*, Redolfo will be angry. She takes out the syringe, and Melosino regards it between them, his expression unreadable.

"What do you remember?" she asks. "*Really* remember."

He hesitates. "What do you mean?"

"Do you know you're a changeling?" she asks. "He thinks you do."

She sees the lies he wants to speak like they're peeking through the windows of his eyes, assessing her: *No, of course not. How could that be? I'm sorry, do you mean changelings, actual changelings?*

But what he says is, "Yes. But I would never hurt you."

She holds up the syringe. "I have an idea," she says, so quietly only the ghosts of Yojiath might overhear her. "It might make him angry, though. So you can't tell him."

"I don't want to tell him anything," Melosino says, just as quietly.

When she holds out a hand, he lays his forearm in it, and she pulls the arm closer, laying the tip of the needle against the swell of a biceps.

"I'm going to tell you about yourself," she says, before she sets the poison, so that he knows what's coming. "Because it isn't fair you don't know."

The skin pops as the needle breaks it, the poison pushed in along with her rebellion. She only wishes someone had done this for her.

"We found you in the canyon of Orozhand," she says. "The others came on you and beat you severely. You were..." She struggles to describe what Melosino looked like, so formless her eyes hurt to see it. "You were in your own skin then. And Redolfo told me to do this. To give you this form. I hope it's not too terrible," she adds. "And I hope you tell me what it helps you remember."

CHAPTER THIRTEEN

Richa wouldn't have thought his night could go worse than his lead faltering, his invitation to Amadea being interrupted, followed by his apartment exploding, but when they got to the Kinship Hall, it got worse with a vengeance.

Before they could get to a quiet room, before he could so much as ask Amadea why she had known to panic at the strange object that had almost certainly been the explosive, Quill and Tunuk caught up to them.

"I don't have time to interview you right now," he started.

But Tunuk took a twist of wood from a pocket and thrust it at Richa. "This is a wooden clavicle," he said bluntly. "Where do you think the bones of Saint Hazaunu are?"

"They're in a vault by now," Amadea said. "At Nanqii ul-Hanizan's house. Where did that come from?"

"You should look into ul-Hanizan's vault," Quill said. "You should look into that right now. And send vigilants to the Hawk's Nest."

"Why?" Richa asked.

"Because a Borsyan separatist has the wooden bones!" Tunuk hissed. "Or at least she had this one and a tooth."

Richa sent the three of them up to his office and went to find someone to go pull in Nanqii and someone to muster a force to sweep the Hawk's Nest. At night. In the rain. No one was going to enjoy this.

He caught Hulvia leaving for the night. "We have a very big problem," he told her. "Those wooden bones might not have made it to ul-Hanizan's vault. We need the guards, the cadets, the priests, and the archivists interviewed, *and* Nanqii ul-Hanizan."

Hulvia scowled at him. "And like before, I ask, do I look like your cadet? Why can't you do this?"

"Because someone blasted my apartment with a trap that made an imperial bombard look like a Salt-Sealing cracker."

Her eyes went wide, her tentacles snapping anxiously. "What? Are you all right? Who the fuck would trap your apartment?"

"I don't know," he said. "But I don't have time to find out *and* figure out why someone just came in carrying one of the wooden bones. Now, I am *required* to tell the imperial liaison that this joint operation, however ceremonial, has gone awry. But as my friend, could you please get someone to pull in that group so we can find out what happened?"

"All right." She looked him over. "Do you need some place to stay? Don't say the ready room—you are too old to sleep on those cots."

Saints and devils—his apartment was *gone*. His space, his safety, his things. "I . . . will let you know. I have to figure some things out first." Like whether he could be safe *anywhere* now.

If you suggest it's Stellano, then everything comes out, he thought. And there was no reason for it to be Stellano. It wasn't his style, and he had no reason to come for Richa after all this time.

But the dog, the knife, the unpickable lock that had to have been picked . . .

You don't know him after all this time, he thought. *That was the point of leaving.*

In his office, Amadea stood behind his desk, looking down at the wooden bone where it rested on a clear space. Tunuk had claimed the chair by the wall, his knees drawn up to his ears, while Quill stood beside him, his arms folded, bouncing nervously on his heels.

"Vigilant Manche's bringing in the people who were in the procession. And Nanqii." He turned to Quill and Tunuk. "Where did the bone come from?"

"A woman dropped it, a friend of Chizid's half brother," Quill said. "I think she's some sort of fabricator and probably some sort of separatist. Her name's Vigdza."

"Why do you think she's a fabricator?" Richa asked.

"Well, obviously she's not," Quill said. "They only allow men to join the Brotherhood. But she was asking Gunarro for advice on some sort of apparatus, like she knew how it worked but maybe wasn't trained enough?"

"What...did the apparatus look like?" Amadea asked.

Quill shrugged. "A cold-magic thing. Lots of tubes and glass bulbs and valves in a sort of nest around a globe."

Amadea met Richa's gaze. It sounded very similar to the thing that had been sitting on his table, the gift left by his unwelcome visitor. Except there had been no cold-magic, no faint bluish glow at the center of that tangle. No power for it.

"She had a boss," Tunuk added. "The first time, he came with her."

Quill made a face. "I don't know if he was her boss."

"*He* certainly thought he was her boss. A Borsyan man. He wanted to know what the device did."

"Can you describe him?" Richa asked.

"Old," Tunuk said.

"Not *that* old," Quill said. "Like forty? Blond hair. Pale skin."

"Face like a skull."

"High cheekbones," Quill corrected. "And strong jaw, I guess you'd say. He had a yellow coat on, although who knows if you can track that. Pretty easy to change your coat."

Richa held his breath. He knew that coat.

"You can't dress like a canary and expect to go unnoticed," he'd argued.

Stellano smirked, the scar at the corner of his mouth making his smile lopsided, his face somehow *more* handsome for it. "I don't want to go unnoticed. I want everyone to know I'm coming." He'd twirled, Egillio barking and chasing the swirl of the coat, the golden fabric shining in the sunlight through the window, and dared Richa, "Tell me I don't look like a gods-blasted king."

Shit, he thought. *Stellano, why are you fucking around with separatists?*

"Are you all right?" Amadea asked.

"Fine," he said, not looking at her. "So that man was there at the temple?"

"No, he was at Gunarro's house yesterday. Only Vigdza was at the temple. We followed her after she dropped that, but we lost her in an alley."

"She *disappeared*," Tunuk corrected.

"All right, well, she dropped that bone. We both saw that. And Gunarro said something about a tooth."

"Where did you lose her?" Richa asked. "What were you near?" Tunuk described a certain bridge off the main street through that part of the city. Richa ducked out and told the cadet to take the address to Hulvia, to ask her to send a detachment down to that neighborhood. "Why were you down there, anyway?" Richa asked when he returned.

"We were trying to find out how Saint Hazaunu got stolen the first time," Quill said. He looked to Tunuk, who straightened up, eyeing Richa in a wary way he could not miss.

"We found out some things about the first time the bones disappeared," Quill prompted. "And Tunuk remembered some things."

Tunuk looked as if he would deny ever remembering anything in the whole stretch of his young life. He looked up, his eyes glowing balefully at Richa. "Maybe some things. I don't know what use they'll be."

"Tunuk," Quill said reproachfully. "Come on."

Tunuk squirmed in his chair. He swung his gaze to Amadea, his eyes dimming.

"I knew the skeleton was fake," he said abruptly. "I mean, not wooden. I realized the catalogues had been changed. I didn't tell anyone because...because I knew it had to do with Qalba and Chizid leaving the archives. They asked me to keep the secret— although nobody bothered to explain what exactly the secret was, thank you very much—but I kept it anyway. I lied to you. I'm sorry."

Amadea moved around the desk to stand beside him. "I'm sorry they put you in that position," she said. "So you don't know why the skeletons were swapped?"

"No," Tunuk said.

"We talked to the generalist who was in the bone workrooms then," Quill said. "Plus Chizid's half brother, and Yinii talked to

Qalba's cousin." He hesitated, looking at Tunuk. "There were...
themes."

"A bunch of aspersions," Tunuk said.

"An argument," Quill prompted.

Tunuk glowered up at the ceiling. "They had a fight. Per thought
it was because Qalba was having an affair. She *wasn't*."

"Chizid got a knife ready for somebody," Quill said. "If he wasn't
trying to kill her lover—"

"Then he killed her," Tunuk snarled. "Just say it! All of you think
that's what happened—never mind it makes no sense, never mind it
doesn't explain how the wooden bones were stolen. Or why."

Quill sighed. "We didn't find the lover. There's also a friend, Toya
One-Saint. We couldn't find him either." Again, he gave Tunuk a
significant look. Again, Tunuk hunched down into himself.

"Do you remember the fight?" Richa asked Tunuk. "If you don't
think it was about Qalba having an affair, what was it?"

"I...I remember there *was* a fight," Tunuk said. "*A* fight. They
never fought. Never. But that one time...right before they...It was
bad. I was afraid. Qalba was so upset she threw up. But...I didn't
know what it was about. I just remembered...Chizid was very
angry and Qalba was very upset."

"How angry? Were you afraid he might hurt someone?"

"I..." Tunuk glanced sideways at Amadea.

"You remembered him saying someone would ruin her," Quill
reminded him. "Per remembered Chizid threatening to kill someone."

"I don't remember that."

"Gunarro did too." Tunuk still didn't say anything, and Quill
went on, "Even if you don't like the idea, you have to admit *something* happened, and when you consider what Gunarro said about her
and Toya—"

"Shut *up*!" Tunuk snapped. Patches of his skin rippled along his
arms, and he clapped hands over them, gasping. Quill shot forward,
pressing his own hands over one of the patches.

"Stay with me," he said, his voice shaking. "We're just talking. I
might be wrong."

Amadea was on her knees, peeling Tunuk's hand gently off the opposite arm. "Let it go," she said firmly. "I know you don't want to have this conversation, but...Tunuk, it needs to come out."

Tunuk stared at the floor between them, his shoulders heaving, his eyes glittering along the edges with sudden tears. "I don't want to talk about Gunarro's stupid theory, all right?" he said.

They were all silent a moment. Then Richa said, "Did you find anything that might relate to a series of thefts from the archives?"

Tunuk tensed again, and Quill said, "Gunarro, the half brother, he immediately assumed we were there because of a theft. That Qalba had stolen something, even before we mentioned the bones."

Richa raised his eyebrows. "So, maybe Qalba was a thief?"

"No," Tunuk said witheringly. Then: "I don't know."

"I ask," Richa said, "because someone was stealing very small artifacts from the archives over a long period of time. Always sorcerer-wrought artifacts. And then a set of wooden bones—a whole sorcerer-wrought skeleton—went missing from the Bone Vault."

"I don't know!" Tunuk said again. "Maybe?"

"Could that have been what they were fighting about?" Amadea asked. "Had Chizid caught her stealing?"

Tunuk shrugged violently. "Maybe she was a filthy thief. Maybe it was an affair. Maybe Chizid killed her and hid the body and threw Saint Hazaunu away. I suppose those are good reasons not to care!" He said this last bit as if he were trying to hurt someone with the words. But the only person being hurt was Tunuk.

"Or maybe she was being blackmailed," Amadea said quietly. "If... if someone was going to ruin her, maybe she was stuck helping them."

Tunuk turned to her, his eyes softening. "Maybe. Maybe...that would be a reason she stole. She...she had people she wanted to protect. Chizid. Toya. Me," he added quietly.

"So it's small things," Richa said. "And then the man—the one who's going to ruin her—escalates. Something changed. What changed?"

Tunuk shook his head. "Nothing. It was all the same. And then the fight."

"A fight so bad she vomited," Quill pointed out.

"Oh," Amadea said. She pulled her hands back from Tunuk, pressed to her waist, suddenly still. "Was Qalba pregnant?" she asked quietly.

Tunuk straightened. "I...I have no idea."

"She vomited after the fight. Maybe that was just the intensity of things. Maybe it's isolated. But...early pregnancy can cause...It's very uncomfortable. I hear."

Richa turned to her in surprise—that didn't sound like something she'd just heard—and Amadea was the one fixedly staring at Tunuk.

"It would be a chance for a blackmailer to escalate," Richa said. "Something more fragile to threaten." Amadea looked askance and brushed her sleeves off—anxious. "We still don't know why anyone would want the wooden bones—then or now. Or who two of our three murder victims are. Or even what Qalba would be blackmailed over."

Richa finally looked away from Amadea, considering Tunuk. "You examined the other skeleton in the archives kind of quickly."

"You were in a hurry," Tunuk said.

"But you could do better."

Tunuk shot a glance at Amadea, fidgeting with the laces of his boots. "I wasn't lying. It's barely 'worked.' It...it was worked enough to get some sense of age and minerals but...I might not be able to tell you anything useful. And I can't tell you a name—it doesn't *have* a name."

"I know," Richa said. "But it has information, and if you can give me information, I might be able to tell you who it was."

Tunuk bunched up tighter. "I have a guess," he said in a very small voice. Then: "Can I...can I not do this alone?"

⊶ ⚎ ⊷

Down in the cold mortuary room, the unknown skeleton lay on a slab of stone, its arms released from their wired poses, the largest of its gems removed. Tunuk knew what he was looking at was an *it*—inanimate, unnamed—but he found he couldn't stop thinking of it as *her.*

Eight steps from the bones, he turned away, the urge to flee too much. Quill caught his arm. "Tunuk, wait."

He felt the bone oozing up through his skin, the spiral ready to envelop him. "I can't," Tunuk managed. "I don't...I don't want to know."

"It's all right," Amadea said, her hand on Tunuk's back. "If it's too much right now, we can wait. We can sit with it."

They were silent for a long moment, an interminable moment, just waiting. Tunuk shook his head, his eyes burning with tears. "What if I can't...? What if it's her and I went about my business all those days, never doing anything? What if it's her and I didn't stop her from dying?"

Amadea took Tunuk's face in her hands. "Do you think Qalba would have wanted you to torture yourself like this? If it is her, then... then we can find out what's on the other side of the answer. But sitting in the middle, wondering... Tunuk, it's too much to ask of you."

"You told me before," Quill said, "it might be kinder if they're both dead. But I think whatever the answer is, it's kinder than you worrying."

They were right, Tunuk thought. He did not want to know, but not knowing was gnawing him from the inside out. He wiped his eyes, feeling foolish. "Thank you."

"You ready?" Richa asked. And Tunuk was not, but he would never be.

Tunuk laid his fingers on the sternum of the skeleton, letting his eyes fall closed. The thrumming moved up through his hands—phalanges, metacarpals, carpals, the puzzle-like bones of the wrists—into his arms, the long bones of his limbs vibrating like plucked zither strings, the bones' song calling back to him. It was whispery and faint, incomplete as if the bones were not quite awake, singing in their sleep. But as he listened, he found the sense of it.

"She... they were thirty-four," he said, his voice sounding thick and husky in his own ears. Was that how old Qalba had been? He remembered buying her honey cakes and wild celery jellies for her birthday one year, saving up for some carved hair sticks another, but the numbers wouldn't come to him. "Thirty-four... four months... eight days..."

He moved a hand to the skull, cupping the pale curve of the cranium with one long hand, his thumb hooking into the left eye socket. "They didn't get enough sun," he murmured, feeling the weaknesses in the bone that were old, grown into it—years of working in the archives? "They're missing a tooth, the right upper bicuspid. They lost it probably four years before they died."

Had Qalba lost a tooth like that? He sifted through memories of her, smiling, laughing, leaning on Chizid as she tried to catch her breath—was there a shadow there in the arch of her jaw? He couldn't remember. He found himself dreading confirmation and wishing for it in turn.

The injuries were subtle—the bones beat the rhythm of an old fracture to the radius, a long-ago crack in the third toe. Tunuk felt the memory eel past, of kicking something too hard to be kicked, the crunch of small bones. The scrapes of the knife on the vertebrae were like a patter of rain behind those, until Tunuk turned his attention that way.

"She..." His voice caught in his throat. "Stabbed. Multiple times. In the neck. It caught the vertebrae in three places. I don't...I don't know..." He wept, his cheeks cool with tears, the howl he couldn't bear to let out trapped in his throat. *Who did this to you?*

The spiral thrummed inside him, a deep sound that reverberated through his own bones, ringing in his skull.

"What's happening?" he heard Quill say.

"Tunuk," Amadea said, "you can stop. It's all right."

But Tunuk didn't take his hands away. The bones weren't Qalba—Qalba was gone. But he owed her this still. He slipped deeper beneath the rhythm, the beat of his own bones matching the remains on the table. The whole skeleton pulsed beneath his hands, bone singing to bone, and Tunuk could feel the hints and deposits that made *this* bone what it was. The pitch, the pattern, they sang of Maqama, of the cavern-towns, of barley and rabbit meat. The bones remembered how they'd lain together while alive; he felt their height—they would have come to the middle of Tunuk's chest. And Tunuk remembered Qalba gathering him close, maternal even though her forehead only hit his sternum.

Come here, shashkii, her voice said in his thoughts, between the beat of the bones. *It will be all right.*

Who did this to you? Tunuk wanted to scream, a violence, a monstrous anger rising up in him. Maybe he was the yinpay—for Qalba he might be the yinpay, something hideous in the shadows, ready to shred the unwary and wicked.

Shashkii, she would have said. *Not that.*

You're gone, Tunuk thought. *You don't know what's best. Maybe you never knew what was best.*

"Tunuk?" Quill's voice came, distant and wary. "Tunuk, I think you should stop."

"What's happening on his arms?" he heard Richa say, panic in his voice.

He felt Amadea's hand settle on his neck, her voice as if far away, saying, "Tunuk," and all of him *wanted* to listen, to turn back, the pull of her was like the spiral—

Instead, Tunuk put his other hand on the skull, cradling the face that wasn't there. He felt the contours of the bone, begged for the memories of the tissue that had lain there. The arch of cheekbones, the rise of cartilage, the swell of the cornual process over the orbits where the horns—

Tunuk pulled his hands off the skull.

Arms aching, vision sliding back into focus, he looked down at the skeleton, frowning.

"What is it?" Richa asked.

"It's not her forehead," he whispered. He turned to the other end of the skeleton, considering the flare and width of the pelvis.

"I think..." He cleared his throat, his grief still choking him. "I...feel like this is a man's skeleton."

"Was Qalba identified as male at birth?" Quill asked.

Tunuk shook his head. "I don't know. I don't...I don't know, but it's not her face." He looked back at the skull. "The horns...I... The cornual processes are usually denser in males, the dark-eye orbit is wider in females—I mean, it's a spectrum. There's not a fucking mold or anything, but..." He laid tentative fingers on the swell of the horns. "These...these are too heavy for her. If I'm remembering right."

And how could he be sure he was remembering correctly, not just grasping at possible answers that meant this wasn't Qalba?

But Richa had crossed the cold crypt to where he'd set his notes and pulled out a paper with the archives' elaborate seal pressed to the bottom of the page. "This says Qalba was born in year thirty-five of the reign of Empress Clotilda. That makes her...thirty-two the year she vanished. That's close."

Tunuk shook his head, feeling a little faint. "If you were just measuring the bone—calipers and things—it would be close, but the bone *told* me. Thirty-four years, four months, eight days. One of these dates is wrong."

"Let's say it's not her, then," Richa said, looking grimly up at Tunuk. "Who are we looking at?"

Quill's eyes widened. "Toya. We can't find Toya ul-Shandiian. This might be Toya ul-Shandiian! Masculine build, Orozhandi—"

"No," Tunuk said. "Thirty-four years, four months, eight days. Toya was probably forty-five or fifty." Tunuk frowned down at the skeleton. "I have no idea who this is." Except it *wasn't* Qalba.

"The lover?" Amadea asked. "Was Toya the lover?"

"No, Toya ul-Shandiian was a friend of Qalba's," Quill explained. "We can't figure out what happened to him. He might be involved, though."

Richa cursed and dragged a hand through his hair. "If he was forty-five or fifty when you saw him last, that puts him at fifty-seven to sixty-two now? Shit. Tunuk, come here and look at something?"

Tunuk followed Richa deeper into the crypt, where the air grew colder and drier still, the other archivists following. Laid out on one of the stone tables was the corpse of an older Orozhandi man, his hair long and gray, his horns dripping charms to Saints Asla and Hazaunu. There was still the faint dent in the side of his skull, the injury healed wrong, but his cheeks, once full and flushed, were gray and slack with wrinkles.

"The peddler?" Quill said, sounding shocked.

"Toya," Tunuk breathed. "*That's* Toya One-Saint."

⌖

The cold air of the mortuary room clouded their breath as they stood over the dead Orozhandi man. The last time Amadea had been in this room, she had been escorting Quill as he viewed his dead friend, and the mark of the Venom of Changelings on Karimo's shoulder had sliced her away from *here* and *now*, falling back through memories she'd tried to keep locked tight.

This time, she had eyes on Tunuk staring down at the dead man, a past she hadn't known about. Tunuk looked lost, confused—his huge eyes glowed up at her. "How did Toya end up with Saint Hazaunu? Why is he dead?"

"We should go back upstairs," Amadea said. They all stared at the dead man, his thin skin bruised, the dark crescent of his third eye peeking out where the lids gaped. Amadea took Tunuk by the arm, gently turning him away, but he jerked away from her touch.

"Why is he dead?" he demanded.

"Upstairs," Amadea said again. "We're not discussing this here."

Richa pulled the covering back up over Toya One-Saint, and they all went back upstairs to his office. "You're not still authorized to draft an affidavit of identity for a corpse, are you?" he asked Quill as he closed the door.

"Absolutely not," Quill said.

"Richa!" Amadea spun to see Yinii pushing through the half-closed door, towing Bucella behind her. Her gaze found Amadea's, and relief lit her face. "Oh, Amadea, we have a problem."

Bucella's dark cheeks were wet with tears, her eyes red and swollen. "They said you'd gone out," she said, her voice high with panic, "and you'd gone to the ul-Hanizan manor, but it was so late, and the rain, and I wasn't sure—"

"What happened?" Amadea asked, catching hold of the girl.

Bucella huffed a deep breath, and when she spoke again, the wobble in her voice was less pronounced. "I took the bones to the vault. Only I realized after that I hadn't told anyone about the borers in the tibia and that I should come by regularly to work on them—it's going to destroy the integrity of the—"

"She went back to the house where they brought the wooden bones of Saint Hazaunu," Yinii said. "And it's locked up tight. No one's there. Worse, it's *not* Nanqii ul-Hanizan's house."

Bucella sniffed. "We brought them to a row house down by the West River. I assumed it was his house."

Dread prickled down Amadea's arms. "Who told you to do that?"

"The priests," Bucella said. "They led the procession there, and then some servants showed us where to put the bones. Only now no one's there."

She looked back at Richa. This wasn't an incidental theft: this was a planned heist.

"Bucella, come with me?" Richa asked. "I'm going to take you to Vigilant Manche. She's getting testimony from the members of the translation procession. If you can help her find that house, it will be very helpful."

Tearfully Bucella nodded and went with him.

When the door shut again, Yinii regarded the rest of them, her fingers pulling at her gloves in an anxious way. "I talked to Oshanna. She showed me something." Her gaze seemed to catch on the plaques of bone still clinging to Tunuk's arms. "Maybe it should wait."

"No," Tunuk said. "Did she tell you why Toya One-Saint might be dead?"

Yinii drew a deep breath. "Not...exactly. She told me he was once ul-Shandiian. That he did something—he was anathema in the house. She wouldn't say what he'd done." She swallowed. "Dushar had a letter. It...was signed by Qalba One-Fox, though I can't verify that. I *can* verify it was written by someone over the Wall."

Tunuk went very still, like a shadow cast by a statue. Yinii looked back toward Amadea, her gaze full of meaning as she added, "It had some...implications about what life is like on the other side too. I don't think Dushar believes in it. I know he doesn't mean to share it. But Oshanna wanted it substantiated, so she showed it to me."

It was all Amadea could do not to ask Yinii *what* the letter had implied—Redolfo Kirazzi, a changeling army, terrifying war machines—

Her memory skipped again—an armory, the strange object, a room plastered with diagrams. *Duke Borcia won't play, so your task is greater than ever. And this is all you have?*

Lira, don't touch it.

Amadea shut her eyes tight. The object had been some sort of weapon—an explosive, that seemed plain enough. And in her memories, it was a weapon Redolfo had been seeking but hadn't managed to perfect. A weapon Tunuk and Quill had seen in the hands of a Borsyan separatist who might have also stolen the wooden bones of Saint Hazaunu.

But nothing she could remember, nothing she could dig out of her mind put those pieces together, and she could not tell if it was for lack of trying or because these things were separate catastrophes, separate tragedies falling at the same time.

Richa returned then, his mouth a grim line. "All right: We've got one theft twelve years ago connected to a murder and the disappearance of three people, one of whom is the peddler, now deceased. Then this theft, which is most definitely planned and connected in some fashion to Borsyan separatists?" He shook his head. "What am I missing?"

Quill looked at Tunuk. "Gunarro said Toya confessed he met Qalba working for the Usurper. 'Making things' for the coup. That would be something to blackmail a person over. Something that might get you called 'anathema,' right?"

Yinii nodded. "Yes. That would do it."

"No," Tunuk said, pacing the room. "It's not possible."

"There was something else," Yinii said. "I asked about the lover, like you said. She didn't think that was likely—"

"See?" Tunuk demanded.

"But," Yinii went on, "she did remember a man visiting while Chizid was gone. A Borsyan man named Stellano Zezurin. Do you know who that is?" she asked Tunuk.

He made a face. "No. She never had a Borsyan man visit. When was that supposed to have happened?"

Yinii shook her head. "I have no idea. She just remembered him being there when Chizid wasn't."

"He was definitely Borsyan?" Quill asked. "Not Orozhandi?"

"Stellano Zezurin isn't Orozhandi," Richa said.

His voice was tight, his expression peculiarly neutral. Amadea's nerves, still simmering from the strange device and the explosion, kindled again. "You know him?" she asked.

Richa nodded, avoiding her eyes. "Yeah, he's a criminal. Ties to Caesura. Slippery fellow."

Quill's eyes widened. "Is that Qalba's lover? Is that why she was stealing?"

"No," Richa said. "Stellano was definitely not Qalba's lover."

Someone rapped on the door, silencing all of them. Richa pulled it open to reveal another vigilant, a round-faced half-Orozhandi woman with her dark hair slicked back into a tight bun, her horns trimmed with silver rings.

"Can I help you, Vigilant?" Richa said.

She stared Richa down for a moment before saying, "I heard you had a guest, Vigilant Langyun. I need to question Sesquillio Seupu-lai about the murder on the road."

"We're in the middle of something," Richa said. Tunuk turned to loom over her, which was only going to make things worse. Amadea took his arm again and firmly redirected him to the chair.

"And I've been trying to get Brother Sesquillio to sit down since you fled the relay station."

"That's *Archivist* Seupu-lai," Quill called.

"Almost," Amadea said automatically.

Richa moved slightly, blocking Quill. "What if I told you I have an identity for your murder victim?"

She narrowed her eyes. "Why, then I'd expect you to tell me and not use it as a bargaining chip."

"I'm asking for a half an hour," Richa said. "I'm in the middle of questioning him myself." But he added, "The peddler's name was Toya One-Saint. Formerly ul-Shandiian. This man just identified him"—he pointed back at Tunuk—"and if your Paremi could draft an affidavit of identity while we finish getting all the information down, they'd probably be ready to take Quill's statements by the time it's finished."

Once more, she stared Richa down, as if she were waiting for something to reveal itself. "That's very helpful of you," she said. "I hear your apartment was destroyed. Fire?"

"Some kind of sabotage," he said. "I'm working on it."

"Seems like someone else should be taking up the investigation. Considering there's *somebody* out there willing to sabotage your home, as you say. And now the wooden bones are missing again?" The woman's smile was joyless as she studied Richa's face. "Where were you this evening?"

"With me," Amadea said. The vigilant looked up as if surprised at the interruption; her gaze flicked over Amadea's sodden, but inarguably official, uniform. "We were at a coffeehouse discussing the wooden bones. You can ask the proprietor. Or the vigilants who arrived after the...damage."

Her brows rose ever so slightly. Amadea did not break her gaze.

"Well," the vigilant said at last. "I'll send the Paremi up here when he's done taking Archivist Seupu-lai's statement." She looked past Richa to where Quill sat. "If you'll come with me, esinor? I'd like to hear about this murder you witnessed."

Quill stood, his expression hard. "Fine. Tell me what you figure out," he added to Richa as he passed. The vigilant closed the door behind her.

"Are you all right?" Amadea asked.

He shook his head. "She's doing her job," he said, in a way Amadea suspected was meant to convince himself as much as her.

Tunuk sprang up from the chair again as the door closed. "You're just going to let her *take* him? You told her about Toya! She can't just take him!"

"I told her about Toya because she's the one actually investigating his death," Richa said. "It would be an insult to my oath not to tell her, not to mention bad for everyone involved. Quill will be fine. What else do you know about Toya?"

"Nothing!" Tunuk said. "He was Qalba's friend. He was addled from a head injury."

Ul-Shandiian's pride is boundless, but his sense less so. Clean it up.

"Did he injure himself while working for Redolfo Kirazzi?" Amadea asked.

"No!" Tunuk cried. "I don't know, but it doesn't make sense. Not for him and not for Qalba! They wouldn't have done that!"

"Then where did they meet?" Richa asked.

"I don't *know*. But you're saying she worked willingly for the worst villain in recent memory—you might as well just call her a monster."

Amadea held her expression very, very still, but the words slid through the armor of her identity like a deftly wielded blade. *You were not willing,* she told herself.

Redolfo Kirazzi, his eyes shining. "We found you in Sestina. They will be so grateful to have you back." Hope blooming warm in her chest, a safety she hadn't thought to imagine before—

Liar, she told herself. She closed her eyes.

"People change," Amadea said. "People have secrets."

"Tunuk, you should calm down," Yinii said, her voice shaking. She kept glancing at Amadea, and there was nothing Amadea could do to get her to stop without drawing more attention to it. "Even if she worked with—"

"She wasn't a monster, and you'd have to be to help the Usurper!" Tunuk said. "And I'm not going to listen to this!" Before Amadea could rouse herself to stop him, he stormed from the room, slamming the door behind him.

Amadea watched him as if from a distance, pulled from her body by the cut of his words. A monster. A villain. A mistake.

I didn't want to. I didn't know better. She thought of Bishamar; *I said no this time.* She curled her nails into her palms, focusing on the pain, focusing on the grain of the floor.

"It's a difficult thing," Amadea made herself say. "To find out someone you trusted was a criminal." She made herself look up, look around. *Wooden trees. Black ink. Blue uniform.* Richa wasn't looking at her, and dread pooled around her heart. She pressed a surreptitious fist to her ribs.

"Yeah," Richa said, a sharp exhalation.

He wasn't in the spiral, Amadea told herself. *He needs some space. It's not because you can't look at him right now.* "I have to get him."

"Don't," Yinii said. "He'll just get angrier if you try to calm him down now." She turned to Richa. "Do you have those palimpsests? The sheets from the . . . where the peddler stored the bones?"

"Yes," Richa said slowly. "They're being held in evidence. Technically under Vigilant Gaitha-hyu's case. Are you sure you can—"

"No," Amadea said.

Yinii flushed. "I am perfectly capable of handling two pages of ink. Maybe he wrote something important? Something he blacked out with other writings?"

Richa looked to Amadea as if asking for permission, and for a brief, absurd moment, she wished she could go back to standing in

the rain under the overhang of the apartment building, held in the
present like an indrawn breath. She wished she did not have to think
of the future and the dangerous things that would spill out from letting Yinii reach for the power that had nearly subsumed her in the
tunnel below the Salt Wall.

She wished she did not have to sit with the knowledge that she
could never, ever cast off the past.

"It has been a very long day," Amadea said. "And we will have
another very long day ahead of us tomorrow. Richa, you have ink
specialists here. Let them do preliminary work. And, Yinii, we can
discuss this when everyone is better rested."

Yinii watched her with an unfamiliar fury. "What about the primate's files? You haven't done anything with those."

"I've started going through them. They're just bureaucracy at the
moment—"

"Just bureaucracy," Yinii said. Then: "There's a sorcerer transfer.
Did you see that?"

Oluali of the Marble, from Alcaic to Sestina. Amadea took a deep
breath, willing Yinii to mirror her. "You saw that. That's . . . I understand that's probably scary, just now—"

"It's abhorrent."

"It is sometimes what has to happen," Amadea said. "And I understand that feels cruel, and maybe it is—we don't know the circumstances. But please, you are not being transferred. You are not under
an isolation mandate. You are not . . ." *Not a sorcerer,* she almost said,
and she could tell Yinii knew exactly what was about to come out of
her mouth.

"Please," Amadea said. "Just . . . for now, I need you to slow down."

A little part of Amadea—a part she had silenced for so long it felt
traitorous to hear it once again—wanted to scream, *Do you think I
like this? Do you think I know how to solve it? I am keeping nothing from
you!* But Yinii only turned and left the room without another word.

"If you want to scream," Richa said, "it's better if we go down in
the vaults. I know that face," he added.

"I feel as if I'm going mad," Amadea said. "Someone stole a relic,
and we have no idea why. Someone was murdered, possibly *inside*

the archives, and we don't know who. Someone blew up your apartment with a device Borsyan separatists were getting tuned up—do you know any Borsyan separatists?"

"Not personally," he said. Then: "You knew what it was."

"No," Amadea said truthfully. "I . . . I knew it was bad, but I don't know why."

Richa studied her. "Maybe it's a pre-Sealing design. Maybe . . . maybe you saw it when you were a kid. Did you ever go to the Usurper's palace?"

Lira, don't touch it.

"I really can't remember where I saw it," she said. "I can look . . . I can ask Ibramo." She *should* ask Ibramo—maybe he knew how far those designs had gone; maybe he remembered Toya One-Saint, or even Qalba.

"I've got Dushar ul-Shandiian on my list to question," he said. "And with two ul-Shandiians suddenly involved with dirty business, I'm all the more inclined. And I might see if the Borsyan noble consul can have a chat. Tell me if he knows a fabricator who might be trying to kill me. And I'll get people looking for her—Vigdza—and Chizid's brother as her contact."

"What about Esinor Zezurin?" Amadea asked. "Is he someone you could question?"

Richa's expression closed, and her pulse jumped—she had gone too far. "I'll deal with that. You should . . . you should both probably go back to the archives. Get some rest. I'll make sure Quill gets back all right."

There was, in that moment, nothing Amadea wanted so much as to go back to her office, to her room beyond, closing door after door between her and the world. All her skills felt in tatters. She could not steady Tunuk, she could not soothe Yinii, she had struck some secret heart in Richa—and after that brief bright point of the coffee, the tempting edge of something in the vestibule of his apartment, it hurt so much more to realize she'd made him close off and not known why.

And beyond all of that, there was herself. She was drowning, and there was no one she could reach to for safety.

Except perhaps Ibramo, she thought. *And you can ask him in the morning.*

CHAPTER FOURTEEN

Quill drummed his fingers on the armrest of the witness's chair, opposite Vigilant Salva Gaitha-hyu. If he closed his eyes, he saw the dead peddler, the lonely bones, layered on top of one another, a patchwork of murders. When he opened them, there would only be the vigilant, stone-faced and implacable.

"Do you want to hear it again?" he asked. He'd described the death of the peddler—Toya One-Saint, he thought—and the discovery of Saint Hazaunu half a dozen times already, and Richa's part in it specifically once again.

Vigilant Gaitha-hyu tapped a stylus against the table before her. "Did you see Vigilant Langyun speak to anyone else when you arrived?"

"The vigilants at the door," he recited. "The innkeeper. The stable hand. He wasn't really in the mood for talking. We even fought about it."

"What about the peddler? Did Vigilant Langyun talk to him?"

Quill sighed. "I think he said 'excuse us' to him when he came to get me. He didn't want anything."

"And while you were talking to the peddler, what was he doing?"

"Unloading our boxes."

"So, while you were talking and he was unloading boxes, are you absolutely certain he didn't talk to anyone besides the two vigilants at the door, the stable hand, and the innkeeper?"

Quill glanced at the Paremi writing out his answers at a table to the side, a young woman with pale skin and angled eyes, thickly curled red hair in a row of puffs down her skull. She didn't look up at him—which was protocol. *Pretend you aren't there.* Quill hadn't taken down testimonies for the Vigilant Kinship in his time with the Paremi, aside from helping Richa the one time, but it seemed an awful lot like recording in court. The same question six times from six angles. The suggestions and prodding to get an answer with some meat to it. He understood, in a distant way, that really all of this was protocol. Not personal.

But by then, he'd been drowning in too many puzzles, too many tragedies. Too much struggling to say the right thing, to guide the right answers. Lies about Redolfo and Amadea and what he knew about Tunuk. He wasn't helping anybody, and he could not keep the protocol going.

"Unless you have an actual question I can actually answer, I'd like to go home," Quill said.

Vigilant Gaitha-hyu paused a moment. "How well do you know Vigilant Langyun?"

"We were almost murdered together," Quill said. "Twice. That tends to make you close."

"Yes. The son of Khoma Seupu-lai, the assistant to the Ragaleate primate, entangled in a conspiracy by one of the Usurper's remnants, at which point he forsakes his oath and swears a new one to the Imperial Archives. That's a lot of hasty decisions and a lot of traumatic events."

"If you say so."

"And how well, after all that, do you *know* Richa Langyun?"

"He hasn't met my mother, if that's what you're getting at," he quipped. "But you should say what you mean."

She smiled at last, but Quill didn't think it was for his joke. "Are you aware that Richa Langyun was for many years a prolific thief in Caesura? That he was named as an accessory to additional crimes, including one very high-profile set of killings?"

Quill paused so long that the Paremi glanced up at him. "I'm sorry?" he said.

"Richa Langyun is a thief. Or he was, before he swore to the Vigilant Kinship. Who knows what he's doing now." Gaitha-hyu peered at him, her bright eyes sharp. "But that business four months ago, that also aligns with him being cast out from the Kinship."

"He was reinstated."

"Do you know why?"

"That would be hearsay."

She nodded, as if she appreciated the point. But then she added, "Has he ever spoken of Stellano Zezurin?"

A chill skittered up Quill's back at the name, the one Yinii had said. "No," he said slowly. "Why?"

"I suppose you aren't all that close, then," she said, "if he's never mentioned the man he shared a home with for five years."

A criminal, Richa had said, when Amadea had pressed him. *Operates out of Caesura. Very ... slippery fellow.* Not a hint of something more personal.

"They were lovers?" Quill asked.

"They were," the vigilant confirmed. "Or maybe they are. Stellano Zezurin is a very crafty and dangerous man, with very wide-ranging enterprises. Did Vigilant Langyun talk to anyone in Ragale? Perhaps by the docks?"

Quill's thought flashed back to Ragale, to long hours inside requesting and collecting and offering up the archives' assurances for Primate Lamberto's papers. Richa hadn't been with him. And then he'd been distracted and quiet all the way home ...

"I don't know," Quill admitted.

"I believe you," she said, "when you tell me he didn't wield the knife against the peddler. At least so far as you could see."

"Why would he even have killed Toya One-Saint?"

"A good question," she admitted. "I've heard the archives have authenticated the wooden bones as being known post-Sealing artifacts ... but then they were stolen again. Which makes me wonder if something else is being hidden."

Quill squinted at her, trying to make sense of that. "What would you hide in a wooden skeleton?"

"Not *in* it," she said. "If you look into Stellano Zezurin's crimes, you'll find a lot of people who are dead for a lot of reasons. I think you have a good enough imagination to figure out why the peddler could be dead, but I think it takes even less imagination to come up with what might happen to confederates in such an endeavor that you'd like to be rid of. I don't think forsaking an oath to Stellano Zezurin is a matter he takes as lightly as even the Paremi."

Quill's thoughts churned as the vigilant returned to protocol: finishing her statement, repeating his location in the city, reminding him not to leave until he was alerted the case was complete. Over and over he found himself playing through the night outside the relay station, checking his memories. How long had he left Richa? Long enough to speak to an assassin? How close had Richa been in the fight over the knife? Close enough to slip between them? He'd never mentioned Caesura, but then Richa wouldn't really talk about himself, no matter how Quill prodded.

This is exactly what you were trying to tell Tunuk, he found himself thinking. *Primate Lamberto and Qalba and now Richa—you think you're going to learn from them, but maybe you're just a pawn.* He hadn't seen it, yet again.

He shook the thought from his head, but it remained, like a splinter he couldn't pull free.

Richa was waiting for him in the hallway outside the interview room, leaning against the wall with a distant expression. He bounced up to his feet as Quill left the room, military straight as Gaitha-hyu followed him out. "All finished," she said. "Do you need the Paremi now?"

"I have it handled," he said.

Her hard gaze studied his face, as if tracking lies across his features. "So you lost the wooden bones."

"We're looking into it."

"You didn't travel with the procession," she went on. "You left some cadets to do the work."

"In the company of six imperial soldiers on an escort task. It was a simple job and an honor."

"But not one for you." She looked him over once more. "You know, I thought you might be a clever criminal, but now I wonder if what you are is a shitty vigilant."

Richa said nothing, but Quill saw his jaw muscles flex as Salva Gaitha-hyu strode away.

"She thinks you killed the peddler," Quill said, still watching Richa's face.

He blew out a breath. "I know. Sorry you're in the middle of it. Come on—I told Amadea I'd walk back with you. And...there's some things we should talk about."

"Oh?" Quill asked.

But Richa didn't confess to Caesura or Stellano Zezurin or thefts or murders—as they walked through the Kinship Hall, he told Quill about how Tunuk had run off, about Yinii's outburst, about how Amadea was fraying. "She kind of...panicked when she saw the explosive," Richa said. "I think she might need more help than she's letting on."

She can get in line, Quill thought, and regretted it. "You have people looking for Vigdza and the wooden bones? What about Stellano Zezurin?"

Richa didn't answer at first, and Quill waited for the brush-off, the *don't worry about him*, the *we don't need to go after Stellano, we have enough here*.

But then Richa stopped walking. "She told you, didn't she?"

Quill looked back, a frisson of panic buzzing in the back of his chest. They were doing this. "Told me what?"

"Salva. Vigilant Gaitha-hyu," Richa said. "She told you about..."

"About Caesura?" Quill prompted. When Richa hesitated, he added, "About your crime-lord boyfriend?"

Richa just stood, watching him, but whereas before, Quill would have worried about how much of his feelings were bared on his face for the vigilant to analyze, this time it was Richa's face laid open like a book.

He was afraid.

"Please."

Richa was afraid, and Quill was suddenly aware that he was being cruel.

"She doesn't have proof," Quill managed. "She just...It doesn't look very good, now, does it? But you didn't. Did you?"

"I didn't kill the peddler," Richa said. "You were *there*."

Quill hesitated. "What about those other things? She said you used to be a thief. That you're connected to some killings?"

Richa didn't answer. "Please," he said again. He swallowed. "Just...don't tell her. Please."

"Salva?"

"*Amadea*," he said forcefully. "Look, I can't...I can't change what happened. The man I was is as good as dead—I killed everything about him. I've held this oath for fifteen years, and that should mean something, but...it still happened." He swallowed. "But I can't...I don't want her to know I was a shitty street thief." He raked a hand through his hair. "Better a shitty vigilant."

Now it was Quill's turn to stare silently. "You're fond of her."

"Yeah," Richa said. "Yeah, I am. And before you tell me that's a bad idea—the consort-prince and being in the middle of a potential attack from beyond the Wall, not to mention stolen bones and separatist bombings—I *know*. I know very well. But...look, I'm not saying to lie to her, I'm saying...I can't—" His voice broke, and he stopped to collect himself. "I can't do this right now. I just need to be me. Please don't tell her I was someone else. I will do it. I know I have to do it. Just not right now."

Amadea's secret sat in Quill's throat, begging to be spoken. But that wasn't his either—and even if he told it, Richa was right. There were so many other things to pay attention to. Sometimes the best thing you could do was trust things would work out in their own time, focus on the problems before you.

"You should talk to her," he said. "Like...really talk to her. Not this...bantering thing you two do. She's...good at listening."

"Fair," Richa said.

"But first," Quill said, "Vigilant Gaitha-hyu suggested you're still involved with Stellano. Are you?"

"Five broken kings, fuck *no*!" Richa said, flushing. "I fled that man, and I have done everything to stay away from him. I don't know what he's doing. I don't know why she cares. And honestly I would die happy not knowing—the man I was is *dead*, and that includes any part that gave two shits together about Stellano Zezurin."

"All right," Quill said. "I believe you. I won't tell Amadea."

Richa shut his eyes. "Thank you."

They continued through the building, out into the entry hall with its massive statue of Vigilant Mother Ayemi. There were fewer people moving through it so late at night: a handful of vigilants heading out on patrol, a few people dozing on benches. Yinii sat near the statue, waiting. She stood when she saw them, then marched straight up to Richa, tapping her amulets as she approached.

"Richa," she said, "you should let me examine the palimpsests."

"No," Richa said firmly. "Amadea told you to go home and rest, and we can talk about it later."

"But I—"

"We know enough. This can wait." He paused. "I do have something smaller." He took from his pocket a crumpled piece of paper, damp and torn along one edge. "It was with the explosive. But it got wet while we were running. Can you separate out the water so the ink doesn't get lost?"

Yinii winced. "Sort of. I can't do that—no one can do that. There's no such thing as water specialists. I don't think, anyway. But I can pull the ink out from the water? It will take a while, and I need clean paper to transfer the ink to. You might want to have a paper specialist examine it if there might be something important about it, but—um—they get really upset when the paper gets damp—" She frowned at the paper. "Can I see it?"

Richa unfolded the strip so the words were visible: *The blasphemous are cast into the desert, their lying tongues bereft of water, and only the mercy of the vultures is theirs.*

"That...that's a curse. An Orozhandi curse. It comes from a reza of ul-Hanizan, a really old book from—it doesn't matter."

"It might," Richa said. "It's an ul-Hanizan phrase?"

"Well, yes, but no. Something that old, it's all of ours, you know? But also the part that might matter is that Dushar ul-Shandiian found a similar note? That one I don't know where the saying is from, but it had a similar...sound, if that makes sense. His said, 'The saint's wrath calls the storm. The vulture is landed in the old cave.'" She looked from Quill to Richa. "It's sort of confusing. I don't think vultures live in caves. But caves are where we put bones? And vultures are the shepherds of the dead."

"Interesting," Richa said. "Thank you. I'll ask the reza ul-Shandiian about that."

Yinii swallowed. "I can be more helpful—"

"You are very helpful," he reassured her. "We'll go after the Borsyans and Dushar and see what's missing. And Amadea will tell me if you're all right to look at the palimpsests." He turned to Quill. "I guess you can get back on your own. If you see Amadea, tell her...well, tell her I said to go to sleep, probably." He turned and started to walk away.

The tension between him and Richa was too thick for Quill to bear. Salva had said they were not close—but they were close enough, Quill thought, that he couldn't leave it like this. He couldn't tell Richa that Amadea had secrets of her own, that those secrets made him doubt she would hold his past mistakes against him, even if Quill's first instinct was to do just that. He thought, oddly, of Karimo, and being the go-between for the shy scrivener and his admirers, and he swallowed against the lump in his throat and gestured for Yinii to wait a moment, before racing after Richa.

"She's not sleeping with him," Quill blurted.

"Who? Yinii?"

"Amadea," Quill said. "She's not sleeping with the consort-prince. I don't think she would, whatever...happened before. But...the archivists, they gossip. A *lot*. They know...she had a past with him, and if something were going on, they'd know. They'd talk. And they aren't. That's all." Richa kept his eyes on the road, saying nothing, so Quill added, "They gossip about you *a little*. Probably more if she's your alibi now—"

"All right," Richa said. "That's enough of that." He nodded awkwardly at Quill. "Thanks."

"You're welcome." Quill hesitated. "Are you worried...Do you think Stellano is here?"

Richa hesitated. "That man you saw, with the yellow coat. Stellano had a coat like that. And it's been fifteen years, that coat might well be rags or all the fashion in Caesura or who knows where. But..." He sighed. "I'm worried. And I'm looking into it."

"If you need to talk, and you don't talk to Amadea, I'm here," Quill said, and walked away before it could get awkward again.

Outside, the streets were slick and full of puddles, dark with night and bluish in the light of dim cold-lamps. *Inky*, Quill thought. "Thanks for waiting for me," he said to Yinii. "I've been wanting to talk to you."

She flashed a quick smile at him through the storm of her expression. "At least you'll actually talk to me. Not tell me to go sit in sequestration."

"I feel like if Tunuk has avoided sequestration, then it's only fair you do too."

"I'm glad you were with him. Tunuk, I mean," Yinii said. "I mean, not that I was glad you were gone. That he wasn't alone." She took a deep breath. "Are you going to leave now? Tunuk's...a lot."

"He's not so bad. He puts up a front, but he does actually like people. He likes you quite a lot." Quill stepped around a puddle, steering her away from it with one hand on her elbow, and then she looped her arm through his, almost hesitantly. "Actually, he's really worried about you," Quill confessed. "I'm a little worried about you."

Yinii's arm around his went stiff. "Why would you be worried?"

"Tunuk thought you were avoiding him because you were sad I left," Quill said. "But you don't want to go out with me, so it's something else—"

"I do, though!" she said.

"You have put me off several times now," he reminded her. "It's all right."

"No...it's..." Yinii pulled her arm back, touched her charms again. "Quill, I just have a lot to figure out. I...I do like you. I like you a lot. Too much maybe, but that's...you don't need to know that. But until I know...what it is..." She fidgeted with her gloves. "I don't want to cut my finger off, but I'm nearly ready to!"

"What?" Quill grabbed her fidgeting hands. "What are you talking about? Don't cut your finger off!"

Her big green eyes were shining with tears—and so tired. Amadea was right, she needed to sleep. "Because I might be a sorcerer, and I don't know if it's fair to have coffee with a boy when I might be a monster that can't control her own spiral!"

"Whoa," Quill said, taking her by the arms. "It's just coffee. And you're not a monster. And can you even be a sorcerer? Isn't that something you know right away?"

She shook her head, her charms jingling. "I don't know. I've looked and looked, and...people don't write this down! It doesn't happen often enough. They say, 'Saint Hazaunu was born in Hanizan Canyon. She could grow wool on the palm trees, and the sheep all followed her as if in a trance.' But no one wrote down when that happened or what happened before it. The sheep couldn't follow her when she was an infant—so when? It's as if you're supposed to just know." She swallowed, as if it pained her. "Fastreda won't tell me how she knew. She told me the way you can be certain is by injuring yourself badly enough that—if you are a sorcerer—your flesh transmutes. If I cut off my finger and it turns into ink, then I'll know."

"And either way, you're down a finger. I feel like you need those," he said. She gave him a dark look. "What about a different sorcerer? That one you found the transfer order for?"

"Iosthe of the Wool," Yinii supplied. "It would be days of travel, and Tunuk's right, most of them don't really want to see people. Fastreda...Fastreda's different."

"Tunuk's also right that she's terrifying. But Amadea wouldn't bring you to her if she didn't think it was safe, right? Can you ask her for help?"

Yinii looked at him as if he'd told a bad joke. "Amadea? Amadea is barely holding herself together."

"That's what Richa said. But...she seemed all right."

"No," Yinii said. "She's been...Look, all the stuff about the Grave-Spurned Princess and Redolfo and now the consort-prince? She's been really stressed since then. She wasn't...doing well during it—she had an attack the first time we saw Fastreda. But she won't stop. I don't think she can. And now the skeletons and this murder and the bones are gone again, and there was an explosion, and Tunuk is courting a spiral? She's trying to do all of it, but at this point, she can only try and make it *stop*. She'll tell me I'm not a sorcerer, and I can't believe her because she probably *needs* that to be true, and then I feel like I have to *make* it true, and I get so angry—"

"Hey," Quill soothed. "All right. It's all right. You don't need to tell Amadea. I think you can handle Fastreda anyway."

"Because maybe I could turn her into ink?" Her voice broke around a sob.

Quill folded her into his arms, slowly so she could pull away if she needed to and so that he could negotiate his way around her horns. "Because," he said as she wept, "you are scared, but you're also... you know who you are."

She pulled away, laughing bitterly. "Were you listening before?"

"Yes," he told her. "Maybe you don't know how you'd classify your affinity or what that means. But you know who *you* are. You might worry about how other people will react or if you're saying the wrong thing, but when it comes down to it, you know what *you* would do. You choose the right thing every time. Fastreda's not going to corrupt you. You're not going to be charmed by a Usurper. You're you. No one should worry about that."

Yinii stared at him, tears on her cheeks, shock on her face. She flushed deeply. "Thank you." Something determined came into her expression. "I want to kiss you."

He smiled. "Well, as established, you choose the right thing every time."

That made her blush harder, but when he leaned in, she did too, her mouth soft, her eyes open and curious for a moment too long. He ran a hand up her back, and she moved closer, relaxed, her own hand reaching to touch his cheek. A moment of sweetness he held tightly to.

The rain began again, driving them apart and into the archives, but that dark and aching sadness seemed to have run off Yinii like the rain sluicing off their cloaks. She was smiling by the time they climbed the stairs to the dormitory. "Get some sleep," she said.

"You too." He leaned in and kissed her cheek. He watched her walk toward her apartment, touching the charm of Saint Asla.

He didn't go to bed, instead walking back into the archives and down to Amadea's office and knocking on the door. Amadea yanked it open moments later, looking alarmed, as if she expected an emergency. She wore a dressing gown, and her dark hair was braided over her shoulder, the crown mussed as if she'd already been in bed. Quill held up his hands in a gesture of calm. "It's all right. I just…I wanted to check on you."

She frowned. "Why? What happened now?"

"Nothing," Quill said. "Can I come in?"

Amadea stepped aside, gesturing him toward the couch in her office. Quill saw the spread of documents across her desk—she hadn't been sleeping. She'd been going through the documents from Ragale.

Amadea took the seat opposite her desk, gesturing again for Quill to sit on the couch. "What's going on?"

There were a hundred things Quill wanted to ask her: *How do I do this?* and *When do you know you're going too far?* and *What is the difference between being someone's generalist and being someone's friend?* But what came out was "Are you all right?"

She stared at him a moment too long. "I'm fine. I'm fine. Are *you* all right?"

"Not in the least," Quill said. "I'm pretty sure I'm terrible at this. I know I'm not keeping Tunuk in line. I managed to make Yinii feel a little better, but I'm *very* uncomfortable thinking of that as anything to do with my oath. I watched a man die a few days ago, and honestly I don't know when *that's* going to fully catch up with me!"

"Quill," Amadea started, "maybe you—"

"Everything is shit," Quill said. "But insofar as it's shit, I don't matter in it. I'm pretty anonymous. But a lot of this—the thefts and the Usurper and what was under the wall and the *explosion* that you panicked about *before* it happened—it's all sitting on you. And I can talk to you about my problems, but you…who do you talk to?"

Amadea blinked at him. "Mostly? I…just get on with it."

"Until you collapse," he said, remembering what Yinii had said, remembering Amadea crouched in the sanctuary of the abbey after they'd fled the tunnel that had been destroyed. "Is that a good idea?"

"It's a better idea than collapsing first," she said briskly. "This isn't normal. And I'm sorry you changed your oath only to get swept up in…three crimes?"

"Five," Quill said. "First, the wooden bones being stolen from the archives. Second, the murder that left the skeleton that replaced Saint Hazaunu. Third, the peddler getting killed. Fourth, the wooden bones getting stolen *again*. Fifth, Richa's apartment exploding."

Amadea folded her hands. "And Tunuk."

"Why did you panic when you saw the device?" Quill asked. "Richa noticed."

She shook her head. "I don't know. I genuinely don't know. I...It seemed familiar."

"Do you think Redolfo Kirazzi had something like that?"

"I don't know," she said again. "I intend to ask the consort-prince when I see him next. In the meantime, do you need me to move you? Tunuk is...a lot of work, and that's when everything is going smoothly."

"No," Quill said. "I like Tunuk, I just...What's the difference between being someone's generalist and being their friend? I feel like when I do what a friend would do, I'm breaking a million rules. When I do what I'm supposed to do, I just end up pushing him away. Making it worse. And then Yinii, I...I know she's not my responsibility, but she's really worried about this sorcerer stuff. And I think I helped her calm down, but...I wasn't being her generalist. I don't think I should be her generalist."

Amadea's eyebrows lifted. "I see. That's...It's a complicated problem. You can be their friend. I think it's better if you are, to be honest, but...I don't think it's what a normal friendship's like. You've always got to be watching out for them. You have to be willing to push them when they don't want to be pushed. I suspect Tunuk will rail at you and claim you've never been his friend, but you have to be willing to do what he needs, not what he wants." She hesitated. "If it's too much—"

"No," Quill said again. Because who would she replace him with? Because he felt like he couldn't give up on Tunuk, not when danger felt so imminent. Because Amadea couldn't take on one more task, even if she wouldn't admit it. "Why aren't you asleep?"

She waved a hand toward her desk. "Someone needs to go through them. And I'm...not tired."

Quill went around to the other side of her desk. Her tortoiseshell cat, Palimpsest, was in the chair, her feet tucked up under her like a loaf of bread. He scooped her up and settled her on his lap. "What have you found?"

"A mess," she said. "It's…everything. Right now I'm sorting them by type. Wills are here. Recommendations are here. Affidavits—"

"I got it," Quill said, still recognizing the files. He picked up a stack from the corner of the desk and started sorting the pages, falling into a companionable silence as years of practice came back into effect. It was nice, for a moment, to do what he had been trained to do, to do what he'd expected in some ways to do for all his days.

Demand letter, will, affidavit—his thoughts wandered to the skeleton lying in the mortuary of the Kinship Hall. Thirty-four years, four months, eight days. There were uncountable reasons you might stab someone, but Quill couldn't imagine any that made skeletonizing their corpse and hiding it in plain sight in the chapel make sense. If you had a dead body and you didn't want it found, why not throw it in the sea? Or bury it in a midden? Or out in the wilds? And if you were going to hide it in the chapel, then why not exchange it with one of the bone skeletons?

Recommendation for advancement, another will, a taxation dispute—maybe that meant the wooden bones had been stolen first, the skeleton made to hide their loss. But then why steal the wooden bones at all? Why spirit them away and leave them to rot under a hovel in the woods? Even if Toya One-Saint had been a particular devotee of Saint Hazaunu, Quill couldn't imagine how he could have gotten the saint out of the chapel alone.

He took out a sorcerer transfer for Oluali of the Marble, remembered Yinii upset.

But Yinii had been angry about a transfer for someone called Iosthe of the Wool. This one was for Oluali del Dizifia, called Oluali of the Marble. From Alcaic to Sestina because of concerns about her safety and welfare.

He frowned. "Do you have the other sorcerer transfer out already?"

Amadea looked up. "Other?"

"Yeah, Yinii found one. For Iosthe of the Wool. This is for Oluali of the Marble." He frowned at the document. "She was really upset about it, actually. I guess this feels different when it could be you."

Amadea set her papers down. "She might not be."

"But she might?"

Amadea searched her desk, not answering, then stood and scooped up a stack from the corner. "Here, these are the ones Yinii separated out. I moved them when I was getting the forms together for Saint Hazaunu. It will be in there." She paused before handing them over. "How sure does she seem?"

"Not very," Quill said, "but...that feels telling. It's not a small thing, her being a sorcerer. If she could say no, she would. Is there really no way to know?"

"No," Amadea said grimly. "Aside from seeing if her flesh transmutes." She went to the shelves in the corner of her office instead of sitting back down. Quill sorted through the documents Yinii had already gone through—they weren't sorted by type, and he could only guess what her method had been. He added Iosthe to the same stack as Oluali, finished, and went back to the stack he'd been working through.

More affidavits, more letters of recommendation, an extension for a court case.

Another sorcerer transfer.

This one cited Ichenda of the Pottery, resident of a town called Biolet in the administrative area of Prodelision near the western sea, was to be moved to Sestina, all the way down near the Salt Wall, due to, yet again, concerns about her safety and well-being.

"Here," Amadea said, handing him a slim dusty-looking book with the Imperial Archives sigil on it, a knotwork of calligraphy that looked almost like a nest. "We should both read this. Chapters eight and nine."

"What is it?"

"Sorcerer protocols," she said. "Just in case. You're right. The chance isn't nonexistent, and...I have been hoping that would change. But there is no wish deep enough to change reality. We should be ready to help her."

Quill looked down at the book. "Would she have to leave?"

"No," Amadea said. "To my knowledge, the others haven't wanted to be here."

Quill held up the new transfer order. "Does that matter?"

Amadea frowned and took the paper from him, reading the information. "Three of them?"

"Are there facilities in Sestina for sorcerers?" Quill asked, afraid he already knew the answer. Eleven sorcerers in the empire, and three of them in the last six months had been bound for Sestina, where the tunnel beneath the Wall ran.

Amadea laid it in the stack. "New plan," she said, heaving up half the remaining stack of papers and setting them beside Quill. "We're just looking for sorcerer transfers or isolation mandates. Put the rest on the floor."

They shuffled the pages, the stack of rejected files growing. But so too did the transfer requests pile grow:

Joodashir of the Salt. From Hyangga to Sestina. Concerns about his safety and well-being.

Thunzi of the Iron. From Isefa to Sestina. Concerns about their safety and well-being.

Ahkerfi of the Copper. From undetermined location to Sestina. Concerns about his safety and well-being.

Anarai of the Silver. From Razaj to Sestina. Concerns about her safety and well-being.

"This is it, isn't it?" Quill said. "Seven isn't a coincidence."

"No," Amadea said. "Richa's friend Corolia said the merchant she knows who sells sorcerer charms has been having trouble keeping a supply. Especially of Iosthe's creations—I don't think he knows where she is. This is already in motion, and it's being done quietly." She spread out the transfer orders. "Who's signing these?"

Quill checked the signatures and the seals. On the left was the primate's seal, on the right, an imperial functionary's. They'd all been signed by Primate Lamberto, but the originating officials didn't match. Two from the Borsyan noble consul, one from the Beminat, one from the Minseon, one from the Ronqu, and two from imperial administrators—it wasn't a pattern exactly, but there was enough there to set Quill's anxiety off.

"So I don't know if you've had to deal with these before," he said to Amadea, "but if I recall correctly, the way these work, you have to have an originating complaint. Someone has to say to the Paremi, 'We want this sorcerer moved for these reasons.' And if you're doing that, you're not going to the primate. You're going to someone local because it's likely urgent. You need the imperial representative who's overseeing the sorcerer's care to sign, and you need the signature of a representative of the noble consul whose protectorate the sorcerer belongs to—or another imperial representative if the sorcerer doesn't align with a protectorate."

Amadea frowned. "So, aside from it being the primate, these aren't strange?"

"No, look, they're missing the first imperial signatory—the person who is the sorcerer's representative isn't here. Primate Lamberto's signed them, but that's not actually necessary—his seal should be enough. And these aren't noble consul functionaries—these are the noble consuls themselves."

"So there's higher authority on two parts of this," Amadea said.

"And nothing for the third," Quill finished. "These are fraudulent, frankly, and worse...I don't think Primate Lamberto could have done it alone. The functionary shouldn't have sealed them as complete."

Amadea stared at him. "Someone else is helping Redolfo Kirazzi?"

Quill picked up the transfer for Joodashir of the Salt, pressing his thumb over the bright green ink of the functionary's seal: the imperial mask, a ring of numbers around it. "This is the same on every one of them."

Amadea picked up one of the other transfer orders, examining the seal. "This is going to be one of the unassigned functionaries. They don't have any of the protectorates' symbols on their seals."

"Useful for hiding," Quill said.

Amadea pressed a hand to her mouth, considering. "I have to bring them to Ibramo," she said at last. "We have to stop the transfers if we can and get them as far from Sestina as possible if we can't."

"Maybe he can find out who that seal belongs to," Quill said. "If we can find another conspirator—" He broke off in a yawn.

"Maybe we can stop all of this without the safety of the empire being compromised." She stood, pulling the belt of her dressing gown tight. "It's late. You should be in bed. Thank you for the help."

She ushered him out, and Quill made his way back to his rooms, still thinking over skeletons and separatists and whether he knew how to help Tunuk. But one thing he felt certain of—he needed to not make that Amadea's problem. Especially if now she was going to chase after the sorcerer transfers herself.

She'd never actually answered his question, he realized, dozing off: *Who do you talk to?*

A moment after Quill had closed his eyes, someone was banging on his door. He opened it to see Tunuk standing in a wash of sun that suggested it was a lot later in the morning than it felt.

"Good," Tunuk said. "You're alive. Come on."

"What?" Quill rubbed his eye. "Where?"

"I'm going to find that fabricator," Tunuk said. "Zoifia already agreed to come with me, and Stavio. I'm going to prove Qalba wasn't involved in this." He hesitated, eyeing Quill. "So are you coming?"

"Are you going to tell Richa what you find?"

"If I find something. Are you coming or not?"

Quill stood a moment, trying to get his bearings. As Tunuk's generalist, he should tell him not to go—he was agitated, and he'd already come awfully close to spiraling once. But as his friend...

What would I want if I were in Tunuk's place? he thought. What *had* he wanted when it was Karimo everyone thought was to blame? He hesitated. Was Qalba more like Karimo or more like Primate Lamberto? They wouldn't find out if they stopped looking, and if Tunuk didn't find out, the wound in him would never heal.

"If you find out Qalba's involved in all this, will you accept it?"

"If you find out she's not, will you?" Tunuk demanded.

"Yes," Quill promised. "But you have to do the same. And we're not getting into any fights with separatists."

"Deal," Tunuk said. "That's Zoifia's job anyway, scare them off. Get dressed, I'll get you a coffee."

CHAPTER FIFTEEN

A re you sure Amadea's all right with this?" Radir asked Yinii the next morning, as she strode into the Kinship Hall again.

"I have my generalist with me," Yinii said, as guilelessly as she could. "Why would she be upset?"

With any luck, Amadea would be so busy with the Imperial Authority that morning she wouldn't even know what Yinii had done until it was finished and settled and everything had turned out just fine.

Yinii had realized several things the night before: First, Amadea wasn't going to help her find out whether she was a sorcerer. She was too like Radir, afraid of what might happen, afraid Yinii might be *uncontrollable*.

Second was what Quill had said: *You know who you are. You choose the right thing every time.* It sent a flutter through her when she thought about it, about him saying that. But hearing the words aloud, that had made them feel true.

Third, she was afraid. That fear of being helpless, of being use-less when the time came, of being shut away from danger for her own good—it bubbled up in her, unable to quiet once she had named it. She would sacrifice so many things, she thought, love and safety and her own good name, if she did not have to feel the helpless terror the Shrike and Redolfo Kirazzi had filled her with when they'd attacked her, stolen Quill, threatened them all with death.

But deep down, she thought she knew the answer: the ink would accept those sacrifices, swallow them into its depths, devour her mind whole, and leave her a weapon, nearly unstoppable.

And when she thought about it, that felt like a comfort. *If they come for me, I will stop them.*

Was that holy? Was that how saints felt? She remembered down in the tunnels, being merged to the ink—it was hers and it was *her* and she was endless. She could not imagine Saint Asla drawing salt from an enemy's body, bursting it at the seams.

But she could, she thought, imagine Saint Asla controlling her skills for the aid of her friends and nation. If the clue had been in salt, Saint Asla would not have sat idly by.

"Is it Amadea's vigilant you're looking for?" Radir asked as she scanned the entry hall.

"No." Yinii went up to one of the vigilants passing through. "Excuse me, esinora, I'm looking for Vigilant Gaitha-hyu? I'm here to evaluate some evidence."

Yinii and Radir were shown to a room, where Salva Nine-Scorpion Gaitha-hyu met them shortly after, looking highly suspicious.

"You're the archivist who was in Vigilant Langyun's office," she noted.

"Yinii Six-Owl ul-Benturan," Yinii said. "This is my generalist, Radir del Sendiri. Vigilant Langyun mentioned there were some documents found with the wooden bones of Saint Hazaunu that needed to be examined by an ink specialist."

"He told you to request them?"

"No," Yinii said, trying hard to keep her voice firm and confident. Saint Asla would not have trembled! "He told me he didn't need me to look at them, but he also mentioned they weren't really under his care. They're under yours. They're palimpsests—layers of writing? And there's a possibility there is something in them that might explain a motive."

Salva tilted her head, considering Yinii. "And he told you not to bother?"

Yinii hesitated. She wanted to see the palimpsests, but she didn't want to get Richa into trouble. "I...I think he was deferring to you. I figured you were really the person I should be asking." She squeezed her hands together to stop herself from touching the amulets on her own horns. "Could you also provide me with some blank sheets of paper?"

Salva left, and Radir whispered furiously at Yinii, "You're going against Amadea *and* the vigilant?"

"They didn't say no," she told him. "They said 'later.' This is later."

Radir leaned on the table, his head in his hands. "They told me you were less trouble than Tunuk."

"Well, Tunuk wouldn't have brought you along," Yinii offered. "And he probably would have also put Biorni in your bed or something."

Salva returned with a stack of clean papers and the case Richa had brought to the archives the day the wooden bones had arrived. She opened it and laid the two pages side by side in front of Yinii, then folded her hands together. "Proceed."

Yinii faltered. "You... you don't have to watch me."

"I do," the vigilant said. "That's evidence. You might be manipulating it."

"I'm not changing the words!" Yinii said hotly.

"And I will testify to that," Salva said. "Proceed."

Yinii pulled one page toward her and removed her gloves.

Radir leaned in and hissed, "If your eyes change color, I am going to physically haul you out of here. All right?"

"All right."

"Try not to need that," he added.

Yinii brushed her fingers over the surface of the first of the peddler's pages, feeling the freshest lines of ink, lifting them gently from the tangle of words to float over her knuckles, up her wrist: *Saint Hazaunu, the eye that watches the weft, and the sentinel that guards the flock, discern within me that which is redeemable and cull the wickedness...*

The line broke, and Yinii coaxed the ink onto a clean sheet of paper, where it slithered into the same down-turned angle it had taken on the original. The ink clung to the slicker, newer paper, and Yinii smiled, imagining it clinging like a little cat to a curtain, afraid of falling.

It's all right, she thought. *That's a fine place for now.*

She ran her fingers down the left-hand edge of the document, trying to find the same layer of ink—the split-scratch of the reed, the dusty memory in the soot of a hillside and dry leaves of a crop rattling in the autumn wind, the most erratic of the handwritings. Even this was old—older than the time Saint Hazaunu had vanished... *from my heart and offer it unto the God Above to burn away...*

Did she imagine it? Or did the penitence echo in the swift strokes of the ink, so quick the script seemed to collapse on itself in places?

...for I have done such wrongs seen such wrongs cursed be...

What was this word? Yinii pulled it out, separate from its fellows, stretching it wide, making the loops of the letters open, the diacritics float away from their places: *for you shall know them by the power of their gifts, by the relics of their affinity.*

"Are you changing it?" Salva asked.

"She can't actually manipulate it like that," Radir said. "She can make it change form, but if she lays it down again, it retains the meaning."

Their words were far off and tinny, but Yinii held them in her thoughts, a counterbalance to the ink, to the faint bitter taste in the back of her mouth.

The light is blinding but in it I see the God Above. The noise is deafening but in it echoes the God Below. The lines hung off her fingertips like chains lifted from a jewelry box, and she draped first one and then the other onto the clear paper Radir slid under her hand.

Yinii felt the edge of light-headedness, the beginning of the roar the ink had taken before, and she paused, sitting with it, listening to it. Then she reached *through* it and peeled up a whole layer of the page:

I was given the tools for salvation or destruction, the water urn and the sword, and I chose the sword. I made my hands into the sword, and the world was set before me, a shining egg. My hands crack the surface of the world. The layers which are not meant to be broken. The light is blinding but in it I see the God Above. The noise is deafening but in it echoes the God Below. In the moment between life and death I see my

soul flensed from my bones, I see the saints take up the tattered rags of
my spirit in their skeletal hands, shining gold . . .

"It's repeating," Radir said.

"It's a prayer," Salva said grimly.

The ink started to crackle, a sound like a building rainstorm, and
Yinii squeezed her hands into fists, holding the moment still. *We're
not doing that,* she said to the ink.

She delved deeper into the palimpsest, feeling Toya's peace fray
and fray with the franticness of his writings, his prayers for absolu-
tion. He had done something terrible, something unforgiveable.

Anathema, Oshanna had said.

Anathema, Toya named himself. *For my sins, I must atone.*

*Ink in her mouth, ink in her nose—the scream and then the wash of black,
char and fat and fluid, that had been the Shrike, but what else should she
have done? Richa was about to die, Quill was about to die, she was about to
die, and the ink was so loud—*

"Yinii," Radir said. "Look at me, please."

He can't help if we don't let him, she thought, and for a moment, she
wasn't sure how she'd meant that. She looked at him, her eyes wide.

He nodded. "All right, you're doing good."

She pulled the ink again, another unraveling weave of words, and
piled it onto the next sheet. When she touched the page next, it was
the final, original layer of writing. She no longer felt fear or contrition in the hand that wrote it, no longer any sense of pain or hesi-
tancy. This was a sure hand, a certain hand.

They were equations, diagrams. There were words, complex and
confusing: *amplification, power decay, reversal of energy.* A shape in the
center that looked strangely familiar.

"Is that a cold-magic lamp?" Radir asked.

Yinii touched the block in the middle, where the cold-magic
should have radiated its divine power into the lamp. Here it was
labeled, *Alternative source must be sized at one and one half comparable
cold-magic. Lifetime is proportionate to mass, much reduced, but functioning.
Organics have best results, but hard to source. Glass is, unfortunately, weakest in this application.*

"What does *that* mean?" Radir asked, peering at it.

Salva looked down at it, her expression as hard as iron and just as cold, and said nothing.

Yinii's stomach tightened. She pulled the second page toward her. Again the layers of guilt and prayer and contrition, covering and covering and covering the base layer, as if to flood it out of mortal sight. Why didn't Toya burn it? she wondered. Why didn't he tear it to pieces?

He left it like an offering below the saint's skull. He gave her what he seemed to think of as the proof of his sins, obliterated by the acknowledgment of his guilt.

Again, equations revealed themselves beneath the words. This time the diagram looked more like a nest, strange tubes bent oddly around a center globe to show their angles and connections. *Burn time* and *exothermic process* and *inversion of established formula*. Here the center was labeled, *Design builds more energy to initiate runaway reaction. Only alternate sources. Glass is non-functioning. Marble is limited. Equations suggest organics might provide necessary energy increase.*

The ink radiated excitement. It radiated pride.

Yinii pulled her hands back. Salva was staring down at the second page as if it had just admitted to heinous crimes—and maybe it had. "Do you know what it is?" Yinii asked.

"You said Vigilant Langyun didn't want you looking at these?"

"I said he told me they were yours," Yinii corrected. *Burn time,* she read. *Exothermic process. Runaway reaction.* "What is this?"

"Thank you for your assistance, Archivist ul-Benturan," the vigilant said, standing and collecting the pages Yinii had made. "You must be tired after all that. I'll be in contact if anything else comes up."

Yinii left the Kinship Hall unsettled, her nerves reaching for ink, whispering all the ways she could turn the cloaks of passersby, the grit between the cobblestones, the blood of the pigeons into ink and into words. She blew out a breath. *Stop it.*

Everything quieted.

"That was weird, right?" Radir said. "Like, I don't know what *you* were expecting to see... This is that dead Orozhandi peddler, though? Why does he have fabricator diagrams?"

"I assume he was fabricating." The Brotherhood of the Black Mother Forest might not have welcomed just anyone into their fold, but that didn't mean their secrets never slipped out through the fences. If Toya had been building devices with cold-magic...

No, she thought. Not cold-magic. Specifically not cold-magic.

His notes had said *only alternate sources*. The lamp was like a cold-magic lamp but with something else powering it. The other object—the weapon, she thought, *runaway reaction*—was only powered by that something else. But what could replace cold-magic? If someone knew that, all manner of things might change.

Glass is, unfortunately, weakest in this application.

And Yinii suddenly understood.

"I have to go run an errand," she said, pulling her gloves back on. "Alone."

Lord Tafad Mazajin, the Borsyan noble consul, was a big man who made the cramped anteroom in the Imperial Complex where he met Richa feel even smaller. He sat beneath a portrait of some Borsyan hero holding a dead vulture in one brawny hand, gesturing for Richa to take the seat opposite. Richa eyed the painting as he slid the box he carried under his chair, thinking of what Yinii had said: *The vulture is the shepherd of the dead.*

"What do vultures mean in Borsyan stories?" he asked idly.

Tafad smiled at him. "The frailty of life."

"Mm. So he's overcoming his own frailty. What about caves?"

"I can't say I know. Can we get to business? You can understand, of course, esinor, that what you're asking about doesn't intersect with my responsibilities. But I'll do my best to assist the Vigilant Kinship, of course."

"If it isn't the noble consul's responsibility, then whose is it?" Richa asked.

"The Duke Borcia would be a much better person to consult if one of the fabricators of the Brotherhood has been using their gifts to commit a crime."

"My apologies," Richa said. "But we're talking about someone who doesn't belong to the Brotherhood."

Tafad's smile tensed, as if he'd smelled something bad but wasn't going to acknowledge it outright. "Anikupika," he said. "The unsworn. That's what we call them. Also known as a sign the Duke Borcia may not be fulfilling his role as the protectorate deserves."

Richa nodded. "You are the former Duke Borcia, is that right?"

Tafad waved this away. "It's been some years since my time."

"Is that why your name tends to come up when we talk about rebel groups aligned against the current duke?"

Tafad laughed, sounding shocked. "I don't even know where I would find the time to involve myself with rebel groups. It's a pity, really, that Ardalai has these difficulties. The Duke Borcia should be strong."

A lot of words that amounted to not answering the question. Richa met them with a placid smile. "That's good to hear. I don't like politics, personally. When they're invisible, that helps the city run smoothly and safely, but it also means no one's terribly sure what's happening under the surface. And when they get loud and unavoidable, it means we're figuring things out. But that's also when people get hurt."

Tafad matched his vague smile. "It's not your world, Vigilant. Stick to the fires."

Richa wondered if that faint sort of veiled threat ever worked. "I suppose I must." He picked up the box beside his seat and opened it on the desk. Inside lay the remains of the device that had destroyed his apartment, retrieved after he'd spent another night in the duty room's god-awful cots.

"This," he said, "is definitely fabricator made. I've had that verified. It also destroyed part of an apartment building on the southern end of the city. We are looking for a person of interest. Maybe two. And if I don't find them and if you don't help me, then my next step is to approach the empress herself. So then the question is, will she be pleased to hear you tried to fob me off on the duke?"

This, he thought, *is how you make a veiled threat.*

Lord Tafad paused, raking a hand through his pale beard. "The empress won't be able to help you. She is locked in her rooms with her ghosts. Everyone knows that."

"And let's be honest," Richa continued. "It's the Lady Sigrittrice I'd end up speaking to. So swap her name into my question, my lord."

That made Tafad pause.

"Do you know a name?" he asked. "For this anikupika?"

"The unsworn fabricator goes by 'Vigdza.'"

He laughed once. "Two of my cousins are Vigdzas, plus a great-aunt and a sister-in-law. This is not an uncommon name."

"But when you pair it with a woman who understands fabricator techniques?"

"Then you are asking me for someone I can't even imagine knowing. This is blasphemous to most people. Did you not say she was speaking to a fabricator? Why not ask him?"

"Tried that. He left town, so far as we can tell." The vigilants had searched the Hawk's Nest last night and this morning, and no one could find Gunarro del Hwana. His workshop was closed up, his house locked tight, and no one would admit to seeing him since the night before. "That's why I'm asking you," Richa said.

Tafad sighed. "You said there were two. Tell me the other person's name so we can finish up."

Richa hesitated. "We have reason to believe Stellano Zezurin is involved."

Something unsettled flitted over the noble consul's features, but then he said, "I don't know this man."

Liar, Richa thought. "Ah, well, he's a member of your protectorate. A criminal in Caesura wanted for multiple offenses. And he's been seen in Arlabecca. With this unsworn fabricator."

"I can see why they are of interest."

"It would definitely be in the noble consul's interest to assist me. I would make certain of it."

Tafad tilted his head. "What was your name again?"

"Vigilant Langyun. Why?"

He shrugged. "Perhaps you will run to Lady Sigrittrice and I will need to know who you are to answer your accusations. Perhaps I wish to commend your thoroughness to the Kinship elders?" His eyes were like ice as he added, "Perhaps if I run across this Esinor Zezurin, I will wish to tell him you are looking for him."

That, Richa had to admit, was a very masterful veiled threat.

Richa left, unsure if he'd given Lord Tafad the impression he was hiring a criminal outside the Kinship or if he'd just been told Stellano would be warned and no good to go after. He did feel sure, however, that the noble consul was happily undermining the current Duke Borcia and probably in connection with the various separatist groups—and that Richa would have a very hard time proving it. That they did so without much care for the Imperial Authority was worth noting, but it did mean the empress was not likely a target.

You, on the other hand, he thought, as he made his way toward the ul-Shandiian manor. Someone had tried to kill him with that explosive. Someone who called him a "blasphemer." It rattled him that he couldn't even guess who might hate him so much, nearly as badly as Salva throwing his past in his face.

Stellano? Maybe he hated Richa that passionately, but Stellano would do nothing so cold-blooded as set a trap and walk away. Stellano would stab you himself and watch the light go out of your eyes if he really hated you. You, your friends, your family if he could.

Richa shuddered. So many years later, he thought, and the kid who'd follow someone down to the doors of demon-hell because they could charm a pack of thieves and insist everything would be fine was long gone from Richa Langyun. He didn't need someone else to have things figured out—he'd figured them out, finally, on his own.

But when he looked at Amadea—worn and weighed down with catastrophes and simply turning herself toward the task—he felt a similar pull, older and wiser and different. He wasn't the same man, after all, but it was there: Someone you could follow into demon-hell. Someone who had it figured out.

Someone who very clearly does not want anything to do with a former criminal, he thought, remembering what she'd said when Tunuk had stormed off. But then there was Quill and the advice Richa avoided and avoided: *You should actually talk to her.*

Dushar ul-Shandiian was out, he was told, requesting an audience with the empress. Oshanna Eleven-Sand Iris was also away, so Richa couldn't ask her any more about the letter or Qalba or Toya

One-Saint. The wind was picking up, cold and mean, and Richa wanted nothing more than the shelter of the Kinship Hall and a hot cup of coffee.

Dushar Six-Agamid appealed as a suspect for the theft of the bones. He'd no more discovered the mistake of the bones, but he'd seized on the opportunity to entrench his power within the Orozhandi ducal authority—and to challenge the authority of the empress. Two of his clan members, Qalba and Toya, were involved in the past troubles with the saint.

But also...the note Yinii mentioned troubled him. If the bombmaker had left one to threaten him and one to threaten Dushar, then what was the connection?

Hulvia intercepted him as he came into the Kinship Hall. "What's the word?" he asked.

"Why didn't you tell me you owned a house?" she demanded.

"What?"

"The row house. The one down by the West River."

Richa shook his head. "I have no idea what you mean. I owned that apartment. The one that blew up. If I bought a house—by the West River? I can't afford a house by the West River."

"It's the one the wooden bones were taken to." She glanced back down the hall. "That road cohort vigilant. Salva. She's definitely got it out for you. And it's not looking good, Richa. What the fuck?"

"Where did she get the idea I own a house?"

"Your name is in the taxation records," Hulvia said. "You're registered as the owner. I saw it myself."

Richa started to protest that there must have been some sort of error, some mistake of identity. But then he stopped. Someone had been breaking into his apartment. Someone had set a deadly trap for him. Someone had made it look like he had stolen the wooden bones.

"Someone changed those records," he said. "Someone's setting me up."

"It gets a lot worse," Hulvia said. "We went looking for the priests. The priest of the God Above? She's dead. Dead for longer than a day. So I don't think she was the one leading that procession to the wrong place, and you are a person of interest in yet another murder."

"But I wasn't there," Richa said. "I can bring in people who can place me well away from there."

"Can you prove you never hired a killer to take the priest out and put on the veil and pretend to be her? Because I think Salva's looking for a conspiracy."

"I don't fucking blame her, but I'm not part of it," Richa said. "What about Nanqii? Did you question him?"

"Swept his house from top to bottom. He doesn't have the bones, and he doesn't have a reason to steal them." Hulvia glanced around the entry hall once. "That ink specialist came in this morning, the little Orozhandi one. She checked the weird pages you found with the bones. Said you'd told her not to bother, but she wanted to help."

"I told her not to bother because the archivist superior said she wasn't well enough."

"Well, it turns out that there's diagrams under all that mess, and one looks a lot like the thing you described blowing up your apartment. Your peddler was a weapons maker. And you told her not to look at it."

Richa raked a hand through his hair, his pulse hammering. The entry hall felt so close and crowded, and he wanted to be anywhere else. "This is specious. All of it has other explanations if Salva'd just ask me."

But she had asked, Richa realized. And he'd shut her down. He paused. "Where is Salva now?"

Hulvia set her hands on his shoulders. "Don't panic, all right? She's talking to the elders."

"Oh, wonderful. That went so well for me last time."

"Last time," Hulvia said, "Lady Sigrittrice was pulling the strings. And she is . . . Well, let's put it this way: she's too busy to give two buckets of slop-water about whether you committed a murder."

"I didn't!" Richa said hotly.

"I *know*." Hulvia folded her arms, her tentacles coiling over one another in an agitated way. Eyeing him. Doubting, Richa thought.

Fifteen fucking years, and it could fall apart so easily.

No, he wasn't going to let that happen. If someone had manipulated the records in the Kinship Hall to look like he owned the row house, they couldn't have gotten to everything. The archives had cadastres—taxation maps—it should be listed in those as well.

"Hul," he said, "you didn't see me."

"What?" She grabbed his arm. "What are you doing? Just go talk to them."

"I'm getting evidence." He pulled free, backing toward the door. "I don't own a house, and I'm going to prove it. But if they ask, I wasn't here. You're not getting sacked again."

"Demoted!" Hulvia shouted. But Richa headed out into the cold day alone and did not answer.

───❈───

"Fuckers! Put your eyes back in your head!" Zoifia shouted at a pair of young men eyeing the group of archivists as they walked through the Hawk's Nest. The sun was bright behind the thick clouds, too diffuse to bother with a sunshade, but the chilly light made Tunuk's eyes ache anyway.

"All right, *this* time, we should agree on a plan," Quill said, rubbing his hands together against the early morning cold.

"It's *fine*," Tunuk said. "There are four of us. Worst case, we scatter."

"Worst case, we find Vigdza, she was the bomber, and she sets off another explosive."

"Nah," Stavio said. "I think worst case, we see Zoifia start a brawl. I think it's funny you asked *her* to come to make yourself less obvious."

"I mean *you*, egg-brains!" Zoifia shouted at the group of young men. "Turn around!"

"So long as we find that fabricator, I don't care," Tunuk said.

It had been a long night for Tunuk. He'd slept and woken thinking about what he and Quill had discovered. Slept and woken thinking about the bones that weren't Qalba's, and where was she now? Slept and woken thinking of the way Amadea had been happy to assume the worst about Qalba.

"Tunuk," Quill had said that morning before they'd set out, "I don't think you should be so hard on Amadea. She doesn't think Qalba's a villain for what she did. I'm sure of that."

"You weren't there," Tunuk told him. "And when we find that unsworn fabricator, it won't matter anyway."

He'd convinced Zoifia to come along as soon as he got back to the archives, thinking a young woman with Borsyan features would get a lot more doors opened in the Hawk's Nest than he would. In turn, Zoifia had invited Stavio, claiming they'd do better with the muscular Ashtabari to ward off "egg-brained bullyboys."

Tunuk...had not asked Yinii. He had considered it, but then he'd remembered her insistence about the letter to Dushar, about Qalba, and he'd found he couldn't. Yinii was one of the ones he had to convince.

They reached the little bridge with its triangular spirals. Zoifia pulled herself up onto the railing, surveying the street beyond like a sentinel on the Wall, wrapping one hand around the bronze post beside her and resting her pale cheek against it with a sigh.

"I *hate* coming down here," she said when Stavio, Quill, and Tunuk caught up. "Tell me what you want so we can get finished fast?"

"You don't want to stop and get some groundnut cabbage rolls?" Stavio teased. "Some beetroot fritters?"

Zoifia made a gagging noise. "The best thing my ancestors did was leave and come somewhere that had better food," she said. "And then they insisted on making the same shit with worse ingredients."

"I like those fritters," Stavio said. "And soured cream—they did give the world soured cream."

"Well, all right," Zoifia said. "Only a monster doesn't like soured cream and fried things." She turned to Tunuk. "Well?"

Tunuk pointed up the street toward the Temple of the Black Mother Forest. "There's an alley up there. She went down it and disappeared. She must have gone into one of the doors along it—I want you to knock and ask."

"And why are we not giving this to the vigilants?" Stavio asked, his tentacles curling around the bronze-work railing of the bridge where he leaned against it. They'd passed several teams, canvassing the neighborhood, speaking with stony-faced Borsyans.

"Nobody here is going to talk to the vigilants," Zoifia said witheringly.

"But they're gonna talk to you?" Stavio asked.

She shrugged. "If they don't, maybe you can punch a door in or something. They'll respect that." She hopped down from the railing. "This way?"

They headed on. As he walked, Tunuk tucked a hand into his pocket where the letters from Chizid and Qalba rode. *There's a little danger,* Chizid had said, *and it's best if none of it stays in the archives.*

The more Tunuk thought about it, the more he thought Amadea was right: Someone had been blackmailing Qalba. Someone might have been making her steal things. Someone had come into the Bone Vault and been murdered, and that had been what Chizid had covered up. That was why he and Qalba had left. It was to protect Tunuk, somehow.

And then, the letter Yinii had found out about. The letter that meant Qalba was still alive. The letter that had not been sent to him.

That hurt, ached in his chest like the wound between his ribs. But he buried it down, bone-deep. *You don't* need *anyone,* he told himself. *A yinpay hunts alone.*

"Hey," Quill said, grabbing Tunuk's arm as they reached the alleyway.

Maybe not alone, Tunuk thought, a little embarrassed. "What?"

"If we find her," Quill said, "we're getting out of here and alerting the vigilants, right? We're not having any sort of a standoff."

Tunuk's thoughts flooded with pain, the assassin cresting the hill, the rapier in his ribs—you didn't always see the standoff coming. "I'm not planning on a standoff," he said.

The narrow street stretched out before them, the buildings on either side crowded over it like they might fall into one another. Most of each wall was unbroken, a handful of doors interrupting the space until another road crossed the end. Tunuk gauged the distance and felt surer of what he'd thought the day before—she couldn't have made it to the other road before he'd gotten here. Which meant she'd gone into one of these doors.

"You have to start knocking," he said to Zoifia.

"It's the height of presumption that I have to do this," Zoifia said. But she went to the first door, rapping right on the chalked bird of prey.

Tunuk thought he understood a little of Zoifia's frustration— what did it mean to be Borsyan when Borsya was gone? When your ancestors had sheared off their roots to come safely to this place, and suddenly you didn't *need* to watch for auguries in the birds flushed from the underbrush or turn to the strongest man in the village, you didn't need to make a nice binding with six or seven lovers or never go walking in the jungle alone? He wondered if the Borsyans had their own version of the yinpay—a monster that grew from a woman who hated beetroot and bullyboys and being ordered around.

But Zoifia was Borsyan enough to know the words to say to the woman who opened the door, to ask about the bomb-maker in a way that didn't imply she was allied with her, that maybe she and her friends were looking to solve the problem of the unsworn fabricator, if that was something the woman was interested in.

"I don't know her," the woman said. "We revere the Brotherhood here."

"Well, if you chased her off, then good," Zoifia said. "My friends will learn from their errors, I suppose." She glowered at Tunuk as the door slammed shut. "It's going to be a lot of this, just so you know. At least until the Brotherhood gets word, and then it will become a lot of shouting."

"Let's avoid the shouting," Quill said.

Three more doors, and no one knew anything. Tunuk was growing agitated, feeling as if his bones wouldn't sit in his skin right. She had come down this alley, and she couldn't have left it if she'd lost Tunuk. He paced back down the alley under the watchful gaze of a trio of blond-haired children, looking for drains or ladders or something he might have missed.

Zoifia tramped back to him after the fourth door, Stavio sliding along behind her. "Are you sure this is the alley?"

"Completely," Tunuk said. He looked down to the far end again—could she have made it that far? Maybe what he misremembered was how far behind he was, how fast she was...

Stavio sucked in a breath through his teeth. Tunuk turned at the sound.

"What?" Tunuk demanded. "What is it?"

Stavio looked up at him, his eyes glittering. "Bunch of bronze in the wall."

Zoifia squeezed in close beside him, brushing her fingers over the plaster. "*Bunch* of bronze in the wall! Couple of pounds! What's it doing there?"

Stavio ran a strong hand down the wall. "There's a seam in here. Vertical. Then a bit here." He slapped the wall at chest height.

Zoifia pressed her cheek to the spot. "Crossbar. Locking mechanism?"

"There's a secret fucking door in the wall?" Tunuk hissed.

"This is when we get the vigilants," Quill said.

"Can you get it open?" Tunuk said.

Stavio exhaled slowly, running his fingers around the bricks. "It's in there kinda deep for me. Sorcha?"

"Let me see," Zoifia said. She set her hands around Stavio's, little sparks crackling in the curls of her hair. Tunuk heard Quill's sharp inhale—the memory of Zoifia's last alignment fresh in all their minds. But this time, Zoifia's breathing only slowed, the sparks firing with a soft, uneven snapping. She traced her fingers carefully around Stavio's, her gaze distant as if she were listening to some faraway speaker.

Tunuk found himself suddenly, deeply envious. There were over a dozen bronze archivists—Stavio and Zoifia were never alone. But more than that, they had each other. Understood each other. They annoyed each other endlessly, drove each other to fits of screaming in alignment...and then came back together, close as siblings in the crèche.

He found himself thinking of Yinii.

"There," she said huskily, tapping on a brick. "That's the one that has the latch mechanism in it."

"Ah," Stavio said. "So it fits like...There, yeah, I see. It needs a..." He looked over at Tunuk. "You got like a...pick? Or a stylus?"

"I have it." Zoifia drew a dagger out of her belt, a needle-pointed demon with a black handle. Tunuk, Quill, and Stavio all pulled back, and she gave them a withering look before stabbing it into a small crack in the bricks, struggling against the mechanism.

"Here. I'm the muscle." Stavio reached over, covering her hand and pushing the blade in one sharp movement.

Something in the wall *clicked*, and the bricks crunched as they swung apart. Zoifia stepped away from the door, as if she hadn't expected it to work. Stavio interposed himself and pulled the gap wide, revealing a dark passage leading down.

"I'll go first," Stavio said, pulling Zoifia's blade free.

"No," Tunuk said, pushing past him. "You can't see where you're going. Just close the door and follow me."

"Vigilants!" Quill hissed. But Tunuk had already started down the stairs, Stavio following.

The stairs bent sharply left, winding around what Tunuk thought might have been the foundation of the apartment building, the ceiling so low he felt his shoulder blades scrape it as he stooped. The light behind them vanished as Zoifia pulled the door closed. Down and down, and around another bend before the floor evened out, Stavio clung to Tunuk's elbow. Tunuk reached back and took Stavio by the hand instead, holding tight.

"You tell me if there's someone ahead of us," Stavio murmured. Tunuk squeezed his hand and moved down the narrow hallway.

It ended in a door. Tunuk pressed his ear to the surface, listening, but heard nothing. He tried the latch, and it opened.

Inside, a line of cold-magic lamps hung along the center of a long, narrow room—if Tunuk stretched out on the ground, he thought he'd be able to touch both sides with hands and feet, but the wall opposite the door they'd entered faded into darkness deeper than even Tunuk's eyes could see. High tables lined one wall, littered with tools, and a few open doorways bruised the left-hand wall with darker shadows. Tunuk stalked forward to peer into one and found crates.

"Will you get the light?" Zoifia said. "Why do they have them hung so high?"

Tunuk reached up and woke the first cold-magic lamp, its light flooding the space, suddenly bright and oddly warm, more like sunlight than the cool bluish light the cold-magic generated. Tunuk blinked, his eyes adjusting painfully at the switch.

Zoifia shut the door behind Quill. Stavio gave a low whistle as he moved into the room. "Somebody's been busy."

Quill followed him over to the worktables, unfamiliar tools spread across the surface. "Are these fabricator tools?"

"Yeah," Stavio said. He picked up a pair of pincers. "I think. What's this?" he asked Zoifia.

"Those are for pinching off the flow tubes," she said.

Stavio eased down the row of tables and picked up another tool, a loop of leather on a wooden handle. "This one?"

"Globe wrench," she said, coming up behind him. "You don't want to grab the glass globes with your hands—they get very hot, very cold, and also shatter."

"Are you fabricating in your spare time?" Quill asked.

"Her uncles are fabricators," Stavio said. "Didn't you know that?"

"And my stupid brother," Zoifia said. She pointed at the tools. "Hammer, obviously. Flow wrench. Calipers."

"What's this for?" Stavio asked, pulling a glass jug from a row of containers toward him. He uncorked it and sniffed, reeling from the smell. "Naphtha." He coughed.

"What?" Zoifia came up and wafted some of the fumes toward her. "Huh. I don't know what you fabricate with that."

Tunuk sidled up beside them, looking at the papers pasted to the wall above the bench. Schematics and notes and diagrams. Stavio pulled the cannister that had sat beside the jug toward himself and uncapped it. "White powder." He opened the next and frowned. "Gritty... gray powder."

Quill leaned in to get a look. "That looks like gunpowder," he said quietly.

Zoifia peered over Stavio's shoulder again. "I don't know what *that's* for."

"For blowing things up," Stavio said. "She *is* the bomb-maker. There's papers too, but I can't see anything. Get the next lamp going?"

Tunuk reached up to the thin glass globe and woke it. And stopped.

It was meant to hold a piece of the Black Mother Forest's cold-magic, a lumpish block of woody material. But that wasn't what he saw, radiating too brightly in the middle of the glass.

It was, in perfect detail, the cuboid bone of a foot, human or Oro-zhandi. Except it didn't thrum to Tunuk; it didn't pulse. It pulled on his nerves with an alien and insistent vibration, the signature of a sorcerer-wrought relic.

Another bone of Saint Hazaunu of the Wool, this time made to glow like the gift of the Black Mother Forest.

And then they heard the door at the top of the stairs slam shut, hurried footsteps on the stairs. Someone else had unlocked the secret laboratory, and they were in for a standoff after all unless they did something quickly.

CHAPTER SIXTEEN

The ink on the soldiers' forms hissed and shushed as Yinii followed them up to the top of the tower. Her own name was on the list—special dispensation from the consort-prince—but they still seemed wary of her, perhaps because she had arrived without Amadea.

A little part of Yinii was still panicking at that—she ought to have gone back to the archives, she ought to have admitted to Amadea what she'd found—but she folded those thoughts into the shushing of the ink. *You always make the right choice*, she told herself.

Fastreda was seated at her table as usual, reading a letter she had tucked into a book, her glass leg shaped like a jagged column of ice today, layers and layers of dripping glass. The *pull* of the sorcerer's affinity felt like a whirlpool as Yinii moved toward her, trying hard to ignore the ink on the letter, the books on the shelves, as it swelled along that current of magic.

Fastreda looked up as Yinii came in—one eye blue, the other pale glass in the crack of the shard-filled scar that ran up her face—and raised her remaining eyebrow. "My shredfinch," she said. "And..." She leaned to look past Yinii at the closing door. "Hmm? No Amadea?"

"Toya One-Saint," Yinii said. "You gave him glass. Was he making weapons?"

Fastreda frowned a moment. "Now where...Ah! Yes! The Orozhandi tinkerer. Fat little rabbit." She peered at Yinii with her living eye. "Why do you bring him up?"

"Did Redolfo have explosives?"

"He had me," Fastreda said dismissively.

Yinii gritted her teeth at that tone—that tossed-away, none-of-this-matters tone. The ink in the books began to rattle with Yinii's irritation, and a wooden inkpot bounced in place on the shelf. She sucked a deep breath through her nose and made her hands into fists. "He was making something else. Why did you give him glass?"

"Because Redolfo asked, and I like making glass." Fastreda sighed. "My shredfinch, you are boring me."

"He needed fuel," Yinii surmised. "He said the glass wasn't working. He asked for glass, though. Glass and marble, and I think... I think that means he was using sorcerer-wrought materials as a replacement for cold-magic. Why?"

Fastreda tilted her head. "That would be foolish. The cold-magic is the gift of the Black Mother Forest. You spit in her eye if you try to improve upon it. I think you are telling stories."

The ink on Fastreda's letter—winter vine char in stinging alcohol—began to peel loose, sliding over the table toward Yinii. She pushed it away, holding it in place. "Did you even ask what they were using you for? Did you just do whatever Redolfo said?"

"I did what I wanted," Fastreda answered. "I wanted to make glass." She leaned forward, dropping her voice. "I will tell you, Yinii Six-Owl, this is why I think you cannot answer my question. That you are asking me this—*why do you let them, why don't you ask*—tells me you cannot imagine being in the same place."

Yinii's mouth flooded bitter. The books shot from their shelf, their ink rising up out of the fanned pages in a swarm, a cloud that swept toward her, winding around her like a scarf, a skirt of midnight.

"I cannot imagine being in the same place," Yinii ground out, "because I would not let myself ignore what was happening! You didn't have to let him make you a weapon! You didn't have to let him bring you down! You could have crushed him—you *chose this*! And if I never understand that, then all the better!"

Fastreda Korotzma studied her, one blue eye, one glass eye wide and wild, and the smile that slid across her face was not cruel, not mocking, yet undeniably sharp—like a slash from a Beminat calligraphy brush, bold and defined. "Then what's my answer, Yinii Six-Owl?"

"I don't fucking *care* what your answer is!" Yinii cried. She felt ink crawling around her mouth, felt the carbon in the rug reaching toward her, and let it ignite on her fury. "I don't fucking care if you think I'm a sorcerer or you don't. I already know who I am."

Fastreda stood, her eyes hungry and elated, her glass leg grinding against the stone floor. She was no taller than Yinii, for all she seemed to fill the room with her presence. "And what do you know?"

Her gloves, the shield against the ink, smoked and crumbled in her hands, pulling water from the air itself to run through her spread fingers. The pitcher cracked, the water flowing into the charred rug, adding to the swirl of ink.

"The ink is *mine*," Yinii said, her voice warbling with the ink. "I could turn the whole world to ink if I wanted to, but I won't, because I'm not a monster like you."

"Aren't you, my shredfinch?" Fastreda asked, and Yinii thought her voice might be trembling too. "We are all monsters in waiting. We are all willing to be terrible for the right price. What happened in the tunnels?"

The ink swept up her, a raiment, an armor—a shield against the pull of Fastreda's affinity. Yinii kept the ink off her, kept it from seeping into her, trying to merge. *You are mine*, she thought, holding the spiral around her. A thudding sound rang out in the room, a garbled sound Yinii lost in the bubble of the ink.

"I don't care that I killed her," Yinii whispered. "The Shrike. She murdered innocent people. She tried to kill my friends. She's better as ink."

"Sometimes you have to be the monster," Fastreda said, as if in agreement. "And sometimes what you must do is choose carefully whose weapon you become."

Her one blue eye shone bright, like freshly poured ink, and she reached through the wetness and the fire to embrace Yinii in her bony arms. "Ah, my shredfinch. My sister—I knew you had it in you. But now, we must fold our wings in." She nodded toward the door.

The pull of Fastreda's affinity bent Yinii's around it. The thudding became knocking, the garbled noises the shouting of imperial guardsmen. There was smoke in the room and so much ink. Yinii pulled all her senses in so quickly her nerves screamed with the effort. The fire went out, the shroud of ink splashing to the floor. Fastreda reached lazily over to the shelf and threw the emptied ink-pot down as the door burst open, guards charging in.

"There was a mess," Fastreda said regretfully to the puzzled soldiers. "But everything's all right now."

<hr />

Amadea arrived at the Imperial Complex that morning wearing her best everyday uniform and the jewelry she'd donned the day before. The golden vulture-wing earrings and bronze hairpins would not convince anyone the faded navy gown was her formal robes, but as those were still damp and pinned beneath her cat, Imp, that morning, this would have to do.

Not for Ibramo, she thought, as if she could reassure the guards who took her request for an audience into the palace proper. *For the archives*.

She waited on a plush bench opposite a tarnished mirror wall. The face that regarded her from the glass looked worn and exhausted, dark circles under the darker eyes. She had slept fitfully, worrying about Yinii and Tunuk and Quill and Richa, about bombs and separatists, about Bishamar Twelve-Spider's knowledge, about Redolfo Kirazzi and what he could do with seven sorcerers.

When the masked attendants, a pair of slim youths in imperial gold, finally arrived to bring her to the consort-prince, all their discomfort radiated from their tense shoulders, their stiff glances at her, as they led her into the palace.

Amadea did not like traversing the residential areas of the Imperial Complex, for the same reasons she avoided Gintanas Abbey. Her memories burst forward in unexpected, unpredictable ambushes. She had never been in this hall before, she would swear it…and then she would turn her head and see a painting and feel a warm sense of familiarity, a vague memory of giggling about the stern-faced man in the mask shaped like a golden octopus. It was unsettling, and with so many puzzles swimming murkily through her thoughts, that sense of unreality, of things not fitting together, set her teeth on edge.

Bishamar's assertion that Lireana survived nudged these broken pieces in her mind. Perhaps they weren't lies, but they weren't hers—the most likely of them was dead, he'd said. She was just a facsimile. Little more than a changeling molded into the shape of the princess.

She had to be.

Then the attendants led her into a room where the Empress of Semilla waited instead of her husband.

Amadea dropped into a panicked curtsy. Beneditta had traded her expansive gown for a trim green suit with narrow trousers in the Minseon style, a golden mask in a chevron shape making a diamond of her nose and pointed chin. Her dark hair was wound up on top of her head, and she stood over a map spread out on a heavy table.

"Leave us," she said to the attendants. When they'd scurried from the room, Beneditta straightened and once more pulled the golden mask from her face. Amadea studied the green stone floor, her reflection in its polished surface.

"Gritta told you to keep the Red Mask from me, didn't she?" Beneditta asked.

"What makes you say that, Your..." Amadea swallowed the title, not sure if she was meant to use it. Gold for duty, green for whim, black for secrets—but nothing for the barefaced acknowledgment of the Empress of Semilla.

"Because I know her," Beneditta said. "And I know she frightens you. She frightens me, too...or she did, until recently."

Amadea lifted her head and found Beneditta watching her, unblinking.

"You said you would find out more for me," the empress went on. "I wish to know what you've found."

"Your pardon, the wooden bones—"

"Yes," Beneditta said, as if they were coming to the point, "the wooden bones. They are connected."

Amadea frowned. "Connected to Redolfo Kirazzi and what he intends? Did...did the Kinship tell you the man who was keeping them had worked for the Usurper?"

Beneditta's fine eyebrows rose. "No," she breathed. "But that does fit." She rapped her knuckles against the map. "I think the theft was engineered by Redolfo Kirazzi's agents. I think it must be. It is so clearly intended to undermine my authority."

"The bones were stolen twelve years ago," Amadea said. "During your father's reign."

"Were they?" she asked. "Or is that what we are meant to believe? Please, Lira—"

"Amadea."

"Amadea. Think about it. Is there anything one could do that would more spectacularly fracture the Imperial Authority? We've never had trouble with the Orozhandi. The rezas might squabble with each other, but they have never given cause for concern. Even when the Usurper was in power, none of the clans sided with him officially—only outcasts."

And spies, Amadea thought, recalling Nanqii and his tale of Bishamar Twelve-Spider procuring a Grave-Spurned Princess.

"And now this?" Beneditta continued. "They cannot countenance the loss of a saint. It is perfect in its disruption. A tale that this is an old theft, an old crime—that only cements things. 'We have been failing our protectorates all along!' But now I know. I have caught him out, you see? And I need your help, I need to find the way to trace this back to him, back to the other side of the Salt Wall, so that I can tell people this is not the doing of the Imperial Authority, this is a trap by the Usurper returned."

Amadea came to stand beside the table, looking over the map. Beneditta had scrawled lines in grease pencil, connections between Sestina and Arlabecca, Sestina and Terzanelle, Sestina and Caesura, Sestina and Maqama. There were names appended to the lines, and Amadea was surprised to find the noble consuls among them.

"Do you think there are traitors among the noble consuls?" she asked slowly.

"There are traitors everywhere," Beneditta said. "My father was too gentle. I don't mean you," she added quickly. "Of course not you."

Amadea considered the network of lines, the names and the cities, facts circling an answer. "Your Imperial Majesty," she said at last, "I don't think the wooden bones are related, unfortunately. I think they are extraordinary, but they are only the failure of the archives in its task."

Beneditta frowned. "The peddler, the man worked for Redolfo—"

"Yes," Amadea said. "But he...if Redolfo Kirazzi was going to ruin your authority with this theft, wouldn't it make more sense to just...deliver the bones to the Orozhandi? To show them the failure and claim the victory?"

"He does not need them on his side," Beneditta pointed out. "Only for them to be turned against me when he reveals...when he reveals..." She swallowed. "When he makes known our terrible secret."

Amadea glanced back at the closed doors. "He doesn't know."

Now Beneditta regarded Amadea as if she were the one rambling through mad statements. "He must," she said slowly. "You were dosed with the Venom of Changelings. If he didn't know before that, surely he figured it out."

It took a moment for Amadea to parse the empress's meaning. Redolfo Kirazzi had given Amadea the memory-altering poison called the Venom of Changelings. Changelings were not affected by the poison, but the Ulanittis, being descended from both humans and changelings, were—albeit with a much higher dose. When the empress was poisoned to hide a murder, it did not replace her memory because the killer had only given her the amount that would make a human malleable—that was how Amadea had figured out her secret.

Beneditta believed Amadea was an Ulanitti. Beneditta believed Amadea was the Grave-Spurned Princess.

"If people discover what has been ruling them..." Beneditta whispered.

Amadea took hold of her arm. "It won't come to that."

A soft scraping sound made her turn in time to see Lady Sigrit-trice stepping through an open panel in the wall. A gold-and-black half mask hid her face, but her hard eyes locked on Amadea as she approached the table. Beneditta went rigid and reclaimed her own mask.

Silver hair, Amadea thought. *Black dress. Red lines.*

"Here you are, Your Majesty," Sigrittrice said with a briskness that didn't cover her irritation. "I didn't realize you'd accepted an audience with Archivist Gintanas."

Beneditta didn't answer, didn't even move to explain herself.

Sigrittrice smiled. "What were you discussing?"

"The security of the Imperial Federation," the empress said crisply.

"Which involves the archives how, exactly?"

"Don't pretend you don't know," Beneditta said.

"I was just telling the empress," Amadea said, "that it's a good thing she cares so much for the safety of the empire. We should be doing everything we can to make certain it's secure. And we are, aren't we?"

"No," Beneditta answered for her great-aunt. "*We* are doing as little as we can." She turned on Amadea. "You said you would find me proof of Redolfo Kirazzi's conspiracy with the changelings. Where is my proof?"

"It's been all of a day," Amadea reminded her, very aware of Sigrittrice's eyes on her. "A day that has unfortunately required me in many different ways." Noble consuls, panicking archivists, secrets in the open, and an explosion thwarting her attempt at a pleasant evening—"busy" was an understatement, and she felt her chest tighten.

Breathe, she told herself, she willed toward Beneditta.

"This should have been your priority!" Beneditta pulled away as she noticed Sigrittrice moving toward her. "This nation is our highest purpose, our only purpose!"

"Archivist Gintanas," Sigrittrice called, "would you leave us? Please. The empress and I have to talk."

"Don't you dare!" Beneditta snarled, though at Amadea or Sigrittrice, it wasn't clear. She took a step back. "Everything is crumbling, and if we don't shore up the weak points—"

Amadea stepped forward, laid a reassuring hand on Beneditta's shoulder, Nanqii's words echoing in her thoughts. *I see the cracks in the foundation.*

"Please, Dita," she said, too familiar again but not sure what else to do. "Have you slept? You can't guide the empire if you haven't taken care of yourself."

Beneditta regarded her warily behind the dark eyeholes of the mask. "Are you doing it too?" she asked, a tremor in her voice.

Pretend she is a specialist, Amadea thought, *on the edge of the spiral*. "You have a problem," she said firmly. "I'm looking for a solution. I don't want you to suffer for something we could easily resolve. But you also must, *must* take care of yourself. Especially now."

Beneditta's eyes welled suddenly. "I fear it's too late for that," she whispered.

The doors jerked open, a burst of protest from the attendants following Ibramo as he charged in. He wore a golden mask, a veil of interlinked stars that fell over his eyes and nose. He took in the three of them—ferocious Sigrittrice, frantic Beneditta, and Amadea, who hoped her panic didn't show.

Ibramo held perfectly still, drawing a careful breath, waiting them out.

Sigrittrice at last broke the silence. "I believe," she said irritably, "your original appointment is here, Archivist Gintanas. What perfect timing. You may go."

⊷ ≡◆≡ ⊶

At the sound of the door opening, Tunuk pushed Zoifia toward the other end of the room, toward the dark doorways. He raced back to the first lamp on light feet and flicked the cold-magic back into darkness before hurrying to the next. Quill was pushing Stavio into one of the last small rooms the light still touched as Tunuk reached up and turned off the lamp, in the same moment the door opened.

Tunuk froze as a dim cold-magic globe shone in the crack of the door, a woman's voice saying, "A moment, esinor, I'll get the lights."

He wasn't going to be able to get to the room unseen—

Tunuk stripped off his uniform, down to the skin, kicking the clothes under the row of worktables, so only the light-devouring shadow of his body showed. He covered his face, peering through the slits of his fingers, and moved back and back into the shadows. He thought, absurdly, of playing hide-and-seek with his siblings, tucking into the deepest shadow you could find and leaping out to surprise the others, only this time, if he leapt out, it would have to be to fight, and his mind brought up the sword in his ribs again.

He stuck to the shadowy rim of the room, moving toward where his friends hid. The first light came on, illuminating the bomb-maker's pale face. She blinked uncomfortably, her eyes adjusting. Tunuk made it to the door of the little room—a closet of a space, four bunks dug into the dirt and laid with wooden boards. Zoifia, looking bright as a beacon, as every scintilla of light reflected off her pale hair, curled up at the very back. Stavio and Quill tried to block her, but to Tunuk's eyes, they were hardly less visible.

Tunuk stepped inside, standing at an angle to block the others from view, imagined himself a shadow only a little too deep, only incongruous if you knew the wall wouldn't cast it.

"I can't believe you work down here," a man drawled.

"It suffices," Vigdza said. "One of the Usurper's bolt-holes, we think. No idea who let him build this—but they're not talking anymore."

Tunuk peeked around the edge of the doorway, still peering through his fingers to obscure the glow of his eyes: the woman who'd dropped the bone, most definitely, and a tall, broad-shouldered human man with pale, gray-streaked hair, wearing a bright yellow coat—the man from Gunarro's house.

Tunuk pulled back away from the edge as the man's gaze swept the room, utter disgust in his expression. "Are you sure about this?"

"Very," Vigdza said. "You saw what happened. They're looking everywhere for the bomber. They knew to comb this neighborhood in particular."

"So did she betray us?" he asked.

"Less a betrayal. More…I don't think she's thinking clearly. I think she only has her mind on revenge."

"Which includes the vigilant? Did he survive?"

"I think so." Vigdza hesitated. "I don't think he was the target, esinor."

"Ah," he said. "You think it was me."

"I'm not asking what you do with your days. But we did meet near there. She might have made assumptions."

"She's managed something brilliant," the man said. The *tink* of a fingernail tapping the glass globe. "The others all burst quite dramatically, I recall. This one only bursts dramatically if you want it to?"

"I can't pretend I understand the equations. She's been working on this for probably a decade. But apparently the . . . organic nature is the difference."

The cage of Tunuk's ribs clutched his breath tight—*probably a decade* was easily twelve years.

It's not her, he thought, ferocious as a yinpay.

"It's absurd, really," the man said, "how many times we must rediscover something, reengineer it. They were so close all those years ago. Now she figures it out again finally—"

"And makes sure every person in Arlabecca knows it."

A pause. "Don't interrupt me, Vigdza. I *loathe* being interrupted."

Another pause. "Esinor Zezurin, you and I both know that Lord—"

At the sound of the name, Quill sucked in a sudden hissing breath.

Everything in the room beyond went still.

"Esinora?" Vigdza called. "Is that you?"

The room swallowed her voice. Behind Tunuk, Zoifia, Quill, and Stavio were so silent he might have thought them dead. Tunuk's attention had locked on to the sound of feet moving slowly toward them, his heart like a wild animal holding him frozen, that horrible moment on the hill outside Sestina replaying itself in his pulse and bones and breath.

This was the moment before he died. This was the moment before everything ended. There was nothing he could do.

He felt the bone plaques rising on his shoulders, buoyed on the surge of his panic, the thrumming rush of bones—in Stavio and Quill and Zoifia, in the fabricator and her boss, in himself. That was what he wanted. Wrap himself in bone, close it all away—

Someone's hand closed on his upper arm—it might have been any of them. He knew it was Quill.

Stop, he told himself. *Breathe. Be here.* If he let the bone take him, it would shine in the light the way his skin didn't—it would reveal them all to Vigdza, and he would fail Zoifia, Quill, and Stavio. He reached up slowly to cover Quill's pale hand with his own and kept his eyes as closed as he could while he watched the fabricator step into view.

She held her lamp up to the darkness, walking the length of the worktables, peering underneath them, looking over each piece of equipment. In her other hand, she held a wicked, well-sharpened knife.

If she comes too close, Tunuk thought, fighting with his fear, *you will just have to leap on her. You will have to do something. Gain them time to run.* He was not the yinpay; he was the opposite of the yinpay—not powerful but weak; not alone but encumbered; not dangerous but in danger. He wouldn't be able to do anything, he thought. He'd just die. The bone sent needles of pain through his skin as it rose, but he made himself hold still.

The light slid past the alcove as she walked, swinging the lamp back and forth. Tunuk closed his eyes and prayed to lost gods that she wouldn't look closer.

"Rats," she said, resheathing the knife at her belt. "They keep getting down here."

"A good sign you shouldn't be playing in the Usurper's footprints," Stellano Zezurin replied. "Fine. Salvage what you can. Clear all this out, and I'll report back. How much do you think she took?"

"It's hard to say. Enough for at least another one. Maybe two. Maybe more."

"Any idea who she might target?"

"You would know better than me, esinor."

Silence. "This is why vengeance is best swift or forgotten," Stellano Zezurin said. "Tafad's not interested in another ul-Shandiian making a fool of him. You know what to do." The door opened again, its hinges squealing. "I'll be at the house by the College of Five Forests when the job's done. Don't make me wait."

Tunuk felt the air shift as he left, the hum of his bones fading out of the discordant chorus. Vigdza uttered something irritable under her breath, then crossed the room again. Within Tunuk's sight line, she stooped to pull a big canvas bag like the one she'd transported the wooden bones in out from under a worktable, then added the containers they'd found the naphtha and gunpowder in, along with the others that had sat beside them. She cinched this shut, then took a pole from the back of the next table, using the loop of leather attached to the end to quiet the cold-magic lamps she had lit. With her own globe in hand, she went back out the way she'd come.

Tunuk didn't move until he heard the outer door shut again, and then he fell to his knees, clutching at his shoulders and hissing curses. Zoifia clambered out after him, crouching down low, patting at his back where he lay sprawled on the ground. "Are you all right?" she whispered. "Are you spiraling?"

"No!" he gasped. Her bones throbbed, an uncanny tattoo. "Maybe!"

"I don't know how you stop yours!" Zoifia said, her voice winding tighter. "I can't...pull your bones away! Or mine!"

"Talk to him," Stavio said. "You have to calm down, bedo."

"Tunuk?" Quill's voice came, another hand on his back. "Hey, it's all right. We're all fine."

"She had a knife," Tunuk forced himself to say. It came out small and reedy, his ribs tight around the words. "I thought I was going to die. I thought I was going to have to throw myself at her and I was going to die." He wrapped his arms around the back of his head and gave a small cry of pain as the plaques of bone shifted, pulling on his skin.

"You saved us all," Stavio said. "Here, Quill, help me sit him up." They maneuvered Tunuk up to lean against the wall. He tried to slow his breath, slow the thrumming. He felt dizzy.

"There's a pole," Tunuk managed. "On the table. Over there."

Stavio moved through the darkness, his hands reaching to catch him against the worktables.

"Nothing even happened." Tunuk gasped. "I shouldn't be panicking."

"That was *not* nothing," Quill said.

"And you weren't supposed to be the muscle," Stavio said. "Get your breath back. I'm going to try and get the lights on. You two keep talking to him. Sorcha, tell some stupid chapbook stories."

Zoifia settled down onto her backside, her legs folded. "Do you want to hear the plot of *Rafiel del Sladio and the Lost Army of Bemina*? It's *so* inaccurate—the jaguar-warriors ride *actual* jaguars. Yinii almost cried! Apparently that's like trying to ride on a big dog or something."

Yinii—saints and devils, he'd been so angry, and she'd been right all this time. And then he'd nearly died not being able to say sorry.

Tunuk looked over at Quill. "You heard what she called him."

Quill nodded. "I heard all of it."

Stavio got the cold-lamp shining again, light filling the room. Zoifia let out a shriek, and Quill pulled away, startled.

"Why are you naked!" Zoifia cried out.

"So they couldn't see me," Tunuk said witheringly. "The light would have reflected on my uniform."

"Where's your uniform?" Quill asked, his eyes averted. Tunuk pointed under the table where he'd thrown the tunic and trousers, and Quill went to recover it.

"You two have a funny way of saying 'Thank you, Tunuk,'" Stavio said. "Honestly, humans have as much skin as anybody else, I will never understand why you act like it's all got to be covered up."

"Your legs are a built-in modesty screen, you dolt!" Zoifia said. Tunuk pulled his uniform back on with shaking hands and had to sit down again. He felt like he might vomit. "What do we do now?"

"We need to get back to the archives," Quill said. "Find Amadea and get word to Richa. That man is someone very dangerous." He hesitated. "Though maybe not as dangerous as the person behind it all."

Tunuk looked up at him, trying for baleful but too shaken to manage. "Don't say it."

"A woman. Who has improved on her work from twelve years ago. Who clearly knew where the Usurper's bunker was." Quill looked at Tunuk, as if he dreaded speaking the answer, and Tunuk felt the bone plaques itch beneath his skin. "Another ul-Shandiian? Trying to finish something?" When Tunuk said nothing, Quill finished, "You know they mean Qalba."

⊷ ⊷⊱⊰⊶ ⊶

Ibramo led Amadea up a flight of carpeted stairs and down a hall that wound around the outside of the building, to a small, out-of-the-way room with two chairs and a low table. She took one of the chairs and rested her head in her hands, trying to order her thoughts and quiet her mind at the same time. It didn't work very well.

He crouched down in front of her and took off the mask, dropping it on the table where the star-shaped links clinked together in a pile. He set a careful hand on her knee.

"You all right?" he asked softly.

"Mostly," she said. "Someone blew up Vigilant Langyun's apartment last night."

"Oh!" Ibramo said. "You weren't *there*, were you?"

"I have a memory," Amadea said, avoiding that entire line of discussion, "of your father talking about a weapon. When I saw the device, I knew it was dangerous." She described it as best she could. "Do you remember anything like that? Some kind of explosive?"

Ibramo shook his head. "No. That would... Gods of the heavens, that would have been very bad."

"Do you remember any Orozhandi working for him?"

Ibramo shut his eyes, thinking. "No," he said at last. "But he didn't bring everyone to Sestina. He had the house in Terzanelle. The apartment in Arlabecca. People he went to, instead of bringing them to him."

"Do you remember him gathering sorcerer-wrought artifacts?"

"No, he had Fastreda." Ibramo's thumb brushed over her knee. "Slow down. Why do you think these are connected?"

Why indeed? She felt as mad as Beneditta in that moment. She covered his hand with hers. "I'm sorry. I don't know if they're connected. I just know they're important." She pulled out the transfer documents. "Primate Lamberto was doing something else for that changeling who had your father's face. Quill and I found *seven* sorcerer transfers in his files over the last six months—all moving toward Sestina."

Ibramo took the papers from her, studying them.

"I don't know if that connects to the stolen artifacts or the bones or someone setting explosives," she said. "But I do know that might mean seven new Fastredas if he can get them to the other side of the Wall."

"But the tunnel's collapsed," Ibramo said. "We've stopped this."

"Good," Amadea said. "Then get those sorcerers as far from the Wall as you can. And then we need to find out who ordered all of these." She pointed to the seal. "One of the functionaries is working for your father."

"I see," Ibramo said. "I'll take care of it."

"Thank you," Amadea said. Then: "You haven't told Beneditta about the tunnels."

Ibramo's gaze flicked over her face, as if he were trying to find the right answer there. "She's busy. I didn't want to make her worry until there was something to worry about."

"She's already worried," Amadea said. "Was that new in there?"

Ibramo stood, paced across the little room, and Amadea stood with him. "If you were to reassure her the Wall is sealed..." she began.

"You give me too much credit," Ibramo said. "I told her the tunnel was destroyed—she sent more soldiers to examine it. Two separate expeditions, and she talks as if it's still passable."

"Maybe she should see it for herself."

"When? She's only one woman," Ibramo said. "It's not reasonable to put all this on her. To make her the one who needs to decide. It would drive anyone mad."

"Do you think she's going mad?" Amadea asked softly.

"No," he said, too quickly. "No, of course not."

Amadea thought of the secret, the lie of the Ulanittis. The revelation that they were all enough changeling to mold with the venoms, to make into perfect rulers—that had driven Appolino Ulanitti to murder his brother, Iespero, and his whole young family. And now Beneditta knew too, and Beneditta was growing erratic.

"She is *the empress*," Amadea said again. "She *must* handle it. That's her purpose."

Ibramo let go of her, pacing in agitation. "And what sort of purpose is it?" he demanded. "We put all our faith and weight on one person, the ultimate voice of the empire. How can anyone fulfill that role, let alone someone appointed to it because of the accident of their birth? She wasn't even meant to have the throne."

Amadea stood as well, full of horror. "You sound like your father right now."

He looked as if she'd struck him. "My father would have watched

Beneditta ensnare herself in the net of her own fears and drown in them," Ibramo said. "We are in danger right now, the cracks in the empire's foundation are undeniable—and whatever the reason, Beneditta is not handling it the way she needs to, and I am worried about her."

Your little stunt at Lord Obigen's memorial, Sigrittrice had said.

I see the cracks in the foundation, Nanqii had said to her.

"She has you," Amadea said. "She has Lady Sigrittrice."

Ibramo looked down at the chain mask puddled on the table. "And she has you."

Amadea dropped back in her seat. "I am too dangerous to be this close to her. You know that."

"You were," Ibramo agreed. "But now? I think now you might be the best thing that could happen to her."

Amadea drew a deep breath, trying to will her fears back down. "Someone...recognized me. Someone knew I was the Grave-Spurned Princess. That hasn't happened before. So, no. It's still very dangerous."

The admission made Ibramo stiffen, alert. Ready to spring. "Who?" he demanded. "Who's threatening you?"

"I handled it."

"That's not a name," Ibramo noted. "Are you afraid to tell me?"

"I'm afraid you're going to try and fix it."

He would—she could already see him striding through that villa, furious and protective. Trying to stand against Bishamar Twelve-Spider's endless reach. That was how they'd always been—a childhood of being terrorized but throwing that fear aside when he could protect her; a recklessness in her when he was the one in danger. But now it was the powers of the Imperial Authority he was talking about wielding.

"I'm not going to let you get hurt," she said.

Ibramo seized her in an embrace, holding her close against him. For a moment Amadea was so tempted by the past, the certainty and the safety of him. She had dreamed once of a future where they fled all the dangers, all the pressures—she had been too young to understand how insurmountable those obstacles were. But now, wouldn't it be simpler? They were wiser and cleverer, and they had so many more resources. She found herself remembering the changeling in the tunnel: *I escaped over the Wall, into the old lands. You should see it.*

You would lose here and now, she thought, and Richa flitted through her thoughts. *You wanted here and now.*

"Right now," Amadea said, still in his arms, "we just have to help Beneditta. We have to figure out what your father is planning and stop it." *And find the lost bones, and find the peddler's killer, and find out what needs to be done to protect the archives.* She thought briefly of Richa's stricken look at Stellano Zezurin's name. The way he'd hidden it under that calm and easy demeanor.

Ibramo sighed, tucking her under his chin. "I will do my best. I don't...understand Beneditta. But I'll do my best."

Amadea pulled away. "She's your *wife.*"

"She's my...duty. I am the consort-prince. I know where I stand. But it would be a lie to say I understand Beneditta the way I understand..." He trailed off, then seemed to muster his courage. "You'll say I sound like my father again, but I don't care: you would have made a good empress. If my father hadn't been involved, I mean. He knew *you* were the right one, even then."

Amadea pulled her hand back. "Don't say these things."

"I'm not saying anything," he argued. "Only that if circumstances were different, you would have been the stronger empress. No one would be wondering what you could be told or what you needed to be kept from. The ducal authorities wouldn't be flouting you—"

"I can barely keep my own archivists in line, and the man I thought was my dearest friend is speaking treason to me!"

"It's not treason, it's the truth!"

"Well, it wasn't the case, and it isn't now, and whatever world put an abbey brat on the throne of the Ulanittis might or might not be better off, but it isn't here and it isn't now. And don't," she said, forestalling Ibramo's response, "say 'What if you're not?' We are done with that. We do not need another empress, we do not need a succession crisis, and what those wars showed us is that when we lack a strong and competent Imperial Authority, supported by their government, we fall to pieces. We are strongest together. We cannot add more cracks."

"The cracks are already there," Ibramo said. "I'm afraid the worst is going to happen anyway."

"Then you need to fulfill your purpose, Consort-Prince." *A flash of Consort-Princess Sestrida, a memory of a mother's alarm.* Amadea squeezed her eyes shut. "Do not let your empress fail, and keep her heirs alive."

"I would never," Ibramo said fiercely, "let something happen to my children."

"Good," Amadea said. "I should leave. I have a lot to do."

She moved to go, but he caught her hand, clasped it to his chest. "If I'm right, if this is too much and everything collapses... what is it that you want?"

She laughed, puzzled. "I want it to *not* collapse."

"No," he said. "I'm agreeing with you in the first place. We can't allow things to fall apart. But neither of us is a god out of legend, an Emperor Eschellado to forge the new path—*if* it falls apart, *if* all these things become moot... tell me what it is that you want."

Amadea drew a slow, steadying breath. What did she want if the world fell apart? What did she want, absent obligation, absent obstacle? Who was she, if the problems were unsolvable? If the weight she carried was swept from her, like a stone tumbled down a river, out of sight beyond the sea?

Would you want me? he was asking. *If we were not the ones to break it, would you and I rise out of the aftermath together?* She could not, she found, even make herself consider it. What would she want? Who was she if the problems were unsolvable? *Nobody,* a dark little voice murmured back.

"I don't want to know the answer to this," she said softly. "I don't think I could bear it." She reached down and picked up his mask. She turned his hand over in hers and piled the linked stars into his palm.

Ibramo looked down at it shining there. He wet his lips. "This is so hard. Seeing you. Knowing that we can't... I still love you," he said, the words tumbling out of him. "I do, I still love you, I have always loved you, and now you're here, and we're not alone like we were, and... I want you to be happy, but I want... I just want."

Amadea shut her eyes. "I know," she began. "Ibramo, I—"

And she stopped, something he'd said catching hold of her thoughts. *He knew* you *were the right one, even then.*

"Amadea?" Ibramo said, concerned. "Amadea, are you all right?"

"There were three of us," she said.

Ibramo had never been good at hiding his thoughts, not from Amadea—the stillness that struck his face had nothing placid, nothing curious in it. It was the stillness of a deer hearing movement in the underbrush.

"What...what are you talking about?" he said.

"Bishamar Twelve-Spider said there were three girls," she whispered, her voice shaking. "And you said your father knew I was the one—did...did you know them too? The other Liras?"

"It doesn't matter," Ibramo said, almost pleaded. "You're the only one. You're the only one left."

In the garden, she had said. *By the fountain*, he had finished. But that wasn't right—they had met in a different garden at a different time, and the girl by the fountain hadn't been her.

"You didn't tell me." She felt untethered, as if she might lift out of her skin, as if the world were plunging away. "You knew—what... what was he doing? Was he ready to replace me? Was he *mixing* us? Which one was I?"

"I don't know!" he cried. "Please! I...I don't know. I...knew. I knew you all separately, I had to pretend each of you was the only one while he did...You all came at the same time from Gintanas, you all were put to the test, and then...it didn't *matter*. You were the one."

"How can you tell me you love me and at the same time tell me it doesn't matter?"

"I made you," Redolfo whispers. "I built you into this. I can end you just as easily."

Her breath was coming too fast; she was getting light-headed. "Is anything I remember true?"

"I'm true," he said. "We're true! And I won't let him hurt you again!"

You can't promise that—the words wouldn't come out of her mouth, and her mouth filled with the sour burn of bile. How could he do this? She had trusted him; she had thought he was the only one she could be certain was on her side—

"I have to go," she said.

She fled down the long, curving hallway, down the carpeted stairs. The ghosts of memories lunged at her, and she kept her eyes on the carpet, feeling as if she were watching herself at a distance, as if she were the specter haunting this place. Ibramo's twin confessions left her spinning. He loved her—he could not love her...he could not love her *right now* in the midst of this. He had lied to her—he had lied to her about something so viscerally upsetting she kept trying to scrape it out of her mind. Her breath became a wild thing, tearing sobs from her chest, fighting her attempts to control it.

Golden flowers, she told herself, her eyes on the carpet. *Turquoise diamonds. Red scrollwork.*

"Amadea! Please! Wait!" Ibramo shouted.

She looked up—she'd gotten turned around, standing at a nexus of hallways. Amadea Gintanas should have been lost. But Amadea knew abruptly where she was—down that hall, turn left, down the stairs, that would take her to the grand entry hall.

She faltered—no part of her wanted to trust these memories, a petty, panicked thought.

Move, she told herself. *Get out of here.*

"Amadea!" Ibramo shouted, catching up as she plunged down the hall, toward the stairs—

"Here, my sweet darling, your mask is coming loose." Warm, gentle hands cup her face, her little hands closing on her mother's wrist—

At the top of the stairs, Amadea stopped, her breath refusing to come, a lost and secret want for her mother unfolding too big and too fast, like a gauzy scarf tugged free of a pocket. She had gone so long believing the memories were false, lies crafted and implanted by Redolfo Kirazzi.

But they were *real*—she had to face that now. They were real and they had happened—but not to her. She was the substitute.

You don't know that, a little voice murmured.

I will never know for sure, she thought.

"Amadea." Ibramo caught up to her. "Please, please let me explain."

"What is there to explain?" she demanded. "What would possibly change any of this?"

Shouts of "Your Imperial Majesty!" echoed through the huge entry hall below, the great murals of the protectorates' founders and the clustered petitioners and courtiers all overseeing the empress sweeping into the space, Sigrittrice in pursuit.

"Oh no," Ibramo said, and stepped closer to Amadea.

At the foot of the stairs, Sigrittrice reached the empress, grabbed her shoulder. "Your Majesty, please, this is not—"

Beneditta whirled, slapping Sigrittrice's hand away. "I am the Empress of Semilla, and I am not someone to test the iron with! You carry out my orders, Gritta, not the other way around!"

Amadea hurried down the stairs, Ibramo following.

"Of course, Dita," Lady Sigrittrice said, holding up her hands in a gesture of calm. She searched the hall, from the staring courtiers to Ibramo and Amadea coming down the stairs. "I want to hear what your orders are. Perhaps we could retire, and the consort-prince—"

The empress jerked another step away. "Don't touch me!" she shouted. "I know what you're doing. I know everything."

In the entry hall, people stared, backed against the painted walls. In their horrified faces, Amadea could see the stories of the Fratricide's madness. Sigrittrice was right—they needed to get Beneditta away from here, now.

A voice rang across the entry hall. "Your Imperial Majesty."

Dushar Six-Agamid ul-Shandiian stood at the far end of the hall, accompanied by a small army of Orozhandi. Amadea recognized the woman who'd represented ul-Tahnaz and the man from ul-Liphiltan, along with their rezas.

"How fortuitous," Dushar continued, still half the hallway away, calling out his demands like a priestess of Alletet shouting for the sun to rise. "We have come—respectfully—to register our formal dispute of your decision to hand over the wooden bones to ul-Hanizan. But since you are here, perhaps we can shorten the process."

Beneditta whipped toward him, her whole body tense as if she might spring suddenly. Sigrittrice once again reached to grab her shoulder. Ibramo moved between Amadea and the empress, trying to shield her.

"This isn't the time," Lady Sigrittrice began again.

And then a roar of sound and light swept away her words.

V

THE GOD THAT WAITS

Summer
Borsya

The farther the girl travels, the more she feels as if she's in a dream. A person can cross the width of Semilla walking the roads in a little less than a month—the world begins at the sea and ends at the Salt Wall, and this is as far as you can go.

But as summer settles in, hungry and humid and full of insects, they are still walking, still crossing a world that keeps stretching on and on like a nightmare hallway.

Redolfo grows thinner, his cheeks hollowing, his eyes burning. When she looks at herself, in the reflection of the water, in the shine of a lost shield, she sees herself growing thinner the same way— older, grown, hungry. She is turning into him, she thinks sometimes, and maybe that's best. Redolfo is the only one who knows what comes next.

At the same time, Melosino has settled into himself, adopting a swaggering step that doesn't feel true to her memories but feels true now to *him*. The girl doesn't pretend this is her baby brother back to life—she's told Melosino what he is, what was done, in hushed voices around the fire, coaxing the truth back little by little. She prefers this, a friend even if she has a hold on him that seems unfair.

Redolfo's made her trap other changelings, and when she does, she holds back a little of the Venom, gives it to Melosino, has him tell her what to say. She lies awake nights, imagining what will happen if Redolfo finds out, swearing not to ever do it again. But when he gives her the venom the next time, she always saves some for Melosino.

"Do you want to go back?" she asks him as they cross a stream, icy cold and shallow as the weather turns. In the ripple of the water, her cheekbones are like cliffs.

Melosino looks up at the sky. "With the others? It's complicated. It's...well, I think it's like this." He nods ahead at Redolfo and his closest guards. "You have a...people who are in power. Redolfo doesn't like that. So there's a war." He hesitates. "I needed to leave. I remember that much. I know there are people I could trust, but I don't remember who they are.

"I remember playing in a garden instead," he adds.

The girl's stomach twists—he has the memories she gave him, instead of his own. The girl wants to ask him if he's happy, but she thinks that might be the wrong question. An indulgent question, a frivolous question—he is alive and so is she, and in a way, they have both won an impossible prize by following Redolfo Kirazzi out into the wilderness. She thinks sometimes of the other girls— one, she knows is dead. She was there when it happened. The other she assumes is dead, and she's glad, really, because Redolfo assumed that was the one who would survive. She hates that other self, that proper *Lira*, in a way that makes her love this wide-open world for not having any trace of her in it.

Out here, *she* is the survivor.

"Do you think about running?" Melosino asks one morning over boiled roots on a valley trail. "I would if you would."

"Don't talk like that," the girl says. "We'd die before we got far."

But Melosino is remembering more and more as Redolfo's army grows—and Redolfo is learning more and more. He's getting better at setting the limits, at locking the changelings into forms and selves that are safe, at making them forget that they can—at any moment—take another shape, act without his permission. And yet he manages to leave them a little more of themselves each time, letting Redolfo gather information about the changeling threat. The girl listens and tests this with Melosino—some of the words seem to pull loose memories, some of the memories let her unlock more.

They number close to fifty when they come through the mountains, always daring the edge of the cold. The forest spreads out below them now, a great basin filled with trees. From where they stand, she can see the fortress cities on their hills, like rocks breaking through the surface of the endless sea of leaves. After the endless plains beyond Khirazj, the forest's lushness slakes a need she didn't know was in her. It is green and green and green.

Except the center. In the center, the god waits.

The Black Mother Forest is the color of a bruise, a black made of purples, layered and deep. Even so far away, the girl can feel the strangeness of it, the distance. This is a place of a different world. It feels as if the forest is a great eye, watching her. Waiting.

"Why are we going there?" she asks Redolfo. She cannot take her eyes off it.

"Do you know the stories of the Black Mother Forest?" he asks.

"I know it's not meant to be just a forest," she says. "It's alive in a different way."

"Indeed. Legend says the Borsyans learned civilization from the Black Mother Forest. Its crow-winged daughters named kings among them and scarred the knowledge of law and architecture and the cold-magic into their very skin. They whispered prophecy to the women until they went mad of it and fled into the woods to mark the places where the hill-cities would be built. When a person seeks a boon, they must first go into the Black Mother Forest and ask for its blessing. It will give you three trials, three tasks to prove your worth. And if you do it wrong, the crow-winged daughters will tear you apart."

The girl can imagine it—birdlike claws ripping flesh, wings flapping, battering her as she bleeds. She shivers. "So the changelings aren't in there?"

"They stay far away from the center," Redolfo confirms. "But that doesn't matter. What matters is what's still there."

Three trials, three tests. And then you may have a boon. "What are you going to ask for?"

Redolfo smiles. "Everything."

CHAPTER SEVENTEEN

Quill left Tunuk to his thoughts all the way back to the archives, but once the door to the Bone Vault was closed, once they were all safe and returned, it couldn't wait any longer. "We need to talk about what we're going to tell Richa," he began.

"There's nothing to talk about," Tunuk said. "It's *not* Qalba."

Stavio and Zoifia settled on stools around the worktable, eyeing Quill and Tunuk both as though waiting for the next bit of chaos. The high shelves around the narrow room crowded close, the cold-magic lamps struggling to light the space. Tunuk went around shaking them each awake with barely leashed fury. Quill sighed. He didn't like being right here, but this was his responsibility. This was what he'd signed on for.

"It doesn't make sense," Tunuk said, biting off each word.

"She was Toya's apprentice," Quill pointed out. "She was helping him after the coup. She had access to his notes. She was probably the one stealing artifacts—for these experiments she didn't get right twelve years ago."

"Who is Toya?" Stavio asked.

"The dead peddler," Quill said. "He was working for Redolfo Kirazzi on something."

"Which might have been a lie and might have been something as innocuous as improving his pistachio yields!" Tunuk countered.

"The fabricator is working with a woman," Quill went on. "An ul-Shandiian woman trying to finish something. Who says she was at least aware of the experiments with the stolen artifacts. That skeleton *wasn't* Qalba's, and Yinii said Qalba sent a letter *recently* to the reza—she's not dead, and she's not gone."

"Wait, what skeleton?" Zoifia interjected.

"The one that was supposed to be wooden, I think," Stavio said.

"Yinii only verified it was from over the Wall," Tunuk said. "It could be a fake. It could be—"

"It could be real, and you'd know that if you gave Yinii the letters you have that you *know* are Qalba's." Quill paused, remembering. "Wait. That one you found in the seaside cabin. What did it say? 'The hunting jackal circles'?"

Tunuk scowled, his dark flesh growing gray in a flush of anger. For a moment, Quill thought he wouldn't tell. " 'The wounded jackal limps along a winding path, but it knows the one it hunts for.' "

"Oh, that sounds sweet," Stavio said. "Trying to get back to its den."

"Sweet?" Zoifia scoffed. "Nothing with a jackal in it is sweet."

"It's got the same style as the note Richa found with the explosive," Quill said. "*And* the note Dushar ul-Shandiian claims he found."

"And so what's your theory?" Tunuk demanded. "Qalba is sending bits of Orozhandi poetic wisdom to everyone she knew? That's not a crime."

"It is if they're warnings that you're going to be killed," Quill said. "Think about it. The first note goes with the bomb—that was definitely meant to kill Richa—"

"Who Qalba doesn't even know," Tunuk said. "And that woman said she didn't think Richa was the target—it was her boss."

"Richa's looking into the theft and Toya's death," Quill pointed out. "He'd be a good person to get rid of. So would the reza, since he's making such a fuss. And they both had notes, whether the fabricator knew or not."

"The reza you claim Qalba asked for help from," Tunuk said. "You're being paranoid."

Quill bristled. "And you're avoiding the obvious. Tunuk, if that note's for you—"

"You've wanted from the beginning for her to be a villain! You decided before we asked any questions that the answer would be

Qalba and Chizid were up to no good—just like the primate! Because if *your* mentor was a monster, then everyone's was!"

"No," Quill said. "But I think I'm a little more experienced than most people in seeing my friend get hurt because he doesn't believe someone he respects could possibly be up to something nefarious! It's been twelve years, and if she's not dead, she's someone you don't know anymore."

Tunuk flinched away from him, curling in on himself. "I think I know her better than you."

"Yeah, I'd have probably fucking said I knew my mentor too before my best friend got murdered by Redolfo Kirazzi's secret assassin because he thought he was helping Primate Lamberto! I'm trying to keep *you* alive because I don't want another friend to die!"

Something broke in Quill as the words flooded out of him, and suddenly all his grief and guilt and helplessness over Karimo's death was rising to the surface, threatening to sweep him away. He clung to his anger, to his frustration with Tunuk—why couldn't he see how much danger he was in? How this small problem was the tiniest fragment of a bigger issue that would destroy them all if they didn't do something about it?

"Wait," Zoifia said. "Did that man pretending to be Redolfo Kirazzi kill the peddler too?"

"No," Tunuk said witheringly.

"You don't know," Quill said. "You don't know and I don't know because nobody *fucking* knows what Redolfo Kirazzi is doing except that it's bad and people are getting hurt, so stop acting like I'm being unreasonable for suggesting the people who helped him before might be helping him *now*!"

Now all three of them were staring at Quill.

"What the fuck do you mean 'what Redolfo Kirazzi *is* doing'?" Tunuk demanded. "They hanged him."

"Saints and devils," Zoifia said, her brown eyes wide as coins. "He's still alive?" She sucked in a breath. "He went over the Wall, didn't he? That's why everyone's muttering about the empress sending imperial soldiers to the Wall and buying up iron charms? Does he have *changelings*?"

Quill faltered—Amadea had said not to tell people. That if people knew, they would panic. And it hadn't sat right with Quill, this idea of hiding dangerous information—if Karimo had just told him he thought the primate was blackmailing someone...

It would be worse, he reasoned, if he lied and told them they were wrong.

Quill drew a long, slow breath before he spoke. "Yeah, Redolfo Kirazzi is still alive. He's on the other side of the Wall. He has changelings. He had a way in—a tunnel under the Salt Wall that we destroyed. Primate Lamberto was working with his agents on something. We're trying to figure out what."

Tunuk blinked at him. "Have you gotten into Zoifia's stupid chapbooks?"

"Hey!" Zoifia snapped. "Those are fun and charming and occasionally educational."

"Yeah, I'm sure you'll need Esinor del Sladio's methods for charming changeling queens in your day-to-day existence. Redolfo Kirazzi was hanged," Tunuk said. "People watched him die."

"They watched a changeling die," Quill said.

"And then what? He just waited on the other side of the Wall for twenty years?"

"Twenty-three," a small voice said. Quill turned and found Yinii still bundled in her cloak, her eyes hollow and red rimmed and full of disbelief. "Are we just telling people now?"

"*You* knew?" Zoifia cried.

"Where have you been, odidunu?" Stavio asked. "You don't look so well."

Yinii hesitated, her gaze flicking toward the back of the workroom. "I'm just going to the chapel. I had...I have some things to think about." She drew a breath. "I found out what Toya was doing. He made the initial bombs. They run on sorcerer-wrought materials—organics, from the sound of it. I tried to get Fastreda to confirm, but...she's not very helpful. About that."

"Fastreda of the *Glass*?" Stavio said, sliding around the worktable, his tentacles pulling against the floorboards. "Yinii, what are you doing? That woman is a *sorcerer*! She's dangerous!"

"She's *helpless*," Yinii said. "They don't even let grains of sand in."

"Because she's a maniac," Stavio said. "Sorcerers are trouble—they're *supposed* to be locked up. This is the one you ought to be fretting over," he said to Quill.

Quill heard the faint rattle of Tunuk's catalogues in their bindings. Yinii's expression was hard and cold as glass.

"You figured it out, didn't you?" he said softly.

Yinii held herself rigid but gave him the tiniest of nods.

In that moment, he wanted to take her hand. He wanted to tell her it would be all right. He wanted to tell her that even though he knew this was something he couldn't really understand, he could be there for her. The ink in the catalogues shook the shelf.

"You know we have to tell Amadea, odidunu," Stavio said. "About Fastreda."

Yinii shook her arms out, as if she were trying to flick water from her fingertips, and the rattling ceased. "Amadea knows. She's the one who suggested it."

Stavio exchanged a glance with Zoifia, as if he must have heard wrong. Quill could see the connections building—if Amadea had suggested it... why had she suggested it... what would be enough to need Fastreda's input. Yinii's closed expression made him think she wasn't ready for any of that.

"Why—" Stavio began.

"She's maqu'tajii," Quill interrupted. "What happened at the Wall, well... You know how bad it is now. Amadea thought it would help Yinii... cope. Amadea knows people. She called in favors."

Stavio's dark brow furrowed. "Favors."

"*Oh*," Zoifia said. "The consort-prince."

"Right," Quill said. "He got Yinii pulled from the lottery to speak with Fastreda."

"So Amadea *is* sleeping with him," Zoifia said. "Saints and devils. I did not expect that."

"No!" Quill said. "They're just... *You* told me about them being childhood friends," he said to Stavio. "She's just been helping him with... with all this Redolfo Kirazzi stuff."

"Are we actually entertaining that?" Tunuk said. "That Redolfo

Kirazzi is still alive with an army of changelings on the other side of the Wall."

"Somehow that changeling got his face, his voice, all his manner-isms," Yinii said. "Enough to fool his son *and* Amadea."

Stavio grunted. "I believe it. That man, he's slippery as an eel."

"They *hanged* him!" Tunuk said.

"I wasn't there. Neither were you." Stavio was still frowning, his arms crossed over his broad chest. "I knew some of this—or I guessed it. I told Bijan that 'cavity' was a tunnel under the Salt Wall. But I don't get what Amadea could help the consort-prince with?"

"Because she's sleeping with him," Zoifia said.

"She *was* helping him before," Tunuk admitted. "The man who said he was Redolfo Kirazzi told her to bring the artifacts. That was in that letter."

Stavio scratched his chin. "Yeah, I heard that part. I figured that's just because she's in charge here, and he knew that. But it's still hap-pening? Why're you helping Amadea track down the Usurper and his changelings?"

"It's important. To the empire," Quill said. "It's just...wouldn't you?"

"No. Why are you helping *Amadea*?" Stavio said. "The consort-prince has an army to order around. He doesn't need Amadea." He frowned and turned toward Yinii. "'He fooled Amadea'—Amadea *knew* Redolfo Kirazzi?"

Yinii turned scarlet. "I don't know."

"She...was in love with the consort-prince," Quill said, repeating the story Stavio had told him months ago. "I think maybe she's still got some fond feelings for him. But they're not sleeping together."

"Yeah, that's why she helps *him*, not why he asks her for help."

"Maybe he's...in love with her still," Quill said. "Maybe he's using this as an excuse to keep her close."

"I believe that!" Yinii said, clasping her hands together. "It's very messy."

Zoifia looked up at the Borsyan lamps, pulling one of her blond curls straight. "If it were a chapbook, she'd know a *secret* about the Usurper. And she'd be promising to tell the consort-prince but dragging it out so that she could woo him at the same time. Then, depending on the kind of story, either they run off together, or he's loyal to the empress and Amadea's crushed."

"It's not a chapbook," Tunuk said, his glowing gaze pinning Quill.

"Yeah," Zoifia said. "If it were a chapbook, she wouldn't *be* Amadea. Amadea's too boring for a chapbook heroine. Or villain. She'd be...a changeling queen. Or the Grave-Spurned Princess in disguise."

"Amadea, the Grave-Spurned Princess?" Tunuk said in disgust. "Are you listening to yourself?"

And then Quill's worst fears came together: Stavio's eyes widened, a gasped "*No!*" escaping him as he clapped a hand over his mouth.

He knew.

Quill held up his hands in a quelling gesture. "Stavio, don't."

Stavio cursed a string of Ashtabari, the language flowing out of him like in a bubbling stream. "The changeling Redolfo was enough to fool her. She was the ward of a highborn house. *That* highborn house! Noniva and all the little fishes, how did I miss this?"

How did Quill stuff these secrets back inside their boxes? How did he undo what he'd done? *Not by saying "don't," you fool!* he thought.

"Miss what?" Quill said. "That she's...probably sleeping with the consort-prince?" Was he really going to cover this up by pretending Amadea and the consort-prince were having an affair? That might be better. Amadea might even prefer it.

But it didn't even slow Stavio down.

"She's the right age. I think," he went on. "Does Bijan know? I will kill him if he knows and didn't tell me."

"Nobody knows!" Yinii hissed. "Stop shouting!"

"Nobody knows *what*?" Zoifia said. "Somebody spill, or I'm going to throw something!"

Silence fell over the workroom. Stavio stared at Quill, as if waiting for confirmation, some secret signal that would say he'd guessed right. Quill found he couldn't say the words. What had he done?

Tunuk set both hands on the table, leaning over to eye Stavio.

The perfect opposite of Tunuk, hunched and huddled over the catalogues—Tunuk, a towering threat, a nightmare enough to scare the secret back into hiding.

"You honestly think," he said in a low, sneering voice, "that Amadea is the Grave-Spurned Princess?"

"Saints and devils!" Zoifia hissed. "That's what you meant?"

"Our Amadea," Tunuk continued, "the kindest, most patient person I know, who has never once given the slightest sense of conspiracy or politics or caring about what people think instead of what needs to be done. What we need done. Why would she, of all people, be a traitor to the empire? Why would she, of all people, hold on to a past that would probably pain her terribly if it were true? Why would you think of telling anyone that our Amadea is a traitor?"

Stavio raised his chin. "Who thinks that girl was a traitor? She was a tool."

"She was a person," Tunuk said, straightening up. "And so is Amadea. So don't gossip about her like that."

Stavio glanced over at Quill.

"Please," Quill said, "you can't tell anyone."

"Who the fuck said I was gonna tell anyone?" Stavio said. "I mean, Bijan—"

"Stavio."

"Look." He pointed a finger at Quill. "I'm not stupid. But you're not either. This isn't the same as discussing whether that vigilant's gonna volunteer to catch her trout or not. Noniva and all the little fishes! She's been Lireana Ulanitti all this time! And you *knew*!"

Tunuk loomed over Stavio. "She's been nobody but Amadea. Understand?"

Stavio stilled, considering Tunuk. "Yeah. She's one of us." He looked back at Quill. "So all that shit about Redolfo? About changelings and sorcerers and such?"

"It's true," Quill said grimly. "Also not for telling people. Nobody wants a panic."

"Shit," Zoifia said.

"All right," Stavio said, "but I have to tell Bijan. That's not up for discussion."

Quill looked up at Tunuk, grateful for the intervention. Tunuk folded his arms again, avoiding Quill's gaze, but he nodded in a way that said he saw it. That he understood and they were all right again.

"Fucking devils." Zoifia shook her head. "Does the empress know?"

"We're not gossiping!" Tunuk snarled. He turned back to Quill. "You found out before the rest of us. Were you at least kind about it?"

Quill hesitated. "I found out because I thought she was the Shrike first, so it was complicated. But honestly a relief, all things considered. I was much less upset about her being Lireana than being the assassin who killed Karimo."

"We have to tell her we know," Tunuk said. "It's not fair. Is she back?"

Yinii shook her head. "I haven't checked."

Quill blew out a breath. "Well, we have to tell her all the other things. Stellano and Toya's notes and..." He didn't name Qalba again, but Tunuk looked down at the floor. "I'll go find her."

But when he left the Bone Vault, walking down the long mezzanine toward Amadea's office, Tunuk caught up to him. "Your friend," he said, low and gruff. "Redolfo Kirazzi did that, didn't he?"

"Yeah," Quill said.

Tunuk was silent a moment. "It's not your fault. If you were thinking that. If that's why..." He huffed a breath through his nose. "You're not to blame, and so you don't need to absolve yourself. If that's why you're helping me."

Quill stopped and looked up at Tunuk. "I was helping you because I wanted to be friends. I couldn't save Karimo. But if I could have, I would have done *anything*. And you're my friend too, whether you like it or not. And you were in danger, so...of course I'm going to do everything I can."

Tunuk nodded. "I do. Like being friends. *Friends*," he repeated. "I don't...Whatever my mothers have said to you, I'm not looking for—"

"Tunuk. I know. We're friends."

Tunuk folded his arms tightly. "Good. Don't," he added, "say anything sappy. You'll ruin it."

"'Ruin it'?" Quill chuckled. "That feels a *little* sappy."

Tunuk sighed. "Qalba wasn't..." He tried again. "People make mistakes. She and Chizid were the best things in my life at that time. And I hate them for leaving. I *hate* that they're gone and they never told me *why*. I'm so *angry* they were hiding things, that they didn't trust me. But...even then, I can't believe she'd leave a note threatening to kill me. I don't even want to believe she's come back and not said anything."

Quill said nothing; he knew better than to push Tunuk too hard.

Yinii sprinted up, clutching her cloak closed. She eyed both Tunuk and Quill as she stopped. "Are you...? I need to talk to Amadea too. I...I have to tell her something."

"Well, then we're all going," Tunuk said. "I have some things to say to her myself."

CHAPTER EIGHTEEN

Amadea's ears rang, the world refusing to resolve. A weight on her, the sharp smell of blood, and the metallic tang of gunpowder and naphtha. Her head pounded, her eyes aching...

The smell of gunpowder from the bombards. Sun glinting off glass soldiers. The urge to run, but where to run? Everything is a battlefield, with only Bylina in the distance, and her ears are ringing with the explosions of the bombards, and if she so much as moves, Redolfo will—

The weight on her shifted, Ibramo raising his head, blood streaming from his scalp, down his ear, his jaw. The air beyond, a smear of smoke and stone dust. His mouth moved, but the words were lost in the ringing in her ears. One hand, shaking, cupped her cheek.

Something exploded, she managed to think. *A cannon, a bombard—*

The shell crashing down, the explosion, screaming and screaming, and Fastreda's stricken face.

Her breath rasped back and forth over her raw throat—too fast, too fast. She had to get up. Redolfo would be furious if she wasn't there, visible, standing—the symbol of the rebellion. She tried to shift, but Ibramo was pinning her down, his arms wrapped around her, and when she pushed against him, pain went racing up her arm. She fell back, pressing her wrist to her chest.

The screaming and screaming, and the glass shatters, refuses, slices up through the mud, screaming and screaming—

The screams echoed around the castle hall. *Why is the battle indoors?* she wondered numbly, even as she remembered, here, now. She tried to turn her head, to take in the room, but the dust and smoke were so thick.

Ibramo rolled off her, panting in pain. Amadea sat up, staring into the smoke, scooting herself across the once-glossy floor to shield Ibramo against whatever was surrounding them.

You're not then, she thought. *Those battles are long gone.*

No part of her body believed it. Her spine pulled itself stylus straight, as if she were still encased in armor, still drilled daily on being Lireana. Redolfo was out there, was too near.

I built you. I made you into this. I could destroy you as easily.

No you won't, she thought. She had to protect Ibramo. She had to run. She had to—

A wimpled hospitaller from the House of Unified Wisdom melted out of the smoky air, a golden-skinned woman with tapered eyes. She looked from Ibramo to Amadea and dropped down next to the consort-prince, a satchel open at her side.

Amadea tried to crawl toward her, tried to explain about the bombards, but someone else took her by the shoulders. She swung an arm at her attacker—and a second hospitaller dodged her hand, held her firm. She tried to pull free—she couldn't be taken, she was being taken—and she made herself hold still. *This isn't happening.*

"Where are you hurt?" the man said, his hands touching her wrist, her forehead. His voice pierced the ringing, echoing like the bombards.

"I'm fine," she said.

"Pain in your chest? Abdomen?" She shook her head, and it felt as if her brain were bouncing in the vault of her skull. "Can you walk?"

"I'm fine," Amadea said, and her voice rang along with the echo of the bombards. "There are people—"

"Esinora, we have it. Can you walk?"

"Ibramo," she began.

"We'll take care of His Highness," the man said. He led her a few steps toward the exit, watching her feet. "There are hospitallers out there who will see to your injuries. Leave along the side here, the floor's damaged in the middle. Go straight, you'll be safe out there."

And then he turned back, melting into the smoky air once more.

Amadea set her hands against the painted wall and edged out of the once-grand hall, out of the battlefield—where did they retreat to? Someone always took her when it got to this point; she wasn't told, wasn't allowed to decide—

It's not a battle, she told herself. And she understood, but her body wouldn't listen, and she was shaking now, her limbs trembling so hard she thought she might fall if she didn't bend all her thoughts into putting one foot in front of the other.

Outside, the air was clearer, the energy chaotic. Hospitallers in green uniforms saw to bloodied courtiers and broken bones. Piled dead bodies. Amadea felt dizzy, her throat raked.

You're breathing too fast again, she thought, but it didn't make it stop. She had to run.

"Over there," one of the hospitallers said, pointing to Amadea's left. She turned and started walking, straight across the field, picking up speed. When the lines broke, if you were slow, you were dead...

You need to get somewhere safe, she thought, and this all parts of her agreed with. She kept walking. The sun dipped lower, and the shadows lengthened, and her mind fought with her memories as they whispered that every corner might have been an ambush, every square a new field of battle, every shadow a place for Redolfo to step out of—but then she saw the fountain with the dolphins... and she knew where her feet were leading her. Safety. The archives.

A little farther, she told herself. *A little longer. You're doing so well, and you're going to survive this.*

She missed the moment she climbed the stairs, the moment she pushed into the entry hall. People spoke around her—guards, the reception archivist—but she brushed them aside. "I have to get to my office," she said.

"Amadea? What happened?" Quill's voice didn't ring like the hospitallers' had; the noise in her ears had faded to a buzz as she'd walked. She was standing at the base of the stairs up to the second level, and he was holding her by the arm, staring at her, furious. She drew back from that angry gaze—

No, she thought. *Worried.*

"I have to go to my office." If she could just get inside, all of her felt sure, she would be safe and she could think. Her head was on fire.

"You're hurt," Quill said. "We need to get to the House of Unified Wisdom. Tunuk, can you carry her?"

Amadea noticed Tunuk looming over Quill, Yinii tucked close to them. "No," she said. "My office. You should be in my office." *You're sounding insane*, she thought. But this was her work and her duty—keep them safe, keep them protected—and she could not shake the sureness that Redolfo was coming, that the Ulanittis were coming. "Please," she said.

"Uh, all right," Quill said. "We need to talk anyway. What happened?"

"Bombards," she said. Then she winced. "Not bombards, they'd never fire bombards in the Imperial Complex."

"Another explosion?" Tunuk said.

Another—Amadea's thoughts hurt as they moved through her head. Another explosion, because the first one...had been in Richa's apartment, and *that* hadn't broken her. She felt so suddenly irritated at the fact her whole body was afraid, that her hands couldn't grasp the keys, that she kept trying to remember where Redolfo was so she could evade his anger.

"Yes," she said. "Someone...It must have been someone... who..."

Quill took the keys off her belt and unlocked her office door, helping her inside and over to the sofa. "Here, sit." He looked back at the other two. "I think she's in shock or something. What do we do?"

Yinii's hands wove together. "Coffee? Cold compress?"

"Fuck that," Tunuk said. "She keeps a bottle of kaibo in the bottom drawer of her desk."

Amadea's hand still trembled when she clutched the glass of kaibo—her wrist still screamed, her head still pounded, and the ringing in her ears still sang around every sound. But the feeling that had seized her body—the sureness she was Lireana again, standing on a battlefield—had faded finally, leaving just that shaky weakness, the thoughts meant for another time and place. She sipped the wild-rice whiskey, felt it burn along her raw throat. "Thank you," she said.

"What happened?" Quill asked again.

She told him about the empress, about Dushar ul-Shandiian. About the sudden sound and light and waking in the smoke with Ibramo pinning her and dripping blood.

Tears flooded her eyes. "I don't know if he's all right."

"But he was alive when you left?" Yinii asked.

Amadea shut her eyes, remembering Ibramo panting in pain. She took another gulp of the kaibo. "I think so."

"The empress?" Quill asked. "Lady Sigrittrice."

"I don't know," Amadea said. "Dushar ul-Shandiian is probably dead, though. He was right in the middle of the field." Her memories overlapped, setting Dushar and his entourage amid Redolfo's glass forces, sweeping confidently toward her.

Quill frowned. "What field?"

Amadea cursed inwardly. "Hall."

"I can't believe they just let you leave," Tunuk said. "You're clearly still hurt."

Amadea looked down at her legs. Her skirt was ripped in a long line across the middle, gaping open like a mouth to show the red tongue of one raw-scraped leg, and her mind suddenly realized that was where the pain was coming from. She took another sip of the kaibo.

Quill pulled the chair that sat before her desk over so he was facing her. "I have to tell you . . . several things that you're not going to want to hear. But they're important. We found where Vigdza—the fabricator—was working. We just came back from there."

Amadea exhaled. "Thank the gods and the saints she wasn't there."

"No, she *was*," Quill said. "Her *and* Stellano Zezurin. And they're not working alone." Quill told her everything they'd found in the underground room—the supplies for more explosives, the hints of who Stellano and Vigdza were working with, and the order to kill her.

"It . . . *might* be Qalba," Quill said.

"Have you told Richa?" Amadea asked, remembering the look of frozen terror that had crossed Richa's face at the mention of Stellano Zezurin's name. If he was here, in Arlabecca...

"We've only just gotten back," Quill said. "And if you were in another explosion—"

"Did you see a Borsyan woman there?" Tunuk demanded. "Was she holding anything?"

Amadea tried to remember, but her thoughts clung once more to the battlefield, the bombards, Fastreda screaming, Fastreda laughing, sharp and specific in her memories, as if it had happened there before the painted walls. The glass raining down, her ears ringing, the Borsyan sorcerer's wild, mad joy slicing through the sound.

"Just Fastreda," she murmured. "It took her leg off. Shattered it to pieces."

"Fastreda was there?" Quill said, alarmed. "She was out of her cell?"

Yinii grabbed his shoulder. "No. She...she lost her leg in the assault on Bylina. Near the end of the coup."

Amadea froze—her head pounding, her thoughts spinning, but the danger was all too clear. Amadea Gintanas had no reason to remember that detail. Amadea Gintanas shouldn't have ever been on a battlefield. "I meant..." she started. What might she have meant? A reza? Lady Sigrittrice? She shut her eyes. "I was mistaken. I thought..."

Quill had gone rigid, and Yinii beside him. Tunuk, bouncing on his heels, looking like he was ready for a fight. Panic crept cold-footed up Amadea's chest.

"I have to tell you some things you don't want to hear," Quill said again.

This was not happening.

Amadea stood. "About Qalba," she said as if finishing his thought. She was Amadea Gintanas; she solved problems. She could manage this. "If she was among Dushar's entourage, she would have been killed. And I didn't see the fabricator, so one assumes this was...an assassination...a...We should get Richa. He should know...and..." She turned to Tunuk. "Tunuk, you are very close to being in alignment, you shouldn't have gone down there...You...Have you—"

Tunuk stepped forward, enfolding her in his long arms and holding her close. "It's not fair," he said gruffly. "That you couldn't tell us. But I wouldn't have either. *Especially* Stavio."

Amadea felt as if she couldn't stay within her own bones. The ringing in her ears increased. "Stavio knows?" she breathed.

"He guessed," Quill said apologetically. "We . . . A lot of things came out. Stavio and Tunuk and Zoifia—they know about Redolfo Kirazzi. And . . . you."

"But they're not going to say anything," Yinii said quickly. "They wouldn't!"

"Stavio *will* tell Bijan," Tunuk said, still holding her, keeping her standing. "But nobody else. You . . . you get to decide what you keep secret."

No, I don't, Amadea thought. Bishamar Twelve-Spider knew and her archivists knew, and it was all spilling out so quickly; she had no hold on her past anymore, and which parts of it were even hers? "I have to sit," she said numbly, feeling as if she would faint.

Tunuk steered her back to the sofa and put the kaibo in her hand. He drew a deep breath. "I'm sorry. I said some things, back in the Kinship Hall . . . I was angry and I was scared, and ever since Stavio guessed who you were, I keep thinking . . ." His voice broke and started again, softer, pleading. "I wasn't saying that about you. I couldn't. You're not a monster, I'm a monster. I'm sorry. Please don't leave."

"You're *not*—" Amadea started to say, but her own voice broke on a sob that wrenched itself from her chest, no more her decision than whatever incautious word had revealed her darkest secret. She could not speak; she could not think of what to say—everything was a nameless, wordless flood of grief and panic.

The stretch of her life where she had not been steered and blown by the decisions and whims of greater forces was really so short. A childhood under the strict rules of the Golden Oblates or the stricter rules of the Ulanitti ruling family—either way cut short by Redolfo Kirazzi and the fathomless plan she was always braced against the next step of. The captivity in Sestina, the fear of the emperor. The early days in the archives swinging between hiding any hint of her

past and flinging herself frenzied at a future that might erase it. How
had she thought those leashes wouldn't wrap themselves around her
again?

They never left, she realized as she sobbed. She'd only chosen how
to put them on herself—chosen what Amadea Gintanas meant and
how she would move safely through this new world. She didn't let
herself remember, she didn't let herself dwell, and she most certainly
didn't let herself *grieve*. She could not be lonely, and she was horribly
lonely. She could not be afraid, and she was more terrified than ever.
She could not falter, not for her charges, and here she was, torn and
bleeding and sobbing snottily into Tunuk's shoulder.

But...he held on to her, like *he* might be sinking. He didn't turn
from her; he didn't think she'd failed him. He was so afraid that *he*
had failed her.

You are not alone, she thought. She had tried to make herself a
guardrail for them, and maybe she still was, but she was more than
that. They cared, maybe as much as she cared for them—and as the
well of panic and sorrow drained away, as Amadea's breath slowed,
she pulled back so she could meet his glowing gaze.

"You listen to me," she said, her voice hiccupping around errant
sobs. "You're not a monster. *None* of you are monsters." Beside her
desk, Yinii was weeping, her arms wrapped around herself. "You've
been dealt a difficult hand, all of you in different ways, and you
are, all things considered, doing very well." Quill, his eyes shining,
looking at Yinii, at the desk, at the kaibo. "Especially when someone is trying to destroy the empire and you are putting yourselves
into danger to stop it."

She was not alone, and *they* were not alone—and Amadea Gintanas might be lonely and afraid and breakable as glass, but as long as
she drew breath, she was a solver of problems.

Tunuk dropped his gaze. "The fabricator wasn't at the palace.
That means...Qalba got the bomb there. We have to find her."

"And we have to figure out what her next target will be," Quill
said.

Amadea fumbled one-handed for the handkerchief in her pocket
and wiped her nose and eyes, her injured wrist still held to her chest.

She picked up the kaibo from the side table where Tunuk had deposited it. "Tell me why you think it's Qalba."

Someone hammered at the door, one of the little runners' voices calling out, the words lost in the ringing of her ears. Quill darted to answer it and returned with Richa.

"Fucking demons," Richa swore, hurrying over to her. "What happened?"

"Someone set off another explosion in the Imperial Complex," Quill said. "They might have assassinated the empress."

"Give me that," he said, gently taking the kaibo glass from Amadea's hand and passing it back to Quill. "This is *not* what she needs right now. Do you have medical supplies?"

"Uh…" Quill looked at Amadea, at a loss.

"Second floor, next to the gold rooms," Amadea said.

"Lie down," Richa said. To Quill he rattled off a list of things to fetch. "All of you go," he said. "You're going to need the hands."

Amadea lay down on the sofa, her head pillowed on a stack of quilts, as her charges raced off.

Richa knelt down next to her, brushing the hair off her face. "Got a deep cut there," he said. "Can you look at me? What happened?"

She looked up into his worried face. Those nice eyes. "I was at the Imperial Complex. Another bomb went off. I don't know…I didn't see if the empress was all right. Or Lady Sigrittrice."

"Well, you're talking fine. Look at the Borsyan lamp?"

She looked up at the lamps, her eyes aching.

"The empress isn't all right," she said. She could do this—one admission at a time. "She wants the Red Mask," she said. "I can't give her the Red Mask."

Richa paused, the significance of that fact clear. The Red Mask meant war. Meant an official and unavoidable declaration that Redolfo Kirazzi, or something like him, was an immediate threat. Meant there was no chance at all to resolve this without bloodshed.

"But if she wants it," he finished slowly, "she'll take it, eventually."

"Exactly," Amadea whispered.

"And you don't know if she was hurt? What about the consort-prince?"

"Yes. Alive, but—" Her voice hitched again, her thoughts on Ibramo lying on his back, panting in pain. "He shielded me. So he's worse than this." She swallowed. "The hospitallers were caring for him."

"It will be all right," Richa told her. He grabbed the bottle of kaibo off her desk and took a clean cloth from the pouch at his belt. He dabbed the whiskey against the cut on her forehead, cleaning the blood. "They should have done this on the scene," he said as he finished. "Can I see your wrist?" He took her hand, lifting it away from her chest, his other hand cupping her elbow so she didn't have to hold her arm up. He rubbed a thumb over the basin of her palm, the thin skin of her wrist.

"Do you feel that?" he said.

She hesitated, staring at his hand, and it was so like that moment in the rain—the edge of something she wanted badly to test. "Yes."

He cleared his throat, as if he'd noticed it too, and quickly touched her fingers to the same result. There was a dark line up the inside of her wrist, and Amadea kept her eyes on it, as he turned her hand slowly, until the pain flared, and she gasped in a breath.

"That is sprained," he said, tucking the arm back against her. He looked askance at her skirts. "I . . . You should clean those cuts. You lost a lot of skin. I can, if you . . . if you're comfortable . . ."

Amadea blushed. "Can we talk while you do it?"

He laughed once. "It's going to sting. A lot. Do you have a pitcher?"

She pointed him back into her bedroom, and he returned with the pitcher and basin from her dresser and the cat, Imp, who leapt onto the desk to watch.

It did sting—worse than the broken floor she'd shredded her skin on. She felt pieces of stone dislodged by the wet cloth, fresh pain with them.

"I would like more kaibo with this," she said through her teeth.

"You have a head injury, so you probably shouldn't have had any." But when he dipped the cloth again, he was gentler. "So, our explosives maker has targeted me and the empress. And Dushar ul-Shandiian got a similar warning note to mine—he might be next. I couldn't pin him down, though."

"Oh. Dushar. He...I think he was right in the middle of the explosion. Maybe he was the target, not the empress."

Richa stopped, a hand on her knee, and looked back at her. "Dushar?"

Amadea explained once more about Dushar's arrival and the place where the floor had been shattered in the entry hall. "If he didn't have the bomb on him, he was very close to the person who did."

Richa sat back, thinking a moment. "I'm not going to lie, aside from the note, I liked him for this. But he's not the sort to sacrifice himself, I wouldn't say."

"No," Amadea agreed. "So if he's the target instead of the empress...that doesn't feel like it's Redolfo Kirazzi."

He worked methodically around her shredded knee. "Did you know Yinii went back to the Kinship Hall and went over those inked-up sheets?"

Amadea cursed. "No. Was she all right?"

"She's fine. I'm less fine. It turns out that there were diagrams underneath, and one looked very much like the explosive we found. He was looking at how to power cold-magic devices with sorcerer-wrought materials. Only now," he went on, "the vigilant from the road cohort thinks it looks like I was trying to keep Yinii away from that information. Like I knew it was there."

"I am quite certain no one knew you could power cold-magic devices with sorcerer-wrought materials," Amadea said, bewildered. "How does that work?"

But in her memories, there was Redolfo. *Duke Borcia won't play. So your task is greater than ever. And this is all you have?*

Lira, don't touch it.

"Your archivists mentioned the artifacts have their own sort of magic," Richa said. "I'm going to assume some unsworn fabricators managed to harness it in its own way."

"Why would you set one off in your own apartment, though?"

Richa shook his head. "Some sort of cover, the way I assumed Dushar might have done with the note? It *doesn't* make sense. But that's something else: the house Bucella brought the wooden bones to, the one that was definitely not Nanqii ul-Hanizan's? Apparently *I* own it."

Amadea frowned. "You own a row house?"

"I most certainly do not," Richa said, soaking more water into a cloth. "But I'm listed as the owner. Someone is trying to set me up."

Amadea took a deep breath. "Tunuk and Quill went off on their own as well. They went down to where they lost that fabricator who had the wooden bones. They found her workshop. And then she turned up *with* the patron they mentioned."

Richa studied her a long moment, and the fear blooming behind his eyes was so hard to watch. "Did they get a name?"

"Stellano Zezurin," Amadea said.

Richa turned from her. "Fucking *demons*," he cursed under his breath. He picked up the kaibo bottle and took a swig from it. "They saw him? They heard that name?"

"Yes. I don't know," she said, "what he's done. Why you... Richa, this isn't some thief you couldn't catch, I can tell. And you don't have to tell me what it is, but... I wanted to make sure you knew. Before they come back."

Richa raked a hand through his hair, turning again, pacing the room to the farther shelves. For a moment, she thought he might leave; there was so much coiled energy in the way he moved, as if he had to run or break apart. But then he stopped, cursed again, and sat on the chair once more. "I'm going to wipe it down with the kaibo," he said. "Keep the rot out."

He poured more whiskey on a new cloth, and Amadea reached over and grabbed his arm with her uninjured hand.

"You don't have to tell me," she said again. "But if you want to... I want to listen."

He considered her hand on his arm, then looked up into her face, wary and worried. He turned from her, toward the task. Amadea sat back on the pillows, resigned to the silence.

And then Richa spoke.

"He's my ex," he said. "And he's a criminal connected to the Borsyan separatists. The vigilant from the road cohort thinks I'm a good suspect for the murder, and part of the reason is she knows I used to run with Stellano Zezurin."

Amadea blinked at him. "Your ex-boyfriend is a Borsyan

separatist? And you used to be a thief? And so you're a suspect in the murder you witnessed?"

Richa blew out a breath. "Yeah, this is a lot all at once, isn't it?"

"How'd you meet him?"

That earned her a look of surprise, and again he did not speak for a moment, long enough she thought he might not, before saying, "Caesura...there aren't a lot of orders established there. It's kind of where you end up if you don't want the protectorates' eyes on you. My parents—my people, going back over the Salt Wall—they weren't who you find in history books. Datong is all massive earthworks and monasteries and canals. Princes on great lizard mounts and reed-sorcerers. You don't read about rice farmers scraping by on rented land or the boat-people rowing up and down those canals, getting out of the city the same night they went in. And you definitely would not read up on my ancestors because I'm pretty sure all of them were criminals, all the way back to before Yakshooka stole crowns for the five founding princes. Except...what else do you do when there's no way to get a leg up? That's not just Datong either, that's everywhere."

He swept more of the alcohol over her ankle, her calf, the sting bracing as all her nerves ignited together and then burnt out.

"So anyway," he said, "a hundred years later, that's all I know. Steal stuff, then sell it or keep it if I need it. When you're working that way, it helps to have friends doing the same. Watch each other's backs. Share your spoils. Anyway, that's how I met Stellano."

"It sounds familiar," she said, and his eyes darted up toward her. "You were vulnerable and so was he. You needed someone to hold on to."

Eyes back on her wounded leg. He took the wet cloth again, cleaning a spot on her knee, another fragment of stone coming loose. "Like you and the consort-prince."

"Maybe some," she said.

He put the cloth in the basin and turned to her, meeting her gaze. "It's not the same. I didn't really care about stealing. And I still have to admit, I don't care too much about people with too much losing a little. But Stellano...Stellano was very comfortable with hurting people. It crept up on me. I didn't realize at first. We had rules and he followed them. He didn't hurt kids, and he didn't start trouble with people we relied on. With family."

Richa fell silent again. Picked up the bottle of kaibo, then went to work on the cleaned part of her knee, still so careful.

"He hurt someone he'd promised not to," she guessed.

"We had a dog," Richa said. "Well, *I* had a dog. Egillio. Big red-haired mutt, all shaggy and sweet. Stellano loved that dog, but...I had a rule. Don't take the dog on jobs. He was big enough and loud enough to scare off other thieves, but he wasn't a fighter, and I didn't want to make him a fighter. But Stellano...he wanted a guard dog. Something imposing. And one day, when I was out meeting a fence, a buyer, Stellano took Egillio with him to go intimidate another thief, a woman he'd worked with in the past but who was pulling in her own gang. Stellano did not like that, and he wasn't going to let it happen.

"But he didn't realize how far ahead she was. She had connections to the Datongu ducal authority, and they weren't looking when Stellano showed up, acting like the fucking Black Mother Forest crowned him king of the thieves. It was an ambush, and he was lucky he didn't die, but...Egillio..." He swallowed. "I had that rule for a reason."

"I'm so sorry," Amadea said.

"It wasn't intentional," he said. "I feel sure about that. But Stellano went to war. He wiped her and her whole little budding organization out. Fucking massacre. And then...then he had the gall to come to me and claim he'd gotten vengeance for me. For my dog. I was so furious. He's the one who got him killed. And I know he was sorry, I know he was heartbroken, but his answer was to kill eleven people and make the whole city panic, drive everyone to ground. I threw it back at him—this was his fault, and it was always going to be his fault, because he did not *care* what I wanted, rules were not for Stellano Zezurin.

"He *exploded*. Called me worthless, called me a coward, said I was holding him back and he'd be better off if I had died instead of Egillio. Which...as he was holding a knife when he said it, led to me getting the fuck out of there."

"Saints and devils," Amadea said. "That must have been terrifying."

Richa nodded in a tight, anxious way. "He was very sorry the next morning, all excuses and apologies, but that was it. I wasn't going to be safe with him, and I wasn't going to ever be happy in Caesura. I packed up, snuck out in the night, got to Arlabecca, and almost immediately got caught stealing by a vigilant."

"Bad luck."

He took another drink of the kaibo before soaking the cloth again. "Mm, actually, it was very good luck. That vigilant, she paid the baker, and she took me back to the Kinship Hall and told me I was going to earn the money back by mopping the floor. And when I was done, she asked if I wanted to earn some more and put me to work hauling papers and pumping water and making coffee. Then errands. And pretty soon...she just asked if I wanted to take the oaths, since I was already doing a cadet's work. And I don't know, on the one hand, it wasn't that different? Here's someone who has it figured out, who's offering to set me on a path. Only...I realized this path, I believed in. I watched the vigilants in this city make things better. Not perfect, not righteous. Just better. And I thought I could do that. I could make up for some of Caesura."

His voice became animated, passionate—she hadn't seen Richa quite like this. *Honest*, she thought, but then hadn't he always been like that? It lit a light, lifting, almost envious relief in her chest. *You could just lay a burden down. You could just change.*

I made you, Redolfo's voice murmured through her memories, *I can destroy you just as easily.*

"It gets a little worse," Richa went on, and some of that fire damped. "The vigilant from the road cohort thinks I'm working for him still, because...I might have picked a few doors open in the course of chasing murderers. Which I should not do," he admitted. "And Stellano is apparently here and possibly putting my name on houses so I look very, very guilty, while having no idea what's going on."

"If he's here," Amadea said, "then we can stop him. We can make him answer for all this. You're not alone."

Richa chuckled once. "He definitely hasn't tangled with the archives, though I think he's outside your usual skill set."

"A thing that keeps changing," she said dryly. "Although I'd rather my archivists stopped charging after dangerous criminals."

He dared another look up at her. "I haven't told anyone that story. Not the whole thing. The Kinship knows I was caught stealing in Arlabecca, and when I took the oaths, I admitted to other thefts, but not... This is new. I hope," he added, "it's not that difficult a thing. To find out someone you trusted was a criminal."

Amadea faltered—this was the moment she should explain. Her archivists knew. Nanqii ul-Hanizan knew—and if he was going to make trouble for her, she would *want* Richa on her side. The words caught in her mouth, though. She didn't know if this was the same kind of forgivable.

"I didn't mean you when I said that," she started.

The door opened again to Quill backing into the room, his arms stacked with bandages and bottles, a sponge in one fist. "All right, I didn't know what a suturing kit looked like, so Tunuk grabbed everything."

"There should be labels," Tunuk said, coming in with a stack of wooden boxes. "Some of these are the same thing, I think."

"I do need help with something else," Richa said. "Amadea says you saw Stellano Zezurin with the unsworn fabricator. Do you think he's still down there? In the Hawk's Nest."

"No," Quill said, darting a glance at Amadea. "He said to meet him at the house by the College of the Five Forests when she... Well, he was implying he wanted Qalba killed."

Richa frowned. "All right, you're going to have to explain some things, and I need witness statements, but first, that fits with why I came here: I need the cadastres. The taxation maps."

Amadea started to sit up, but Richa turned, holding up a hand. "You're not doing it."

"I have it," Quill said.

"Have you got the sedative?" Richa asked. Quill set his load on the desk, and Richa fished out a dark glass bottle the length of Amadea's palm. He held it out to her. "You are going to be a lot happier if you sleep for a bit. Especially while I sew you up," he told her. He cleared his throat. "When you're ready."

Amadea took the bottle, testing the weight in her hand. There were so many things she needed to say, but everything was moving so quickly.

Quill gave her a knowing look. "We'll handle things. You should take a rest."

Amadea handed the bottle back. She could take a rest. She could trust them for a few hours. Maybe she even needed to. "Could you open this? My wrist."

CHAPTER NINETEEN

The cadastres of Arlabecca filled pages and pages of the huge bound books the archivists hauled out of the shelves and stacked on the table for Richa to peruse. Each spread of paper was marked on one side with a meticulous map of a city section, on the other with lists of names that matched the symbols on the shapes that lined the winding edges of roads.

Quill and Tunuk and Yinii and Zoifia and Stavio all crowded into the records room, an audience Richa didn't want and did not know how to disperse. But at least it made finding the house by the West River simpler.

Quill slid the book toward him, the map open. "Here."

Narrow rectangles in a row followed the slow bend of the river. Richa tracked a finger down the row to the last of these, the one Bucella had described going to. He marked the number, then went down the list of names and valuations.

Richa Langyun.

He read it and read it again. It was still his name.

"Five broken kings," he cursed. This was a lot worse than he'd expected.

"What's wrong?" Yinii asked. "Can we help?"

If his name was on these records, then it wasn't just that the Kinship's records had been changed—this wasn't like the skeleton catalogues, meant to fool a few specialized observers. Someone had purchased this house in his name, paid taxes in his name. Someone had set this up a long time ago.

And Richa could not lie to himself—he knew who that had to be.

"There are two things I need," he said slowly. He pressed a finger to the row house on the map, as if holding it in place. "First, I need to know when this house changed owners. How many years has it been listed as mine?" He hesitated, not wanting to explain, not wanting to admit to what he thought was going on. He said to Quill, "You told me Stellano Zezurin said he'd be at the house near the College of the Five Forests. Can you get the cadastres covering that area?"

"Yes," Quill said, reaching for the stack of Arlabeccan maps. "What are we looking for?"

"We're looking for another of my houses," Richa said grimly.

The archivists divided the tasks with an efficiency that was a credit to their oaths. Yinii and Zoifia went through the cadastres hunting for the area near the College of the Five Forests, while Stavio and Tunuk fetched the older books, the history of Arlabecca by way of its tax revenues.

Quill watched him. "Do you think it's possible he's trying to lure you in?"

"Why would he bother?" Richa said. "It's been fifteen years, and we didn't part on good terms. Plus, he tried to blow me up."

Quill shook his head. "He didn't do that. They made it sound like Qalba was acting without permission. In fact, I have to give Tunuk that much: Stellano thought *he* might be the one she was targeting. Not you."

"In my apartment?" Richa said, but then he stopped. The dog icon, lying on its side. The knife on the table. The feeling that someone had been in his space—not an accident, not a mistake. He swore. "In my apartment! He was in my apartment!"

"Stellano?" Quill said. "I thought you hadn't seen him?"

Richa rubbed his arms, still feeling the intrusion on his skin. That apartment had been *his* space, *his* safety. "I haven't. Somebody broke in. Somebody who can pick a very expensive lock." Somebody who thought it would catch his attention to tip over the red-furred dog icon that looked like Egillio. "I'm going to kill him," Richa said.

"Not if Qalba gets to him first," Quill said. "So she saw him going into your apartment, assumed he was staying there, and planted the explosive with the expectation it would kill *him*. You were incidental."

"So does she know Stellano's not dead?" Richa said. "This might be our only chance to pin him down."

Tunuk and Stavio returned with stacks of the previous cadastres. Richa turned through them, watching the maps shift in minute ways—an alley closed here, a building torn down there. Five years ago, he'd owned this house. Ten years ago, he'd owned this house.

Fifteen years ago, he had not.

"That lines up with the first theft," Richa said. "And the murder." It lined up with Oshanna ul-Shandiian claiming Stellano had been here, in Arlabecca. That feeling of intrusion, of the space around him warping into something *almost* real, but not quite, crawled over him.

"I still don't remember him," Tunuk said stubbornly.

"Why's he got it out for you?" Stavio asked.

"Here," Quill said, foisting a stack of cadastres into Stavio's arms. "Can you put those back?"

Richa gave him a grateful nod and turned back to the two young women making their way through the neighborhood around the College of the Five Forests.

"I don't see you listed in any of these," Yinii said.

"What about 'Stellano Zezurin'?" Richa said.

Yinii winced. "We looked for that. No."

"He definitely said the house by the college," Zoifia put in. "Maybe you should just start knocking on doors."

"Maybe it's farther out," Yinii said.

"Maybe it's not in either of our names," Richa said. Which left the whole world of possible names available. He raked a hand through his hair.

"Maybe Lord Tafad?" Quill asked. "Or someone you knew in Caesura?"

"Oh." Zoifia flipped back a page, ran her finger down the list. "Do you know someone called Egillio?"

Richa startled. "Egillio?"

"'Egillio Caesura,'" Zoifia read. "I thought it was kind of an odd name. Like an orphan name, but for a whole city—that's weird."

"Egillio Caesura," Richa repeated.

She pushed the book toward him, her finger tapping the name on the list. There it was. The back half of a house over a shop. Stellano's attempt at being clever.

"You shit," Richa said. "Stellano, you absolute *shit*."

"What is it?" Quill asked. "What's wrong?"

"That's where he is," Richa said. "In a house owned by my dead dog."

⊷ ⇥⊹⇤ ⊶

Yinii helped stack the cadastres up to reshelve, as Richa excused himself, address in hand, to race back to the Kinship Hall. He'd recruited Stavio and Zoifia to come give their statements about seeing Stellano—more evidence, he hoped, for the vigilants to move.

Tunuk had slipped out behind them, and Yinii sighed. It was probably better to leave him to himself. Maybe she was going to have to do a lot more of that.

She looked down at her hands, still bare, the cuffs of her sleeves stained from the ink she'd made in Fastreda's cell. She tugged the ink loose and let it coil around her index finger before she nudged it onto the table, the shape of her cuff reproduced on the scarred wood.

"Hey," Quill said, beside her. "You all right?"

There wasn't an answer Yinii felt she could give him. Were you all right if you felt as if you were only halfway into your proper skin? If a part of you felt relief at knowing yourself and a part felt terror about it?

"Yes and no," she decided. She wiped her hands on her skirts. "Should we go check on Amadea?"

"No, let her sleep." Quill pulled a bottle of ink out of his pocket. "Here. I took it from the storeroom."

Yinii frowned. "What's this for?"

"I read some of the protocols for sorcerers," he said. "You're not actually supposed to be kept from your affinity material. That's a difference between specialists and sorcerers: you have to be around it, or you *will* make it. From what I've read, it actually seems like it's impressive how much ink you *haven't* made in the last couple of months."

Yinii looked down at the bottle, the ink inside a distant whisper trapped in the glass. "Did you tell Amadea?"

He hesitated. "No. But I talked to her about what she's been doing. About telling you that you can't be a sorcerer. She's the one who suggested I read them."

Yinii rolled the bottle in her hands. "I was thinking about just not telling anyone."

Quill frowned. "Why?"

Yinii touched the amulet of Saint Asla and sighed. "I thought the hardest part of this was figuring out if I had crossed some boundary, if I had enough affinity to change the way I talked about it. But then there are all these *protocols* and rules, and the Imperial Authority can just decide I can't be in the archives anymore. Amadea cares about us, but she cares about rules—what happens when they don't fit together? What if I just want to be me?"

"Yinii, no one's going to take you away. Amadea agrees."

"That's very easy to promise. What happens when the rezas find out? What happens when they decide I should be in Maqama where they can keep an eye on me?"

"You ink them," Quill suggested.

"Don't, that's horrible."

"Sorry. I only meant...Look, I think you should tell people, but you're right, you don't need to tell everyone. And I think Amadea will agree."

"You think she'll agree not to inform the Imperial Authority I might be a sorcerer?" Her throat tightened. "I think...I think that might be why she was...She's been acting like this was so impossible. Like I couldn't be a sorcerer, how absurd that would be! But... maybe it was because she knew. She knew it was a whole different sort of difficult.

"Being atnashingyii is already hard," she said softly. "I can't even guess how to be a saint." She thought of the chapel, the cool, hollow space. The saints all watching. Yinii wondered if someday her bones would be among them, her fragile flesh run off them, seeping into the ground as ink. There would be little hiding from the rezas at that point.

Quill moved to stand beside her, putting his arms around her, and she eased into him. "I'm not going to pretend I know anything about that. And I'm not going to pretend it will be easy. But...I think you should tell Amadea. Maybe Radir if he's going to stay your generalist, because otherwise he's going to have no idea what to do. And I think you should tell Tunuk."

Yinii ducked her head, looking down into the hollow of their two bodies, and as much as she'd bristled at Amadea's insistence that no one could know her secrets, she felt at last that she understood: it wasn't so much the telling as the not knowing what came next.

"What if he hates me?" she whispered. "What if he's afraid?"

"He's not going to be afraid."

"You don't know that. People are. People made them sacrifices and outcasts and weapons, and now they just get locked up and moved around and—"

"And those people aren't Tunuk."

She thought of Amadea sitting on the couch, bleeding and so pale Yinii couldn't imagine how she was still standing, still alive. Clinging to her secret, her safety—her control. But hiding it, that wasn't really safety. You had to be alert all the time; you had to lie all the time in a hundred tiny ways. Yinii feared being locked away, being isolated, but if she hid this from everyone...that would be like locking herself away.

Yinii pulled away from him a little, holding up the bottle of ink. She worked the stopper loose with a thumbnail, breaking the wax. A ribbon of ink rose out of the bottle, curled around her thumb and over her palm. She shut her eyes, listening to the murmur of the ink, feeling it soothe her tattered nerves.

"You're right," she said, and let the ink slide back into the bottle. "Amadea and Tunuk. And...Amadea can tell Radir, maybe. Maybe Zoifia. But not Stavio."

"Not Stavio," Quill agreed, his arms still looped around her. "How long do you think Amadea is going to be asleep for?"

"Richa said a couple of hours."

"Do you want to go get a coffee?"

Yinii smiled, her cheeks aching. "Yeah. Yes. Yes, I'd like that."

He took her by the hand, and they wound their way back through the archives. Maybe things were scary and complicated, and maybe she didn't know what exactly came next. But right now, this was nice. This was what she wanted. And maybe Amadea was right: she didn't have to decide things for a lifetime.

"Where do you want to go?" Quill asked as they came through the big opal-decorated doors into the entry hall.

"There's a place down by the square with the dolphin fountain," Yinii began. Then she stopped.

An imperial soldier stood in the half-open exit, talking to Mireia. She nodded along, looking grim, and when he left, she gestured at the door guards to pull the entrance shut. She turned, glancing down at Yinii's hand in Quill's as she did.

"Sorry, my dears. You're going to have to change plans."

"What happened?" Quill asked.

"Another explosion," Mireia said. "The Borsyan noble consul is dead. The Imperial Authority has declared a curfew. So go have yourself a little coffee in one of your apartments. Nobody's allowed out while they sweep the city."

⁕—✦—⁕

The Chapel of the Skeleton Saints was curiously silent as Tunuk entered, as hollow and empty as an unadorned rib cage, as still and tense as an indrawn breath. The middle of the day, there were usually at least a half dozen Orozhandi making their prayers, but as Tunuk walked the long circuit of the chapel, he found no one but the saints, their many bones and many rhythms drumming on his pulse in a strange symphony.

At the end of the long hall of the chapel, Saint Hezetha of the Sandstone stood against the last pillar, a chisel and a grindstone in her hands, bright green gems in the orbits of her upturned skull. Her bones *hummed* as Tunuk looked up at her, the transformation into a relic bringing them a voice.

"It's her," he said, testing the words. "It's Qalba, and I can't change that."

Not that he hadn't tried. Not that he hadn't done everything he could to avoid it. Quill had been right. Qalba had been a villain, and maybe Chizid too.

But they were alive—or Qalba anyway. He found he didn't know how he felt about that, which might be the most ghoulish thought he'd ever had. But there it was.

He walked back down to the gap that had held the false Saint Hazaunu and stood before it, the wooden skeletons of Saints Doba and Tabith still posed beside the gray shroud that covered their missing companion's place. The wood said nothing to Tunuk. He glanced up at Saint Jeqel of the Salt holding the column on the left, the bones pulsing a long, slow beat. He took out the note he'd found in the cabin: *The wounded jackal limps along a winding path, but it knows the one it hunts for.*

"She might have lied to me about the Usurper," he said, testing the words again. "Amadea lied, so really anyone might have." He flinched at the words—it felt different, but it wasn't that different. Not nicer, but not that different, if Qalba hadn't told him that she had worked for the Usurper, that she was now tangled up with separatists.

That she had been entangled with them even back then—that had been what Stellano had meant, not being fooled by an ul-Shandiian again.

Tunuk paused, rolling the words in his head. That hadn't been quite what he said—

The doors to the street opened, footsteps echoing across the chapel's polished floors. Tunuk turned and found himself facing Oshanna Eleven-Sand Iris ul-Shandiian.

She looked as shocked to see him as Tunuk felt. Grief hung on her like a shroud, like the long, pleated white tunic she wore, the mourning ribbons in white and yellow wrapping her horns and binding up her reddish hair. Her face was no longer full and spotty, but hollow and tense as the empty chapel.

"Tunuk?" she said.

"Oshanna," he said. "Welcome to the chapel."

She blinked at him, her piercing eyes red rimmed and unreadable. She looked back behind her, as if someone might be following. As if she were gauging how fast she'd have to run to get away.

"Sorry about your reza," he added.

She started to speak, then seemed to think better of it. "Dushar was a complicated man. He made a lot of enemies. Hurt a lot of people. This was always a possibility. He should have known." She sounded angry at Dushar, angry at someone for taking him away—and Tunuk knew how that felt.

"My nest-father was killed a few months ago," he said. "We didn't get along. He...was complicated too."

"I'm sorry for your loss." She sniffed, as if she'd been crying. "I just came to—"

"Right, sorry," Tunuk said, stepping aside.

Oshanna went into the alcove and knelt before the saints and the gray shroud. She pressed her forehead to the ground, her shoulders shaking with suppressed sobs, and Tunuk did not know where to look.

After a moment, Oshanna lifted her head, pressed her folded hands against her forehead, murmuring under her breath. He sat down next to her, waiting until she paused.

"Were we friends?" Tunuk asked abruptly.

She turned her head and looked hard at him. "When did my father die, Tunuk?"

Tunuk considered telling her until two days ago, he had completely forgotten Nimar Eight-Myrrh even existed. In fact, he was still having a hard time placing him. "All right," he said. "Not friends. I didn't think we were, but Yinii...Yinii made it sound like I misunderstood. I do. A lot."

"We were the same age in the same place. I don't think poorly of you..." She let out a shuddering breath. "Your pardon, it's... it's today. Sixteen-Spider. That's when he died. And I wasn't even with him. I loved him so. Maybe I would have grown to see him as a complicated man, too, eventually, but he was really the only one who understood me, and he was taken far too soon."

This Tunuk remembered a little bit: Oshanna bragging about her father as they walked from the archives. *My father is brilliant. My father is strong. My father is going to be reza one day.* He'd thought it was childish, even as he could sort of remember retorting at one point, *I've got four fathers, and none of them sound as insufferable as yours.*

"Do you know who might have...?" He cleared his throat. "I heard a rumor that Qalba might not be dead."

She turned to him again, again hard-eyed as one of the saints standing over them. "I don't know where you would have heard such a thing."

"Do you think it's true?" he asked, pushing past her bluster.

"It would be foolish of her," she said. "But then she was always foolish. Easily led."

Tunuk frowned. "Qalba?"

"What would you rather I say? That she fell in with a bad crowd? That she listened to the wrong people?"

Redolfo Kirazzi, she wasn't saying. *Stellano Zezurin*. But the part that bothered Tunuk was less the "bad crowd" and more the idea that stubborn, steady Qalba was foolish and easily led. And really, he thought, that was the part of all this that had given him the most trouble: not that Qalba had done wicked things, but the stories people told to explain it. She wasn't someone looking for power or revenge or the approval of Redolfo Kirazzi. If she'd done terrible things, she'd done them because they were necessary.

"If she did anything like that," Tunuk said, "I think she was trying to protect us."

"Yes, well, she didn't do a very good job, now did she?" Oshanna pursed her mouth around her anger. "I would like to finish my prayers. Do you mind?"

Tunuk stood, backed away to the table displaying the fragmented bones of Saint Zobeii of the Gold, the rhythm of them erratic and slow as a dying heartbeat, almost lost in the chapel's silent syncopation. Standing here, with his affinity rising, Tunuk could hear the gap left by the skeleton that wasn't Saint Hazaunu and wasn't Qalba. He wondered sometimes if the bones noticed each other, if Saint Zobeii's bones perhaps recognized the absence of that skeleton of a dead man, thirty-four years, four months, and eight days old.

Tunuk frowned. Thirty-four years, four months, eight days...

It was Sixteen-Spider. He worked his way backward through the Orozhandi calendar, through twenty-day months that had nothing to do with the moon—Spider, Citron, Horse, Baboon, Scarab, Myrrh. Eight back from the sixteenth day...

Eight-Myrrh. As in Nimar Eight-Myrrh ul-Shandiian.

Tunuk's breath caught. The bones' thrumming surged along his nerves.

What had the fabricator said? *I don't think she's thinking clearly. I think she only has her mind on revenge.*

And Qalba didn't have vengeance on her mind—she wasn't the sort; she'd fled instead of fighting. Maybe she'd been a criminal, and maybe she'd helped a monster, but when it came down to it, she'd wanted freedom and she'd taken it.

Almost: *What do you want me to do? I can't just stop talking to him.*

Qalba had been afraid. That he remembered. Angry and afraid, and when Richa had pointed to the thefts, the only thing that made sense, if they were Qalba's crime, was that someone had forced her into that corner. If she had been responsible for the theft of Saint Hazaunu, then something very bad was happening and someone she couldn't escape easily was doing it.

But not a lover—never a lover.

Hey, shashkii, will you take Oshanna down to the pancake shop?

Every time, every time—because Nimar was there, because Qalba was making Tunuk leave, because the conversation wasn't one he ought to overhear, because she wanted to keep him away from Nimar. She wasn't close with her family, and yet here was this young cousin who came around, whom Tunuk was always sent off to entertain. So her father could talk to Qalba. The daughter who was so enamored of her father she'd never question why she and Tunuk couldn't be there.

Another time, another scheme—*It's absurd, really, how many times we must rediscover something, reengineer it. They were so close all those years ago*—another ul-Shandiian building weapons off Toya's broken notes, while Qalba tried to keep them all safe until she couldn't.

Tafad's not interested in another ul-Shandiian making a fool of him, Stellano had said. And Tunuk had assumed that meant Qalba, meant Qalba had slipped his grasp when she'd fled.

But if it had been Qalba before, then it couldn't be Qalba now and still be "another ul-Shandiian."

And it didn't have to be Qalba before if Nimar ul-Shandiian was the one who brought trouble to the bones.

Who would you become the monster for? He thought of how afraid he'd been to read the bones, how he knew down deep that if it were Qalba, if someone had killed her, all the darkness, all the ghoulishness in him would come pouring out and he would find that person and *hurt* them. He thought of how afraid he'd been when they'd gone. How adrift. How easy it would be to never leave that place.

An apprentice hurt enough to bend all that knowledge toward vengeance, an ul-Shandiian woman who knew what had happened twelve years ago, and a death that made a monster of her. A death she would punish with her father's gifts.

Oshanna Eleven-Sand Iris made the last of her bows and set a folded paper in the tray meant for offerings, alongside other prayers and coins and fragments of pottery. She stood and straightened the pleats of her tunic. She wiped her eyes with a handkerchief from her sleeve and turned to face Tunuk.

You have to stop her, he thought. *You have to catch her. You have to pin her down.* If he was right, she was dangerous, and he had no idea who else she meant to kill and who might die in the process.

The door to the chapel opened, a guard stepping in with one hand on his sword. "Esinora Oshanna? You need to leave. The Imperial Authority just declared a curfew." He held up a letter with a tasseled seal. "They gave us permission to bring you back to the manor."

Oshanna made a face. "How annoying. Thank you, Ilyas. I'll be right there."

Tunuk's gaze locked on the guard's hand on the sword, and his heart seized stiffly around the memory of another blade in his ribs, the footsteps of the fabricator advancing into the shadows. The guards were ul-Shandiian; he couldn't be sure they'd side with him. If he died, he'd die alone, and no one would know what she had done. What she still might be doing.

"Well," Oshanna said. "It was nice speaking with you, Tunuk. I have a lot of preparations to make. Travel to see to." She sighed. "I will be glad when this is all finished."

"What will you do now?" Tunuk asked.

Tears sparkled in her eyes, and she sniffed. "I will get through this and see what lies on the other side."

"Esinora?" the guard called. "We really should go."

Tunuk eyed the paper in the offering tray. He thought of the bones with the knife scars along the cervical vertebrae, the feeling of a sword parting his flesh. He didn't want to die, and he didn't want to die alone, and he did not need to.

"Goodbye, Oshanna," he made himself say. "A best evening and may the stars align beneficently."

"Thank you," she said, her teary eyes burning with an unsettling intensity. "I think they will."

When the doors to the street closed again and the guards turned the locks, Tunuk lunged for the offering tray, plucking out Oshanna's folded promise. He glanced back once more to be sure she'd left and then unlocked the door to the Bone Vault, sprinting up the stairs three at a time.

He saw Yinii coming into the unlit workroom, her dark-eye open. She spotted Tunuk as he rushed to meet her and dropped Quill's hand behind her.

"Can you check ink?" he asked, before she could say anything. "Are you allowed to check ink now?" He pulled the letters from his pocket, spreading them on the table, and removing the one from the seaside cabin and the letter Qalba had left. Quill woke the cold-magic lamps, flooding the room with a cool light that made Yinii shut her dark-eye and Tunuk flinch.

"Sorry," Quill said. "What's going on?"

Tunuk held the two letters out to Yinii. "First," he said, "I don't think these are the same writer. Can you check? They're about twelve years apart, if that matters. This one, it's a note Qalba left me, and this one, I found it when I went on respite."

Yinii took the paper, unfolding it and reading the line. Her dark-eye flashed open once in alarm. "Tunuk, was this for *you*?"

A rush of heat bloomed over Tunuk's throat and shoulders. "Maybe. Why?"

"'The wounded jackal limps along a winding path, but it knows the one it hunts for,'" Yinii read. "Tunuk, that's a *threat*. The jackal is coming after the one who left it alive."

Tunuk peered over the top of the paper. The words were crawling like ants over Yinii's fingers in lazy loops. "I thought...I thought maybe it meant coming home."

"Definitely *not*," Yinii said, sounding worried. "It's from a famous letter to the reza ul-Nymand, back in the canyons, before the Wall, when he had left the army of ul-Shandiian to— It doesn't matter," she amended. "It means the speaker is coming for revenge, and the implication is that they don't care how long it takes or if they die while getting it." She took the other one. "This one's Qalba's?" She brushed her fingers over it, the lacy letters of Orozhandi script brushing their tails around her touch. Yinii smiled sadly. "She...she was very careful writing this. Very focused."

Yinii set both pages on the worktable, shaking the clinging words free from her hands. She considered both for a moment, and then the ink lifted, the letters turning in midair. She frowned at each, then stuck out her hands, pulling both into her palms, where they lay like snakes in the nests of her hands.

"Different pens," Yinii said, her voice taking on a wet sort of warbling. Tunuk's bones *pulled* toward her, and he fought to keep his breath in its own rhythm. "Different moods. This one's angry, so *angry*. This one's...sad...and afraid. And hopeful." She brought her hands together, the lines chasing each other in ever-speeding spirals, until one slipped over the other, a single serpent of text winding around and around Yinii's cupped hands. She turned her palms, pressing them together, catching the lines between them.

Then suddenly she pulled them apart, dumping each separate letter back onto its page. She looked up at Tunuk. "No," she said. "They're not the same writer."

"Aren't they both from Qalba?" Quill asked.

Tunuk didn't answer but handed Yinii the folded-up offering. "This one? Does it match the threat?"

Yinii unfolded it. "'Their sins shall be punished, their springs shall turn foul, their crops will wither, and their children cry out, parentless, but the gods will turn their faces from these betrayers.' All right, wow—um—Tunuk, what is this?"

"Are they the same?" Tunuk said again.

Yinii peeled the ink apart again, a flourish that made Tunuk step back, eye Quill. She was definitely *not* supposed to be doing *this*. But as quickly as he recognized that they should stop her, Yinii dropped the ink, the letters reshaping themselves on both pages.

"Those are the same," she said. "Very much the same. Where's the other one from?"

The confirmation made something unknot in Tunuk's chest that he hadn't realized was squeezing so tightly. "It's from Oshanna ul-Shandiian. She's the bomb-maker. And I don't think she's finished."

VI

THE BIRTHPLACE OF MONSTERS

Summer
Borsya

The girl knows little about the Black Mother Forest: It is the birthplace of magic. It is the birthplace of monsters. It is where Redolfo's plans all turn and the place, she thinks, she is most likely to die, after all this. It is not to be trifled with, and she knows this down to the marrow of her fingerbones.

The Black Mother Forest, she thinks, knows more about her: she is a ghost, a liar, a husk of someone else. She is an interloper in a thousand different ways, and as they near that strange center of the forest, she can feel the presence there assessing her, finding her wanting.

Redolfo doesn't seem to sense the same presence—or perhaps he meets it as an equal, a king marching toward a fellow monarch's court. She cannot see the dark center any longer through the thick growth of larches and spruces, the quiet crunch of leaf fall, but she feels it waiting for them as they avoid the ruined hilltop fortresses, cross the remnants of centuries-old roads that still carve gaps between the trees.

Those roads don't lead to where Redolfo is heading.

They leave most of the army near an abandoned outpost, where there's some measure of shelter. Redolfo, his brother, his assassin, the girl, and Melosino will travel on. The ground is damp, and the girl's shoes are worn to ruin. With her little knife, she cuts the remains of cloth stolen from far-off Orozhand into strips and wraps her feet, trying to keep them dry.

Melosino takes her hand as she stands, pulls her close. "This is dangerous," he whispers, too quiet to be heard. Redolfo is watching, so she smiles at Melosino.

"We'll be all right," she promises. Or at least, she thinks, they'll be no more in danger than they'd be alone out in the world, and those are their choices.

When the forest changes, there is no mistaking it. The birdsong grows quiet, and the trees all transform: their bark black and smooth as skin, their leaves heart shaped and deep as a bruise, a shadow against all the green that surrounds them.

Redolfo stands a long moment, regarding it. A king observing the ceremony of a rival court. He holds out a hand to the changeling shaped like his brother, who puts the bag from Orozhand into it.

"Shall we?" he says, and they head into the forest.

The girl makes it a few steps in, when Melosino grabs her arm.

"We can run," he whispers. "He's distracted."

"What?" She pulls her hand away, looks ahead to Redolfo pressing on toward the heart of the forest, trailed by his guards, their crunching footsteps lost in the distance. She feels the Black Mother Forest watching her. "What are you saying? Where would we go?"

Melosino glances back toward the forest, toward where Redolfo has vanished between the trees. "Listen, I...I didn't forget everything. I remember what I was before."

"I know," she says. "I helped you—"

"Lira, *listen*. The ones he's talking to, the ones he's keeping aware. They're—" He says a word her ears refuse to hear, a sound like water running through a glass funnel that is shattering simultaneously. She shakes her head, not understanding. "They are the *enemy*," he says.

"The enemy of who?" she asks.

Melosino hesitates. "He's dangerous. What he's doing is *dangerous*. For all of us."

Lira takes a step back. "I'm just supposed to trust you?"

"You have to," he says. "We need to go."

"Where?"

"Away. Back to the—" And again, a word that is not a word. A word that is chaos.

"Changelings?" she says.

"You won't be hurt," he says. "I promise."

The girl has heard this before—she has said this before. *You won't be hurt. We'll be all right.* They are easy words to say. "You can't promise that."

"I can promise you *will* be hurt if you stay," he says. She takes another step back. "No, no, I didn't mean it like that."

In the tree behind him, a little brown bird hops along a black branch, scattering moss it tears up as it passes. It flutters its wings, leaping to the next branch, and the flash of red feathers under its wings surprises the girl.

It sits, studying her with tiny black eyes, as if waiting to see what she'll do next.

"He wouldn't want you to help Redolfo," Melosino says. "Your brother."

"My brother is an invention," she retorts.

"And you aren't?"

The words cut through the core of her, all her shared secrets sharpened into a weapon aimed for her heart. *I am the one who survived*, she wants to say, but her mouth won't work.

She wraps her arms around herself, her breath coming quickly. What Melosino is asking is worse than anything she could imagine— even as a little part of her thinks he should go, he should be free. But if she leaves Redolfo's side, she will be like a leaf adrift in the rising flood—she cannot return to Semilla. She will not survive the changelings.

More of the little birds have joined the first, the red under their wings flashing as they land.

"I can't," she says.

Melosino steps toward her. "If you're not coming, I can return for you. But I am coming back with the hunters."

She shakes her head, the words not making sense. "The what?"

"He cannot be allowed to live," Melosino says. "Not now. I've left messages on the trail. I don't know if they've found them yet, but I think we're near enough to their territory."

It's as if he's told her he plans to pull down the moon—what will the world be without a moon? What happens to the brother who defies the gods? "Please," she begs. "You can't. I don't have anywhere to go."

"With me," he pleads. "You can trust me."

But these again are easy words to say. This is not her brother—this is a creature of destruction and disorder, even if she loves him. Even if she hurt him first. The forest watches. The girl shakes her head—she knows what she has to do. Melosino huffs out a breath and turns to go.

The birds on the branch start calling, a piercing, screeching sound. Melosino flinches away from it. Picks up a rock and throws it at the screaming birds. The girl feels the forest shift, angry.

Three tests, she thinks, taking out her knife. He doesn't turn, doesn't notice as she marks the soft place where his ribs won't protect him. *Three trials. You're the one who survives.*

CHAPTER TWENTY

Amadea woke, muzzy and aching, the back of her tongue still bitter with the sedative Richa had given her. She touched her forehead gingerly, found a bandage there covering the stitches she dimly remembered him saying she needed. She climbed out of the bed she didn't remember getting into, favoring her torn leg. That was bandaged too, her ripped-up uniform taken away. She had the memory of Yinii helping her into her dressing gown, of concentrating hard on not talking, the memory of Richa saying something low and soothing...

She pulled herself to her feet, limped out into her office.

Bijan leaned over her desk, his magnification goggles on, his braids tied in a bundle at the back of his head. The Flail of Khirazj, or what remained of it, lay on her desk on a fabric-covered board, pieces pinned in place. He looked up as she came through the door, pulling up the goggles.

"You all right?" he asked.

Amadea laughed, her throat aching. "No. Is there water?"

"Sit. I'll get it."

She pulled out the chair behind her desk, opting for nearness over comfort, and sat contemplating the pieces of the Flail of Khirazj. It would need rebuilding, most of the wood replaced, but Bijan had pinned the rubies in place and matched the faience beads that had been saved to their places as described in the catalogues.

"You can give it to the glass workrooms to sort," she said, nodding at the beads.

He handed her a cup of water. "I'll let them check my work."

She and Bijan had started in the archives within a year of each other—her as a generalist, him with a late-discovered corundum affinity. Rubies and sapphires had been rare in the world before, but they couldn't be found at all in Semilla—a corundum specialist was both incredibly valuable and incredibly limited in their tasks. Bijan had taken to generalist training to fill his time. Amadea would have been hesitant to say she'd made friends in those days, but Bijan, steady and curious, had been the closest.

"Sorry," Bijan said, putting up his tools as Amadea gulped the water. "I was in the middle of this when Stavio grabbed me. He and Zoifia went with the vigilant to explain *what* they were thinking when they ran off with Tunuk to hunt for separatists." He shook his head. "I haven't gotten the whole story. I don't know if I want the whole story. That man is going to be the death of me."

Amadea smiled. "I think you told me once he was 'vibrant.'"

"He is," Bijan said, smiling, as he slid calipers back into his apron. "Just sometimes vibrant spills over into 'impulsive.' And sometimes impulsive runs in a pack."

Amadea stared into the water cup. "Did you talk to Stavio already?"

"About running off with Tunuk?"

"No."

Bijan sat down in the chair opposite her desk. "Did something happen?"

Somehow, it was easier to look at the Flail—broken, barely the relic that had been carried out of Khirazj. Barely the weapon Redolfo Kirazzi had wielded. *Redolfo, flail in hand, looming, looming. Lireana on the floor, on the carpet, the good Alojan carpet, and she's both a million miles away and close enough to hear the beads clink together as the flail swings.*

She had been so afraid of it once, and now it was splinters. Sandy glass beads. Chips of gold. The rubies were the only thing that seemed unchanged. The rest of it would have to be rebuilt on the memory of the thing.

"Bijan, when Stavio comes back, he's going to tell you the truth: when I came here, I lied," she said. "I wasn't leaving the abbey for the first time, looking for an oath, and I wasn't recommended by the day-sisters, and I wasn't Amadea Gintanas." She made herself look up, meet his dark eyes. "I was...I was the...I was the Grave-Spurned Princess, and I was trying to start over. Stavio found out, and I won't make him keep a secret from you. And...I'm...hoping this doesn't change things."

Bijan studied her, and Amadea found she was holding her breath, bracing against the moment. Was this ever going to be easy? Would it ever not feel dangerous? But if she couldn't tell steady Bijan, then who would she be able to let into her secret?

No one, a little part of her whispered. *You must tell no one.*

Bijan sighed. "How mad are you going to be," he asked, each word carefully chosen, "if I tell you I guessed this?"

Amadea stared at him. "What?"

"I mean, I didn't guess it as in I would have gossiped about it," he said. "But...I wondered. The timing. The way you talk. The business with Ibramo Kirazzi."

"There's no business with Ibramo Kirazzi," she said. "Especially not now." Grief and fear and longing all surged together in her—was he all right? And did she love him? And how could he keep such a secret? How? She shut her eyes, slowing her breath, pressed the nails of each finger into the meat of her palm, one by one.

"Do you want to talk about it?"

"No. I'm sorry. I don't mean to burden you with all this—"

"Amadea," Bijan said patiently. "I'm *offering.* We talk about my problems all the time."

"You don't have problems like this," she said, with a broken little laugh. She thought of what Quill had said—*Who do you talk to?* She thought of what she would tell Bijan if their roles were reversed: *I am here to help you, I am here to solve problems.*

"I almost told Richa," she blurted. "I ought to tell Richa. Only I can't stop thinking about what happens if he doesn't understand—if he understands too well. It could be dangerous. Or it could just be too much."

Bijan raised his eyebrows. "Are you seeing him?"

"No," Amadea said quickly. Then: "I...I don't do that. I haven't since...It doesn't seem fair to lead someone along and not tell them."

"So tell him," Bijan said. "If he's going to run, you should find out he's going to run now, before you're in so far it's going to hurt a lot more."

Amadea nodded. "And then one more person knows." She swallowed. "I have to be careful. Lady Sigrittrice—"

"Look, I'm not Vigilant Langyun's biggest admirer," Bijan said. "But do you really think he's going to run off and tell Lady Sigrittrice you told him about your past? That doesn't seem like his sort of foolish." He tilted his head, considering her. "When is the last time you took respite?"

"Respite is for specialists."

"Yeah, remember how I also took generalist training? That's not true."

"I don't know that the archives can spare me."

"They're definitely not sparing you much these days," he said, nodding at her bandaged forehead. "You're not doing anyone any favors if you run yourself into the ground. And anyway, it would probably be better for everyone to learn to handle themselves a little more."

"And when something goes wrong?"

"There are three other archivist superiors in this building," Bijan pointed out. "And Mireia." He shrugged. "I could do some of it."

"You're a specialist."

"I'm happily married to a *bronze* specialist. I have plenty of practice with generalist techniques. But," he added, "you get to decide what you want to do."

Amadea blew out a breath. "I'm not sure what I want rises above what I need to do."

The door to her office burst open, Quill, Yinii, and Tunuk pouring in. "We figured it out," Quill said. "The bomber."

"It's not Qalba," Tunuk said. "It's Oshanna ul-Shandiian. We have to get a message to Richa."

"Wait, slow down," Amadea said. "Why do you think...Oshanna ul-Shandiian? She...No, she was the reasonable one. In the noble consuls' meeting."

Tunuk thrust two notes onto her desk. "These match," he said. "That one Oshanna wrote."

Amadea took them—they reminded her of the note Richa had found with the explosive. Poetic and threatening.

But it was a thin comparison. "These are not explosives," she pointed out.

"The skeleton in the chapel matches the age of Oshanna's father," Tunuk said. "Thirty-four years, four months, eight days. He was there, he died at the right time. She's been mourning him ever since."

"It's the only thing that makes all the pieces make sense," Quill said. "Someone stabbed a person and hid him in the chapel. Which is bizarre—it's always been bizarre. Why hide a body in such a complicated place? And the only people who could plausibly exchange that skeleton and not leave a record of it are the bone specialists. But again, why bother? There's a whole room of bones upstairs. Scatter them around. Label them as something else and lose them. There are so many options that have so much less risk."

"That is odd," Bijan said.

It had been a puzzle from the moment they'd discovered the skeleton. "So how does knowing who it is change that?" Amadea asked.

"Because of the wooden bones," Yinii said. "If someone wanted to steal Saint Hazaunu, they couldn't have just taken her. People would notice immediately if one of the saints were gone, even a less popular one. They would need a substitute."

"So Qalba and Chizid killed Nimar to cover up the theft of the wooden bones?" Amadea asked.

"No," Tunuk said. "Maybe."

"Let's assume Richa's guess was right," Quill said, "and Qalba was the thief in the archives. She's taking sorcerer-wrought artifacts for the same sort of research Toya One-Saint was doing for Redolfo Kirazzi: making alternate cold-magic."

"All right," Amadea said, glancing sidelong at Tunuk. "Do you think she was assisting Toya?"

"I don't know," Quill said. "But what matters here is she's *not* the one doing the research. It's actually Nimar Eight-Myrrh. The one cousin who keeps visiting her. She *is* being blackmailed—get these artifacts, or I'll tell what you did before."

"Or what Toya did," Tunuk added. "She would have tried to protect him."

"The notes Richa found with Saint Hazaunu had diagrams of something like a lamp and then a device like the explosive," Yinii said. "It wasn't just weapons. Nimar might not have even started out working on those. Just alternate cold-magic."

"And either way, nothing's too bad," Quill said, "until he gets the Borsyans involved."

"Wait," Amadea said. "Why do you think there were Borsyans involved?"

The three of them exchanged a look. "Mainly," Quill said, "because Oshanna blew up the Borsyan noble consul's residence, and now the whole city is under curfew while they search."

"What?" Amadea tried to stand, and her leg screamed at the sudden movement.

"Sit!" Tunuk said. "They won't even let us out of the building right now. No one's traveling without a special pass and escort."

"It's a guess," Quill said again. "I know. But there's a chain here—Vigdza works for Stellano, who worked for Lord Tafad in secret. We had that all figured out. And what Stellano said in the underground lab was that Lord Tafad wasn't going to appreciate being made a fool of by another ul-Shandiian. For that to be true, he had to be involved back then *and* now."

"Why?" Bijan asked. "He's the Borsyan noble consul—why is he making weapons? Why would he try to replace the cold-magic? Most of their political power comes from the fact they control the cold-magic."

"Have you *met* the Borsyans?" Tunuk demanded. "That gives *the Duke Borcia* power because he's the head of the Brotherhood, and they're the source of the cold-magic and the fabricators. So everybody wants to be the Duke Borcia."

"Twelve years ago," Quill said, "Tafad Mazajin had been deposed. He wasn't the duke, and he wasn't a noble consul yet. And right now, he wants the ducal authority back. Both times he might be looking for an alternative to the cold-magic."

"*Something* changed," Tunuk said. "Something escalated. Something made stealing the wooden bones of Saint Hazaunu seem like a good, viable idea, and replacing them with a substitute would have had to be part of it at the very start, because Yinii's right: it would have been noticed immediately."

"But Qalba can't bring herself to do it," Amadea said, following the line of thought. "Maybe Nimar's escalating because now she's pregnant, now she's more vulnerable, but he also wants those artifacts. Now."

"Because he has a partner who wants results," Quill said. "Who can give Nimar access to fabricator tools and techniques and funds too: Lord Tafad."

"He just walked up and asked Lord Tafad to do business?" Bijan asked.

Yinii fidgeted. "I...don't want to speak poorly of a dead man, and a reza at that, but...Dushar Six-Agamid was known for being controlling. And devious. And generally unpleasant, but mostly power hungry."

"And Oshanna *blew him up*," Tunuk pronounced. "He was part of this."

"The deal can't be just between Nimar and Tafad," Quill said. "Why would Tafad ever hear him out? Nimar brings it to Dushar, Dushar brings it to Tafad. They know each other. They exist in the same circles. They can help each other cement further power."

Amadea thought of the way the two men had blustered at each other in the noble consuls' meeting. The way she'd thought even then they must have had history, other battles, other spats. Other schemes that had fallen to pieces.

"Is that how Stellano Zezurin enters into it?" she asked. "He's the one who comes to the archives and speaks for Lord Tafad?"

Tunuk shook his head. "I don't know if he ever came here. Oshanna is the only one who said so. I think he only went to Nimar—and he's definitely working with her now."

"*That's* why Richa's apartment was trapped," Quill said. "Because Stellano is on her list—Richa thinks he was in the apartment at least twice. Oshanna must have thought he was staying there."

"Stellano, Dushar, Tafad, Toya," Yinii listed, "they all were involved with the scheme that took advantage of her father's perfection of his experiments and led directly to his death."

Bijan frowned. "So who killed Nimar?"

"Chizid and Qalba would be two of the few people who can tell us if we're right because it might have been either of them defending themselves," Quill said. "Arguably, it could even have been Toya One-Saint. We don't know. But it happened in the archives. It had to have."

"So Nimar is killed, by your version of things, in self-defense," Amadea said. "They skeletonize him and swap the bones out. Toya takes Saint Hazaunu. Chizid and Qalba leave. Why? You were right at the start—getting rid of the body would be so much simpler."

"Because there was this plan to swap the bones," Quill said. "That's the piece we missed. And if Tafad and Dushar knew about the plan, when Nimar disappeared, they would just come and press Chizid and Qalba again to do it. Maybe they'd even have figured out they were the ones who killed Nimar and have something new to use as blackmail.

"But if the plan was always to substitute the wooden bones so you could turn them into alternative cold-magic and weapons," Quill went on, "and Nimar vanished, but you went to the chapel and saw the swap had been made? Maybe you just assume Nimar is the one who crossed you. Maybe you spend all your time looking for that wayward son."

"Maybe you start spitting on his name," Yinii added quietly. "And maybe his daughter is listening, and maybe you're making a whole new enemy."

"And then, when the time is right," Quill finished, "when she can find her own way to follow in his footsteps, she kills the ones she thinks killed her father with his own invention."

"But not Toya," Amadea said.

Quill threw up his hands. "I don't know why she didn't blow Toya up. Ask *her* why she didn't blow Toya up! But more importantly we have to get out of the archives and tell Richa!"

Amadea traced the path of their claims, the connections it solved—the identity of the skeleton, the ways the murders were connected. There were still questions, but it was enough to interest the vigilants, surely.

"Do you think she's after Stellano Zezurin, then?" Amadea asked. "Is that the end of her list?"

Tunuk shook his head tightly. "I think she's got one more." He tapped the letter he'd left on the desk. "I found this in the respite cabin, by the seaside, but I don't think it was meant for me," he said. "I think she's going to end this going after Qalba."

The curfew would not lift until morning, so there were no runners to carry a message to the Vigilant Kinship until then. Tunuk spent the night too restless to sleep, pacing the archives. He wasn't alone—clusters of archivists loitered along the iron railings, in the hallways of the dormitories. All whispering about the explosions, the curfew, the imperial soldiers and vigilants in the streets.

"It feels like the war," Bijan murmured. They had gone out onto the promenade on the third story, overlooking the square where a half dozen uniformed guards paced the streets. "Lockdowns and soldiers and not knowing what's coming next."

"I hope Zoifia and Stavio are all right," Yinii said, worrying her hands. They were still at the Kinship Hall, held back by the curfew.

"Me too," Bijan said.

"I think the biggest risk is them getting bored," Quill said. "They're safe in the Kinship Hall."

"Probably come back with fresh gossip and new chapbooks." Bijan sighed. "I hope."

Bijan went to bed, and then Quill, with a low conversation and a discreet kiss for Yinii, and then it was just Yinii and Tunuk, standing on the dark promenade looking out over the city. Yinii kept fidgeting with her hands, her amulets, looking out over the city with her day-eyes, then her dark-eye as if she were trying to work herself up to saying something.

Tunuk cleared his throat, his eyes on the palace, far up the hill. "Quill was lying about why you're seeing Fastreda, wasn't he? It's not because she's maqu'tajii."

"What makes you say that?" Yinii asked.

"Because I know you. If this were just about meeting a maqu'tajii, you would have met her and then given up your spot. Make sure everyone has the chance."

"Well," Yinii said, "that...yes. That's just polite!"

His bones ached, and he made himself look her in the eye. "Is this why you're avoiding everyone? Why you're avoiding me?"

She ducked her head. "Something happened in the tunnel under the Wall."

"You spiraled."

"I...spiraled in a way I shouldn't have. Or that Amadea thought I shouldn't have. It was...I think something changed after that. Like I was holding something in too hard and now...now it's..." She looked up at Tunuk. "I'm a sorcerer."

No you aren't, Tunuk wanted to say—it was such an absurd comment. Yinii was the most powerful of the specialists he knew, but Yinii was Yinii. There was nothing perilous about her, nothing otherworldly—

But he caught himself, feeling quietly for the pull of Yinii's affinity, the tug on his own that would come around a sorcerer. To his surprise, it was there, hiding in the thrumming of the bones, a pull from nowhere like a great breath drawing out the pulse he expected.

He thought of those lost rituals his fathers spoke of, and the yinpay, transformed by its loneliness. He thought of the saints in the chapel, their bones so far from the ones they'd cared about.

"What does that mean?" he said. "Are you leaving?"

She shrugged, and he saw how very scared she was. "Not if I can help it."

Tunuk pulled her close, folding her into an embrace. She pressed her forehead to his chest and wrapped her arms around him as well.

"If anyone tries to take you from the archives," he said thickly, "I will...pull their bones out."

She laughed and wiped her face on the back of her sleeve. "They're not worked. You can't do that."

"Who said I was going to use my affinity?" He released her. "I'm going to ask you something stupid, and you have to swear not to tell me it's really stupid. Will you promise not to ignore me while you and Quill have your romance?"

She turned pink. "I...It's barely a romance. I don't have any idea what I'm doing. Do you think he can tell?"

"Of course he can tell," Tunuk said. "*I* can tell you don't know what you're doing. But he likes you." He hesitated. "If it's too much to ask, that's fine."

"I'm not going to ignore you. Why would I ignore you?"

"I mean, it's normal to prioritize."

"You're my best friend," Yinii said. "And...maybe I haven't been available but...you really thought I'd ignore you for some boy?"

Tunuk threw his hands up. "I mean, yes?"

Yinii tucked in close beside him. "Tunuk, I don't want to be insensitive," she said, "but...that's a really Alojan thing. I'm not going to stop having friends just because I like Quill."

"What? Alojans have friends. My parents have friends. Do you know how many people were at Obigen's memorial?"

"Right," Yinii agreed, "but...how many people went out for lunch with him? How many people did he sit and talk to? Who did he go to if he was angry at one of your other parents? And when your parents have really liked someone, how long before they invited them into the nest?"

"I don't know," Tunuk said. "I didn't keep his social calendar." But he knew the answer—his parents spent time with one another. And maybe something about that seemed inevitable to Tunuk.

"I don't mean you have to live like that," Yinii said. "But...I think that's why your parents worry. It's what they know. They don't understand that you have plenty of friends who care about you, who take you to your favorite pancake shop and listen to you complain and make sure you have what you need. Who you check on and hug and tell jokes with. You just don't live with them. Or...do...other things."

"Hmph," Tunuk grunted, feeling embarrassed but also...better. "All right. Fair." He looked sidelong at her. "You know you have to be able to say what 'other things' are before you can do them with your new boyfriend."

Her cheeks darkened further. "I...can say it. I just don't want to."

Tunuk snorted and put an arm around her. "I missed you," he admitted. "I'm glad you worry about me."

Yinii leaned against him. "I'm glad you worry about me too."

———— ⊷⊷⊷ ————

When the pieces come together, Richa thought, *everything moves fast*. The work of the vigilants was slow and cautious and thoughtful—it had to be.

But when you showed up with two witnesses who put Stellano Zezurin in Arlabecca—in league, even, with the person wreaking havoc in the city with fabricator-designed weapons—and when you handed over the address to what was almost certainly his safe house, things tended to pick up the pace.

Salva eyed him warily. "Where'd you get this?"

"Being a shitty vigilant," he said. "Those witnesses heard him say he'd meet the fabricator at the house by the College of the Five Forests. I went through the taxation records. There's a half-flat owned by someone who has the same name as his dog."

"His dog?" Salva asked skeptically.

Richa hesitated. "My dog. My dog that he killed. That row house isn't mine, but I'm willing to bet he did that to prod at me. I think he did this too. And if the Borsyan noble consul is dead, I think you have to go after Stellano quickly."

She reached up and turned one of the rings on her right horn, still eyeing him. "What changed?"

Richa hesitated again. He had decided he wasn't interested in unburdening himself further. He wasn't even sure how he had managed to tell Amadea, only that in the moment, it had felt safe and right, as if nothing bad could come of her knowing. And...nothing had. She'd understood, she'd promised to help, and she hadn't looked at him like he wasn't someone she knew.

It had seemed so impossibly terrifying, only the day before, when Quill found out and Richa felt his control over his own history slipping through his fingers. More than anything, he thought, it said something about Amadea. About him and Amadea.

"I didn't think you were right," he said. "I didn't think he'd come here. But I trust my witnesses. And I see how it fits together now."

Salva raised an eyebrow, her forehead shifting around the swell of her unformed dark-eye. "I still think you're a shitty vigilant."

"And I think you're a self-important asshole. But we're a Kinship, and we help each other help the empire." He eyed her right back. "You were sure Stellano was involved, but it wasn't the murder, I don't think, because we didn't even know who the victim was—a knife in a peddler at a relay station is a tragedy, but it's not a marker. I think you were looking at me already, but even then, you jumped very fast on one circumstantial moment. There's plenty of other points in my recent career you could have pushed on if it were just about me.

"So I think," he said, "this is about the wooden bones. That's the distinctive part. But nobody knew those were missing—there's not a ring of archives thieves. I know, I checked. So you didn't think those were from this side of the Wall—you couldn't have, because all the saints on this side of the Wall are accounted for and haven't been reported missing.

"The ones that aren't," he said, holding her gaze, "are all back in Orozhand. You thought the peddler's saint had been smuggled from over the Salt Wall. Which means, I think, Stellano has become more of a reckless idiot than he was even fifteen years ago, which *is* the last time I spoke to him, and he's found a way to smuggle things past the Salt Wall. Tell me I'm wrong?"

He said it like a request—because truly, Richa wanted nothing more than to be wrong about *this*. The Salt Wall kept the empire safe, kept the changelings out, and it was bad enough that Redolfo Kirazzi had made a passage under it; if Stellano was risking that for artifacts or drugs or Aye-Nam-Wati even knew what—

"*Around* the Wall," Salva said grudgingly. "We think he's got people sailing around."

Richa swore. The Salt Wall was well guarded, the tunnel at Sestina an extraordinary thing. Fishing boats that plied the waters off Semilla went through strict protocols upon docking that had not slackened over the century—iron for every hand, a dip in the salty water before coming back to land. The changelings had never attacked by sea, which led to the assumption the salt water was enough to harm them—but if a changeling came aboard a ship that had pulled up on some other shore, who was to say they couldn't manage to board without touching salt?

"We need to move now," she said. "Would you kindly inform Vigilant Manche that we need the Imperial Authority alerted? They haven't lifted the curfew, and I don't want anything to slow us down."

Richa held up a hand. "You've got this. I don't want to be involved with catching him beyond here."

"Do I look like a fool?" Salva asked. "You've been very accommodating, Vigilant Langyun, but there exists a scenario where I was right from the beginning, and you are setting a very dangerous trap."

"You still don't trust me?"

"Not really," she said. "You can meet me downstairs."

Which was how Richa came to be standing, just after dark, up the street from the building where his dead dog lived, where Salva Nine-Scorpion could see him. The streets were quiet, the cobbles shining with rain and his breath clouding on the cold air.

"It's pretty clear he's connected with the person planting explosives," Richa had warned Salva. "He's trying to take her out, and I'm pretty sure the reverse is true too."

The vigilants had been briefed on the appearance of the explosives, creeping in close and careful. Richa's nerves built and built—no one knew how the things went off, whether there was a trigger or a timer. Any moment now, there could be another flash, another roar, another rain of debris.

Any moment now, there could be Stellano, dragged into the street in his canary coat, finally brought low, and Richa didn't want to see that any more than the next explosion. Right now, on the cold and empty street, he felt numb—he ought to be afraid, and he ought to be angry, and maybe part of him ought to feel some sorrow, some worry that someone he'd loved very much was also in danger. But the numbness persisted, and he didn't want to let go of it. He wanted Stellano to stay the problem of the past, the problem of Caesura. The problem of Salva Gaitha-hyu.

He could just see her, a block ahead, across the street from the house, watching the forward forces surround the building, check the exits. Every once in a while, he'd see her pale face flash toward him, making sure he was still there.

"Have the imperial guards found the bomb-maker yet?" he asked the vigilant standing beside him, a human woman with short brown hair and pale skin.

"Not yet," she said, repacking a medical kit she'd just checked. "The curfew's on until morning at least. The gates are all closed, and the waterways. Hopefully they catch them soon enough."

A shout rang out, and the vigilants near the building burst into movement—away from the structure. The air ignited, then cracked, a sound that shattered Richa's ears, and the building rained down in pieces around them.

The other vigilants sprang into action, medical kits in hand. Richa moved to follow, but a hand around his biceps stopped him, the sharp point of a weapon pressing to the muscle of his lower back.

"Hey there, Pigeon," a throaty voice said in his ear. "It's been a long time."

Richa started to turn, but the knife pressed harder, and Stellano clucked his tongue. "No, no, no—you had your chance to do this nicely."

Ahead there was smoke and rubble and shouting voices. There was his Kinship in danger. "How'd you get past the perimeter?"

"No stupid questions either." Stellano pulled Richa backward, into the alley, and finally let him turn around and face him.

A measure of that numbness shattered. Some part of Richa fluttered awake with the memory of this man, his cocky smile, his sure hands, his constant presence all returned.

The greater part of him flooded with fear—Egillio and the knife and the threats. Worse: Stellano was dressed as a vigilant.

"Where did you get that uniform?" Richa asked.

"I said don't ask stupid questions." Stellano looked him over. "Well. I was wondering if you'd ever come find me. I hate being ignored."

"You were in my apartment," Richa said, clinging to what was left of that numbness, searching for an escape. As tight as the alley was, he didn't think he could get past that knife. There was no attacking first—Stellano had him trapped.

Stellano smirked. "I wondered if you'd noticed. It's a bit of a dump, isn't it?"

"Since your friend got to it, yeah, I'd have to agree."

Stellano laughed. "I missed you. So here's how it's going to go: I think it's pretty clear, against a maniac murdering her way across the empire, I'm a petty kind of prize. You want to get rid of her, and so do I. And I know where she's going next, assuming she thinks this little stunt did the job. You get me out of Arlabecca, and I'll take care of your problem."

"Can't do that," Richa said. "They already think we're working together. I help you out and I'm the one getting thrown in the Imperial Prison. Besides, that's all pretty squarely against my oath."

Stellano snorted. "Your oath. As if your hands are so clean." He smiled, a cruel curl of his lips, and looked Richa over again. "The uniform suits you, though. Nice fit."

Richa kept his eyes on Stellano, on the sharp knife he still held carelessly in his right hand. He wasn't going to stop Stellano here—and he knew the clock was running out. Stellano wasn't so foolish to stand around waiting for the vigilants to come catch him, waiting for an answer from Richa.

But if Richa agreed...

"If I get you out," he said slowly, "you'll put down the bomber. Can you make it clear she's working alone? This wasn't connected to any political movement? That would make it worth it. My superiors would be very happy if everyone thought it wasn't political."

"Easy as lifting a drunk pilgrim's purse," Stellano said. "Come on."

"We can't do it now," Richa said. "I have to go make a show of *being here*. If I leave, they'll send runners to all the gates, and they'll be looking for both of us. Just make yourself scarce. Tomorrow. If they haven't caught the bomber—"

"They won't," Stellano said.

"If they haven't, then where should I meet you?"

Stellano eyed him, and for a moment, Richa worried he would

see a trap, refuse to go forward. Maybe gut him like he'd promised fifteen years ago and go about his business.

"The north-bound gate," Stellano said. "The one in the old wall, not right at the gate, mind—there's a fountain near there with one of the old emperors in the middle. Sunset's nice—tricks people's eyes, adds a bit of romance. Show up then, get me through the gate, your problem's solved."

Richa nodded stiffly. "All right. I'll do it."

Stellano laughed once, pressing his tongue to the point of an eye-tooth. "Just like old times."

"No, it's not," Richa said.

Stellano's laughing eyes went cold and cruel. "Well, I hope not too much like old times, since that would mean you're about to run like a coward." He flipped the blade over in his hand. "Here, Pigeon. Wouldn't want you to get into trouble."

He swung it backhanded as if to slice Richa across the throat, but Richa caught his arm, pushed it down, away from him. That's when Stellano's fist came up hard under Richa's chin, slamming his head into the stone wall behind him, hard enough to make him see stars. He let go of Stellano, his hand pressed to his skull.

When Richa could see straight again, Stellano was gone.

CHAPTER TWENTY-ONE

The next morning, Quill went down to the entry hall, ready to sprint to the Vigilant Kinship himself, only to find Amadea standing before the open doors, giving a runner in imperial livery a coin in exchange for a pair of letters. The bruise over her right eye and cheek was lurid, and she held her splinted wrist to her ribs, but she was standing at least. She slit the first open as he caught up to her.

"What is it?" he said. "Did they catch her? Are we allowed out? Is the empress alive?"

"The curfew ends in an hour," she said, skimming the letter. "No one has said anything about the empress, good or bad." Amadea held up the message. "This one's from Richa," she said. "He says they've got a plan to catch the bomber and Stellano in place, and we should just stay where we are until tomorrow."

Quill took the letter. "Does he know it's Oshanna he's looking for?"

Amadea shook her head, opening the second message. "Unclear. I'm assuming he's on top of things, but I can send..." She trailed off, her attention on the letter in her hand. Quill noticed the imperial seal dangling from it.

"Is everything all right?"

"No," Amadea said slowly. "Lady Sigrittrice wants me to come to the palace."

"I guess that means *she* didn't die in the explosion," Quill said. "Might be nice to make an announcement." He peered over Amadea's shoulder. "Does she say why?"

"'Duties to the empire,'" Amadea said. "Which I am coming to understand is how she says 'You don't need to know.'" She folded the letter back up. "Obviously there are many things that concern the empress right now."

"Is she actually going insane because there might be changelings?" Quill asked. "That's what people are saying."

Amadea blew out a breath. "People will talk. We have to focus on finding the answers to help the empress, and we've done that by finding the sorcerer transfers."

"Should you be up and walking that much?"

She flashed the imperial seal at him again. "Do I have a choice? Besides . . . I need to talk to Ibramo. If he's all right."

"Do you think he's found the functionary?" Quill said.

She swallowed as if her throat was tight. "I think he has probably been recovering from that explosion. But . . . I don't want it to get lost. We need to make sure those plans are completely stopped." She tucked the letters under her arm. "I'll hire a carriage. I can stop at the Kinship Hall on my way to the palace and make sure Richa knows about Oshanna. You . . ." She blew out another breath. "Take care of Tunuk, please. He's going to be . . . agitated."

"Can I get him out of the archives?" Quill asked. "Or do we have to stay put?"

"As soon as the curfew is lifted, I think getting Tunuk outside is a very good idea." She reached into one of her apron pouches and pulled out a small purse of coins. "Here. Whatever you two need."

It took little convincing to get Tunuk to leave his room for the promise of pancakes and only the vaguest mention to include Yinii. While Yinii fetched her cloak and Tunuk retrieved Biorni, Quill paused at Bijan and Stavio's apartment beside hers to report that the curfew was being lifted, and so Stavio and Zoifia would likely be back soon.

"Do you want to go get pancakes?" Quill asked.

Bijan shook his head. "Be careful out there."

"The Kinship's got this," Quill said. "And Oshanna's not targeting us."

"That's not what I mean," Bijan said. "If you have to put a curfew on a city, that means things are bad. It's not about catching one terrorist; it's about keeping everyone off the street. I'm going to guess people weren't happy about being afraid of the bombs, but they're going to be even angrier about the curfew and the gates being closed."

As they walked to the pancake shop, Quill didn't see any outward signs of unrest. But it was clear from the way people moved, glancing furtively around them as if any of their neighbors might be trouble, from the way many of the shops they passed were still locked up tightly, that something was shifting in the city.

The pancake shop was open and selling but not letting anyone linger at the tables. They wrapped the spongy flatbreads around chunks of honeycomb and raisins and folded a second around the bottom so they could be eaten walking, then shooed the archivists away.

"At least it's a nice day," Quill said. The rain clouds had cleared, the sun low but bright. He let Tunuk lead the way, wandering nowhere in particular, the conversation about nothing in particular.

Which was all right, Quill decided. You needed a moment, now and again, of not thinking of the terrible things.

And then they reached the hill that sloped down to the eastward gate, the road to Terzanelle. A crowd of people, waiting to pass through, filled the street, and from here Quill could see the road beyond the city's wall, winding out into the flatter farmlands beyond. On to Terzanelle.

On to where Qalba had said she could be met.

They had been wandering here specifically, Quill never realizing it.

"Tunuk," he began.

Tunuk wiped the crumbs off his uniform, staring at the gate, the rabbit skull tucked under his opposite arm. "Do you think she's alive?" he asked. Then: "Do you think she'd be angry to see me?"

Quill didn't know the answer. Really there was only one way to know the answer—to find Qalba and ask her directly what the hell she'd been thinking.

"You can't get through," Yinii pointed out. "The gate's closed."

She was right. The crowd wasn't a line—the crowd was a protest.

A row of vigilants held the gate, walls of sandbags making the passage into a minor maze.

"Only official imperial business!" one of the vigilants shouted over the buzz of discontent. "There's still a malcontent on the loose! You need to disperse!"

"Maybe after all this," Yinii said, "maybe we could go. I don't know where we'd get the flag of the reza ul-Shandiian, but...maybe we could ask around about her."

"If she's still there," Tunuk said. "If they're all right. If..." He trailed off, peering at the crowd.

A rider on a horse moved through the crowd toward the gate: Oshanna ul-Shandiian, mourning ribbons wrapped around her horns. When she reached the gate, she handed down a leather folio with a tasseled seal to the vigilant.

A moment later, the vigilant handed it back. Oshanna nodded her thanks and nudged the horse through, winding around the passage of the sandbag walls.

"Shit," Quill breathed. "They don't know."

Tunuk broke into a run, but when he reached the massed crowd, now shouting at the vigilants even more angrily for having watched this woman pass easily by, he slowed, as if moving through mud. Quill and Yinii hurried after him, squeezing behind in the wake he left, until he could shout to the vigilants.

"Why did you let her go?" Tunuk demanded.

"Esinor, step back," the vigilant said again. "The gate is closed until further notice unless you have imperial permission."

"Why does *she* have imperial permission?" Tunuk said. "She's the—"

"That wasn't imperial permission!" shouted a man Quill couldn't quite see. "That had the ducal seals!"

"The reza ul-Shandiian is dead," the vigilant said. "She's traveling to notify the clan members in Terzanelle."

"That's not his business," his comrade said. "Move along, please. We still need to keep people from congregating here."

"She's the one you're looking for!" Tunuk shouted. "You absolute idiots!"

"Esinor, you need to calm down, and all of you need to disperse! No one is getting through! Everyone *go home* before you make yourself a target of this maniac!"

Quill pulled Tunuk back through the crowd of people who drifted from the gate, still lingering angrily within sight of the exit. There was no going that way.

"We should go back to the Kinship Hall," Yinii said. "Tell Richa."

"By then she'll be halfway to Terzanelle!" Tunuk said. "She's going to kill Qalba, and these idiots aren't listening, and if we don't—" Tunuk gave a sharp cry: a lacework of bone had erupted on the back of his hand, reaching for Biorni.

"Breathe," Quill reminded him, taking the rabbit skull away. "Give me a moment."

Oshanna was on horseback and had already gotten a head start. If they could reach the relay station between Arlabecca and Terzanelle, they might be able to get horses and warn vigilants and catch up to her before she could signal Qalba and kill her, and maybe carry on to Chizid too. They couldn't get through the gate without permissions, but this was a crisis, and crises were not by their nature well planned. There would be edge cases, Quill reasoned. People who were more trouble in the city than outside.

He looked at the bone spreading on Tunuk's hand, then over at Yinii. He handed Biorni back.

"Follow me, and look scary," Quill whispered.

He marched up to the vigilant at the lead, a human man with medium-brown skin and curly brown hair. The vigilant held up a hand. "Esinor, the gates of the city are closed unless you have—"

"Yes, I know," Quill said. "But I have a problem. I need to get these two to Terzanelle."

"No one is to leave the city," the vigilant began.

"You mentioned," Quill said. "But I'm from the archives. These are two specialists in alignment. They're about to *spiral*. Do you know what that means?"

The vigilant looked nervously over Quill's shoulder at Tunuk. Quill took another small step forward, lowered his voice. "She's just an ink specialist, but he's a *bone* specialist. I really can't have his affinity getting out of hand here. I need to get him *away* from people. There's a respite cabin near Terzanelle, and I'm supposed to transport him—I was supposed to leave last night, but we honored the curfew—and I can't get imperial permission. The line is already halfway across the city!"

"He's gonna have to just wait it out," the vigilant said hesitantly.

Quill looked at Biorni, at the patch of shining bone on Tunuk's arm, and winced. "I don't know if you understand. Once it starts, it's almost impossible to stop." He dropped his voice to a whisper. "Do you have any idea how painful it is to have your bones pulled out?"

"No," the vigilant said, still staring at Tunuk.

"I don't even know if they've gotten the travel permissions figured out for this—stand in line all day, find out it's too rare, it slipped through the cracks. Meanwhile..." Quill gave the vigilant a significant look. "It's really down to bad timing. I can't imagine it's making *your* jobs easier."

Another vigilant came to stand next to the first. "We're not supposed to let you through."

Quill smiled affably at her. "Really, we're navigating the same waters. Orders from on high, and you're just trying to protect the city. I'm just trying to prevent people from becoming...boneless puddings. We don't want more panic, do we?"

Tunuk loomed behind him. Quill heard Biorni's jaw start chattering again.

"I don't think anybody wants that," the first vigilant said.

"Look, what if you search us?" Quill said. "I don't have anything more dangerous than a penknife on me. You can even report back to the Kinship and the archives and even the empress that we went this way. Vigilant Langyun knows we're supposed to go this way. But I don't want to be responsible for triggering his spiral and..." He trailed off, letting the vigilants imagine what could happen when Tunuk spiraled.

The vigilants met in quick conference, and a thorough search of their persons later, all three of them were ushered through the gate.

The road to Terzanelle stretched east over gently rolling hills, and Oshanna was nowhere in sight.

"Do you think they're going to tell Amadea we left?" Yinii asked nervously.

"I'm counting on it," Quill said. He looked over at Tunuk. "Sorry I let him think you were a danger."

"Don't be," Tunuk said grimly. "I feel a little dangerous at the moment. Let's go."

⸻ ✦ ⸻

Sundown wrapped the city in shadows, the chill of the daytime plunging deeper as the dark crept in, not enough heat in the stones. Richa pulled his fur-lined cape close around him and eyed the gathering shadows. He'd come early, not wanting to be surprised, and Stellano hadn't arrived yet.

Richa wanted to believe the self of his past was dead, but as he stood in the dark, the thief in him was waking up. How to be unobtrusive, how to seem at ease, how to parse all the sounds of the city into opportunity or danger. He wasn't worried that Stellano was late. They'd done this before—Stellano would be winding his way in toward the fountain, checking for vigilants, making certain Richa hadn't crossed him. He wouldn't find anyone.

"He spotted you closing in soon enough to escape that perimeter," Richa had told Salva the night before, once they'd returned to the Kinship Hall and assessed the damage—to Salva's assumptions and Richa's skull. "He's going to spot anyone watching within a few blocks."

"Agreed," Salva said, though she clearly didn't like it. The remains of the safe house had yielded the body of the fabricator, Vigdza, but not much else in the way of clues or evidence.

"We're better off setting an ambush down the road," Salva said. "You meet him where you're meant to, convince him you're on his side, and try to get more information about how his work was directed by Lord Tafad and where he's working from now. How far this smuggling business extends."

"And where is Qalba One-Fox." Richa went to rake a hand through his hair, caught himself when he remembered the bruise. "Where are you setting the ambush?"

"A mile out. Right before the road forks toward Ragale."

"*A mile?*" Richa said. "What happens if he doesn't head where we're expecting?"

Salva studied him. "Look, I misjudged you before. I'll admit it. Your oath is to this city and this empire and these people, as much as mine. But you know as well as I do, we can only plan so far. If Esinor Zezurin outwits us, then you will just have to prove how much you aren't a shitty vigilant."

The curfew had come down again, opening the Kinship's entry hall to the fury of a crowd of people. They were afraid, and nothing the orders or the empress or the ducal authorities were doing was helping that.

The sun set, the darkness lengthened. The light of a single cold-magic lamp hanging over the fountain hardly pierced the shadows. The cold started to seep into Richa where he leaned against the stone wall. And still no Stellano.

What happened if he didn't show up? What happened if he did? Richa didn't like Salva's plan at all—did she understand he had never, ever been able to control Stellano?—but he didn't know of a better one, and this was not only their path to stopping the passage of goods and people around the Salt Wall but also to finding Qalba and stopping the bombings before anyone else got hurt.

Footsteps brought Richa up straight, all his nerves alert. But it wasn't Stellano who melted from the shadows. Ibramo Kirazzi, masked in black velvet, strode over to Richa, limping on his right leg.

"Your Highness," Richa said, "you can't be here." He looked for guards, looked for attendants—Ibramo was alone, and that was even worse.

"Where's Amadea?" Ibramo asked, low and urgent.

"In the archives?" Richa said. "What do you mean?"

"Gritta summoned her to the Imperial Complex," Ibramo said. "She didn't arrive. I went to the archives, she's not there, but they said she'd left this morning saying she was going to the palace by way of the Kinship Hall. And the vigilants didn't see her. I got them to tell me you were here—"

"They should *not* have done that. Your Highness, you need to leave, right now." If Stellano arrived, if the consort-prince were here—

"I know she's angry at me, but the empress…" Ibramo drew a sharp breath. "It's very bad. We need her. And she needs to know, I think she was right about the sorcerer transfers—someone filed changes, moved them again."

"What are you talking about?" Richa asked.

"The primate's papers," Ibramo said. "She found seven orders to transfer sorcerers from their current locations to Sestina, all sealed by an unidentified functionary. I didn't find the functionary—there hasn't been time—but I tried to halt the transfers, and they were all already changed, all going to the coasts. They're not finished."

Richa regarded the consort-prince with dawning dread. "You think your father is trying to kidnap sorcerers?" Stories of Fastreda of the Glass, of her terrible armies endlessly re-forming, rose up in Richa's thoughts. *Of the Iron, of the Silver, of the Pottery*—how deadly could those other sorcerers be if you bent them to your will?

"Where is Amadea?" Ibramo said again.

And Richa finally realized what the question meant—she wasn't in the archives, she hadn't gone to the palace, and she hadn't arrived at the Kinship Hall. She was missing.

"Shit," he said. "Where…where would she go? If she was called away, or—"

More footsteps, the grind of grit on damp cobblestones, the uneven steps of someone hauled along.

Richa had the good sense to reach up and yank Ibramo's mask down to hang around his neck, crumpling the symbol of the consort-prince in the hopes he'd seem to be just a wealthy Khirazji man in an odd scarf. A moment later, Stellano, still in the stolen vigilant's uniform, stepped into the light of the cold-magic lamp illuminating the fountain, dragging Amadea with him.

Richa's chest seized at the sight of her—he knew those bruises, the splinted wrist, that limp, none of those were Stellano's doing. But the knife against her throat, the faint quiver of her pursed mouth, the horrible fragility of Amadea in that moment—he could kill Stellano for that.

"Richa, I'm sorry—" The press of the knife cut her off.

"Oh good," Stellano drawled. "You brought a friend too."

"This wasn't the agreement," Richa said. If he moved too fast, too foolishly, Stellano had only to flick that blade, and she'd be dead. The plan was to get him moving, get him onto the road, into the ambush, but every moment he had that knife pressed to her neck was an eternity.

"I needed security," Stellano said. "In case you decided to tattle to your Kinship. This seemed like something you cared about, so I just waited to see if she'd leave. Hopped in a carriage, silly thing. You didn't think I was just going to trust you again?"

Richa spread his hands. "You didn't think I might not want to tell the Kinship I'd bargained for an extrajudicial murder? Nobody's here. Let her go."

Get him walking, get him talking, keep him on the path—but all these plans that were meant to keep the city safe, keep the empire from threats seemed far away and foolish. *Maybe there's something you care about more than the oath*, Richa thought.

Stellano nodded toward Ibramo. "Who's he?"

"A friend in the wrong place," Richa said. "You don't need either of them for this. It'll be harder to get out of the city with four. In fact," he went on, "you give her to him, and we can walk out of here nice and easy."

"Gonna disagree with you there, Pigeon. I don't like loose ends." Stellano smiled. "So you can either figure out a way to get all of us out the door, or I'm going to have to cut both ends short. And before you two start making any sort of calculations about how fast I am with this knife, do keep in mind that even if you'd survive that tangle, she's not going to."

Richa glanced at the consort-prince, who blessedly had kept his mouth shut, his body still. Ibramo returned the look, silent and determined, and gave Richa the smallest of nods. He was with him.

"Through the gate," Richa agreed. "Then you let them go."

"We'll see," Stellano said. "We have a lot to talk about." He jerked his head back the way he'd come. "The carriage is that way."

Ibramo and Richa went first, Stellano following behind with Amadea. "How's this going to work?" Ibramo said under his breath.

"He's got to see reason," Richa murmured. "This is too many hostages."

"Anytime you want to test me," Stellano called, "I'm happy to drop that number by one."

The carriage was tucked against a closed-up apothecary shop, the horses anxious and prancing, the driver similarly cagey. Stellano ordered them all inside, and there was a moment when Richa thought he might be able to kick Stellano away from Amadea, back out the carriage door—but in the same moment, he pictured the drag of the knife, the spray of blood.

Be patient, he told himself. *Be wary.*

"Let's go," Stellano called to the driver. The horses took off, the carriage lurching. Amadea gave a little cry as the sudden motion threatened to pull the blade against her skin, but Stellano kept it exactly where he meant to. He clucked his tongue. "Don't you worry. I'm very good with this. Tell her, Pigeon."

"I've already heard," Amadea said, her voice calm. "He's told me a lot about you."

"I'm sure it was all very fair and reasonable," Stellano said disdainfully.

Richa looked out the window of the carriage. "We're going the wrong way. This isn't going to lead to the northward gate."

"Oh, we're not going north," Stellano said. "We're going east." He pulled his handsome face into a moue. "Were your friends expecting me to go north? Pity."

Richa could have cursed—he'd known Salva's plan had holes, and he hadn't pressed her hard enough to sew them up. Now he was left scrambling, forming a plan as the circumstances shifted from underneath him, unable to communicate with his allies.

He met Amadea's eyes. *I am so sorry*, he thought to her. *I am so sorry.*

At the eastward gate, the carriage halted. Stellano took his arm from around Amadea's shoulders, tucking the blade low against her waist where the vigilants wouldn't see it.

"Go ahead, Pigeon," Stellano said. "Make nice."

Richa stuck his head out the window, nodding to the other vigilant. "Evening."

"Gates are closed," the vigilant said. "Unless you've got a pass."

Richa handed over the imperial pass he'd been given to get through the northern gate. "Didn't Vigilant Gaitha-hyu send word we were passing through this way? We have a report there are separatists in Terzanelle connected to the bombings."

"Nobody told me anything," the vigilant said. "This is for the north gate. How many people are in the carriage?"

Richa cursed under his breath. He'd hoped the message would come across, but Salva hadn't prepared these vigilants for her move against Stellano. He pulled his head back in. "I need your help," he said quietly to Ibramo.

Ibramo's gaze slid to Stellano, seeming to weigh the knife, the threat, the possibility that Stellano knowing who he really was would make things worse. They could alert the vigilants? Stellano might kill Amadea faster than that.

Richa opened the door as Ibramo pulled the black velvet mask back up over his eyes. The vigilant stuck his head in, considering Stellano smiling blithely, Amadea sitting ramrod straight.

"Oh," the vigilant said, surprised. "Are you the archivist superior? Are you going after those archivists from earlier? The one with the spiraling bone specialist?"

Amadea's face was still as porcelain, but Richa knew inside she must be panicking. "It's related," she said, her voice tight. "When did they come through?"

"This morning," the vigilant said, looking over to Richa and then Ibramo. He froze, taking in the black mask. "Oh."

"Is there a problem?" Ibramo said.

"No," the vigilant said. "No, sorry. Sorry." He handed the document back to Richa. "So sorry."

The carriage jerked into motion again, and Stellano watched Ibramo, his eyes dancing as he recognized the symbol of the consort-prince. "Well, well, Pigeon," he said. "Interesting company you're keeping these days."

The carriage rambled on some ways, but they hadn't gotten out of sight of the city when shouts echoed outside. The carriage halted again, the restless horses squealing.

"What's this?" the driver said.

Richa lifted the curtain from the little window: the left side of the carriage was crowded by imperial guards, most on horseback, a quartet dismounted and holding crossbows ready. Stellano leaned toward the window, his knife still pointed at Amadea. "Interesting," he said again. "Your doing?"

"No," Richa said, his pulse rising.

"We have orders to arrest the consort-prince, Ibramo Kirazzi, and Amadea Gintanas, also called Lireana Ulanitti, the Grave-Spurned Princess, for conspiring with Sigrittrice Ulanitti to commit treason against the Imperial Authority," shouted a voice beyond the carriage. "And we have reason to believe you're traveling with them. Dismount the carriage."

For a moment, Richa stood in two worlds at once, his past overlapping his present. Here was the vigilant, the call for assistance from an allied order. The warning of danger, of dysfunction, of the sparks that would ignite a fire if they weren't smothered. A chance, he thought, to explain—because they all wanted the same things here. The Imperial Guard was mistaken.

There, though: the thief, the survivor, the boy full of adrenaline eyeing all the exits because being caught was unthinkable, intolerable, and that shouted order meant the trap was closing quickly. Treason was beyond him—a distraction, a shield.

He turned to Amadea, the words still sliding into place—*also called Lireana Ulanitti, the Grave-Spurned Princess*—as if she might have a plan, might know the way out.

Amadea's porcelain expression had shattered—she looked haunted, terrified. And all Richa's thoughts slammed back together. It was true, and here he was, and there wasn't time to weigh his decisions.

"We need to get out of here," he said.

Stellano withdrew from the window, regarding his companions with a spreading smile. "Pigeon," he murmured, "do you remember that time in Razaj?"

The memory came fast to Richa—a job gone bad, a flight out of the port city, a runaway carriage, a whole lot of arrows. "Stellano. No."

"Oh yes," he said, sheathing his knife and coming to his feet.

"You can still drive a carriage, right?" He threw the door open without waiting for an answer—there wasn't time, after all.

"Hold tight," Richa said to Amadea, and clambered out the opposite window as fast as he could, up and over and into the driver's seat.

Stellano emerged from the carriage, seized hold of the roof, and swung out, kicking the two guards on foot in the face. As their heads snapped back, their grips on their crossbows loosened, and he hooked one with a heel, kicking it back into his grip.

Richa didn't watch the rest. He slid into the empty driver's seat and took the reins. He whipped the horses across the haunches, and the carriage launched into motion. The horses blocking the road shied at the sudden movement, but Richa whipped the carriage horses on.

He looked back to see the guards pursuing, but Stellano clung to the carriage roof with not one but two crossbows and a spilling quiver of bolts.

"How the fuck—" Richa started.

"I'm very good!" Stellano shouted back, laughing, and fired a bolt at the pursuing guards.

Focus on the road, Richa told himself. The horses would catch up to the carriage; the guards were better armed and trained for this. If he could get a little distance, a little space—

There. The road went up over a sudden hill, curved along the cutbank of the river, behind a stand of trees, and headed toward Terzanelle.

"Hey!" Richa shouted. "Gotta jump! Once I pass the trees!"

"The river?" Stellano shouted back.

Richa didn't answer—if Stellano didn't like stupid questions, he shouldn't ask them. Richa knotted the reins around the carriage frame, hoping the horses would keep running.

"Get the prince," Richa shouted to Stellano, then swung down the side of the carriage, to yank open the door. He reached for Amadea. "Come on, give me your good arm."

He pulled her to him, covering the back of her head as he jumped free, rolling down the grassy slope and plunging off the edge of the bank and into the swift and icy water. She clung to him as they both kicked up, into the air, gasping.

He heard Stellano and the consort-prince break the water and glanced back, making sure Ibramo could swim, injured as he was. But in the moonlight, he saw them both, Stellano and the consort-prince, carving through the water, back toward the high cutbank. Richa towed Amadea there, and the four of them huddled close beneath a moss-patched log washed against the steep bank, listening to the thunder of hooves riding on after the runaway carriage. He did not move until they'd faded into the distance.

Amadea clung to him one-armed, her injured wrist tucked to her chest, her glassy gaze on the river beyond the pale curls of strange moss drooping down from the jammed log. She was shivering, her breath erratic, panicked.

"Are you all right?" he asked.

"I didn't," she managed. "I didn't. I was still helping her."

The empress—the Red Mask, the danger over the wall, Lady Sigrittrice, and the rumors of the empress going as mad as her uncle. "I know," he said calmly. "You're not the treasonous type."

Her gaze slipped to him, watching him out of the corner of her eye, all wariness. Because she was the type, a little, if she was the Grave-Spurned Princess. *Saints and devils, five broken kings.*

This wasn't the time. They needed to get out, Richa thought. Make for the opposite bank, get to where the guards wouldn't track them. "Any ideas?" he whispered to Stellano.

"There's a sheep barn a few fields that way," he said, nodding at the shallow slope of the opposite bank. "Warm up, dry off without a fire, maybe."

"One at a time," Richa agreed. "You all right to run?"

Ibramo made a face. "I've been better. But I'll make it. Amadea?"

"I have her," Richa said.

"Let's go," Stellano said, and dove down under the water, swimming across the flow of the river. Ibramo waited a moment, then followed.

Richa waited until Ibramo climbed up the other side without alerting the guards down the road. Amadea still wouldn't look at him.

"This...this is why you're always holding people at a distance, isn't it?" he said quietly. "Why you found it so easy to forgive my past? Why you knew about the venom?" He paused. "Why you're so protective of your archivists? You don't want anyone to use them the same way. You can't change what happened, but you'll do every-thing to keep someone else from the same sort of pain."

She swallowed as if it hurt. "I'm just me," she whispered. She looked at him again, sidelong. "I wanted to tell you. I tried, I did, but I was—" She drew a long, shaking breath. "The only good rea-son I kept it from you was that this was supposed to keep you safe, and now? Now...I didn't turn on the empress," she said, even softer. "I didn't, I swear."

"I know," he said. Whatever other surprises came out of this night, he was certain down to his marrow that wasn't going to be one of them: she wasn't a traitor. "It honestly didn't even cross my mind that you would. For starters, where would you find the time?"

That startled a laugh from her, and she looked on him with such gratitude, such relief that it suddenly felt absurd that he'd ever felt like she held him at a distance. She bit her lip, as if considering, and they were so close, she was so solid in his arms.

There was a time when all of Richa yearned for someone who had figured it all out. Someone he would follow down to demon-hell, just because they didn't break their stride. He had wondered, a little, if that was why he couldn't stop thinking about Amadea Gintanas—an old habit, an old wound, an old gap you couldn't fill on your own.

But Richa—all here, all now—knew she hadn't figured it out. She was holding all the broken pieces together, a shield against grief and harm, just the same as him. Which meant she wasn't a bad habit, an easy plaster for that old gap in him. She was herself, and all these feelings were his.

The words all tangled together in his mouth, the feeling too com-plex to speak. *I am falling in love with you for you*, he thought.

"You should run," she said, her voice steadier. "You should go back to the city. They can't blame you, you were abducted—"

"I'm not going to leave you," he said. "I couldn't."

Her protests faded, a soft sort of surprise washing over her face as he felt some of the tension go out of her. He pulled her a little nearer, the only sound their breath and the water lapping around them—

A short, sharp whistle sounded from the other side of the river, like the call of a nightjar—but Richa recognized the signal. Stellano was getting impatient, and probably for good reason.

"We need to go," he said.

"Right," she said, looking out toward the river beyond the hanging moss. "Can you follow close? I'm not sure how well I can swim like this."

"Here—hold tight and I'll tow you. Spare your arm."

She started to move around behind him, but she froze as she did, her eyes on the log. "Wait." She reached out and grabbed the pale curly moss, knotting her fingers around it. She pulled...and it did not budge, but her weight lifted off his arms before it tore suddenly, and she slid back down.

"What is that?" Richa asked.

She held open her palm, rubbing a thumb across the pale fluffy fibers. They rolled together, tangling into a bundle. "It's wool," she said gravely. "Wool growing out of the log. Someone brought a sorcerer this way."

CHAPTER TWENTY-TWO

The sheep barn sat alone on the edge of a pasture, locked up tight for the night, but the sheep seemed to have broken free of the building, the door splintered apart, the herd of them pressed against the fence a hundred feet off, looking at the river. Amadea regarded them, rolling the wool she'd yanked free of the log between the fingers of her splinted hand. *Iosthe of the Wool*, she thought. A sorcerer. A sorcerer who crafted organic wonders. The perfect material for Redolfo's weapons.

Amadea squeezed through the broken entryway and dropped to the straw-strewn floor while Richa cleared space to build a small fire. The pungent smell of the sheep hung moist and ever present despite their far-off bleating. She wanted quiet; she wanted a rest. She wanted a moment alone with Richa. She wasn't getting any of that.

In truth, it was taking most of what Amadea could manage not to just give up. The empress had named Amadea a traitor—she hadn't even been declared that during the Usurper's coup. She had only been following Sigrittrice's orders—orders she'd been unconvinced were the right course of action. She'd promised Beneditta proof, not realizing Beneditta had gone too far to wait for proof.

You are never going back to the archives, she thought, and she swallowed a scream of rage and frustration that burned in her throat. What did she want if the world fell apart? She wanted her refuge, her safety, her archivists, it seemed.

The one with the spiraling bone specialist—Tunuk had left through the eastward gate, and that meant only one thing. The fire crackled to life, its warmth sliding through the physical chill of her wet clothes. She shed the outer layers, laying them by the fire to dry. *Dry straw, blue cloak, green river weed*, she recited. *Start with the small things.*

"That guard said a bone specialist went ahead of us," she said. "That means Tunuk and the others must be going after Qalba. She said in her letter that Dushar should meet her in Terzanelle. I need to catch up to them. If Tunuk's spiraling..."

"Who's Qalba?" Stellano chimed in. "Another traitor?"

Richa turned to him, his eyes narrowed. "Your confederate. The one trying to blow you up."

"Not Qalba," Stellano said. "My ul-Shandiian this time is called Oshanna."

"You didn't know." Amadea shot to her feet. "She's still out there. Oh, saints and devils—Tunuk thought she was going to go after Qalba. That's who they're following." She cursed again and again. So much for small problems. "I have to go after them."

"Doesn't sound like you're going anywhere," Stellano said. "The Imperial Authority's on the hunt, and they'll find you in Terzanelle just the same as Arlabecca."

"He's right," Ibramo said, fury rising in his voice. "But that brings us to the question: Why are we even discussing this with the man who kidnapped Amadea?"

"Because, Your Highness," Stellano said, "you don't want me to run back to the guards. It's not often I'm the least wanted person in a room, and I don't think you want me to put that distinction to use."

"He's right," Amadea said, cutting off further conversation. "And he might be useful. I hope you appreciate, though, esinor, if you try anything with that dagger again, you are likely to regret it."

He laughed once. "If it pleases you to think so."

"Saints and devils," Richa spat. "Look, considering we all know what Yinii can do if she has to, we have to hope those three will handle their own trouble. Why does the empress think you two are traitors? Why has Lady Sigrittrice been arrested?"

Ibramo shook his head. "Dita...the empress has been growing agitated. Amadea saw. We all know there's a threat beyond the Wall, and the more Sigrittrice tries to tell her it's fine, the more Dita pulls away."

"And she won't listen," Amadea said, remembering Beneditta's violent reaction to Lady Sigrittrice's attempts to calm her down.

"She worried Gritta was controlling her," Ibramo said quietly. "That she couldn't be trusted. I assured her Sigrittrice has nothing but the empire's best interests in mind and therefore Beneditta's... but I don't think she believed me. Obviously," he added bitterly, "since she's decided I'm a traitor and in league with Sigrittrice of all people."

Something small and shrinking in Amadea shied away from the image of Ibramo and Beneditta speaking so closely, so intimately. *That is his oath*, she reminded herself. *That is his role.*

That's his wife, she thought. *And she's turned against him.*

"I didn't have time to look for your functionary," Ibramo said. "The hospitallers didn't even want to let me leave the House of Unified Wisdom. I told Sigrittrice when I came back, which is when I found out she'd sent for you, and you hadn't shown up." All the worry and fear he'd felt shone on his face as he looked up at her, and she wanted so badly to take his hand. "That was more pressing."

Instead, Amadea held up the wool. "I think we have evidence at least one has already been moved again. Iosthe of the Wool. From Endecha to Sestina to Terzanelle?"

"Do you think Lady Sigrittrice is working with your father?" Richa asked. "Do you think she ordered the sorcerer moved after you told her?"

"No," Amadea answered quickly. She thought of what Sigrittrice had said in the little room during Lord Obigen's memorial. *We are meant to rectify the natural failings of a monarchy. We are made to be perfect, just rulers, to devote ourselves to the good of Semilla. To resist the urge of tyranny and self-enrichment.* She was as designed for the Imperial Authority as Beneditta was. As Lireana had been.

Ibramo gave Amadea a dark look. "You can't be sure. She's a power unto herself—and she's been happy enough to ruin lives and meddle in what shouldn't concern her."

"I..." Amadea faltered. She couldn't explain—not without

speaking the Ulanittis' secret. But that secret changed the nature of everything they were dealing with. Beneditta was acting in what she believed were the best interests of the empire. Sigrittrice had been acting in the best interests of the empire.

Appolino Ulanitti, the Fratricide, Lireana's uncle who had left her for dead among the bodies of her family—he had been acting in what he believed were the best interests of the empire too. Every Ulanitti was shaped with the Venom of Changelings and the Venom of Khirazj to be an ideal ruler, a dedicant to the empire—but then, each Ulanitti was a person of their own. Ibramo was right; it was folly to set the whole empire on one person. Which was why Semilla wasn't really settled on one person.

Amadea lifted her head. That had been Lady Sigrittrice's role. Shape the emperors and empresses, make them what they need to be. Mold them with the venoms and then train her successor to carry on the art.

If Sigrittrice died on the hangman's noose, then the secret died with her.

And that secret might be the only way to save Beneditta from herself.

"Is Sigrittrice in the Imperial Prison?" she asked.

Ibramo shook his head. "I assume so? Unless Beneditta's had her executed already."

"No, she'll want a trial. She'll want to sway the public to her side." Amadea stood and paced the edge of the fire, forming plans. It would be dangerous; it would be difficult. It would mean breaking several promises, to herself and others. She stopped before Stellano.

"I need you to get back into the city," Amadea said. "I need you to carry a message to Bishamar Twelve-Spider at Nanqii ul-Hanizan's residence. Can you do that?"

Stellano raised an eyebrow. "Are you friends with the reza ul-Hanizan, esinora?"

"We have mutual interests," Amadea said.

"But I'm not sure you and *I* do," Stellano said. "What's in it for me?"

"A pardon," Ibramo said.

"Your Highness, I don't think that's wise," Richa said.

"Right in one, Pigeon," Stellano said. "Why would I accept a pardon from the consort-prince, who is not merely out of favor with his wife but actively being hunted as a traitor to the Imperial Authority? Your pardon's not worth sheep shit."

Amadea stepped closer to him. "You're not a fool," she said. "I am well acquainted with men who are not fools. Your patron is dead. Your name is on the Kinship's lips. Who knows how many people marked you stealing that carriage? And beyond that…" She tilted her head, studying this man. "You don't *want* to disappear. And that's your other choice: disappear completely."

Stellano raised his chin. "I'm very good at disappearing."

"But not permanently," Amadea said, remembering what Richa had told her—a man who needed to be seen, a man who wanted to be adored. She found she hated Stellano, hated what he'd done to Richa, but he was the tool she needed right now, and even a hateful man was a person.

"It's horrible," she said, "being left aside, being ignored. Being erased. And right now you're connected to two very high-profile criminals. You can't just go back to the way things were."

"I could turn you in," Stellano said. "The Grave-Spurned Princess. People would certainly talk about me then."

"And no one would ever trust you again, would they? Because that's a very high-profile betrayal, and you're in a business that runs on very fragile trusts. But… break into the city? Help stop a coup? Opportunities abound, and maybe more importantly, stories." She set a hand on his arm, turning him toward the fire. "Imagine it. You would be beyond patrons. Beyond pardons."

Stellano grew still a moment, watching the fire. Then he turned that sly smile toward Amadea. "She's entertaining, Pigeon, I'll give you that. What's the message?"

Amadea drew a deep, steadying breath. *Gray uniform. Yellow straw. Hot fire.* "Tell Bishamar Twelve-Spider that I will accept his offer, but I need him to retrieve Lady Sigrittrice from the Imperial Prison first. Whatever means necessary." She hesitated. "And if possible, retrieve the sorcerer Fastreda of the Glass with her."

"What?" Ibramo shouted, coming to his feet. "You can't let Fastreda out."

"Your father is collecting sorcerers, so Fastreda's going to be on his list," Amadea said. "And even if he isn't, Emperor Clement spared her in case she became useful to the Imperial Authority—do you think there is a moment where Beneditta is more likely to decide a glass army is very useful?"

"What happens if Bishamar won't deal?" Stellano asked.

"Then we are no worse off than before," Amadea said, "and he doesn't get my help."

"All right. And where do I report back?"

The sorcerer transfers, Tunuk, Oshanna, the proximity of the Salt Wall—there was only one place she was going right now. "Terzanelle," Amadea said.

"The Imperial Guard will be heading there," Richa said. "That's the nearest city. If they don't find us in the meantime, they'll search there." He turned to Stellano. "But you have a boat in Terzanelle, don't you?"

Stellano's smile sharpened. "I think you'll find I own nothing of the sort."

"I think you'll find the Kinship's already on to that little trick, and you can stop pretending you're clever. Name the boat."

Stellano smirked and turned to Amadea. "It's a little dhow called the *Cormorant*. I can't promise it will be in port—it's a busy ship—but when I get back, I'll track it down and put out the word that it's ready to sail." He smiled. "And if it's in port, I suppose you can make yourselves comfortable, so long as nobody sees you aboard."

"Thank you," Amadea said.

Stellano picked up his jacket, grimacing at the still-damp lining. "Is it true?" he asked, sounding more curious than worried. "Is Redolfo Kirazzi alive and plotting?"

"That's our current theory," she said.

"Dark days, then," Stellano said. "Here's hoping the reza ul-Hanizan is in a listening mood." He turned to Richa. "Pigeon." And he swept out into the night.

"You can't trust him," Richa said as soon as Stellano had gone.

"I think I can trust him exactly this much," Amadea said. "I think he'll go to Bishamar if only because it suits him to sate his curiosity, and I think the reza ul-Hanizan can manage Stellano Zezurin." She tugged the sleeves of her damp blouse down as if straightening them might make the wet clothes less uncomfortable. "And he needed to leave before I said anything else."

"What did Bishamar Twelve-Spider offer you?" Ibramo asked, his voice full of dread.

Amadea glanced at Richa, not wanting to say it aloud. "He wanted assurances. A spare if Beneditta goes mad."

"He's the one?" Ibramo cried. "He's who recognized you? Fuck!"

"I know I'm late coming to this," Richa said, "but are you telling us you just agreed to stage a coup with the reza ul-Hanizan?"

"Not a coup," Amadea said. "He says he wants to keep things stable. He wants to keep the Orozhandi safe. That he only wants to acknowledge me if Beneditta can't hold the throne anymore. To be regent. I don't want that either."

"But you've offered it to him," Ibramo said.

"Because we need to help Beneditta," Amadea said. "I think we can stop this. But we need resources. And I wasn't planning on breaking anyone out of the Imperial Prison, so we use the tools at hand, which means Bishamar Twelve-Spider."

"How is that supposed to help Beneditta?" Ibramo demanded.

Amadea's stomach knotted tighter. "Because there's something you don't know. Something I swore never to tell for the safety of the empire, but... at this point, it's more dangerous to keep it a secret.

"I accidentally found out the Ulanitti family are part changeling," she said. "Including the empress. They were like that before the changeling horde; they've always been that way—it was intentional. That you could shape someone into a perfect ruler if they were mal-leable." She was talking too fast, afraid to stop. "They're locked, like changelings, when they're born. Sigrittrice is the one who does it. She said that... the Fratricide... Appolino went mad when she told him so that he could be the next one to handle the venoms. He tried to undo it, to see what he was without it, and... and he decided the only way was to wipe out the line.

"Beneditta is trying to do what's best—she can't do any differently. But...this is getting out of hand. We need to find her proof, and we need to make sure Sigrittrice doesn't take the secret with her, or we're going to have a lot of problems."

And maybe, an uncomfortable little part of her said, *maybe you need to remold Beneditta into what this empire needs.*

"Saints and devils," Richa breathed.

"Was this done to my children?" Ibramo demanded.

Amadea flushed—she hadn't considered that part. "They...Sigrittrice made it sound like when they're born, they're not...they're more like changelings. It had to be done."

"It had to be done, but no one bothered to tell me?"

"They don't tell anyone," Amadea said. "Beneditta didn't know either. It's hidden, very carefully."

"They don't tell anyone," Ibramo said, his voice growing tighter and tighter, "but *you* knew. You found out. And you didn't tell me." He pulled a mask from his pocket, shoved it back in. "You'll excuse me, I find I need some air," he said stiffly, and stormed out of the barn.

"I will be right back," Amadea said, darting after him, pushing past the broken board. "Ibramo!"

He was striding across the field, toward the milling sheep. "Ibramo, wait!" she shouted again. She caught up to him. "Ibramo, I know—"

"No, you *don't,*" he said, angrier than she could ever remember. She fell back a step. "You were livid I didn't tell you about the other two—the other two who are dead and gone and not a threat to you at all—and all the while you've been keeping this from me."

"That is not the same—" she started.

"It's *worse,*" Ibramo said.

She wanted to scream at the stars: *You don't know what it's like— you don't know, and you can't.* But was it so different? The prince and the princess were what they were—there was no unmaking their natures. There was no smoothing it over, no making it palatable. Better to swallow the truth.

"I thought I was protecting you—" she started.

"Why are you always the one who decides how to protect us, Lira?" Ibramo burst out. "Why are you the one who makes these choices? We don't need to discuss what Bishamar Twelve-Spider wants, I don't need to know about my children, we don't need to discuss Gritta's offer—you just go martyr yourself and say it couldn't be helped?"

Amadea drew back. "What are you talking about?"

"You abandoned me," Ibramo said, furious tears streaming down his face. "Do you ever think about that? You have been hurt in a thousand different ways, but you're *not* the only one. *You* decided to leave. *You* decided I had to marry Beneditta. *You* left me to fend for myself." He looked away, over the backs of the sheep. "We took care of each other. We always took care of each other. And then you were gone." He swallowed. "And now you are not thinking of me, you are not thinking of my heart or my safety or my duty. So don't tell me you are."

You don't know what it's like, you don't know, and you can't. She had not imagined Ibramo's life after her as anything but better. How could she have? She had been seventeen; she had been so afraid, so heartbroken, so sure it was all her fault, all her dangers dragging him down. She had only wanted to make sure nothing hurt him—that was how they were. Him, throwing his fear aside when she needed protecting; her, reckless when he was the one in danger.

All these excuses felt as flimsy as straw.

"Maybe," she said, "maybe you need a walk—"

"Don't talk to me like I'm one of your archivists."

Something angry flared inside her, small and bright. "I'm talking to you like you're a *person*, Ibramo. What do you want me to say? This is all really shit. It's really *shit*. There's no way around that, every part of this is unfair and cruel and absolute, irredeemable *shit* that no one can change. I am sorry. I am sorry I didn't talk to you. All I am good for is solving problems, and right now, there is nothing I want more than to do just that, but I can't fix this—and you can't either."

The fire in her, small and spitting, guttered out, and she was just so very tired. "I have never wanted more to give up," she confessed.

"To lie down and surrender and accept that this is my fate. But I know if I do that, my archivists, your children, this country—all of them will suffer. So I can't. And if I am making mistakes, then...all I can ask is that you see I'm trying."

Ibramo regarded her for a long moment, and she saw in him all the same grief, all the same weariness—and all the same persistent fierceness.

"Who told you," he said quietly, "that you were only good for solving problems?"

"Circumstances," she said. "I don't know that I wish things could have been different. Not really—there is so much we would both lose that I wouldn't want to take away. I wish, though, that they were different now. But...here we are. With the world falling apart."

"Not if we can help it," he said. He reached out and took her hands in his—a comfort, she told herself, even if an old thrill whispered through her fingertips "Terzanelle. Find the sorcerer. Find your specialist. Find somewhere to lie low while we figure out if Sigrittrice..." He exhaled hard. "If Bishamar can't get to her, you have the texts. About the venoms."

"And I have no sense of how to dose the empress," Amadea said. "It can be our emergency plan." She swallowed against the lump building in her throat. "I'm sorry. I'm sorry for abandoning you. I..."

"I'm sorry I brought it up like that," he said thickly. "We were kids. You were scared." He touched her cheek, turned her face toward him. "We would have managed much better, you and I, if it happened now."

Kiss him, the flutter in Amadea's chest urged, and Ibramo leaned ever so slightly toward her—*No*, she thought. *Stop.*

They were older and wiser, and there was a world to keep from falling to pieces. She stepped in and hugged him instead—maybe too familiar but decidedly safer, she thought.

"Come on," she said. "We'll start by finding the sorcerer."

⊷⊶ ⊠⊹⊠ ⊶⊷

Beside Arlabecca, Terzanelle was a youthful city, what had once been a solid little fishing village grown with the influx of refugees and the buildup of soldiers so near to the Salt Wall. In the distance, Tunuk could see the fabled barrier tapering away into the low mist of morning that hid the churning sea and the world beyond. Tunuk knew there were jagged rocks of shining white, like teeth threatening to shred unwary ships, where the Salt Wall continued out into the sea. The sorcerers' magic infused that salt and iron into something stranger, something greater that kept the treacherous shoals of the Salt Wall from washing away.

It was daybreak by the time he and Yinii and Quill reached Terzanelle, that mist easing back down toward the sea as the sun rose higher. The buildings did not reach so high as Arlabecca's, only a story or three, and they sloped, whitewashed and red-roofed, down steep-cobbled streets to a harbor where the masts of fishing boats poked free of the fog.

Tunuk shivered, not just from the chill. Terzanelle felt like a place between worlds, a way station between safety and peril.

"We need a plan," Quill said. "And as much as I'd like to go rest in an inn for a day, I think we can't risk it."

"She's going to head for the harbor," Tunuk said. "If she wants to lure Qalba in, she has to fly the flag of the reza off a ship in the harbor."

"And hang a green-glass lantern from the prow," Yinii added.

"So she'll be there," Tunuk said. "Waiting. We just have to find the right ship. And stop her." He hesitated, fidgeting with Biorni. "How do we stop her?"

"Depends what she's doing," Quill said.

"I think we can assume," Tunuk said. "She's got a pretty clear method to her vengeance. I don't think she's suddenly going to poison Qalba's coffee."

"So we need to find the ship, then find the explosive and...stop it?" Quill said. "Do we know how to stop it?"

Tunuk shook his head. "Do I look like a fabricator?"

"What if...?" Yinii said. "What if I just...?" She dropped her voice. "What if I *ink* it?"

Quill and Tunuk exchanged a glance. "I don't think you can make all of it into ink," Tunuk said. "There's glass and copper tubing—"

"Copper makes blue ink," Yinii said. "You have to oxidize it." She blew out a breath. "But the glass, right—I'll have to leave that."

"It's also full of naphtha and gunpowder," Quill said. "And when you made ink before, you made fire. If you make the other parts into ink, that will set everything off."

"Oh." Yinii bit her lip. "Right, then...what do we do?"

Quill looked at Tunuk. "So we just go down to the docks and stop her?"

"That's not a plan," Tunuk said. "But I don't have a better idea."

They wound their way through the slowly waking city, and by the time they reached the harbor, the mist had risen in scraps and patches enough to see across the churning sea to where the sun rose golden in the east. All along the docks, the little fishing boats were preparing to cast off. None of them flew the skull-adorned flag of an Orozhandi reza. The smell of the sea, old fish, and drying seaweed mixed with the electric scent of the Salt Wall, and Tunuk pulled the collar of his shirt up over his nose.

Somewhere in this city, Qalba might be waiting. Somewhere across that water, maybe Chizid and their child waited. How did a person survive on the other side of the Salt Wall? How was Tunuk going to react if he saw either of them again?

Yinii took out a bottle of ink and coaxed the black liquid in ever-thinning loops around her fingers, bending the path into script. *You will know them by the power of their gifts, by the relics of their affinity.*

"What do we do if she isn't here?" Tunuk murmured, his gaze scouring the boats as they departed.

"If she isn't here," Quill said, "then we have time to track down the vigilants."

"Look," Yinii said. "That's it."

At the end of the dock was a sleek cargo ship, large and meant for sailing around the peninsula, up to Ragale and Tornada and back. Its sails were folded up tight as it rocked at anchor, and from the highest mast flew the same flag that had hung on the ul-Shandiian manor—a red field, the saint's skull. At the farthest point of the prow, a green-glass lantern gleamed. The gangplank had been pulled aboard, the side of the ship a wall before them.

"I'll go first," Quill offered. "See who's up there. Boost me up."

Tunuk handed Biorni to Yinii and made a stirrup of his hands to boost Quill up to where he could grab hold of the railing.

Yinii cradled the rabbit skull, and when Tunuk turned back, he could feel the pull of her affinity tugging on his, making the thrumming of the rabbit skull faster, more insistent. The ink around her wrists shifted, wrote a new prayer: *Saint Hazaunu, guardian on the clifftop, the eye that watches the weft, and the sentinel that guides the flock, grant me a measure of your vigilance, your compassion.*

She looked up at him, her eyes a shade too dark. "Promise me something? I...I don't know what will happen. In the tunnels, that was bad. That was very bad. I...I lost myself. I hurt someone. That can't happen again."

"We're not going to let anything happen," Tunuk said. "Quill read the protocols."

"I don't think the protocols include things like stopping a madwoman who's bent on killing you," Yinii said. "It's a different level of stress." She looked up at Tunuk, and for a moment, her eyes were shining black as Alojan bone. She blinked, and they were green again. "So please don't let...don't let me forget to stay myself. I don't want to be Fastreda."

"You're not going to be Fastreda," Tunuk said, squeezing her shoulder. "You can't make ink out of seawater. So if you spiral, I will dunk you like a sailor coming into port, and right here, the water is disgusting. But I love you, and that's what I'll do. So if the ink is getting too much, think about all the old seaweed you will be covered in when I haul you back out."

Yinii shuddered, her shoulders twitching as if she could shed the imagined ribbons of seaweed. "Thank you," she murmured.

Quill stuck his head back over the rail. "No one's here," he hissed.

"What?" Tunuk reached to climb up himself, then remembered Yinii and lifted her up to Quill. He took Biorni and scrambled up after. The ship's deck was empty, gently rocking with the waves.

Tunuk went to the prow, where the required lantern hung, its piercing light washing out in the rising dawn light. He felt for the odd tug of nerves that the bones of Saint Hazaunu sent through him, but either there was no device on board, or it was too far away for him to sense.

"Maybe Qalba hasn't had a chance to see the signal," Quill said. "Maybe Oshanna went to find somewhere to wait."

Tunuk didn't answer but scanned the horizon. Far off to the east and the north, the smudge of land blurred the edge of the world. He traced a path across the choppy waters back toward the ship they stood on and out again. Across the horizon and back. How far would you have to sail to see a signal? Where would you come to shore?

Not here, he thought. Not where all the other boats were gathered, where people might ask questions about who you were. Qalba would pass any tests of salt and iron, but she wouldn't want to draw attention—

He stopped, stretched out on the prow. The ship was in the last berth along the harbor, but farther down, where the land broke off in chalky cliffs, there was a bit of beach. A jetty extended out into the water, another mooring point for incoming ships built of timber and stone. But no high-masted dhow anchored on the jetty—only one of the little fishing boats, its sail tugging against the ropes that tied it.

Standing at the boat's side were two people: an Orozhandi woman in mourning white with her back to Tunuk and another with her hands raised in submission as she backed toward the fishing boat, a tattered orange cloak hanging from her shoulders.

CHAPTER TWENTY-THREE

Iosthe of the Wool's trail was easy to follow, though not as easy as it would have been in the light of day. The moonlight caught on patches of the strange wool growing off trees and logs and even leaves leaning low over the river, but the path was muddy and shadowed, and more than once, Amadea stumbled and nearly went into the water.

When the sun broke over the horizon, they had reached where the river rushed down toward Terzanelle, the red roofs of the city still dark in the gloom, the fires on its watchtowers burning bright. A little onward the river split, the larger part flowing away from the city at an angle. At its vertex, there was a dock for unloading cargo heading to Terzanelle and then down to a shallower estuary below where the larger ships could be turned and sent back upriver.

But there was no miraculous wool. No sign of the sorcerer.

No sign of Tunuk or the others either. Which, Amadea admitted, was probably best. If there was something to see, that would mean something catastrophic had happened.

Richa came to stand beside her. "We'll find them," he said. "And...Quill's with them. This is his oath, right?"

"For their affinity spirals, I'll take the comfort," she said. "For Oshanna, that makes me more worried."

"They must have kept going down the river," Ibramo said. "It empties out a little ways down where they turn the riverboats."

They followed the towpath along the river, as it widened and slowed and worked its way toward the sea. Though Amadea's thoughts still drifted toward Tunuk, she knew rescuing Iosthe was her oath as well—all three of their oaths. Protect the vulnerable. Guide those wrestling with the affinity magic. Stand for the purpose of the empire—to preserve what the world and people's worst natures threaten.

They hadn't lately been exemplifying those oaths, Amadea thought, not in specific ways, considering the flight from Arlabecca, considering sending Stellano off, considering her requests to Bishamar. And so she felt a heavier responsibility to Iosthe, a sort of penance. This had happened because the people who should have been alert to it were not.

Amadea would not let anyone else be made into a weapon for Redolfo Kirazzi.

The river ended in a lagoon, the muddy water held back from the ocean beyond by a strip of sand and scrubby salt-briar. A wooden shack with a dock perched on the shore, a trickle of smoke rising from its chimney. A single riverboat was drawn up alongside the house, in the shadow of a conical stone tower, its outside rugged with uneven stones. A fire burned atop it, a marker for the estuary.

"In there," Ibramo said.

"No." Amadea pointed at the tower. "If they want to be careful, they'll have her in there. She can't make stone into wool. Only organic things."

Richa squinted at the tower. "One door. Probably guarded. In fact, if there's not someone sitting right against it, I'll eat the boat." He nodded at the fire at the top. "I think in through the top is the only way that's going to work."

Amadea looked at him. "Can you climb that?"

Richa sucked air through his teeth. "Maybe? Did it all the time when I was twenty. We'll need a distraction, though. Can't have them looking up at the wrong moment."

Ibramo nodded, studying the tower. "It's pointless to wish for soldiers, but I wouldn't mind a force with me right now."

"We don't even know if they're aware they're carrying out Redolfo's plans," Amadea pointed out. "And if they are, they're certainly trying to hide it. What if you just knock on the door and make demands, Your Highness?"

"Then they will most definitely wonder where my soldiers are," Ibramo said.

Amadea considered Richa. "If it's the both of you? You're both armed, if it comes to it, and they won't have heard the orders to arrest Ibramo. You'll get their attention—a vigilant and the consort-prince."

"Then who's climbing the tower?" Richa asked.

"I am, of course."

"Your wrist is sprained," Richa pointed out. "And I don't recall you having a misspent youth climbing buildings."

"This is not so vastly different from the scaffolding in the sorting facility," she said, eyeing the uneven stonework, the slanting sides. "It might be even easier. And the splint is holding."

"It's not safe," Ibramo started.

"None of this is safe," Amadea interrupted. "But you two will be more convincing together, and I have a little more experience handling someone with affinity magic in a high-stress situation."

"Fair point," Richa conceded. He looked at Ibramo. "If we need it, I assume that sword's not an ornament?"

Ibramo fished a gold mask from his pocket, his eyes locked on the tower. "Not a bit."

They made their way around the lagoon, along the shoal, and up to the tower. Amadea's confidence at being able to scale the stone wall faltered as she reached the base. The wall was much steeper than it had seemed, the stone green with moss in places.

Redolfo's voice skipped through her thoughts: *Lira, don't touch it.*

Just like the scaffolds, she told herself, and set her foot on a protrusion of stone.

"You've got this," Richa murmured, as he and Ibramo circled the tower's other side.

It was slow work, the rocks sharp on her palms, her injured arm fine for balance but useless for pulling her higher. Once a patch of moss sent her foot sliding, and for a moment, all of her was panic. But she leaned against the curve of the building, pushing herself higher and higher with each step.

The roof was abandoned as she'd hoped, the bonfire high and

bright. She could hear Ibramo's voice below, but the rush of the ocean blurred it into smoothness. There was an opening in the tower's floor and handholds carved into the stone of the wall inside to make a ladder. She listened for a moment, not hearing movement, before descending.

The room below was round, filling the width of the tower, and absolutely bare, except for an iron hatch in the floor and a Borsyan cold-lamp hanging above.

And the sleeping body of middle-aged woman, her dark hair pillowed under her head, her linen clothes thready with magically grown wool: Iosthe of the Wool.

Amadea hurried to her, but before she could reach the woman, Iosthe sat up, her eyes snapping open. She had a narrow nose with a sharply curved bridge and honey-colored skin, her huge gray eyes locked on Amadea's wool cloak.

"You're Iosthe del Sepharin?" Amadea asked.

The sorcerer nodded, reaching out for the cloak. "Please," she said, her voice high and light and hungry. "Can I see it?"

Amadea pulled the cloak off and wrapped it around her. Iosthe shuddered in a pleased way, wrapping it closer. "I'm here to rescue you. We have to go now." Amadea helped the woman to her feet. "Can you climb the ladder?"

Iosthe did not seem to hear Amadea. Worse, when Amadea steered her toward the ladder, her steps wandered and stumbled, one leg buckling. Amadea caught her. "Did they give you something? Some kind of poison?"

Iosthe only sighed, and Amadea's cloak began to unweave itself into curls and coils. Definitely drugged, Amadea thought. There would be no getting her up the ladder—there would be no getting down the tower either.

Yarny tendrils of wool twisted together as her cloak unwove itself, stroking Amadea's arms where she held Iosthe. *Every tool at hand*, Amadea thought.

She turned Iosthe around to face her. "I need you to work the wool."

A bright grin broke the sorcerer's face. "Oh good. I want that too."

Amadea looked up at the hatch in the ceiling. "Can you make

something that will help me pull you up through there? Or...something you can climb?"

Iosthe looked up at the square of lightening sky, blinking as if it confused her. For a moment, Amadea panicked, considering the iron hatch, the dangers of the way down.

Then the sorcerer flung her hands upward, Amadea's cloak unraveling to fibers. The wool twisted and spun itself back together in a score of thick strands that braided around Iosthe like a harness. They shot up through the hole, anchoring somewhere out of sight, and began weaving back together behind Iosthe, lifting her up onto the tower roof like a fish pulled up in a net.

Amadea stared, awestruck at the easy beauty of Iosthe's craft, the smooth workings of her affinity. She climbed up the stone ladder and found the sorcerer standing at the edge of the tower, the tatters of the cloak waving around her like kelp in the current.

"Can you help me get you down?" Amadea asked. "We need to get away from here and quickly."

But Iosthe wasn't listening. She was looking down at the ground, where Richa and Ibramo were surrounded by a half dozen men and women with blades.

"She's there! The jetty!" Tunuk shouted, vaulting back over the side of the boat and breaking into a run, Biorni tucked against his chest out of habit. Quill and Yinii called after him, but he couldn't stop, couldn't wait. Could only hope they would stay back from any explosives.

His long legs devoured the distance, propelling him along the rocky beach, up the boards of the jetty. He was not careful; he was not quiet—he didn't care. In that moment he wanted Oshanna to know he was coming for her.

Oshanna turned as his feet struck the boards, just enough to show what she held before her: a horned girl, lean and lanky, with reddish undertones to her brown skin and a faint swell between her horns where her dark-eye would have grown. A knife pressed to the side of her throat. Tunuk stopped short, the rabbit skull thrumming along all his racing nerves.

"You really shouldn't be here," Oshanna said. She pivoted, stepping so she could see both Tunuk and Qalba, dragging the girl with her.

"Tunuk?" Qalba said softly. She was thinner than before, her muscles hard, her face weathered. But it was her—it was undeniably her, whole and fleshed and here.

And in a lot of danger.

Tunuk held Qalba's frightened gaze. *Who would you become the monster for?* he thought. He swallowed down the fear. His gods might be rotting on far-off mountaintops, but he thought of the prayer Yinii had scrawled across her wrists and forearms: *Saint Hazaunu, guardian on the clifftop, the eye that watches the weft, and the sentinel that guides the flock, grant me a measure of your vigilance, your compassion.*

"And yet here I am." Tunuk turned to Oshanna. "I realized it was you. Why didn't you tell me?"

"Why didn't you tell anyone Nimar Eight-Myrrh's skeleton was hidden in the chapel?" she shot back. "We all have our secrets."

"Because I didn't know it was him," Tunuk said. "All I knew was that *she* had abandoned me and left some poor dead soul behind." He took a careful step forward, his hands spread. "If you had suspicions, you might have told me. We could have gotten answers a long time ago."

Oshanna hesitated. "For all I knew, you were just like them."

"I'm a lot more like you," Tunuk said, thinking about how Oshanna had changed with her father's death, thinking about how he might have changed. "He was your world. The one you counted on to watch out for you, and then he was gone. You were abandoned without anyone explaining. Do you actually think I don't know what that feels like?"

Hurt washed over Qalba's face, but Tunuk made himself think, made himself turn back to Oshanna, who said, "He didn't abandon me—they took him. They murdered him."

"That's not how it happened," Qalba said.

"I said shut the fuck up," Oshanna snapped, pressing the knife more firmly to the girl's throat. "What do you want, Tunuk?"

"Closure, I suppose," Tunuk said. "I mean, you got to take Dushar out. Lord Tafad. Toya."

"Toya was an accident," Oshanna said. "He was like you—unfortunate but not responsible."

"But you killed him."

"I was traveling to Endecha to find out where my supply of materials had gone, and there he was. In the relay station. I couldn't believe it." She looked up at Tunuk, her dark eyes shining. "I wanted him to know. I wanted to tell him I'd re-created his life's work. He wasn't as happy as I'd expected."

Qalba cursed a string of Orozhandi Tunuk couldn't catch.

"Oh?" Oshanna said. "Is 'self-defense' only a viable explanation when you're the one wielding the knife?" She spat at Qalba's feet. "Get in the boat or the girl dies. Tunuk, you want closure, get her in there."

Tunuk glanced at the little boat. In the bottom, one of the tangled devices sat, Saint Hazaunu's talus sending vibrations out from the globe, frosting the copper tubes as the energy built. There was also a chain, bound to the hull, and a pair of shackles.

Qalba stepped, shaking, into the little boat. Oshanna nodded at Tunuk. "There you are. Put the shackles on her and shove it out to sea."

Tunuk set Biorni down and moved carefully toward the boat, stepping inside its rocking hull. He lifted the chain and the shackles, meeting Qalba's gaze. "Everybody is going to see this. The whole harbor will know."

"Good," Oshanna said. "It will keep them busy. Hurry up—it takes an hour to build up the right energies, and we're getting close."

Tunuk crouched down in front of Qalba. He took her hands and set them in the shackles. Pale bone erupted along her jaw, and she flinched. "Please," she whispered. "Please. I'm sorry"

Somewhere, in the depths of Tunuk's memories, there was surely some whispered phrase, some clue he could give her that he wasn't what he was pretending to be.

Lah-aada, lah-diiqad, hiimqoqim yaa b'eh bimehem'ooqaliithem, hiimqo-qim yaa b'eh naaqitajiihem qitsilii. Her last message filled his thoughts up, useless, worthless. *You will know them by the power of their gifts, by the strength of their affinity.*

You will have to trust me, Tunuk thought. *The way you didn't before.*

His gift was the yinpay's; his strength, how easy it was to believe he
was nothing but ghoulish.

"I don't hear the latch clicking," Oshanna said.

He snapped the shackles closed, one after the other. "What's with
the girl?" he called back to Oshanna. "Are you really planning to do
the same thing they did to you?"

"Oshanna, I swear it wasn't—" Qalba shouted.

"I don't fucking care," Oshanna snarled back. "You've already
said it all. He was the bad one. He was making the weapons. He
was blackmailing you. He attacked you. Wouldn't that all be so convenient, except I don't believe a word of it. He hadn't figured out
how to trigger the explosives—you made sure Toya wouldn't tell
him that—I'm the one who solved that, I'm the one who finished
his work, because you and the Borsyans and Dushar killed him for
making a better cold-magic.

"Untie the boat," she said to Tunuk. "We'll make certain she pays
for what she did to both of us." When Qalba started to protest again,
Oshanna added, "Or I can kill the girl. You choose how you suffer,
Aunt Qalba."

"Shashkii, please," Qalba whispered. "I'm...I'm sorry for how
things went."

His heart twisted as she searched his face—hopeful, fearful.
"Maybe," he said slowly, "you should have trusted me?" He stood,
and climbed from the boat, and started unlooping the moor line,
unhurried. He glanced up the jetty—Quill and Yinii were making
their way down the beach.

Time to be the monster you know best how to be, he thought.

"So," Tunuk said, lazy with the moor line, "it's different when
you make an orphan, is that it?"

"It's an unfortunate situation," Oshanna said. "I still have to find
Chizid—he hid my father, after all. Then I'll be finished. And then
maybe she'll have a chance, not growing up with killers for parents."

Oshanna was close—close enough to grab with his long arms—but
the girl was still there, between them, and the memory of the sword
in his ribs was so hot and bright he could taste blood in his mouth.

"Didn't work out great for you," Tunuk said.

Oshanna's burning eyes widened in surprise, but she kept the knife still. "My father was a good man. He was making the world better—leaving the old ways behind."

"That's a funny way to say 'destroying a holy relic,'" Tunuk said. He was running out of rope. *Come on*, he thought. *Come at me*. "Were you really stupid enough to believe all this nonsense was going to lead anywhere new? Your saints would be appalled."

Oshanna laughed. "Do you think the saints would want us to sit in our memories and weaknesses? Saint Hazaunu would have gifted Nimar Eight-Myrrh with her wool if she were still alive. Saint Qilbat would grow sacred wooden figurines to power our new works. The bones are worth more with a purpose given to them."

"Oh yes, I'm sure the rezas will line up to thank you for the desecration. The ducal authorities all held on to their power through the collapse of the world—you think they wouldn't take this too?"

"They would have to," Oshanna said. "My father knew that. I know that."

"Oh?" Tunuk said. "Then who was meant to replace Saint Hazaunu originally, Oshanna?"

Her face went still, so full of hate and rage. "I don't know what you're talking about."

"They wanted the bones," Tunuk said, dropping the rope, keeping Oshanna's attention on him. "He was going to steal Saint Hazaunu. But for all you're so certain the rezas would come around, there was clearly a plan to replace her. So who was supposed to take Hazaunu's place when this was Nimar's plan? Was it Qalba? Was it some poor fool who was in the wrong place at the wrong time, being such a tempting sacrifice? What happened if it worked? Who was next?" He looked her up and down with disgust. "Maybe it was you. Because I don't think your father ever actually cared what happened to you. You were just a shield."

Oshanna lashed out at him with the knife, slashing across his chest. The wound stung, screamed, but he pushed past it, reached out with his long arm, and shoved her shoulder away, breaking open her grip on the girl. Qalba's daughter squirmed free, and Tunuk pulled her past him, shoving her up the jetty.

Oshanna swung her knife at him again. Qalba screamed. Tunuk dodged, his foot catching in a rotten bit of board. He slipped and fell backward, his ankle tangling in the boat's moor line. For a moment, Oshanna loomed over him, her white mourning ribbons fluttering in a breeze off the water. He kept his eyes on her as he struggled to kick off the rope. *Come on, do it, I'll go down fighting.*

But she only bent down to grab the loosened rope and tossed it out to sea. Then Oshanna turned toward the sound of the girl running slap-footed down the jetty, toward the sound of weaker prey and greater plans. Panic swelled in Tunuk, and he lunged after her.

Oshanna made it two steps before Tunuk's hand closed around her ankle, and he yanked her legs out from under her. She fell stretched out on her belly.

"Leave her alone!" he snarled.

Oshanna rolled, her knife still in hand, furious as she turned on Tunuk. "I have time to handle all of you," she said.

And Tunuk felt Yinii's affinity yank on him like a sudden spiral.

—·— ▆◆▆ —·—

The world shifted around Yinii as she raced after Tunuk, the shapes of objects becoming suggestions, promises of ink she could pull into being, scribe the whole city with. *Or make the whole city ink*, she thought. *So easy.*

No, she thought. *Focus.* She held up her hands and made the ink from the bottle shift, the script becoming a prayer to Saint Asla. *Grant me a measure of your wisdom, your sureness.*

The pull of her affinity narrowed down as they ran up the rocky beach, the sand, the stones—nothing that could become ink. Her nerves threw her affinity wider, reaching reaching—

She found Quill—and the ink was in him too, all her nerves so aware of the fluids and fats and pigments that could be made. *Not that, not that*, she told it.

The jetty—all wood and water, ready to burn, ready to blend—stretched out into the sea. At the end she could see Tunuk, see Oshanna. See a young girl fighting to get free. See the boat bobbing alongside and a woman straining against an iron chain. Feel the pulse and pull of Saint Hazaunu's bone somewhere in that boat.

Red ink, she thought, the iron touching the edges of her affinity, delight in her heart. Oshanna's knife flashed out as the girl broke free and started running. Tunuk seized Oshanna's heel, and she fell forward.

Focus, she told herself.

The boat began to drift, wood and iron and flesh and linen and hemp, glass and copper and the bone of Saint Hazaunu—all caught in the waves.

"The bomb," she made herself say. "Quill, it's in the boat."

The running girl drew even with them. "Help!" she cried. "Help, she has my mother! She chained her in that boat!"

The ink in her reached for Yinii—oils, fluids, pigments. Yinii squeezed her eyes shut. *All of you, be quiet!*

"Get back to the harbor," Quill told the girl. "Hurry!" He squeezed Yinii's shoulders. "Do you think you could make ink of just those shackles? If she can get free—"

"I don't know. It might be...I might have to reach for a lot more of the magic. I'm worried I won't come back."

"All right," Quill said, holding her gaze. "How about this? You can tell this time, you can tell it's getting away from you?"

"Yeah," Yinii said, hearing the wet warbling on the edges of her voice.

"Hold my hand," he said. "Squeeze it twice if it's too much. I'll do the rest. I won't let go of you."

Her mouth was burnt bitter, ink flooding over her tongue. But she didn't shove it away, didn't push it down—she sat with it and slipped her hand into Quill's.

And she turned her mind toward the ink.

It wasn't like in the tunnels—not quite. It didn't feel like slipping under the tide anymore, more like sliding into a warm tub of water or slipping into her own true skin. That shift again, from people and objects to what could be ink, what could not be ink. Delight surged through her at the long stretch of char just waiting under her feet, the shapes of solvents and pigments moving over it—

No, she told herself, told the ink. *We only need red.*

Rubrication, a swath of emphasis—her focus sharpened and she reached out as far as she could, touched the boat—the slick, oily wood of it, the waxy fabric of the sail, the fat and flesh and char and iron, oh, so much if she just sorted it right—

Red, she told the ink, told herself. *We need red.*

She reached farther, sinking her senses into the distant iron, feeling it fray and flake and become rust. She needed solvents, though—there was fat near, easy to pull.

No—she reminded herself, that ink was a person. *Pull the water.* She drew on it, drawing the fluid away from the heavy salts, the bits of sea. A wash of red floated up the sails, made a beautiful labyrinth of a pattern.

The relic of Saint Hazaunu pulled back at her, the gift of another sorcerer making its own little eddy in the currents of her affinity. Yinii drew her power back, drew her attention away. The boards around her crumbled into char, the waters swirling up out of the sea, washing up her skirt, circling her in lines and lines of Orozhandi curses.

"She's free," Quill said, and for a moment, Yinii smiled, thinking he meant herself. But then a part of her remembered the boat, remembered Qalba. Remembered the bomb she could not break into solvents and pigments, still sitting in the bottom of the little boat.

CHAPTER TWENTY-FOUR

Richa could not watch Amadea as she scaled the tower, every part of him afraid the next thing he heard would be her body hitting the ground. Ibramo, on the other hand, didn't seem able to look away. "We ought to wait a moment," Richa said quietly. "Give her some time to get to the top."

"Agreed." Ibramo took off his cloth-of-gold mask, smoothed the edges, retied it in place. "So," he said, as if they were sitting down over coffee, "you and Amadea seem to be...working together well."

"I think so," Richa said.

"Good. That's good." Ibramo looked up at the tower again. "I just want her to be happy."

Richa did not respond—a lie, but not one meant for him. He wanted to ask about the Grave-Spurned Princess. About the other lie, the "childhood acquaintance." About where she'd come from and whether that terrifying revelation about the empress might apply to her too.

But instead he said, "What's the plan here?"

Ibramo sighed. "She's right: we don't know whether they're innocent pawns or my father's lackeys. We should figure that out. And we should keep them away from the sorcerer and Amadea."

"Agreed. So: bluster until everyone comes out?"

"And hope they don't see through it before she's clear of the tower," Ibramo said, drawing his sword and sliding it back into the scabbard as if testing the blade. "She's nearly to the top. Let's go."

Richa went ahead and pounded on the door, as if he needed

someone on the very top floor to hear it. "Open up," he bellowed. "Imperial business!"

The door opened, and a man stepped out, eyeing them both warily. When he spotted Ibramo, he straightened. "Your Highness? Uh, what...what...?"

"I've been told that a sorcerer known as Iosthe of the Wool was brought here," Ibramo said. "I've come to retrieve her—she is required in the capital."

A woman eased around the man, one hand on a sword hilt. "We just arrived," she said. "We were waiting to hand her off to the next...associate." She looked Ibramo over once, then Richa. "Would that be you?"

"Who told you to meet the transport here?" Ibramo demanded, sounding irritated, sounding in charge. "She wasn't meant to go to Terzanelle. Someone is meddling. I want everyone involved out here—whoever is responsible for this disaster needs to answer for it."

Richa kept his hands loose, his stance calm, but he watched the man and the woman, all tight and guarded.

"We had orders," the man said.

"From whom?" Ibramo demanded.

They looked at each other. "The usual way," the woman said. "They didn't mention you, Your Highness."

Ibramo stepped forward, something dangerous in his long frame. "Why would they?" he asked in a low voice. The woman stepped back. "Where are the others?" he asked.

"Are you...Who are you working for?" she said.

Something in her tone sent the hairs on the back of Richa's neck prickling. Ibramo fixed a withering look on her. "Who do you think?"

The man narrowed his eyes. "'There is no one who goes away and comes back again,'" he said, as if quoting from something. A passphrase? Richa kept his eyes on the man, ready to move.

Ibramo paused. "'But a fair welcome is given to him who follows the river of life to its end,'" he said, as if this were obvious, and Richa relaxed a little. Ibramo held the man's gaze. "Get the sorcerer and stop stalling."

Neither moved for a moment. Then the woman leaned back into the dark of the tower and jerked her head.

"You study well, Your Highness," the woman said. "But we're not singing the funerary songs. And you know perfectly well who comes back from the grave."

Five more kidnappers filed out of the tower, fanning out to encircle Ibramo and Richa.

Ibramo cursed, drawing his sword. Richa moved outward, forcing their line to follow, scanning the ground for a better weapon than his knife—

The big man who'd stood in the door disrupted his search, an axe cutting down toward Richa. Richa dodged to the side, grabbing the man's wrist as the axe came down and twisting hard, forcing the man's grip to break. He shoved him away, sending the man stumbling into the next kidnapper, and scooped up the axe.

A cry of pain—Ibramo's sword came down on one of his attackers' hands, sending up a spray of blood. The consort-prince didn't pause, forcing back another. There were too many. Richa risked a glance up at the tower and saw Amadea coaxing a dark-haired woman wreathed in waving yarn toward the edge. She needed more time.

He gritted his teeth and settled the axe in his grip as the big man untangled himself from his partner and charged at Richa.

An arrow whizzed past and sank itself in the side of the man's neck. Richa moved, turning so he could see where the archer was and keep an eye on the kidnappers—on the opposite shore, two of them. Two more arrows zipped through the air, another burying itself in the chest of the woman who'd held the door. The kidnappers broke—some retreating to the tower, some scattering along the shore.

Richa took advantage of the chaos, racing around the tower to where Amadea and Iosthe descended. Wool wrapped the sorcerer like a harness, the strands extending and knotting around the projecting stones, lowering her smoothly down the tower while she stared up at the clouds with a beatific expression. Amadea followed, slowly, carefully.

Ibramo came running up. "Where did those archers come from?"

"I don't know," Richa said. "We need to move." Iosthe slipped down the side before them, her feet settling lightly on the ground. Richa recoiled without meaning to—the eerie waving wool made him want to keep far away. But he held out a hand. "We need to go, esinora."

She blinked at him. "Of course," she said, setting her hand in his. "You should know, I'm not myself just exactly."

The shouting of the kidnappers within the tower revealed they'd discovered the sorcerer was gone. Amadea hit the ground hard, leaping from too far up. Ibramo caught her under the arms, and they started up the hills, toward Terzanelle.

As they came up over a rise, however, the archers blocked their path. One was a dark-skinned man with gray in his curls and a short-trimmed beard, the other a dark-haired woman with huge, strangely blue eyes and golden skin.

"Hold it," the man said, training an arrow on Richa. "You aren't taking her."

"We're not giving her to you," Amadea said.

The blue-eyed woman looked at her companion, then back at Amadea. "Does this happen often?" she asked in an oddly childlike way.

The man didn't answer. He was staring at Amadea's uniform. "You're an archivist." He lowered his bow. "Which ones?"

Amadea frowned. "Which what?"

He let out a small, rough laugh. "Which workrooms? Which affinity?"

Amadea hesitated, as if measuring the danger in answering. "The southern wing."

A broad grin split the man's face. "I'll be damned. I'll be damned. Wait." He tilted his head, peering at her. "You...you were in the gold rooms? No, bronze. You were in the bronze rooms."

The blue-eyed woman looked from her companion back to Amadea. "You know each other!" she said. "So she's not—"

"She's all right." The man looked over at Iosthe. "I think. Unless you're working for them?"

"We're getting her to safety," Amadea said. "We're not the ones kidnapping sorcerers."

"Good," the man said. "We came to intercept them." He held out a hand. "I'm Chizid del Hwana. This is Nell. We..." He looked over their faces again. "It's complicated, and we should get somewhere safe. I can explain better once I find my wife."

Amadea began to answer, but out on the horizon, a plume of black sprayed into the air, a geyser of inkiness on the other side of Terzanelle.

The girl screamed and screamed. Tunuk and Oshanna struggled, their bodies thudding against the jetty's boards, but Quill made himself stay focused on Yinii, focused on her hand in his. Out on the water, the fishing boats that had been heading out to sea were turning toward the jetty, drawn by the shouts.

Into the reach of Oshanna's last bomb.

"You can't turn it to ink," Quill said to Yinii, ink swirling all around her. "The naphtha, the gunpowder." The explosive was sealed up too—getting it wet wouldn't be sure to disarm it. He risked a look at the water, at Qalba swimming for the jetty, freed of her shackles—but still very close to the bomb. "Can you push it away?"

"How far?" Yinii's voice warbled wetly as the ink dripped from her mouth.

"Far as you can?" Quill said. He glanced at the boats. "Away from everyone?"

Yinii hesitated. Her eyes were green when she looked back at him. "Don't let go, all right?"

"I'm not going anywhere," he promised, and squeezed her hand once.

There was nothing in Quill that could sense the spiral, but as Yinii drew on her affinity, he could feel the absence of that sense, as if he should know why the wood began to smolder all around them, why the water pulled toward it like a miniature tide. She rose, and rose, on a swell of ink, his arm pulled to its full reach, and ink was pouring out of her mouth, out of her nose. She stretched out a hand, reaching for the boat.

The sails ignited, crumbling into dust that washed into ink. The red from the chains crawled free and added to the dark swirl, building beneath the bomb. The boat came apart, becoming an island of ink, lifting itself free of the seawater and lifting the bomb with it.

Yinii was panting, shaking. The boards beneath her crumbled, added to the building ink, and Quill leapt up onto one of the pillars. Every part of him screamed to yank her down, get her back to the beach and the sand and the things that weren't ink.

But she hadn't squeezed his hand. And the bomb was still there.

You have to trust her, he thought.

She pulled the jetty apart, board after board, adding to the cloud of ink lifting the bomb up. Her arm shook in his; her whole body trembled. He didn't dare look away.

The jetty crumbled, splitting in half, a wave of ink pouring into the terrible storm growing beneath the bomb that bobbed in its midst like a ship lost at sea.

He heard her exhale softly, as if satisfied at a job well done. And the ink burst upward in a geyser, the stream of it launching the bomb high, high into the air.

Yinii's hand twitched in his—once, twice.

Quill pulled down hard, wrapping an arm around her. He leapt over the side of the jetty into the deep water meant for the cargo ships. The freezing water forced a shout from him, and then water closed over their heads.

Oshanna twisted, the knife still in hand, and smashed her heel down on Tunuk's clutching fingers, over and over, until his grip around her ankle broke. She glanced back once at where the girl had run, then shoved to her feet.

He pushed up and lunged at her again, getting his arms around her chest and pulling her backward. Oshanna stamped hard on his foot. Pain and hot panic washed over him, pulsing with the pull of Yinii's affinity and nearly breaking his grip, but he held tight as she twisted and bone plaques sprouted all across his chest and arms, locking joints and stiffening his limbs.

If Tunuk had been a bone sorcerer, what wonders would have

been at his fingertips? Could he have grown armor of bone for himself instead of the fragile, painful plaques that erupted without intent or reason? Could he have wrapped Oshanna in bone and stopped her frantic twisting, kicking movements?

She slashed at his arm, shattering the plaque there to dust as the blade skipped off it, then coming down again, to bite deeply into his skin. He pulled away, but with the thoughts of Yinii and Quill and the girl down the jetty toward the shore, he managed to shove Oshanna back with his uninjured arm, knocking her off her feet again, toward the water and the end of the jetty.

Bleeding, seething, terrified at the edge of the spiral, Tunuk planted himself between Oshanna and the others. "If you know what's good for you," he snarled, "stay down."

He was not the yinpay—if he had been the yinpay, he would not have been afraid, he would not have been worrying about the people behind him. He would not hesitate to devour Oshanna down to her shadow, and he would not be clinging to the hope that if he held Oshanna off for long enough, surely—surely—Quill and Yinii would be here soon, or the vigilants or—in a deep and ridiculous part of his thoughts—Amadea.

But no—he wanted them here and helping, but as Oshanna scrambled up again, as the knife flashed, he also wanted them far, far away. The memory of the sword in his side pulsed along his ribs, spreading more bone plaques as the spiral wrapped nearer.

"You're not going to ruin this!" Oshanna cried, her bones erratic and clattering against the rhythm flowing through him.

"And you're not going to bring him back!" Tunuk retorted. She moved to dart around him, and he met her. The knife flashed out again, and Tunuk threw his bone-shrouded elbow into the strike, the plaque shattering under it. She slashed again, and this time he stepped into it, letting the knife plunge toward his chest, where it cracked apart the spread of bone there, skipped over it, and sliced his shoulder.

Every part of him hurt, every nerve in him pulsed with the echo of the bones and the cuts bleeding darkly down his skin. But Tunuk couldn't stop, couldn't scream, couldn't let her pass.

Tunuk's spiraling affinity swelled, the pulse becoming a frantic tattoo. The jetty groaned, moving suddenly with the waves, in a way it hadn't before. Oshanna's eyes widened, staring past him. "Saints in the canyons," she breathed.

Tunuk risked a glance back and saw boards crumbling to char, rising into a tower of ink and Yinii streaming black and red and weaving all the streams together like threads into knotwork epics.

You will know them by the power of their gifts, by the relics of their affinity, Tunuk thought. She really was a sorcerer.

Or, he supposed, turning back to Oshanna caught awestruck by Yinii's display, a saint. Whatever practicality, whatever easy disrespect she'd given to the wooden bones of Saint Hazaunu, it wavered in the presence of Yinii Six-Owl ul-Benturan, the only living saint in generations, performing a miracle.

Tunuk seized the moment and tackled Oshanna to the boards.

The air rushed out of her in a grunt, but she twisted her arm down, slamming his bleeding forearm against the jetty and forcing him into a roll. He tangled his legs around hers—he wasn't going to let her up, not until that bomb was dealt with, not until the others were safe.

She drew back an arm, aiming the knife at his eye, and he caught her wrist with the hand of his injured arm. She put all the weight of her body and her fury against that blade, and Tunuk's grip shook, his nerves shrieking to the fingertips as bone spread over his knees, his calves. Oshanna shifted, untangling herself from his locked legs, and leaned harder against the knife, against his bleeding shoulder.

A splash, a thump—

And Qalba suddenly loomed above Oshanna, sopping wet and holding Biorni by one forked horn.

Qalba dashed the rabbit skull against the back of Oshanna's head with an ugly *crunch*. Oshanna screamed and whipped up, her knife ready. Qalba swung again, hitting her in the face with the rabbit's vicious teeth first. Blood sprayed over Tunuk as Oshanna went over sideways.

"Get away from him!" Qalba shouted. "Shashkii, swim for shore!"

Oshanna got to her feet again, though swaying now, her teeth and the whites of her eyes bared and brilliant. Qalba circled as if to draw her away from Tunuk, panting and trembling—

Oshanna lunged from the swaying jetty, and Tunuk pushed himself up with all his strength into her path, shoving her and the knife she wouldn't drop away from Qalba. Oshanna stumbled, slipped on the rocking jetty, and fell harder than Tunuk had expected, her head slamming down into the metal cleat the boat had been tied to.

She twitched once, then lay still, all the jangling in her bones fading to something soft as waves on the shore.

"Tunuk!" Qalba cried, coming down beside him. She wrapped shaking arms around him. "Oh, are you hurt? Did she hurt you? What were you thinking?"

Tunuk looked at her numbly, not sure what to say. "I couldn't let her past," he managed. "Is she dead?"

Behind Qalba, he saw Yinii's swirling ink suddenly shoot into the air, the explosive atop it, glinting in the rising sunlight. Carried up and away and—

The geyser faltered, the bomb seeming to hover as it continued its path up and up and up, a tail of vapor faintly visible, as if it were steaming hot...

It takes an hour to build up the right energies, Oshanna had said, *and we're getting close.*

"Move," he said. "Move!" He seized Qalba around the ribs in the same moment, his arm and shoulder electric with pain as he flung them both into the water, just before the explosion rolled over them.

⊷⊷ ⩥⧫⩤ ⊶⊶

Tunuk remembered little of the immediate aftermath. The cold water on his skin. The dragging weight of his own body as he pulled himself up the rocky beach. Ink on everything, splattering black like an apocalyptic rain. He remembered Yinii and Quill embracing him, Qalba embracing him. Biorni clutched in his hands, though he hadn't remembered grabbing him. They had hurried to the city, away from the smoking ruin of the jetty, away from the boats and away from the vigilants rushing that way. They found the girl, and then Amadea was there—*How? When?*—weeping, pretending she wasn't panicking, and Chizid and Richa and the consort-prince, and everyone rushed Tunuk down to the docks, to a little boat in a cheap slip.

Oshanna remained, still outstretched on the end of the jetty. Alone. He felt nauseous thinking of it.

Later, on the little boat, in the cabin, sailing he knew not where but wrapped in blankets and bandages with Biorni cradled in his lap, Tunuk thought back the chapel, to the moment when he thought he'd understood Oshanna, how she'd come to this—Nimar had set the stars for her, as Uruphi would say, much as Qalba and Chizid had for him. And then he'd been taken, much the same as Qalba and Chizid had been. That fear, that loneliness, that sense of disorienting confusion and even betrayal that came in the wake of it—it changed a person, if they weren't careful.

Tunuk had to admit it had probably changed him for the worse. Those first years of finding his place, of figuring out how to be himself had been critical, treasured. The aftermath... well, maybe there was a reason he couldn't keep a generalist. And maybe that was his fault, as much as Oshanna's insane plan for revenge couldn't really be blamed on her father getting himself killed enacting his own insane and dangerous plans.

Tunuk cradled Biorni's cracked skull against his chest and felt the overlapping pulses of the broken bone, now put to new use and echoing with a new voice. After all, there'd been the baby to consider, the girl they had named Hazaunu, after the hidden saint.

But...

Tunuk turned Biorni to face him. He was angry still—hurt and angry. They had their reasons, he understood their reasons, and still something seethed in him. He'd missed them, mourned them. He'd fought *so hard* to clear Qalba's name, and now they were here, and they were alive, and they were so happy to see him, and he could not silence the part of him that wanted to snarl and sneer and hide away. He had settled for going down into the cabin of the little boat, while the others argued in hushed tones about what happened next.

Tunuk found he could not even *think* about what happened next.

"Maybe I'm as broken as you are," he said to Biorni, testing the thought. The *thrum* didn't change, and Tunuk sighed. "You're going to be insufferable now, aren't you?"

"I think he's earned a little insufferability," a soft voice said.

Qalba stood there, her arms folded, her expression worried. "Can I come in?"

"It's your boat," Tunuk pointed out.

She sat down beside him, saying nothing for a long moment. "Do you want to meet Hazaunu?" she asked, not looking at him. "She's asking."

"No, thank you," Tunuk said. "I'm not exactly my best right now."

"I wanted to thank you again. For saving her. And...that young man," she said, "your generalist, he told me what you did."

"Which part?"

"Most of it," Qalba said. "That you...Tunuk, I can't believe..." She stopped, as if trying to keep herself from crying.

"That I thought you were dead?" Tunuk said sharply. "That I lied to Amadea about the wooden bones? That I nearly got myself killed chasing after the woman who wanted you dead?"

"That you still defended us—me," she said, and the tears broke free, "after all we did to you. I have regretted every day—*every day*—leaving you behind. I knew we couldn't ask you to come with us—it was so dangerous, and you couldn't break your parents' hearts like that, I know you. I knew you," she amended, softer. "And we couldn't tell you why—it would make everything more dangerous if they thought you knew where we were. But of everything, I regret leaving you alone the most."

Tunuk nearly pointed out she'd killed her cousin and worked for the Usurper, so did she really regret leaving him *the most*? But he caught himself. He was hurting, but she was too. And if there was a future where they weren't both in pain, it did not come by way of him being sharp and cruel to protect his own heart.

"Well," he said, his voice thicker than he'd have liked, "it's a good thing you didn't actually leave me alone. I have friends. People who care for me. Amadea."

She smiled through her tears. "I see that. They all seem wonderful."

He turned Biorni over, ran a finger along the crack in the parietal bone, feeling the thrumming working its way up through his own bones, nudging it back into rhythm with itself and healing the relic he'd made his own.

"I don't know how we...talk now. It's been twelve years. It feels like you just left."

"'All great things pass in a moment and an eternity,'" Qalba recited. "We'll find our way, shashkii. If you're willing."

Tunuk nodded, not trusting himself with the words. Qalba reached over and took his hand in hers, slowly so that he could pull away if he wanted. But he let her, intertwining their fingers and leaning against her.

"I'm very glad," he said quietly, "you aren't dead. All three of you."

"Mama?" A small voice near the door spoke. The girl—Hazaunu—stood there, half hidden by the doorjamb. "Baba wants to know if we can all come down yet. Nell's getting...agitated."

Qalba sighed. "Baba wants to know, or you want to know?"

Hazaunu shrugged in a jerky way. She was all limbs and joints—he could practically hear her long bones growing. Her large eyes kept flicking from her mother to Tunuk. To Biorni.

"Can I see it?" she asked boldly.

"Shashkii," Qalba said sternly, "I know you're excited—"

"I didn't pester him—I asked about the skull!" she protested. "It's pulsing and it's *interesting*. Are you fixing it?" she asked Tunuk.

Tunuk blinked at her. "Are you a bone specialist?"

Hazaunu touched the little charms hanging on her horn. "Yes," she said, a little warily. "Like my parents. It doesn't always happen that way, I know that."

"Listen," Qalba said, squeezing his hand and coming to her feet, "I have to help Chizid with Nell. We're going to need the cabin for her—if the bones are too loud after all that, I can make you a nest on the deck?"

"It's fine," Tunuk interjected. Hazaunu inched inside the room.

"If she bothers you," Qalba said, looking significantly at her daughter, "tell her so, and she will leave, won't you?"

"Yes, Mama."

Qalba left the cabin, and Hazaunu sat down on the bench beside Tunuk, tucking her legs up under her and eyeing Biorni in a covetous sort of way.

"I'm not giving you my rabbit skull."

"Who said I wanted it?" Hazaunu asked, folding her arms against her, as if Biorni might leap into them otherwise.

Tunuk held Biorni out. "You can work on one of the cracks."

She reached out and touched the crack that split the zygomatic arch with careful fingers, petting it as if it were a butterfly's fragile wing. "They talk about you," she said, so softly he almost didn't hear her. "All the time."

Tunuk made a face. "Why?"

"About how you were. About how I should be more like you." Bone spidered over the crack in the arch, building with each touch. "I used to wonder if you were my brother. But I guess not. Not in the usual way, anyway."

"Not in the usual way," Tunuk agreed.

Chizid came through the door, guiding the woman Nell, who had been wrapped in oilcloth from her head to her hips, as if she were an easily spooked horse. Chizid offered Tunuk a weary sort of smile as he guided Nell to the bench beside Hazaunu. "You all right?" he asked.

"I've been better," Tunuk said. Then: "I will be better."

Chizid grinned. "That's good to hear."

Nell tucked her legs up and wrapped the oilcloth around them, shivering. She poked her face out through the folds.

"Do you want some more?" Chizid offered.

"No," she said nervously. "I want to be alert. Have you checked this boat thoroughly? There's no leaks? None at all?"

Chizid smile turned rueful. "All boats have a little leaking. But there's nothing to be afraid of."

Everyone followed. Quill and Yinii tucked in close to Tunuk. Amadea and Richa, the consort-prince and the dozing wool sorcerer sat on the other side of the cabin. Chizid crouched down to sit on the floor, while Qalba stood, looking as if she wanted to be anywhere else at all.

"This," she said, "has gotten very complicated. But I think we need to all be clear on what's happening and what we're planning to embark on. To begin with, where we're sailing."

"I assume it's not Tornada," Tunuk replied.

"You went over the Wall," Amadea said. "That's where you escaped to. That's where you're heading?"

"Yes," Chizid said. "It was... Well, everything got very dangerous very quickly. What's a little more danger?"

"But you made a life there?" Richa asked. "You seem like you survived, even thrived."

"We weren't alone," Chizid said.

"It's not like they tell you," Qalba said. "Not exactly."

"Hold on," Quill said, fumbling with his wet clothes. He pulled out an iron charm, shaped like a grimacing cat. He took it off and thrust it at Qalba. "You came from over the Wall. You need to prove you're safe."

Qalba hesitated.

"She went in the salt water," Tunuk said. "Leave her alone."

"No, shashkii," she said. "I said we'd tell all of it. I said we need to trust one another." She took hold of the amulet, laid it across her palm, and showed it to Quill. Then she handed it to Chizid, who did the same and tried to hand it back to Quill.

"There's four of you," Quill pointed out.

Chizid reluctantly handed the charm to Hazaunu, who took it, looking around confused at everyone else.

"Does it do something?" she asked. She tried to hand it to Quill.

"Give it to Nell," Quill said.

The woman beside Tunuk went even more rigid. He turned with dawning horror.

"No," Nell said in a small, shaking voice. "Please. Put it away."

"Are you a changeling?" Tunuk demanded, pushing away from the woman wrapped in oilcloth. She blinked at him with her weirdly blue eyes, as if he'd spoken gibberish.

"Hey, it's all right," Chizid said, though whether to Nell or Tunuk, it wasn't clear. "We're all friends. We're all on the same side."

"That's the first of it," Qalba said. "We're not alone on the other side, and they're not all the same." She turned to Amadea. "And the rest... the rest is that, of late, it's getting much worse for all of us. And I think someone from here needs to see exactly how bad."

VII

WHAT FEEDS THE FOREST

Summer
The Black Mother Forest, Borsya

The girl follows the trail of broken branches and footprints in the dirt, never looking back at the marks she leaves, never looking back at the body lying dead in the leaf fall. The red-winged birds flock alongside her, chasing her steps, but they don't sing their awful song again. The leaves shiver as she runs, as if the trees are hissing at her.

She hears wings rushing through the air behind her, but she doesn't look back to see what they belong to. The trees change again, their dark limbs knobbed with a round, glowing blue fungus that looks almost like eyes—or perhaps it's just the feeling of the Black Mother Forest watching her, assessing her that makes her think that.

Three tests, three trials, she thinks.

Stay or go.

Protect Melosino or protect Redolfo.

She dares a look down at her hands, dark with greenish blood, then back at the path behind her, the marks of her passing, the smears of blood she's left. There will be a third trial before her, and she needs to keep her mind focused on that.

A wind races through the leaves, a sound like waves crashing on the shore. The air feels cooler as more and more of the trees are covered in that blue fungus, those searching eyes. She keeps her own eyes on the faint and fainter footprints until she cannot find them anymore. Until she is moving forward through the watching trees and the gathering birds by feel alone, too afraid to slow down.

The trees clutch closer to her path, nearly blocking the way. The sound of wings drowns out the leaves' hissing. She will die here, without a third test, alone in a distant land, in the mouth of a god who finds her wanting.

And then...she reaches the heart of the forest, the breath of the waiting god.

The two locked changelings stand outside a clearing as wide as a city road where the leaves do not fall. Redolfo kneels in the center, the bag from Orozhand discarded behind him, the bones of the saint laid out in the bare dirt, pieces of the strange fungus strewn among them.

He looks up as she crosses the boundary, alert and angry, but then he sees the state of her clothes, the blood on her hands, and his gaze turns surprised. Pleased, perhaps.

"There are hunters coming," she says.

"Let them," he says, gesturing at the grove.

The girl follows the sweep of his hand. The trees that surround the clearing are the largest she's seen yet, as big around as her circled arms. Still smooth midnight bark, still the heart-shaped leaves that shiver like a hiss, still the blue fungus, knobby and glowing all along the branches like strange pustules.

But here, there are bones.

Skulls scream in the folds of trunks, glowing fungus rooting in their eye sockets. Elbows protrude like lopped-off branches where the wood has enfolded them. A hand still strapped together with sinew reaches from a hollow, as if its owner is trying to pull free. Every tree she can see holds a skeleton within its wood.

"What is this place?" she whispers.

"Fastreda used to tell me," Redolfo says, a quiet reverence in his story for once, "that she was 'not so old as to be fed to the forest.' A

Borsyan saying. She thought it was metaphorical. They're sorcerers, I think. And if I'm right..."

He looks down at the bones and the fungus. Something moves there, wriggling below the earth. She hears him suck in a breath, and they both stare as tiny seedlings sprout from the dirt, their roots creeping over the offered bones. They grow quickly—spurred by magic—and Redolfo takes out his knife and cuts the dirt around them, wrapping the seedlings, bones and all, in strips of cloth, before returning them to the bag that held the saints' bones. The forest shivers all around them.

"What are you doing?" the girl asks.

Redolfo smiles. "Taking what we cannot find within the Salt Wall. I should think the forest would like to see the world as well, don't you?"

The sound of wings comes again—the wind of something's passing, shivering through all the leaves. The girl turns as the changeling guards cry out, as two terrible shapes plunge into them, bearing them to the ground by their throats. A third creature lands between the fallen guards, entering the clearing on feet not meant to tread the earth.

She is sleek with black feathers, her wings held high as if to emphasize her size, the ease with which she might rise in the air. Four legs that end in vicious talons, extend with too many joints, pick their way over the dirt. Her feathered neck is too long, her eyes too large and too yellow, her mouth too wide and far too full of teeth as she tilts her head too far to one side and inhales.

"A crow-winged daughter," she hears Redolfo whisper, and at the shock of his voice, she knows this, too, he expected to be metaphorical.

The crow-winged daughter speaks, a language full of clicks and long vowels, a phrase full of fury.

The girl shakes her head in confusion. "What does that mean?"

"It's Borsyan," Redolfo says. "She asks why we're here. No one has come here in ages." He answers, but the crow-winged daughter only looks at the girl.

"What did you tell her?" she asks.

The crow-winged daughter speaks, her eyes unblinking on the girl. Redolfo starts to answer, and the creature retorts. The girl can hear the changelings torn apart by the crow-winged daughter's sisters.

"I told her we've come for the gift of the Black Mother Forest. She says we can't take it yet. She says you have only begun to pay the price."

The girl spreads her hands, green with the blood of the only brother she can be sure she had, and she wants to weep, wants to vomit, wants to give herself to the crow-winged daughters to be torn into pieces.

The crow-winged daughter lumbers forward, her wings still held high, to sniff the girl's face, and the girl, for all her fear, for all the teeth that are there, just inches from her skin, holds still. If she falls, then Redolfo falls, and then everything has been for naught.

The creature speaks again, revealing more rows of tiny razor teeth, a blackened tongue. Redolfo interprets the words: "Give me your name."

The girl blinks. She doesn't have a name—she lost it. The first in the swirl of memories, the second to that other, better her. She is no one. But she cannot say this, not with Redolfo listening, not to the crow-winged daughter with her many teeth, her vicious talons, her too-long neck.

Three tests, she thinks. *Three trials.*

Stay or go.

Melosino or Redolfo.

No one, or...

The crow-winged daughter's sisters crowd close to her, their muzzles greenish black with the blood of the changelings. The little red-winged birds crowd the branches of the skeleton trees.

She is the one who survived, she thinks. She is the one who can still survive. She is the one Redolfo will have to choose. And why shouldn't she be? Why shouldn't *she* be the one? Why couldn't she be the princess who survived, the heir to the throne?

"My name is Lireana Ulanitti," she tells the crow-winged daughter. "I have come for the gift of the Black Mother Forest so I may retake my empire. I have passed the trials. I have given you sacri-fices. And now I will leave."

There is something in her voice, or perhaps in her stance. The crow-winged daughters all fold their wings tight and sidle backward as she takes hold of Redolfo by the arm and, like a princess—like an *empress*—leaving her court, strides from the forest out into the world, a seed of righteousness, of vengeance, unfurling in her heart.

CHAPTER TWENTY-FIVE

In the back corner of the Imperial Archives, Bijan del Tolube's workshop had become a clandestine meeting room.

"She wouldn't do this," Stavio said stubbornly, his writhing tentacles belying his nerves. "Amadea isn't a traitor."

"Right, but where is she?" Zoifia demanded, perched cross-legged on Bijan's worktable. "She wouldn't just run off either."

"Maybe they caught her," Radir said, worried. "Maybe she's already in prison."

"And Yinii?" Zoifia demanded. "*You* were supposed to watch out for Yinii."

"I'm not a miracle worker! Yinii's probably with Quill and Tunuk."

"Who are where?" Stavio demanded. He turned on Bijan. "Bedo, what do we do?"

Bijan remembered the coup and the war, the way the authorities' clashes had trickled down. He had been a child then, a quiet observer, and not the one anybody looked to for help. Now Amadea was gone, and Mireia was being watched, and everyone was afraid. "We need to be careful," he said. "They searched Amadea's office, so they might come back and search the whole archive."

Zoifia snorted. "What would they find?"

"Depends," Bijan said. "If the empress already thinks we're the enemy? Whatever she wants to find. That's what I mean when I say we have to be careful."

The bell high on the wall started jangling, the summons to the head archivist's office. They all stared at it. "I don't think I ever heard that ring," Stavio said.

"Maybe she has a ruby emergency?" Radir suggested.

"Why are you this stupid?" Zoifia demanded.

"Stay here," Bijan said. He leaned close to his husband. "*Please* keep them calm."

Stavio kissed his cheek. "I'll do my best. Don't get arrested."

"I'll do my best." Bijan made his way down to Mireia's office, keeping his thoughts away from what she might say, what he might hear. *There is no point in worrying*, he told himself. *Find out what it is first.*

Sunlight sliced through Mireia del Atsina's office windows like facets of a gem reflecting out in sharp angles. Mireia sat behind her enormous wooden desk, looking as if the last week had aged her beyond even her many years. Opposite the desk, a woman in a tailored green gown sat, her dark hair pulled back in an artful bun, her long eyes enhanced with an edging of kohl, the scent of jasmine heavy in her perfume.

A functionary? Bijan wondered. A noble from the farther cities?

"Archivist del Tolube," Mireia said. "This is Esinora Khoma Seupu-lai of Hyangga."

The woman stood and took Bijan's hand in a firm grip. "A pleasure, archivist," she said briskly. "Where is my son?"

"Oh," Bijan said, glad he hadn't tried to guess. "You're Quill's mother."

"Yes," she said with a tight, impatient sort of smile. "He's apparently forsaken his oath, and now I hear he's run off. The head archivist thinks you might know—"

"Have you heard from Quill, Bijan?" Mireia asked.

"He...went with our bone specialist to Terzanelle," Bijan said, repeating the report sent by the vigilants. "I'm sure they'll be back soon."

Khoma searched his face. "Why did they go to Terzanelle?" she asked. "No one's offered me that information."

"I believe because the bone specialist was at risk of an affinity spiral. There's a respite cabin near there."

"Where they are not. So where is my son? And if you don't know, who should I be asking?"

Bijan hesitated. "I'm not sure, esinora. But we want him back, too."

A commotion rose from the entry hall. Mireia came to her feet, swallowing a curse half spoken. "Excuse me a moment, esinora," she said, hurrying out of the office. A moment later, he heard Mireia cry out, "Your Imperial Majesty." And both Bijan and Khoma Seupu-lai hurried from the office, coming up against the railing that over-looked the floor below.

The empress of Semilla, shining as the Salt Wall in a suit of white tapered trousers and a flowing jacket, stood looking up at Mireia as she descended the stairs, her face hidden, her entourage all armed soldiers.

Bijan made a hobby of knowing the imperial masks—there was a language behind them, and he appreciated the empress's wit, her cleverness in choosing which to wear. He'd chatted often with the gold specialists about what she took from the vault and what it meant for who was in favor or what challenge she was making. He wouldn't pretend to know all the masks, but he was familiar with most.

The mask Beneditta wore was nothing Bijan knew. It was ugly, patched-together fabric on a full-face base, only her dark eyes show-ing. Red velvet, red brocade, red wool, red cotton—it looked like raw flesh stitched together.

Beneditta had been forbidden the Red Mask, and so she'd made her own.

"Lord on the Mountain," Khoma Seupu-lai breathed beside him. "The rumors are true."

"Your Imperial Majesty," Mireia said again, hurrying down the stairs. "What... what is it?"

Beneditta stared at Mireia for a too-long moment, and Bijan had the urge to bolt, to run back up to his workroom, to get Stavio out of here. Memories of the coup, of the war boiled up in his thoughts, and they needed to be anywhere but under the gaze of that terrible mask.

"I require the assistance of the Imperial Archives," she said, her voice muffled by the makeshift Red Mask. "I need you to locate something, for the good of the empire. I trust, Head Archivist, that I can rely on your loyalty."

⋯ ⊫✦⊐ ⋯

Sigrittrice Ulanitti sat alone in a narrow room at the peak of the Imperial Prison tower, tabulating all her sins. There were things she had done and things she had left undone. Things she had chosen that had turned out to be wrong and actions she had taken that were for the good of the Imperial Federation but that, set aside from that noble mission, taken out into the cold light, were inarguably wicked.

Sigrittrice had sent a message to Beneditta, begging for forgiveness. She had sent a message to Ibramo, pleading for an audience. She had sent a message to Archivist Gintanas, saying if she ever had any love for Semilla and her protectorates to find a way to carry a letter to her grandniece, Djaulia, to bear the secret out of Sigrittrice's inevitable grave.

She had heard back nothing.

Sigrittrice sighed. No one was coming. Beneditta had made certain of that—even the guards only slid her dishes through a gap beneath the door. Everything was falling apart. She had miscalculated for the second time in her long life.

She shut her eyes, remembered Appolino, who should have taken up the responsibility, always in his brother's shadow, never his mother's favorite. But Sigrittrice had loved him in her own way, loved him for his curious mind and his careful words. Loved him even when he'd grown into a moody, dissatisfied man.

This, she thought, sat among the worst of her sins—she, who had spent her whole life assessing risk, had mistaken the risk in Appolino to horrific effect. So many terrible things flowed down from misunderstanding that her nephew had become dangerous to the empire she had been created to love above all else.

A key rattled in the latch, and Sigrittrice's heart leapt—this was it, then. She stood, proud and erect. She might be going to the noose, but she was still an Ulanitti. She was still the granddaughter of the great Emperor Eschellado.

The guard who opened the door was a young Orozhandi woman, peering in wide-eyed and nervous. "You...you have a visitor, esinora," she said. Then, to someone behind her, she whispered, "You must be quick, Reza."

"It won't take long," Bishamar Twelve-Spider said, pushing past her. "Thank you, shashkii." He eyed Sigrittrice with bright brown eyes. "Gritta. You're looking well, all things considered." He leaned heavily on his cane as he came into the room, followed by that silver-haired grandson of his, who pulled out a chair for the reza.

"Pardon me if I don't stand on ceremony," Bishamar said, sitting down. "Time is short, and I'll need to conserve my energy for the climb back down. Nanqii, put the bag on the table and go wait outside."

The younger man did as he was bidden, giving Gritta an obnoxiously knowing smile as he set a heavy sack on the table in front of Bishamar. Once he had gone, she narrowed her eyes. "What are you doing here, Bish?"

"A favor," Bishamar said.

"What favor do you owe me?"

"Not a one." He sniffed. "I owe Amadea Gintanas."

Panic bloomed in Sigrittrice's chest. "What is she doing for you?"

"You should worry about that once you've escaped," he said. "There's a rather mouthy boy waiting to spirit you away to Terzanelle. I'm sure the archivist will have further information for you if you find her." He took out a handkerchief and patted either side of his dark-eye. "She's very convincing."

"What did she tell you?" Sigrittrice demanded.

"That she could not possibly be Lireana Ulanitti," he said. "That you said she could not possibly be Lireana Ulanitti. That it would be a very dangerous thing if I suggested she was Lireana Ulanitti. But...again, she's very convincing, I think, and that's what matters here."

"Think about who you're confessing this treason to," Sigrittrice began.

"A traitor in the imperial tower?" Bishamar asked. "A...very convincing traitor."

Sigrittrice froze. For a moment, they just stared at each other, assessing—two exceptionally canny people who had been masters of their spheres for a long, long time.

"What do you want?" Sigrittrice asked.

"I want my people safe. I want my empire sorted out. I want not to hear that people are afraid of our grandparents' perils. And that doesn't happen with you hanging by the neck."

"It happens with Lireana on the throne, is that it?"

"It happens," Bishamar Twelve-Spider said with exaggerated patience, "because someone, somehow solves the problem of Beneditta. I think you deserve that chance. I also think," he went on, "you ought to have another conversation with Amadea Gintanas."

Unbidden, the face of that young girl rose up in her thoughts, her eyes red rimmed, her pallor ashen. *Let us go, we'll disappear, I'll never even say that name again. I'm not a threat.*

"She is not Lireana," Sigrittrice said stubbornly.

"She wasn't the one I had my coin on," Bishamar said. "But you know I don't mean *that*." He heaved himself to his feet. "Now, before we get distracted discussing how I know things and why I know things and what I will do with my knowledge, let me redirect us to this moment: You need to get out of here. You know how to get out of here." He patted the sack on the table. "I leave you with this to do as you please, but I would remind you that a weapon left in your enemies' hands will be turned on you soon enough."

"Beneditta is *not* my enemy," Sigrittrice said.

"I think she'd disagree there, shashkii." Bishamar patted the sack again. "Now, your guard out there is ul-Hanizan, so she's willing to let me have a word, but she's going to lock your door as soon as I'm out, so I suggest you make up your mind quickly." He smiled at her. "It's nice to see you again, Gritta. I do hope it's not the last time."

He turned and began to make his slow way toward the door. Sigrittrice pulled open the mouth of the bag, expecting to find coins or blades or, knowing Bishamar's reputation and hers, poisons.

"Sand?" she asked, running a handful of the grains through her fingers.

Bishamar looked back over his shoulder. "Sand. For now."

And Sigrittrice understood.

There were many sins Sigrittrice Ulanitti knew would hang against her when her soul made its way through the gates of the afterlife. Always for the good of the empire.

And for the good of the empire, she would have to bear a few more sins.

"I don't enjoy it," she said to Bishamar. "I want you to know that."

"Doesn't make much difference to me," the reza ul-Hanizan said, reaching the door. "Only matters if you do it." He rapped sharply on the exit.

Sigrittrice scooped up the bag, cradling it in the crook of one arm, and moved, pushing up past Bishamar as the door opened. The guard's eyes widened in surprise, her hand going for her weapon, but Sigrittrice's own hand shot out and touched the girl's bare cheek.

"You darling thing," she said, feeling all the fear, the excitement in the young woman, the hope, the worry. "You credit to the empire. You have done such a magnificent job following orders. But this exercise is over. Stand down."

The woman's eyes searched her face, puzzled. "This was an exercise?"

"Of course it was," Sigrittrice said, pulling on that hope, pulling on that excitement with everything in her. This wasn't the force of the venoms—something in Sigrittrice sang to the girl's emotions, and they shifted to match that song. "Can you imagine me being named a traitor? But that was the test: Could you be perfectly loyal to the empress?"

The girl smiled, nodded. She raised a fist in salute. "I . . . I won't lie, esinora, I was surprised. I'm glad it was all an exercise."

Sigrittrice flicked her gaze to Bishamar and his grandson, who looked absolutely baffled but wise enough not to say anything about it. "Where did you say your . . . mouthy lad was?"

"Carriage across the street," Bishamar said, smiling like a cat full of cream. "Nice vigilant boy."

To Terzanelle. Sigrittrice did not want to think about what that boded. "Why don't you help the reza downstairs?" she said to the guard. "I'll inform the others and retrieve my mask." She hitched the heavy sand higher up on her hip. "You've done a great service, and the empire thanks you."

A firm stride and a furious expression did more work than any affinity Sigrittrice bore in her. But the guards, already on edge, already afraid, took more as she passed—a firm grip, a strong will, a calling to the working life had already done on them. Were they not this empire's loyal guards? Didn't her explanations of exercises, of tests make more sense?

They would, for the moment.

Her mind felt as if it were sizzling in a pan by the time they fetched her mask of gold, her keys, her rings. They handed them over gladly—everything was going to be all right. The cell they opened reluctantly, but everyone in the Imperial Complex knew there was a reason this cell was here, a reason the glass sorcerer had not been executed with her coconspirators. And after all, they were at war.

Fastreda Korotzma looked up at her, amused and puzzled. She crossed her glass leg over her other ankle, dragging the sharp point of it over the ground in an irritating way. "Ah, Lady Gritta. To what do I owe the pleasure?"

Sigrittrice opened the bag of sand and dropped it on the floor between them. Fastreda's living eye lit hungrily.

"What is this?" Fastreda crooned. "Is it the empress's turn to beg a glass army?"

"No," Sigrittrice said. "I'm the one asking. Your empire needs you. If you're willing."

Fastreda's sharp smile spread, and her hands reached out, the sand glowing, condensing. It rose in a shimmering spiral of glass, ready to become whatever the sorcerer wished. Fastreda licked her lips and gave a frantic laugh.

"You know the right way to ask," she said, beginning to shape the glass. "And I always know who to choose."

The story continues in...

Books of the Usurper: Three

Keep reading for a sneak peek!

ACKNOWLEDGMENTS

Sometimes books are just *demons*. They are difficult to wrestle down, they keep changing shape, and you would sell your soul to make them behave. I had thought that at this point, I was done with demon books (in multiple ways)! But, book, you were such a demon.

There were points when I did not think I would finish it. Thankfully, there were many people in my life who made sure the demon did not win.

Thank you always to my family. My sons, Ned and Idris, for their occasionally thinning patience but general sweetness; my husband, Kevin, for his endless support—we make a great team, Boy. I love you three so much.

Thank you to my sister, Julia, without whom we simply wouldn't manage. A rock and a whirlwind and truly phenomenal.

Thank you to my wonderful friends who helped untangle problems of timing and arcs and motivations: Kate, Rashida, Corry, Rhiannon, Shanna, and the ever-patient Susan. Thank you to Treavor for letting me bounce hypotheticals off him and to B. Dave Walters for listening to and untangling my "conspiracy board" ramble as I reoutlined the entire thing on my whiteboard—I love you and I love your faces. And thank you, Tangerinos, for just being excited about this book.

Thank you to Yang-Yang, voice from above and all-around good friend, for much wisdom. Thank you to all my Con Artists for coming to Concentration Check while I wrestled this book. I hope you keep wrestling yours down and you don't forget to rest!

Thank you to the whole DS Discord, especially Jorge for the wonderful art and Ben for being an endless well of excitement. I'm so glad I get to know you!

Thank you to my editors, Bradley and Tiana, who gave me the critical early feedback to see where things had twisted around. Thank you to my agent, Bridget, who reminded me that second books are often demons.

Thank you to everyone who had a hand in making this demon into a book I am so proud of. There are more folks than I can possibly name involved in the process, and I appreciate every single contribution so much.

extras

orbit

meet the author

Kevin Goodier

ERIN M. EVANS is the author of seven Forgotten Realms novels for Wizards of the Coast, including the 2011 Scribe Award winner *Brimstone Angels*. In addition, she is the former editor of the Eberron novel line and has written fiction for the RPGs *Shadow of the Demon Lord, Monarchies of Mau,* and *World of Aetaltis,* as well as dialogue for the MMO *TERA*. Erin graduated from Washington University in St. Louis with a degree in anthropology and currently lives in the Seattle area with her husband and sons.

Find out more about Erin M. Evans and other Orbit authors by registering for the free monthly newsletter at orbitbooks.net.

if you enjoyed
RELICS OF RUIN

look out for

Books of the Usurper: Three

by

Erin M. Evans

I

A SEED OF PURPOSE

Late winter
Beyond the Salt Wall

For two hundred days, Redolfo Kirazzi has not spoken of Semilla. The girl Lira has marked them one after another on her walking stick since they fled the Black Mother Forest. She knows him well enough to know he is planning, but if the empire of outcast nations beyond the Salt Wall lingers in his thoughts, it does not cross his lips.

It must, she tells herself. One day, it must.

In eight rough clay pots stolen from the ruins of a forest tower, eight skinny trees with black bark slick as silk reach toward the sun, the buds of bruise-dark leaves all along their scant and twiggy branches, the winking eyes of glowing fungus only tiny pin-pricks along their trunks. Lira pokes a finger into each pot, tests the moistness of the soil. She shifts them so they sit in the bright light of noon, letting them soak up sun while they can. She doesn't know what the transplants of the Black Mother Forest need to thrive—she's figuring it out, day by day, the same way she figures out herself.

Once she was the princess, the eldest daughter of the emperor. (*Once*, her thoughts hiss, *you were a fortunate orphan, a nothing, a discard.*) Once she was the tool in reserve of Redolfo Kirazzi, once duke of the Khirazji Protectorate, now outcast, usurper. Once she was only a girl who survived.

Now she is Lireana Ulanitti, rightful empress of Semilla.

Lira cannot say where they are now—away, afar, high on a plateau that looks over the land below. Redolfo keeps the map to himself and his followers give her a wider berth than before. Only *she* went into the Black Mother Forest with Redolfo and came back out. Only *she* sacrificed the changeling she'd given her brother's face to their plans, their future. Only *she* spoke her name to the terrible crow-winged daughters.

It is as if it has marked her. But Lira doesn't mind. She's chosen her path, chosen her future. She knows what must be done, and so does Redolfo.

The seedlings are the beginning—they will grow into the trees that harbor the fungus the Borsyans of old called the cold-magic. With the cold-magic, she reasons, they can make weapons. With weapons they can arm a force to take Semilla. And with the right message they can gather an army large enough to break down the Salt Wall and claim her birthright.

She imagines the weapons as she makes her way back to the main house, imagines great siege engines propelled by glowing blue light, bombards filled with magic, sprays of blue fire that—perhaps—that melt the Salt Wall.

"We will get to that part later," Redolfo has assured her. "That's not for now."

The house is built of bent cedar trees and stones, elk hides and grass and mud. It was Redolfo who remembered old histories, old drawings. These are Ronqu houses in a way. The cedar, the stone base, the hide walls—but the Khirazji insist no house is finished until everything is slicked smooth with mud. It keeps the temperature even, they insist. Lira has to agree: the narrow space, crowded now with half a dozen people, is warm as she could wish.

All the people in the room are people. All the changelings are asleep, lying in torpor as the winter sits on the plateau, stubborn as a cat. All the floor space between them is covered in maps drawn on the scraped skins of the plateau's sharp-hooved mountain goats with the little flicking tails.

Lira eyes these, hunting for symbols she knows, sigils that mark the path to Semilla.

She feels Redolfo watching her, warning in his dark eyes. She meets his gaze in a way she never could have before she saved him from the crow-winged daughters. Before she took her name back.

"If that's where they are," the woman beside him is saying, "we'll be a month walking before we reach them." Her skin is dark as Redolfo's, her hair in long curls, and she wears a gold collar that looks like a peacock biting its folded tail, which Lira quietly covets.

"Might be better to go now," the man nearer to Lira says. He is paler—not perhaps as close to old Khirazj as Redolfo, who would have been the Son of the River if the changelings hadn't destroyed the world. "Get there as they're waking up."

"You're going to find the changeling court?" Lira asks. Everyone startles.

Redolfo frowns, the slightest indication of his annoyance. "Lira," he says patiently. "This isn't for you."

"Why not?" she asks, her boldness a new coat she's still delighting in. "Why would you court them except to ally with them, and why would you ally with them except to increase our army?"

The others exchange glances, and Lira's boldness falters. "Why are you seeking them," she asks, her voice smaller, "if not to take Semilla back?"

Redolfo stands, crosses the room and takes her by the arm to walk her back out into the cold bright day. "Lira," he says again, like her name is a command, "I will say it once more: the world is wide and we have many tasks before us. Many opportunities before us. You can see, I hope, that we're not ready to return to Semilla."

"Not yet," she says.

"Not yet," he agrees. "It's not something I intend to do without knowing the outcome. And so we need allies, yes, but—"

"But the changelings," she begins.

Redolfo doesn't yell, doesn't strike her, doesn't seize hold of her arm again. He merely stops, regarding her coldly, and Lira knows enough to close her mouth around her protests. "I'm sorry," she manages.

"You're bored," he says. "You've lost your friend. I suggest you make a new one."

"The changelings are all asleep," she says, and does not let herself think of Melosino.

"Then find a person to be your friend," he says. "Or a plant if you must. Leave me to plan your grand return." He turns to go.

"I can be useful," she says, desperate for him to stay.

He does not look back, but says, "You're very useful, my dear. Just not in this. Never in this." And Lira stands and watches as he returns to the house of mud and bent cedars, unable to name the tangle of grief and shame that sinks roots into her heart, sends runners through her memories.

CHAPTER ONE

Year Eight of the reign of Empress Beneditta
Arlabecca, the Imperial Federation of Semillan Protectorates
(Twenty years later)

When Sigrittrice Ulanitti was fifteen, her favorite uncle put a needle full of venom in her arm and told her she was calm.

That was important, she would find out later—he had not *asked* her to be calm or even *ordered* her; he did not tell her she *would be calm*. He said simply that she *was*. Such that shortly after the burn in her veins faded, when he told her that she, like all her family and all the Ulanittis before them, was not entirely human, but carried the blood of the changelings that had nearly destroyed the world, Sigrittrice took the information in stride.

After all, she was calm.

"It won't be permanent," he said of the change, as they walked through the gardens of his villa near Pentina. "I wasn't very specific. But it will help, and you'll know now that this is who you need to be. You have a lot to learn."

"Yes, Uncle," she said, not really believing him. She knew in some way that she had been different before, that something had changed—that perhaps she *shouldn't* be calm. Her father, Emperor Soraxio, had died two months ago, and she hadn't been calm then. She had wept and wept and soaked her white masks, and Clotilda had ordered her to go to Pentina, to Uncle Torvatro's villa, if she couldn't behave in a way that befitted her station.

Torvatro Ulanitti had been her father's advisor. The younger son of the great Emperor Eschellado, Torvatro was a quiet man, stout and serious, with gray in his mustache and in his dark hair at the temples. That day in the garden, he wore a white mourning mask too, a patch around each eye in the shape of a dove in flight.

Sigrittrice liked that he always listened to her when others found her easy to overlook, so much younger and less charismatic than her older sister, the newly crowned empress of Semilla. She liked that he was happy to tell her who the portraits in the imperial complex were of, and teach her how to say things in the many languages that had spread across the empire since his youth. He would stay to the edges of her father's court, observing, but if Sigrittrice asked him what he was watching, Torvatro always told her.

That day, he paused beneath one of the rosebushes that lined the wall of his garden. In the summer heat, the scent was thick and powdery. He touched a bud, pale orange and only half-opened. "Gritta, I want you to succeed me."

Sigrittrice frowned. "Haven't I? I'm the empress's sister, you are—were the emperor's brother." That thought made her mind skip—Clotilda was empress, but if Clotilda was *also* part changeling—

"No, not like that." Torvatro said. "I am...well, you could say I am the caretaker of the Ulanittis. I am the Warden of the Line." He smiled at her, the skin around his eyes crinkling in the hollows of the mask. "And so will you be."

"What does the Warden of the Line do?" she asked. It *sounded* important. Like someone who did a lot more than watch the court from the edges of the room. She did not think Clotilda would appreciate her little sister intruding in the business of ruling—they didn't get along very well already, mostly because Clotilda was a bitch.

"Avert catastrophes," Torvatro said. "You see, we're made to be perfect, just rulers. To prevent the weakness inherent in a monarchy. But in itself, the method is its own weakness—especially now." He plucked a leaf, dark with spots of mildew from beside the bloom. "No one can know the truth. Fortunately, you and I are uniquely positioned to make certain that happens."

"How?" Sigrittrice asked. None of this was making any sense. "Because no one notices us?"

Torvatro smiled and pointed to her as if she'd made a very clever connection, which only made her more frustrated. "No one notices you because you want no one to notice you."

Sigrittrice thought it had a lot more to do with Clotilda being a bitch, but since her sister was the empress, it seemed impolitic to say so. Torvatro took a pair of garden shears from the pocket of his coat.

"Have you noticed that?" he asked. "People do what you want, Gritta." He clipped a deadhead and dropped it into a basket at their feet.

"No, they don't."

"They do," he persisted. "It's hard to spot because you want mostly to be left alone, and that looks the same as no one paying the slightest mind to you. That's perfect, really." He turned and smiled at her. "You don't believe me."

"No, Uncle. I think either you're teasing me or you're working up to some lesson about how I should best support Clotilda. Which isn't fair—I haven't done anything wrong."

He chuckled. And then he set a hand on her cheek.

Later, Sigrittrice would remember this too, when she stood in Torvatro's position and knew what was happening under her own hand—the way that, when he told her to grab the rose stem, her thoughts slid sideways first, and the way she tumbled after them. Everything her uncle said made *sense*—that she wanted to touch the rosebush, that she didn't feel the thorns stabbing her hand, that she was *happy* the blood dripped from her palm—

She shook free of it with a start and tried to fling the rose to the ground, but it caught in her skin. Torvatro took her wrist gently and pulled the prickles free.

"Do you know what affinity magic is?" he asked, offering her a handkerchief.

She took it gingerly, every part of her expecting a trap. "Of course I do. Everyone knows. People can talk to things. Specific kinds of things."

" 'Worked materials' is the usual term. Do you know what that means?"

Sigrittrice shrugged. "Metal. Cloth. Wood, but carved wood, not trees really. Unless…maybe sorcerers do things with trees."

She looked down at her hand, the red pinpricks of blood sharp against the paleness of her palm. It itched, like the idea growing in her thoughts. "People . . . are people a worked material? Is that why you asked?"

Torvatro chuckled once. "Ah, Gritta. You are perfect. Yes. Although it doesn't seem to be an affinity that makes itself known in the general population. Whether changelings have it too or not, I couldn't say. But sometimes, every generation or so, an Ulanitti is born with this specific affinity." She looked up at him and found his expression grim. "It can't be more than once a generation or so, you understand? And it can never be the Imperial Authority. It's too dangerous."

Sigrittrice was calm, so calm. "Are you going to kill me?"

"Not you," Torvatro said. "You would have to make a very bad mistake for that to make sense."

"I make a lot of mistakes," Sigrittrice warned him. "Ask Clotilda."

"Well, you're human. Mostly." He chuckled again. "Come on. Clean your hand up and we'll start your lessons."

orbit

Follow us:

f **/orbitbooksUS**

X **/orbitbooks**

▶ **/orbitbooks**

Join our mailing list
to receive alerts on our
latest releases and deals.

orbitbooks.net

Enter our monthly
giveaway for the chance
to win some epic prizes.

orbitloot.com